NEVER FORGET

NEVER FORGET

A Veteran's Journey For
Redemption & Forgiveness

A Novel

ANDY ADKINS

ISBN: 978-1-7363878-0-1 (Paperback)
ISBN: 978-1-7363878-1-8 (Digital Edition)

This novel is a work of fiction. Several of the World War II and Vietnam War battles, locations, and events are real and historically accurate. Every character, all dialogue, and plot are products of the author's imagination or are used fictitiously. Any resemblance to actual persons, living or dead, businesses, companies, or locales is purely coincidental.

Published by Andy Adkins, Gainesville, Florida
www.azadkinsiii.com

COVER PHOTO CREDITS:
Cover Design – Jared Adkins
Cover Top – Officers of Company H, 317th Infantry Regiment, 80th Division; Saint Avold, France; December 1944. (A. Z. Adkins, III Collection)
Cover Bottom – U.S. Army UH-1D helicopters airlift members of the 2nd Battalion, 14th Infantry Regiment, 25th Division from the Filhol Rubber Plantation area during Operation "Wahiawa," northeast of Cu Chi, South Vietnam, 1966. James K. F. Dung, SFC, Photographer. (National Archives)

A VETERAN

Whether active duty, discharged, retired, or reserve,
a Veteran is someone who at one point,
wrote a blank check made payable to
"The United States of America"
for an amount of
"up to, and including, their life."

THAT IS HONOR

Welcome Home
We Will Never Forget

ALSO BY ANDY ADKINS

A Veteran's Journey, Volume 1
A Veteran's Journey, Volume 2

Three Years, Eleven Months, & 29 Days:
But Who's Counting

You Can't Get Much Closer Than This:
Combat with the 80th 'Blue Ridge' Division World War II Europe

The Lawyer's Guide to Practice Management System Software

Computerized Case Management:
Choosing and Implementing the Right Software for You

Part I

WHY ARE YOU HERE?

What did he know?
I'm the one who fought in Vietnam, not him.

1 - The Phone Call

"Reilly.

"*Psst*, Reilly.

"You okay up there?"

The jungle in this part of 'Nam was denser than Tom remembered. He was out front, leading an eight-man patrol on a routine search and destroy mission. It was the best place he could be to protect his squad.

The patrol moved silently along the narrow footpath. Tom's eyes darted ahead, searching for any movement or disturbance. He strained to listen for any unusual sounds—a snapping twig, a bird, or an animal calling out.

Wait! His right hand shot up with a clenched fist, signaling the rest of his squad to freeze. What was that sound?

He spotted an enormous rat scurrying a few yards to the right off the beaten path. Tom relaxed, looked back at his slack man, and smiled. "There it is," he mumbled. They'd been through this drill hundreds of times.

After spending two days in the bush, his squad looked ragged and tired, and were definitely on edge. It was during the return trip that a lot of men died in an ambush because they'd let their guard down. But not Tom, and not his squad. It wasn't safe until they were back in base camp in Lai Khe, Vietnam. They knew that SPC4 Tom Reilly would get them there, just as he had many times before.

The patrol reached a clearing within a few minutes. In a hushed voice, Tom let his men know they'd take a short break, but to stay alert. The grunts quietly broke out their C-rations. Two of them set a defense perimeter watch, making sure someone always had eyes and ears on the surroundings. Several leaned back and closed their eyes, knowing they'd wake in an instant if needed.

Tom checked his watch and map, then signaled his squad to get ready to move out. He was again on point, leading the patrol.

Nearing their base camp, Tom spotted a figure beside a tree, thirty meters ahead, pointing something in their direction. He signaled his squad to take cover. Everyone immediately jumped off the footpath.

It was too late. First one shot, then another, then an angry burst of fire from an AK-47 automatic weapon. Shots came from everywhere. Tom's squad was surrounded and in the middle of an ambush.

He looked back. His slack man was down, killed instantly with a round through his helmet. The back of his head had been blown out—blood and brains everywhere. He ran toward the others, calling their names, but no one answered.

Where is everyone? Why won't they answer? He called again, but had no voice. There was no sound, only the movement of his mouth. It was almost as if Tom Reilly didn't exist...

"HEY, REILLY. You okay up there?"

Tom reached for his weapon, ready to fire. Unable to put his hands on his rifle, he snapped out of his dream. He shook himself awake, like he always did when these flashback dreams occurred.

"Yeah, I'm fine, Jim. Just taking a break. I'll be down in a few."

He looked toward the foothills. From the rooftop, he took in a spectacular view and breathed in the cool early spring air from atop a two-story house he'd just finished painting. The vast expanse of the West Virginia hills was a stark contrast to the thick jungles in Vietnam.

He hadn't slept much the last few nights—nothing unusual for him. Though today, his head throbbed, the beginnings of a headache inching up the back of his neck, courtesy of one too many nights lacking sleep. He wasn't sure why. Last night was different. Perhaps a premonition which left him wondering what the future might bring.

God, he wished he could go back in time, *before...*

Tom took a deep breath and lit a Marlboro cigarette, trying to clear his head. His hands were slightly shaking.

He slowly climbed down the ladder, trying to let those memories fade into oblivion, but knew they'd always be with him, night and day. Reaching the ground, he was once again grounded, safe, and in the present.

After retracting and taking down his extension ladder, Tom carried it over and strapped it onto the roof racks of his charcoal gray Ford F-150.

"Tom. We're headed over to Bobby's Hideaway. Want to join us for a beer?"

"Thanks, Jim, but I'll pass."

"Big plans?"

"No, just the usual."

"By the way, Tom, how's your boy doin'?"

"Chris is a freshman in high school."

"No shit. Already?"

"Yeah. Time flies."

Tom lit another cigarette, leaned back against his truck, and turned the conversation around. "How's the family? Everybody enjoying an early spring?"

"You bet. It's been a bitter winter. Too much snow for me. Kids love it. But me? I prefer the warmer weather. I know you grew up around here. You're probably used to it."

"I did, but I'm ready for warm weather, too."

Tom smiled. "Lots of new homes going up around here."

His coworker smiled, knowing what that meant. "2001's gonna be a busy year for us."

"See you on the next site, Jim. Have one for me."

"Will do."

Tom climbed into his truck, ready to end the day with an ice cold drink. His thirst would have to wait, but home wasn't far away. Besides, it was daylight, and the day was still gorgeous.

He rolled his window down, lit a cigarette, and contemplated taking a long drive, but decided against that. Chris would soon be home from school, and while they weren't the best of friends, he still felt he needed to be there for him.

DEMENTIA. ALZHEIMER'S.

After gently hanging up the kitchen phone, uneasiness settled in Tom Reilly's gut, something he thought he'd put behind him years ago. The nursing home administrator had tried to explain a few things, but Tom was so surprised, he didn't hear much after her words, "your father."

A million thoughts ran through his mind. At the forefront was *why now? Did he even want to see him again?* He'd almost told the administrator, "No way, no how."

It had been over twenty-five years since Tom had spoken to his father—an angry parting that had left them both with bad blood, just like every other time. Except *that* last time *was* the last time.

Tom reached for his Pittsburgh Steelers shot glass and poured a full shot of Kentucky bourbon, dumping it into a glass with only a few cubes of ice. He reached for a bottle of opened club soda, then gently placed it back down on the counter. Pouring another shot of bourbon, he slowly added it to his glass, filling the rest with club soda, and then gently stirring the concoction with his finger.

Tom's world just flipped upside down.

He lit a Marlboro, inhaling deeply before taking a sip of his drink. His thoughts drifted back to the last time he and his father, Ed, were together.

Tom had fought in the Vietnam War. Like many of his generation, he'd volunteered to serve his country. But upon returning home in 1969, his country wasn't the same as when he'd left a year earlier. A lot had changed, and not necessarily for the better. The war changed him. It changed his country. And... it changed his father.

After returning home from the war, all Tom wanted was to be left alone. The Vietnam War was a waste of time, money, and men. His father *strongly* disagreed with him and argued that *"America was right to fight a war to prevent the spread of Communism."*

Ed Reilly had fought the Germans in Europe in World War II, came home and made something of *his* life: a family and a career. Tom should've been able to do the same.

What did he know? I'm the one who fought in Vietnam, not him.

For a simple man trying to live a simple life, Tom now faced a complicated situation—his father's debilitating illness.

I don't know anything about dementia or Alzheimer's, he thought to himself. *How can I deal with that? Have another drink. Isn't that how I work through my problems?*

As he finished his second—or perhaps it was his third—toddy, Tom's teenage son, Chris, came home. The front door slammed behind him as he headed straight to his room without even a quick, "Hello."

Back to his computer. Same old son, same old shit, just a different day. I guess we've lost touch with each other over the last few years.

"Chris, can you come into the kitchen?"

"Be there in a minute."

Even though Chris and his father didn't talk much—they tolerated each other by avoidance—he was respectful, even for a high school teenager.

His son's, *"Be there in a minute"* annoyed Tom. He wasn't in a good mood, especially after *that* phone call.

"Chris. Now!"

I guess I'll pour another drink. On second thought, maybe I'll hold off… for now.

Tom's wife had died years ago in a car accident, when Chris was a toddler. His drinking had always been a point of contention between them. He didn't think he had a problem. *She did.*

"What's up?"

"I just got off the phone. Your grandfather is not doing well."

"I thought you guys hated each other," Chris said without hesitation, taking a seat at the kitchen counter. He grabbed an apple from the fruit bowl and took a big bite.

Chris had never met his grandfather. He knew there had been a major falling out between them before he was born. He didn't know why, and frankly, didn't care.

"We haven't spoken for years. This came out of nowhere. He's in a nursing home up in Pittsburgh." Tom paused a moment with a sigh. "He has Alzheimer's. They asked me to come up to help make some decisions about his treatment.

"They obviously aren't aware of our current relationship," Tom said with a sarcastic chuckle. "I don't even know how they found me, let alone who I was."

"I've heard of Alzheimer's, but what is it?" Chris asked, taking another bite of apple and grabbing a napkin to catch the dripping juice.

"I'm not exactly sure. I know it usually affects older people and has something to do with memory loss. They become forgetful, even forgetting things that happened that same day."

"Bummer." Chris stopped chewing and eyed his father. "Are you still mad at each other?"

That surprised Tom. He didn't think of it as being *mad*. More like, *we just don't like each other.*

"I'm not sure if we're still mad at each other or not," Tom admitted quietly, as if talking to himself. "I just got tired of his crap. Your grandfather always harped on my life, always told me what I should and shouldn't do. He never appreciated what *I* stood for or what *I* wanted to do."

"Kind of like how you tell me what *I* should and shouldn't do."

That sent a shiver down Tom's spine. He'd never thought of it like that. *Was he becoming his own father?*

Before his father could respond, Chris asked, "Are you talking about the Vietnam War?"

Tom took in and released a long breath.

"That's part of it. There's more, I'm sure. But that was always the main problem between us. Just because he believed in *his* war didn't mean I needed to believe in *mine*. I didn't believe in the Vietnam War back then. And to this day, I still don't believe we should have been over there."

It was obvious Tom's attitude toward the war had been tainted over the years.

"Deja poo, Dad." Chris rolled his eyes.

"What the hell is that supposed to mean?" Tom glared at his son.

"I've heard this crap a million times. You make these generalizations, yet you never talk about it. Give it a rest." Chris finished his apple and tossed it in the garbage can.

There were only two things Tom purposefully kept from his son. One was the details of his service in Vietnam, and *anything* associated with that period of time. The second was his father, Chris' grandfather. Chris was aware of both, but considered them taboo.

Tom wanted to avoid having this same argument again. He lit another cigarette. "Well, I've got to decide whether or not to visit him. They asked me. I… I guess I should go." He paused before continuing. "I have no clue what to say to him after all these years.

"I'm in between jobs right now and can take time off from work." Tom was a house painter and his own boss. He mentally calculated the time he'd need to take off.

"I think I'll visit him by myself this first time. I'm not even sure he's aware he has a grandson. In his current state of mind, with this memory loss, it may make matters worse. Can you stay with some friends while I go?"

Chris' expression changed. Tom thought he might be disappointed he wouldn't be able to meet his grandfather. But Chris simply said, "I can hang out with Rachel after school."

"Good," Tom replied, trying to remember if Rachel was a friend or a girlfriend. "I'll be home in time for supper."

2 - Sterling Oaks Retirement Community

After making sure Chris would be okay staying with his friend after school, Tom walked outside to a cool morning. He raised the garage door and once again admired his prized 1967 Pontiac GTO. "Time for another ride in the country," he said out loud to no one in particular.

He fired up his baby, shifted the four-speed manual transmission into reverse, and carefully backed out. Putting his car into neutral and setting the parking brake, he stepped out to close the garage door—he didn't have an automatic opener. *Never have, never will. Keep life simple.*

He'd planned his trip the previous night and had a map beside him on the seat. He didn't use a fancy Garmin GPS, just a Motorola flip phone. It suited Tom fine, and best, it was paid for.

Sterling Oaks Retirement Community was located in Canonsburg, Pennsylvania, southwest of Pittsburgh, where he'd grown up. It was a straight shot up I-79 from his home in Morgantown. Tom estimated an hour and a half drive, as long as he didn't get lost along the way.

The sun was bright with only a few outlying clouds on this early spring day, but a cool nip still hung in the air. The plan was to spend only an hour or so at the nursing home, then back in time for supper with Chris.

Pulling onto the northbound ramp of I-79, he tuned the radio to his favorite station, "Pittsburgh Oldies," and lit a cigarette. He was in his safe place now, driving his original blue, two-door GTO hardtop—nicknamed "Sunshine"—listening to 60s and 70s oldies, and smoking a Marlboro. Life didn't get much better than this.

A few minutes into the trip, Tom's thoughts turned to the last time he and his father had been together. It wasn't fun—it hadn't been for years. The fighting started not long after he returned home from Vietnam. He refused to talk about the war to anyone, *especially* his father. He'd been awarded the Bronze Star Medal and two Purple Hearts—the same as his father during World War II. But he didn't want to remember *anything* about that damned war.

His father had served with General George Patton's Third Army in World War II. Tom knew he'd been an infantry rifleman and had fought in the Battle of the Bulge, but he never talked about the war… not *ever*. That generation rarely did. Whatever Tom knew about his father's experience came from his aunts and uncles and what he'd read in books and magazines.

He'd asked his mother several times, but she said it was something they simply didn't talk about. That was it. After a while, Tom quit asking.

But growing up, his father was his hero. The soldiers had won the war and returned home to careers and to raise families. Yet, all he'd say to Tom was, *"We just did our job."*

CRUISING UP I-79, alone with his thoughts and listening to his favorite band, Creedence Clearwater Revival's *Bad Moon Rising*, Tom almost missed the turnoff to Canonsburg. He slipped into the right lane quickly enough without causing anyone to slam on their brakes. This was Pittsburgh. People here drive a little different than in West *by God* Virginia.

Once off the interstate, Tom racked his brain trying to remember if Sterling Oaks was a right or left turn. Like most veterans though, he had excellent directional instincts and turned left on a whim. After a mile down the two-lane country road, the first billboard appeared: "Sterling Oaks Retirement Community, *Aging with Dignity*."

Tom chuckled to himself. It seemed the older people got, the less dignity they cared about—himself included.

He turned onto a curvy, two-lane road with well-maintained shrubbery, blooming roses and wildflowers, and manicured lawns on both sides. *Snazzy place. Ed must have done all right to end up here.*

He approached a security booth with two lanes leading into the facility and both boom gates lowered. A sign indicated the right lane was reserved for residents and family members who had a bar-coded decal on their window. The left lane, closest to the security booth, was for visitors. An American flag flew high next to the booth.

Tom slowly pulled up to the gate just as a uniformed guard walked out to greet him.

"Good morning, sir. Welcome to Sterling Oaks Retirement Community. How may I help you?" The tall and lanky, white-haired guard's eyes widened, clearly impressed as he stared at the car, *not* at Tom. His name tag simply read, "Earl."

"Good morning. I'm Tom Reilly, here to visit my father, Ed Reilly. He's a resident here." The words spoken out loud weighed heavy on his tongue: *a resident here.* He slightly shook his head, wanting to enter with minimal disruption. Tom didn't like talking to strangers, especially those in uniform. He usually tried to avoid conversation.

Earl looked at Tom and replied, "Let me check to see if they're expecting you, Mr. Reilly. It'll take a moment." Earl retreated to the guard booth and quickly returned with a visitor's pass.

"You're on the visitor's list, Mr. Reilly.

"Say, is this a '66 GTO?"

"'67."

"Nice set of wheels. Mind if I ask you what you've got under the hood? 389?"

Tom didn't want to waste time chit-chatting with the security guard. But when someone with a bit of antique car knowledge showed interest in his GTO, he always seemed to find time.

"Nope. 400 cubic inches with a four-barrel Rochester carb," he replied proudly.

"She's a beauty."

"Yep. She's all stock except for the headers I put on her. I've taken care of her since 1967."

"You've had her since '67?" Earl stepped back and took in the full ambiance of Tom's prize possession. "Wow, and to see her in such fine shape. You really know how to take care of cars, Mr. Reilly."

"My father taught me all about cars when I was growing up. He bought this for me after I graduated from high school."

"Impressive. I won't take any more of your time, Mr. Reilly." Earl handed Tom his pass. "But I'd sure like to look under the hood sometime when you have a few extra minutes."

"I'll do that."

"When you get past the guard gate, keep to the right at the fork. You'll see a sign to 'Reception.' Someone will be at the front desk to assist you."

"Thanks."

Tom drove along another curvy, uphill road for a quarter mile, passing both houses and duplexes, and what looked like administration buildings. He saw a sign on the side of the road with an arrow pointing to the right: "Administration and Reception."

He turned in and found a parking spot near the front entrance. Two four-story structures stood next to both sides of the Admin building—almost like bookends to the main building. Tom assumed they were resident apartments. The visitor's parking lot was about half full, but he noticed two things: all the cars were almost new and most were four-door sedans.

As soon as he walked through the double glass doors, a young, blond-haired receptionist seated behind the counter greeted him. Tom's nose slightly twitched as her delicate perfume reached his nostrils.

"Good morning, sir. Welcome to Sterling Oaks Retirement Community. I'm Margie. How may I help you?"

It sounded more like a rehearsed sales pitch than a greeting. Tom wasn't in the mood to discuss what she was selling. Instead, he politely replied, "I'm Tom Reilly and I'm here to see my father, Ed Reilly."

"Hello, Mr. Reilly."

Before Margie could continue, Tom interrupted. "Tom. Please call me Tom. Mr. Reilly sounds too much like my father."

"Tom it is, then. If you'll follow me, I'll take you to our meeting room. Ms. Myers would like to meet with you first before you visit your father. It's routine here, especially since it's been a while since the two of you have seen each other. You will probably notice changes in your father's demeanor."

Demeanor? What the hell was that supposed to mean? This wasn't the plan. I was going to show up and go to my father's room and that was that. Tom narrowed his eyes. *Interesting that they'd neglected to mention any knowledge of their less-than-friendly relationship. Unless… they didn't know.*

Margie led him down a wide hall to a small, well-furnished conference room. A square mahogany wood table and four dark, vinyl-padded captain's chairs were perfectly centered in the middle of the room. Shelves of old classics and new books lined the edge of the room, along with several Renaissance-style paintings and photographs. It reminded Tom of an old Sherlock Holmes movie.

"Ms. Myers will be with you in a few minutes. May I get you coffee or something else to drink?"

"Yes, coffee. Black would be nice. Thank you."

Tom waited patiently, hoping the coffee would arrive before Ms. Myers. His wish was granted as Margie quickly returned with a smile and a steaming cup. As she left the room, an image flashed through his mind—Lai Khe, Vietnam, and the welcomed smile of a Red Cross Donut Dolly.

"Mr. Reilly?"

Tom returned to the present and stood to meet Ms. Myers.

"Welcome to Sterling Oaks Retirement Community, Mr. Reilly." Ms. Myers smiled as she extended her hand.

"Please. Call me, Tom."

"Certainly, Tom. I'm Michelle Myers. We spoke earlier on the phone. I hope you don't mind, but I wanted to discuss a few things with you before you met with your father. I understand you have not spoken to each other in several years."

"Try twenty-five years," he shot back, his jaw tensing shamefully.

As they sat down at the table facing one another, Tom noted her professional appearance. She wore dark slacks and a long sleeve light blue button-down shirt. Her brown hair flowed across her shoulders.

"I'm sorry to hear that," Ms. Myers responded, almost if she expected to hear more of an explanation. "But that's the past, and I'm here to help deal with the present and the future. I may tell you things you already know and, if so, my apologies. I don't know where else to start except at the beginning."

Ms. Myers cleared her throat. "Your father has been a resident at Sterling Oaks since 1997, when we first opened. He is one of our founding members. Until a few weeks ago, he was very active in the community, well-liked and well-respected, and generally a pleasure to be around."

"And now?" Tom politely interrupted, raising his eyebrows.

"Well, that's why I called you. A few days ago, one of our Security Team members spotted Ed walking outside, seemingly confused. He loves to walk around the campus and is always comfortable outdoors. When the guard approached and asked if he could help, Ed became adamant that the guard was trying to restrain him. In fact, Ed became, shall we say, quite defensive and belligerent. Certainly not the Ed Reilly we've come to know."

Tom's lip curled up slightly. He remembered at times, his father could be "quite belligerent."

"All of our Security Team members are well-trained and aware of our community residents. In most cases, they are also familiar with their backgrounds. The guard knew Ed had fought in Europe in World War II. He picked up on the fact that your father *thought* he might be back in Germany. That's an initial sign of memory loss or dementia. At least around here."

After listening to Ms. Myers' story, Tom asked, "So my father thought he was still in the war and the security guard was a German?"

"Not necessarily. Once the guard observed Ed's irrational behavior, he spoke to him using a calmer voice, asking his name, if he knew what day it was, and where he was.

"You see, Tom, we train our Security Teams to first try entering the patient's *realm of reality*, and then help them find their way back to the real world. In other words, we try to first bring the resident back to the present *mentally*, then get him back to the facility *physically*.

"Within a few minutes, Ed realized he wasn't in any danger, he was here at Sterling Oaks, and could carry on a normal conversation with the guard. All the while, not remembering a thing about what had just happened."

Ms. Myers paused as she shifted in her seat, changing gears.

"At that point, it's our policy to seek professional help. That's where I came into the picture. I'm the resident memory specialist here at Sterling Oaks. I spent time with Ed and diagnosed him with early stage dementia. That would also account for the temporary memory loss he experienced earlier.

"Once we have that diagnosis, we notify family members. Only in this case, Ed wasn't sure where you were, so we had to do a little digging to find you.

"And that, Tom, brings you up to date."

Tom hesitated, first staring out the window, then turned toward Ms. Myers. "Wow, that's a lot to digest. I'm not sure what to say."

"No need to say anything, Tom. I wanted to let you know how your father is—he's doing fine, by the way. When you visit him, you probably won't notice any difference…" Ms. Myers stopped short, realizing what she'd just said.

"I mean, you shouldn't notice any peculiar behavior. Dementia is a strange condition. It doesn't affect everyone the same way. In your father's case, you will need to first come to terms with whatever separated the two of you, before you can determine the next steps."

Ms. Myers passed several brochures across the table. "I have some literature that describes dementia. Please take and read it when you have time. It may help you better understand your father's condition and what to expect in the future as the dementia progresses.

"Unless you have any questions, let's go see your father."

They walked down a long corridor leading to the memory unit of Sterling Oaks. "Ed actually lives in an apartment in another building, but because of his recent diagnosis, he is temporarily in our memory unit."

The last time his father had seen him, Tom had let his thick brown hair grow long, down past his shoulders, but kept in a neat ponytail. He'd also grown a full beard. He couldn't remember if it was because he wanted to be left alone, or if he was trying to distance himself from his recent life as a combat soldier. He wasn't alone. Many Vietnam veterans grew their hair long in protest after they returned to *The World*.

Tom was the same size and build as when he first returned from the Army. He still wore old, faded blue jeans and a basic, solid color t-shirt—that hadn't changed since 'Nam, though he sometimes wore flannel shirts on cooler days. He hadn't seen a need to change his wardrobe, since he rarely went anywhere other than work and the supermarket.

In fact, when he worked at his father's appliance business soon after returning from the war, he'd called him out on it time and time again during those first few years home. *"Customers don't trust men with long hair, wearing jeans."*

Since then, he'd cleaned up, cutting his hair much shorter and neater, though it was thinning on top with strands of gray. He also now sported a well-groomed goatee, with a slight hint of silver. He wondered if his father would notice.

"Here we are. Ed is in room one-nine-six-seven." Ms. Myers gently knocked on the open door.

"Good morning, Ed. You have a visitor. It's your son, Tom."

"Who?" A rough-sounding, yet familiar angry voice emitted from the room.

"Tom. Your son, Tom."

Ed Reilly didn't say a thing, but stood to see his new visitor. It took a few seconds for him to realize that Tom—the son who'd stormed out of his life years earlier—was standing in *his* room.

"Hello, Tom," Ed said with no emotion.

"Hello, Ed. It's been a while."

Tom couldn't bring himself to say, "Dad." Over the years, he'd convinced himself that his father simply didn't exist.

"Yes, it has. How long? A dozen years?"

"More like twenty-five," Tom flatly replied. He wasn't sure how else to respond.

Ms. Myers sensed the awkward silence and chimed in. "I'll leave you two alone. I'm sure you have a lot of catching up to do. If you need anything, I'll be down the hall in my office."

"Thank you," both said, almost simultaneously.

She then caught Tom's eye and asked quietly, "Tom, would you stop by my office before you leave?"

He acknowledged with a quick nod.

After Ms. Myers closed the door, Ed motioned to one of the two chairs in the small room. They sat down facing each other, almost defensively. Two war veterans, ready for combat.

"You look like shit," Ed stated, lobbing the first volley of insults. What else could you say to a son who had walked out of your life over two decades earlier?

"You don't look half bad yourself," Tom fired back with a long judgmental look. His eyes narrowed.

A few moments passed before Ed asked, "Why are you here?"

3 - Your Father Has Alzheimer's

With a furrowed brow and an angry scowl, Tom was steaming as he hurried down the hallway. His fists were clenched tight, and his jaw was stiff. Looking for the nearest exit, he reached into his shirt pocket and pulled out a Marlboro—he needed a cigarette, bad.

He quickly walked right past Ms. Myers' office, forgetting he was supposed to stop on his way out.

"Mr. Reilly. Mr. Reilly. Tom!" Ms. Myers called out as Tom tried to escape.

Tom slowed his pace and stopped. Turning as he lit his cigarette, Ms. Myers caught up with him. He was a man on a mission and obviously didn't follow rules.

"Tom, can we step outside? There's no smoking in the building complexes."

Tom's eyes darted about; he was eager to leave. But something in Ms. Myers' voice was reassuring.

"Sure. Lead the way."

They walked in silence down the hall toward a double-door exit. Ms. Myers used her name badge to open the security door. A few feet away, another door exited to a large, well-manicured courtyard, surrounded by colorful, blooming pink and white azaleas. In the center was a huge, multi-tiered flowing water ceramic fountain, designed to match the appeal of the vegetation. To one side and strategically located for shade were several young cherry trees with new buds ready to bloom.

Ms. Myers pointed to a wooden bench under a small shade tree.

"We can sit over here."

Tom's instinct told him she'd had this conversation before and knew it was better to have it away from her office and the constant noise in the memory unit. He could tell Ms. Myers was searching for the right words. *She probably knows more about Ed than I do.* They both sat down at opposite ends of the bench.

"Tom, would you be surprised if I told you that your father has talked about you—a lot—over the past few days?"

Tom glanced at Ms. Myers, his eyes flashing for a quick moment. "Yes, as a matter of fact, it would. I have no idea why on earth Ed wanted to see me, especially after not hearing from him all these years." Tom struggled to remain calm.

"We weren't aware that Ed had a son until just a few days ago—he kept that to himself. In fact, when we asked about his wife, Louise, he didn't want to talk about her death either. Those memories were obviously still painful. All Ed would tell us was that she died of a heart attack in the 60s."

Tom remembered that fateful day—that entire life-altering year. Looking out toward the green foothills, he took a long puff and exhaled a cloud of smoke before replying.

"I was in Vietnam when I got the news. I flew home for her funeral."

"I didn't know that, Tom. I'm very sorry."

After a few moments of respectful silence, Ms. Myers sat up straight and stated, "Tom, your father has Alzheimer's disease. Do you know what that is?"

"It's a loss of memory, I think." Tom lit another cigarette, staring straight ahead.

"Sort of. You are probably familiar with the term, 'senility.' As people age, some things may begin to give out. It could be their sight or their hearing. It could also be physical, such as knees or hips. Not everyone experiences these problems, but the odds increase as you get older.

"In your father's case, he is *physically* fit. But he is beginning to lose his memory." Michelle cleared her throat. "Unfortunately, it's something that is irreversible."

Tom listened carefully, but continued to avoid eye contact.

"There are four types of dementia—Alzheimer's disease is the most common. Sixty percent of dementia cases are Alzheimer's. In the U.S., one in nine people older than age sixty-five have Alzheimer's. The odds increase to one in three when you reach eighty-five."

Tom heaved a big sigh while staring at the ground. "Why are you telling me this?" It was obvious he still harbored an animosity toward his father.

"Because the Ed you saw today—perhaps the same father you parted ways with years ago—is *not* the same Ed we've known here at Sterling Oaks. He asked us to call you. He's frightened, and he's confused. He knows he is not well, and I sincerely think he wants to make up for lost time with you."

"Well, he certainly didn't show much *affection* a few minutes ago," Tom replied defensively as he looked up at Ms. Myers. "It was the same hate-filled argument we had years ago that split us apart."

Tom's gaze turned intense and animated. "What the hell am I supposed to do? He told me the same thing, using almost the exact words he said twenty-five years ago. '*Get the hell outta here. I never want to see you again.*' Whatever I say or do, it seems it's always the wrong thing."

Tom paused a moment then ventured. "Besides, it won't matter. He won't remember anything, right?"

"Actually, Tom, neuropsychological research suggests the emotional memory of individuals with dementia or Alzheimer's disease remains intact. The patient can remember when they've been treated cruelly."

What kind of mumbo-jumbo bullshit answer is that? Tom almost blurted out loud.

Ms. Myers sat straight up and looked directly into Tom's eyes. He felt a lecture coming on.

"People with dementia have mood swings. Some swing wider than others, but almost everyone experiences these swings. Ed is in what we call, 'stage one,' or early dementia. That means he not only forgets things, but he's also lost interest in activities he's enjoyed in the past. It's a disruption of his normal routine, yet he may not realize it.

"He has always loved being with people; that is until a few weeks ago. I've noticed he is slowly drawing into himself and spending less time with others out in the community, even some of his close friends. These are all signs of Alzheimer's."

Tom was listening, but fought the urge to interrupt with questions.

"It's not uncommon for someone at his age to realize he's no longer invincible. Many World War II veterans think they'll live forever, or at least a very long time. They are *never* ready to slow down. It is probably one of the basic instincts that helped them survive the war.

"Your father is no exception. When someone faces memory loss and is diagnosed with dementia, it often sends a shock they've never experienced. That invincibility begins to fade when they realize they have a limited amount of time left in their lives. At that point, they often want to make amends for things they may have said or done, or with people they may have hurt."

As he listened to Ms. Myers' descriptive analysis of his father's condition, her calming voice began to lessen his anxiety, putting him at ease. He shifted position on the bench, turning to face her.

"How long does he have to live, Michelle?" Tom asked, not realizing this was the first time he addressed Ms. Myers by her first name.

"There is no defined timeline, Tom. From a statistical perspective, the average time from onset development to diagnosis spans about two-and-a-half years. We assume the incident several weeks ago was the first indication of dementia, but we aren't certain. After the initial diagnosis, people may live for months or for years."

Tom shifted in his seat, his eyes narrowing. "Are you saying he only has a couple of years left to live?"

"No, that's not what I'm saying." Michelle took a deep breath. "There are many factors to consider and unfortunately, the approach is to wait and see. The only certainty is that Alzheimer's is not reversible and there is no known cure. Memory fades, and eventually, the body soon follows.

"Ed is at the early stage. His memory will drift in and out. He wants to make amends with you, Tom. That I can tell you for sure. It's up to you to figure out how to do that.

"There will be times when he's coherent and other times when he's not. You *will* get frustrated with him when you try to speak with him about certain things. We know there are triggers that bring back certain memories, some of which may set the patient off, but they are all individualized."

Tom leaned back on the bench, took out another cigarette and stuck it in his mouth without lighting it. "What can I do?"

Michelle offered a faint smile.

"Come back next week and visit your father again. That will give you both time to digest what's going on and for you to better accept his prognosis. It will also give you time to figure out what you need to do to clear up whatever caused this riff between the two of you."

Michelle took a card out of her pocket, turned it over, and jotted down a phone number. She handed it to Tom. "Here's my business card. My personal cell number is on the back. Call me anytime if you have questions. And please, call to let me know when you'll be back."

Tom glanced down at her card. It was plain white with the Sterling Oaks Retirement Community logo and neatly lettered, "Michelle Myers, Psychologist, Ph.D." The title didn't mean much to him other than she was probably smart.

After a few moments, both stood and shook hands.

"Thank you, Michelle. Thank you for what you've done for my father and for me."

"My pleasure. I look forward to seeing you again next week.

"One last thing, Tom. A wise person once said, *'You can't control what other people do or say. The only control you have is how you react to what they do or say.'* Try to keep that in mind while visiting your father."

Tom recalled a time when he attended Sunday school as a kid— The Golden Rule: *"Do unto others as you would have them do unto you."*

He turned and headed out of the courtyard, which led directly to the parking lot. Lighting his cigarette, Tom glanced back over his shoulder at Michelle and gave her a quick nod and a smile.

4 - Why Here, Why Now?

Tom walked up to his car and opened the driver's side door, but didn't get in right away. He peered out over the top of his GTO and past the trees just starting to gain their early spring leaves. His eyes focused on the distant hills.

Even with the rounded bales of hay neatly stacked and wrapped in plastic alongside the fence line, it was still a magnificent view. It reminded him of his younger, worry-free days, happily roaming the hillsides near Pittsburgh at his grandparent's farm. It was a long time ago, many years *after* his father returned from a war and years *before* Tom went off to his war.

He caught himself reminiscing, wishing once again for those days when he and his father were truly father and son, back *before* Vietnam.

Tom climbed into his car, closed the door, and rolled down both front windows. He was safe again—safe from life's displeasures and disappointments. He cranked Sunshine up and smiled, listening to the steady hum of the perfectly tuned engine. He had taken great care of his car—it was his pride and joy. His father had taught him that no one would take better care of Sunshine than he.

The interior looked almost as pristine as the exterior. The wood-grain padded panels and multiple gauges sparkled like they did when he first drove it home. While Sunshine didn't smell like a new car, he'd installed air fresheners to help dissipate the lingering cigarette odor.

Tom put the car in reverse and backed up slowly, shifting gears, and being careful to not pop the clutch. Even though his GTO was still stock, its 335 horses would easily spin the tires.

He lit another cigarette and turned on the radio. Bob Dylan's *Blowin' in the Wind* played on the Oldies station.

Yes, 'n' how many times can a man turn his head
And pretend that he just doesn't see?

Tom reached over to change stations. He hated protest songs with a passion.

He eased down the winding road toward the interstate. Slowing as he approached the guard shack, the automatic gate lifted. Not seeing Earl, he continued on his way. Back on the interstate, he headed south toward Morgantown.

His thoughts soon returned to his recent visit. His father didn't look like he did when he last saw him in the mid-70s. He had aged, but then, so had Tom.

Ed stood tall and did not slouch like a lot of older men his age. His hair had turned silver gray, but as well-groomed as Tom remembered. His eyes were still deep brown, now with bushy white eyebrows. Ed's once-menacing glare had softened to one of a kinder, older gentleman. That was until Tom pissed him off again.

He didn't know how the same old argument restarted, but soon after Ed asked why he was there, Tom tried to feign his actual feelings. He simply told him someone from the retirement community called.

What he hid from his father was that he wasn't sure he wanted to see him again. The last time they spoke—years ago—was hateful. He'd heard that time *should* heal all wounds. But it's difficult to face a man— especially your *own* father—who'd told you more than once, *"You're a fucking disappointment."*

That was long ago, but the words still stung as if freshly spoken. He thought he'd buried that memory for good. But after seeing his father today, that argument snuck back into the forefront of his mind. His father would *never* understand why he hated the Army, he hated Vietnam, and he felt let down by his own country.

Tom snapped out of that downward spiral—he'd been there too many times. Passing the turnoff to Washington Township, he lit another cigarette and turned the radio back to the Oldies station.

A Whiter Shade of Pale was playing.

We skipped the light fandango
Turned cartwheels 'cross the floor

He forced his thoughts to return to the beauty of the day as he and Sunshine cruised down the interstate, but his father was still with him.

What was he going to do about Ed? Did he really give a rat's ass about him, especially after all these years?

He was struggling to find the answer, when he thought again about Michelle's comment, *"The Ed you saw today is not the Ed we know."*

Could it be his father had changed? Could it be he wanted Tom back in his life, even though he said again, *"Get the hell out!"?*

"You can't control what other people do or say. The only control you have is how you react to what they do or say."

"'A wise old man,' my ass," Tom said out loud. Dr. Michelle Myers is a well-trained, mental health professional and knows how to deal with people—people of all ages—*and* their family members. However, that thought stayed with Tom.

She also mentioned mood swings were a symptom of dementia. Is that what he saw earlier today, a mood swing? "What the hell is a mood swing, anyway?" He was talking to himself again.

Yet, when he first walked into Ed's room, there was a different look about him. Something told him maybe his father really wanted to get past their past.

Tom's thoughts soon turned to his mother, as they often did when he was confused. She had been taken at the prime of her life. From what he remembered, she had dropped dead of a heart attack while shopping in downtown Pittsburgh. He only knew what his father had told him, but he'd been heartbroken. He still couldn't understand why… *why his own mother?*

Tom missed her more now than ever. He wasn't sure why. Perhaps it was because he'd just seen his father and after another ugly fight, he looked for his mother's comforting love.

He barely noticed, but The Beatles *Let it Be* played on the radio.

And in my hour of darkness she is standing right in front of me
Speaking words of wisdom, let it be

As Tom neared his exit to Morgantown, he slowed down to get off the interstate. It didn't take him long to get home—traffic wasn't bad.

He pulled into his driveway, set the parking brake, and got out to open the garage door. He wasn't sure if Chris was home or not—there weren't any tell-tale signs. He'd grown accustomed to Chris coming and going on his own.

After pulling Sunshine into the garage, Tom stepped outside and stared up at the cloudless sky, as if he were looking for a sign from above. Seeing and hearing nothing in particular, he closed the garage door and walked into his house.

5 - Grandfather Reilly

Chris Reilly was a typical 15-year-old: shy and socially awkward. While he had recently started his first year in high school, he was already bored. He felt he knew more than his new classmates and his teachers. From an academic point of view, high school—at least the first few months as a freshman—wasn't a challenge.

He spent most of his non-school time at home on his computer: playing games and reading. The few books in his room were almost all related to school. In fact, there weren't many books in the house. His father didn't read much. Most of what Chris needed to know, he found on the Internet or in the school library. And he enjoyed being a computer nerd.

His mother died when he was only two years old. He knew she had been killed in a car crash driving home from work, but not much else. There were only a few pictures of her in the house. From what little his dad had told him, she was a nurse and was passionate about her work in the hospital intensive care unit, caring for her patients as well as their families.

Chris was a loner like his dad, and could count his close friends on one finger. But he didn't mind. He was still at that age where he generally liked people, but didn't like to be around crowds. The middle school and high school cliques turned him off. He simply didn't like to hang around people who acted like someone they weren't. In his mind, that accounted for almost all high schoolers.

Chris and his father rarely saw eye-to-eye on things. His dad tried to let him be his "own man," as his father often mentioned. But at times, Chris felt distant from him. His father had always been there, but didn't seem to want to spend "quality time" with him when he was growing up. Even though they played a little sports—mostly baseball and basketball outside in the yard—he felt they were worlds apart.

He knew his father had fought in the Vietnam War. But other than being a veteran, he knew *nothing* else. His father *never* talked about the war and whenever Chris asked, Tom always changed the subject. It was as if he wanted to erase that part of his life.

Chris was also aware that Tom's father had fought in World War II, but little more than that. He was also aware that his dad *never* talked about *his* father. There had been a falling out, a "meltdown" as his father said once after one too many drinks, but that's all he knew. After a while, Chris simply quit asking.

Whatever he knew about World War II he'd learned in school and from his computer games. His history class teacher, Mr. Johnson, was also a Vietnam veteran. That's all he'd reveal about his past, too. But the way he taught history and spoke about the battlefield, especially World War II, Chris could sense that Mr. Johnson had been in combat. It made Chris want to know more about the wars—*both* of them.

IT WAS THE WEEKEND following Tom's first visit to Sterling Oaks. Weekends were usually quiet and casual, but this Saturday was special. This day, Chris would meet his grandfather for the first time. Normally, he would sleep in, then either be on the computer all day or hang out with his friend, Rachel. But his dad insisted he go, and he agreed, albeit somewhat reluctantly.

However, he loved to ride in his dad's Pontiac GTO. While Chris was only in his first year of high school, he appreciated that this was a bitchin' ride. He knew a little about older muscle cars from surfing the Internet. One thing was for sure, though—*this* GTO was more than just a car. When his dad drove *this* car, he was a different man.

About twenty minutes into the trip, Tom lit a cigarette, cracked his window, and broke the silence. "How's school?"

Chris stopped tapping his foot to the music and sat up a little straighter. "Fine. Why do you ask? You *never* ask me about school."

"I know, but I figured since you're meeting your grandfather for the first time, it might be good to know how things are going. That's all."

"They're fine, Dad," Chris replied with a hint of sarcasm in his voice. "I'm keeping my grades up. At least, I'm trying to."

"What's your favorite subject?" Another annoying question.

"You mean besides computers? I like math and science the best," Chris answered dryly but also added with more enthusiasm, "I like our history teacher, too—Mr. Johnson. He makes boring history interesting. He's a Vietnam veteran, too, Dad. Like you, he doesn't talk about the war except what's in our textbook."

Tom absorbed that comment with a deep breath and an exhausted sigh.

So my son is learning about the Vietnam War. There's no way you can teach what happens during war to a high schooler from a book. Hell, if our own government couldn't understand it, how can anyone who hadn't been there know what it was like?

Tom kept those thoughts to himself, but his son sensed he may have said something he shouldn't have.

A few minutes later, Chris changed the subject. "Dad? What did Granddad do in the war? I mean, I know he fought the Germans, but did he kill any?" Chris' history class was currently studying World War II.

"Chris, one thing you don't want to do—*ever*—is to ask a veteran if they'd ever killed anybody, even if it was the enemy." Tom realized he'd raised his voice and wondered if he was protecting his father or himself. "Of course he killed Germans. That's what a soldier does." He didn't mention he'd also killed—Vietnamese.

Tom calmed down and shared with Chris what little he knew. "Your grandfather was in the Army infantry. He never talked to me about the war, so all I know is what I overheard and what I learned when I was in school.

"He was a rifleman with the 80th Division and fought in the Battle of the Bulge."

Tom glanced over at his son. "Have you ever heard of the term, 'Baptism of Fire'?"

"Only in some movies I've seen. Isn't that, like, the first time you fight the enemy?"

Tom smiled. "That's right. For the 80th Division, and for your grandfather, they hit the shores of France about two months after D-Day in early August. They marched inland and after a few days, his unit ran into their first battle—their *Baptism of Fire*—in a place called Angers, France.

"He was wounded twice—once by shrapnel during the Battle of the Bulge. I think he was also shot when he was in Germany. He received a Bronze Star, but I'm not sure for what. There's a lot more, but like I said, he *never* talked it.

"I asked my mother a few times, but she said that was one subject they didn't talk about. I never understood why, but she just said, *'Your father has his reasons.'"*

"*You* never talk about the war, either," Chris mumbled under his breath, but Tom heard it.

It wasn't long before they reached the exit to Sterling Oaks. Tom hung a left and as he neared the guard shack, he noticed Earl was not on duty. *He must not work on the weekends.* Instead, a younger security guard slowly emerged. He didn't seem to wear his uniform with the same pride and confidence as Earl did.

"Good afternoon, sir. Welcome to Sterling Oaks Retirement Community. How may I help you?"

Tom smiled to himself. *These security guards must have attended the same Dale Carnegie School of Courtesy—they all make the same introduction.*

"I'm Tom Reilly and this is my son, Chris. We're here to visit Ed Reilly, my father."

"Just a moment while I check, Mr. Reilly." The guard yawned as he slowly made his way back into the guard shack. Unlike his first encounter with Earl, Tom thought he may have interrupted this guard's naptime.

Tom had called Michelle the day before to let her know he would be up to visit Ed this weekend. She said that would be wonderful and thought he would appreciate it. She also mentioned she would be in her office and looked forward to seeing him again.

"Here you go, Mr. Reilly. Just place this Visitor's Pass on your dashboard. Park anywhere that's not marked 'Reserved.' I assume you know your way?"

"Yes sir. Thank you."

Tom eased the car forward as the gate lifted. This guard didn't notice—or at least, said nothing about—his car. That was fine with Tom. His mind was focused on the upcoming visit with Ed.

When he pulled into the parking space, he turned off the ignition and turned toward Chris. The backlight of the morning sun was such that he noticed for the first time his son had a hint of peach fuzz. His short hair was dark brown and soft, like Tom's at that age, but his light brown eyes and square chin belonged to his mother.

Why he was thinking this, at this moment, was a little troubling—he couldn't quite put a finger on it. *Could it be he is taking his only son to meet his grandfather for the first time and he wanted Ed to be proud?*

"Chris. I need you to understand something."

"Sure, Dad. What?"

"I don't know much about this Alzheimer's disease. From the information Ms. Myers gave me, I know it affects a person's mind. The grandfather you meet today may not be the grandfather you were supposed to know growing up.

"We've had our differences in the past. But now… *now*, things are different. I'm only telling you this because I want to make sure you understand your grandfather may be happy, sad, or just plain angry. I don't know what his mood will be today."

He rubbed the side of his face with his hand. "When I visited him earlier this week, we had another argument, and I left angry, swearing I never wanted to see him again."

"Then why are we here today?" Chris stared out the front window, not wanting to hear a lecture.

"After I left, one of the health care professionals explained how this disease affects the mind. She said your grandfather was normally a pleasant man—something *I* hadn't seen in a long time. But he insisted I come. I'm not sure he knows he has a grandson. I just want you to be prepared in case he is… angry."

"I understand, Dad. I'll just sit in the back of the room and be quiet."

"That's not what I'm saying, Chris. I want you to talk with him if he wants. I want you to get to know him." Tom paused.

"I guess what I'm trying to say is that I haven't been through this before and I'm not sure what we're supposed to do, but he said he wants to see me—us—again."

"Ok. I think I understand." Chris looked over at his dad with a confident smile. "Let's do this."

They walked into the complex through the double glass doors, heading straight for room 1967, where Ed and Tom first met— *fought*—earlier that week. When they arrived, the door was open but the room was empty. Tom walked back into the hallway and looked around, confused.

Michelle had seen them walk past her office and came out to greet them. "Good morning, Tom. It's good to see you again. And who is this handsome young man standing next to you?" Michelle smiled, making Chris feel a little uncomfortable.

"Hi Michelle. This is my son, Chris."

"I didn't realize you had a son. It's a pleasure to meet you, Chris. I'm Michelle Myers." She extended her hand to shake Chris'.

"Ed is back in his apartment, Tom. I should have mentioned that when you called earlier. He was only in the memory unit for a short while. I'll walk you over there."

Down the hall, a turn left, another left, past two small empty dining areas, then onto an elevator to the third floor, and a right turn down another hall. The sound of alarms and buzzers faded as they walked away from the memory unit and the skilled nursing wing. *Geez, this place seems like a maze.*

As they walked from one wing of the building to another, Tom noticed the carpets changed colors and patterns as well as the wallpaper and general décor. It was almost like entering a different building, yet they were still in the same facility.

"I'm glad you know where you're going, Michelle. I would be lost trying to find my way."

"You get used to it, Tom. It's quite logical once you understand how the community is laid out. We have two main apartment buildings with two hundred units for our independent living residents, both one-

and two-bedroom. We also have thirty villas and another thirty club homes on the campus.

"In addition, we have a memory unit—that's where we first met. We call it the 'Memory Support Neighborhood.' It sounds a little friendlier for the residents. We also have an assisted living wing and a skilled nursing unit.

"When someone retires to Sterling Oaks, they can easily move to another unit as they age and need additional assistance. They can remain here for the rest of their lives. It's the same community and they still have the same friends who age alongside them. We offer quite a diverse culture for anyone and everyone."

Aging with Dignity, Tom almost said out loud.

"And here is Ed's apartment, three-five-nine-eight. I'm sure he will be happy to see you again. It was nice to meet you, Chris," Michelle said with a broad smile. "Tom, please call me next week. I'd like to hear how today's visit goes."

"Thank you, Michelle. I will."

Tom knocked on the door. While they were waiting, Chris whispered, "I think she likes you, Dad."

Tom shot Chris a strange look, his eyes narrowed. He didn't notice anything. Yet…

Ed Reilly opened his apartment door to greet his son and grandson. Michelle had mentioned Tom would visit today, so Ed was expecting *him*. He smiled and said, "Good morning," and motioned them in.

Closing the door, Ed turned and looked squarely at both men. Chris was as tall as his dad and looked a little like him. "Hello Tom. And who is this?"

"Chris is your grandson. He's fifteen and a freshman in high school."

"Hello," Chris said cordially, not knowing what else to say.

Ed stepped forward and stuck his hand out to shake Chris'. His grandfather had calloused hands and a powerful grip like his own father.

Without looking at Tom, Ed said with a hint of enthusiasm, "I'm glad you came today. Please take a seat."

Entering Ed's small apartment, Tom immediately recognized several familiar pieces of furniture, pictures, and knickknacks from the old house—the house he grew up in. On the end table, next to Ed's La-Z-Boy recliner, Tom spotted a picture of his mother.

It was evident that Ed didn't want another fiery episode. Tom recalled what Michelle had said earlier. *"You can't control what Ed says or does, but you can control how you react to him."*

I wonder if Ed remembers our visit last week.

Before sitting down, Tom turned and faced his father. "Ed, I want to apologize for raising my voice last week. I wasn't sure what to say, it had been so long, and well… I just wanted to say I'm sorry."

"No need for apologies, Tom. Let's let bygones be bygones."

He remembers.

An awkward silence filled the room as Tom sat on the couch next to Chris. As he settled in his recliner, Ed spoke first. "I moved to Sterling Oaks in 1997. I was one of the founding members. We've been growing steadily over the past few years. I guess there are more older folks now needing a place to retire. I've made some wonderful friends. Most of them are still around." Ed shifted his position.

"I guess you knew I sold the business? Since you left and had…" Ed glanced at Tom, "gone your own way, I didn't have anyone to pass it along to. So I retired and travelled—quite a bit, actually. That got old after a while and I was tired of taking care of the old homestead. It was just too big for one person. When Sterling Oaks opened, I thought, why not? So, I moved in and have enjoyed being here ever since. There's a lot going on all the time."

Tom had the impression Ed wanted to avoid any discussion about their past relationship, or that they had been estranged for over two decades. He decided not to stir the hornet's nest again.

Ed asked if they would like a tour of his apartment. Both stood up at the same time. "Sure."

"It's only a one-bedroom, but that's all I need. I sold most of the old stuff—stuff I didn't need when I moved to this apartment, but I kept a few personal things." Ed led them down the hall.

The walls were covered with pictures of Ed and his wife, Louise, Chris' grandmother. There were also a few photos of Tom when he was younger, and others of his grandfather at various places he had visited while traveling around the world. On the other side of the hall, another set of photos, certificates, and citations covered the wall—all about World War II.

The old photos of his grandfather fascinated Chris. He then spotted one toward the end of the hall that was color, not black and white. "Is this you, Dad?"

Tom turned around and instantly recognized a photo of him with several buddies in Vietnam. He had the same photo at his house— buried in the bottom of a desk drawer.

"Yes, that's me when I was in Vietnam with the Second Battalion of the 28th Infantry." Tom's voice was pure monotone. "I haven't thought about Vietnam in a long time," Tom lied.

Chris looked at his grandfather. "Dad never talks about the war."

Tom glared at Chris and repeated sarcastically, "Yeah, my father *never* talked about the war, either."

Ed sensed the tension in the air. "Well, that's the grand tour, including the 'Me Wall'."

"What's a 'Me Wall'?" Chris had never heard the term.

"It's a wall covered with pictures, certificates, and awards—all about 'me'," Ed proudly replied while gesturing his thumb toward his chest.

"Besides, if you can't dazzle 'em with brilliance, then baffle 'em with bull." Tom and Chris both laughed out loud, settling back on the couch in the front room.

Over the next few minutes, Ed asked about Chris' school, what subjects he liked, and if he played any sports. Chris answered he liked math and science and he had a cool history teacher, but didn't go into detail. Ed asked if Chris was into football and if he liked the Steelers. Chris said all the right things—he was beginning to warm to the older gentleman, his grandfather.

A few minutes later, Ed looked at Chris and asked the same question, "What subjects do you like in school?"

Both glanced at Ed oddly, but Chris simply replied, "I like math, science, and history." That seemed to satisfy Ed, but Tom wondered why he asked Chris the same question twice.

It was almost noon. Ed asked if they would join him for lunch. "Let's go hang the feed bag." That brought a chuckle.

Tom looked over at his son, who spoke up immediately. "I'm starving." That settled it. They were on for lunch.

Ed had no problem finding his way to the dining room on the first floor. "Three, please," he said to the young man at the head station. "Follow me."

They all ordered from the menu, and the waitress promptly brought their drinks. "This doesn't look like a retirement community, Ed," Tom said. "In fact, the menu looks pretty good."

"They have a variety of meals here and the food is always first class."

A few minutes later, an older, dark-haired woman cautiously approached the table. She was smartly dressed and wore a gorgeous smile. "Hi, Ed. It's wonderful to see you. I missed you the past few days. How have you been?" Tom could tell at a quick glance that she was old school—prim and proper with kind eyes. Much like he remembered his own mother.

Ed immediate backed up his chair and stood. "Hi Ester. I'd like you to meet my son, Tom, and grandson, Chris. They're visiting from West Virginia."

"Hello, Tom. Ed's talked a lot about you."

Tom's jaw dropped. *Why would Ed talk about him if they hadn't spoken to each other since 1975?*

Tom stood and gently shook Ester's hand. "Very nice to meet you, Ester."

"I won't take you from your company, Ed. I just wanted to come over and say 'Hi.' Please come see me when you can. I miss you," Ester said, looking directly into Ed's sparkling eyes. Both Tom and Chris noticed.

"I will, Ester. Thanks for stopping by."

After Ester walked away, Ed observed Tom and Chris staring at him, expecting an explanation. "She's my girlfriend," Ed explained with a wink and a smile, not elaborating any further.

Tom and Chris looked at each other. Then Chris smiled. "Way to go, Granddad!"

Tom was confused, not with Ed, but with his own feelings. He found himself torn between missing his mother and happy for Ed to have a companion, but he didn't dwell on it.

It wasn't long before their lunch arrived, which they all hungrily dug into. After a few bites, Ed asked, "How's the grub?" Tom mumbled his was good, and waited for Chris' response.

"It's a lot better than what we get at school."

Ed smiled. "Better than C-rations, too. Right, Tom?"

Chris watched his father to see how he'd reply to his grandfather's remark. "Much better, Ed," was all he said.

It didn't take them long to finish their lunches. They ate quickly with minimal conversation. "If we're done with lunch, let's blow this popsicle stand," Ed said as he backed his chair up. Chris noticed his dad smile, something he hadn't seen in a while. He enjoyed this new "language" his grandfather was introducing to them.

Ed wanted to show Tom and Chris around Sterling Oaks, so they walked directly outside from the dining area. It was another gorgeous spring day in the western Pennsylvania foothills. Ed took the long way around the community campus, sticking mostly to the sidewalks alongside the streets.

It was obvious to Tom that his father could get around with no problem. Tom questioned Michelle's story about the guard discovering him wandering aimlessly.

They walked by another couple of residents and greeted them with a courteous, "Hello." After they passed, Ed joked, "They're a couple of more inmates that live here." Chris chuckled at that comment.

Back at the apartment, Chris was antsy and explored more of the small apartment. He stopped at the end table, staring at something he hadn't seen earlier. "What's this, Granddad?"

Ed got up and walked over. "Your grandmother made this for me not long after I returned home from the war. It's called a 'Shadow Box' and contains my Army medals and unit insignias. Do you know what any of these are?"

Tom leaned in and listened carefully. While he knew about Ed's shadow box, he'd never heard these stories.

"I was wounded twice. This is my Purple Heart ribbon. The small oak crest on the ribbon signifies the second wound. The Bronze Star was awarded to me for charging a machine gun nest, tossing in a couple of grenades, and taking out the Germans who were shooting up my unit. The other medals are World War II campaign medals."

"What's this one?" Chris asked, pointing to another medal in the center of the shadow box.

"That's the Combat Infantry Badge," Ed said. "All Army infantry soldiers that fought against an enemy have one. Your dad has one, too. Did you know that?"

Chris glanced proudly over at his dad, who tried not to be obvious. Sensing the tension again, Ed changed the subject. He gently placed the shadow box back on the table and settled down in his recliner.

"I went over to Europe in 1995 for the fiftieth anniversary of the end of the war. It was the first time I'd been back since the war ended. I went with a group of other World War II veterans from the local American Legion. It was a great trip.

"The last time I'd been over there was in January 1946. There was a lot of death and confusion, and we just wanted to get back home as soon as we could. We'd been over there for almost nineteen months, between fighting the war and serving as the Occupation Force.

"Anyway, the French and Luxembourgers loved us. They treated us like royalty—great food and drink, and lots of ceremonies. They even unveiled a half dozen new memorials for my old division, the 80th. They served us champagne for breakfast, champagne for lunch, and champagne for dinner. It was great!"

Ed's voice changed to a more somber tone.

"I even visited one of the old concentration camps we helped liberate. I wasn't sure if I wanted to visit that evil place again, but I went along with the other veterans on the tour bus.

"Afterward, I was glad I did. Several camp survivors were there to greet us. By the end of the day, there wasn't a dry eye among us. We were all crying. They were so thankful, not only to have survived the horrors of the concentration camp, but to meet some of the soldiers who helped liberate them.

"I had taken over two of my Pittsburgh Steeler 'terrible towels.' Everybody went nuts when I swung them around over my head, like I do at football games. I gave a Steeler towel to one of the concentration camp survivors.

"He had lost everything, including both his parents, their parents, and all of his brothers and sisters. He was the only survivor in his family. I just can't imagine."

Ed sank back in his recliner and rubbed his eyes. It was obvious that memory pushed him deeper in thought, and his face slightly changed, almost like he was smiling at what he had accomplished during his life.

He was getting tired and closed his eyes for a moment. Tom and Chris decided it was time to go, so they stood and said their goodbyes. Ed hugged them both, something Tom hadn't experienced from his father in years.

Tom said he would be back in a week or two, depending on work. He had a big job coming up and needed to make sure he could get the work done while the weather held.

"I enjoyed meeting you, Granddad. Thanks for lunch," Chris said with a wide grin.

ON THE RIDE HOME, Tom and Chris rode quietly, thinking back on the man they had just met—father and grandfather—and both wondered when they'd see him again.

"Dad?"

"Yes, Chris?"

"Granddad seemed normal to me, except that one time when he asked me twice about school. That was weird. It was almost like he forgot what he had just asked."

"I noticed that, too. That may a sign of Alzheimer's. But he seemed perfectly normal when we talked about World War II."

"Yeah. He certainly remembered details about the war."

Chris asked, "Did you also see all the Post-it Notes around his apartment? I saw them after lunch."

"No, I didn't, but maybe that's just something older people do."

Tom wondered if he'd just witnessed several different signs of Alzheimer's. He'd have to ask Michelle about that. The thought of her brought a slight smile to his face.

6 - Reconnecting

Tom had a day between jobs, so he drove up to Sterling Oaks again, unannounced. It had been more than a week since his last visit—a great visit by any measure. He was, however, still cautious about the type of relationship he and his father might have. It had been a long time since his meltdown and he wondered if it was his fault or his father's.

Chris was in school. Tom didn't need to worry about keeping him entertained on this trip, though he thought the three of them connected well last time.

The drive up the interstate was a little rainy, but Tom cruised along smoothly in Sunshine. All guys had nicknames for their cars and Tom was no exception. He was proud of his GTO and kept it clean, waxed, and most important, fine-tuned. He knew it was valuable. It was original and in mint condition. But he had no intention of selling it... *ever*. It was worth far more to him than any amount of money anyone could offer.

As he pulled up to the guard gate at Sterling Oaks, a familiar face, Earl, approached his car. "Good morning, Mr. Reilly. Nice to see you again. I assume you're here to visit your father?"

Tom was a little annoyed—*why else would he be here?* But he didn't raise the question. Instead, he smiled with a, "Yes, sir."

Earl returned with his Visitor's Pass. "Do you know why the skeleton didn't go to the dance?"

Tom furrowed his brow and gave the security guard a strange look. He wasn't sure what kind of question that was, but Earl seemed bored, so he played along. "No, Earl. Why didn't the skeleton go to the dance?"

"Because he had no body to dance with.

"Do you know what a turkey's favorite dessert is?"

Without waiting for an answer, Earl smiled and said, "Peach gobbler.

"I've got more…"

"Thanks, but let's not use them all up today."

Tom shook his head, relieved he didn't have to listen to any more corny jokes. He was sure Earl had a thousand more. He seemed that type of person.

After parking in his usual spot, Tom walked in to first see Michelle, hoping she'd be in her office. When they last spoke on the phone, he reported an enjoyable visit with his father. She seemed pleased to hear that, but asked Tom to let her know when he would visit again. He realized he'd forgotten to call her about today's visit.

He thought back to Chris' earlier comment, *"She likes you, Dad,"* but quickly dismissed it. She was a professional and just doing her job to make sure everyone was as comfortable and welcomed as they could be.

Michelle's door was wide open, so he quietly knocked and poked his head in. She was on the phone, but smiled as she waved him in, pointing to a chair. He took a seat in front of her desk.

Tom looked around the room and immediately felt relaxed with the cozy surroundings—nicely decorated, and comfortably used. Michelle had put a professional woman's touch on her office furnishings, including floor lamps, plants, and plenty of open space. He strained to read the three university diplomas that hung on the wall behind her desk, but couldn't focus on the small print. *Maybe I need glasses.*

When she hung up the phone, she rose, as did Tom, walked around, shook his hand, and took the seat next to his.

"Good morning, Tom. This is a pleasant surprise." Michelle's smile was warm and inviting.

"Good morning. I had the day off and thought I'd come see Ed." Tom's voice sounded excited, like a kid on a new adventure. "We had a great visit last time when Chris was with me. How's Ed?"

"He's fine. I probably didn't mention this before, but we've assigned a 'Care Team' to him. It's standard procedure when someone has had an event."

"What's an 'event'?" There was a little worry in Tom's voice.

"It can be any number of things. In Ed's case, the event was when the security guard first found him wandering the grounds and confused. Even though he's in this initial stage of dementia, we need to make sure he doesn't wander off somewhere he shouldn't. It's not uncommon in these cases. All we do at this early stage is monitor his whereabouts."

"Has he experienced any events other than that initial one?"

"No, not that we've observed."

"That's good, isn't it?" Tom gently sighed as he relaxed in his chair.

"Of course. Unfortunately, we expect things to progressively decline over time," Michelle said in her professional voice.

"The only thing Chris and I noticed during our visit was that Ed repeated himself a couple of times."

"Oh?" Michelle raised her eyebrows. "Tell me more about that, Tom."

"Well, Ed asked Chris about school and sports and Chris told him what he was into. A few minutes later, Ed asked him the same thing. It's as if he forgot he'd already asked that question."

"Interesting. That's not uncommon though, when a person with early stage dementia repeatedly asks the same question. We hadn't observed that, but I'll make a note of it."

"One more thing, Michelle. Chris wandered around his apartment more than I did. After we left, he said there were a lot of Post-It Notes scattered about. Is that unusual?"

"Not really. Many older people need reminders for certain things, such as taking medication, classes they want to attend, and people they may want to see or call. They often use Post-It Notes. I wouldn't worry too much about that, but if you see anything else that seems out of the ordinary, please let me know."

Tom hesitated, then smiled. "How can I tell if something is out of the ordinary, Michelle? My father and I haven't seen or talked to each other for over twenty-five years. I don't have a clue what might be normal in his life right now."

"Excellent point, Tom," Michelle replied with an acknowledging grin. "I guess if you observe anything out of place, so to speak, then let me know. Deal?"

"Deal."

As Tom stood to shake Michelle's delicate but sturdy hand and thank her again, he noticed she didn't wear a ring on her left hand. Neither did he, but he hadn't realized it before. He didn't think twice about it, though. He was ready to see his father.

TOM FOUND ED'S APARTMENT, missing only one hallway turn. This time when he rang the doorbell, Ed promptly answered the door.

"Well, isn't this a pleasant surprise? Good morning, Tom."

Tom smiled. *Who was this strange man in front of him?*

"Hello, Ed. I had the day off and thought I'd drive up."

As soon as Tom walked into the foyer, he sensed someone else in the room.

"Ester, you remember my son, Tom?"

"Good morning, Tom. Nice to see you again. Ed and I were just talking about you. I hate to leave as soon as you've arrived, but I've got an appointment I don't want to miss. I'll leave you two boys to catch up. Nice to see you again."

Ed gently closed the door after Ester. Turning around, he said softly, "Ester is a good friend. Her husband died about a year ago. He was a wonderful friend, too.

"Please, have a seat and take a load off your feet."

Tom cracked a smile. That was something his father often said while he was growing up, not only to Tom, but to everyone who came in their house.

"What brings you to Sterling Oaks?"

Tom thought twice before answering and chose his words carefully. "I was thinking about what you did after I… you know, after I left… *abruptly*."

Ed looked thoughtfully at his son before responding. "Well, a lot. My business took off in the eighties—enough to open a second appliance store and hire additional employees and repairmen. I had quite a successful business.

"When I reached retirement age, someone approached me to buy the business and made me an offer I couldn't refuse. Since you and I parted ways, and you had left, I didn't have anyone to leave it to or take over. So I took the deal."

Tom was listening, looking out the front window, wanting to light up a cigarette, but knew there was no smoking in the apartment.

"I'm sorry, Ed, but at that time, I didn't like myself very much and I couldn't stand to be around people. I know it was painful for you, but I just needed time to find my own way. I guess, in a way… I'm still looking."

After a few moments, Ed suggested they go outside for a smoke, surprising Tom. He didn't think his father smoked anymore.

They took the stairs down to the ground floor. Ed commented this was one of his ways of staying in shape. They walked outside to a different, yet similarly designed, courtyard than the one Tom and Michelle had sat earlier. There were more bird feeders scattered throughout this courtyard and Tom heard several Goldfinches battling it out near a feeder.

They found a couple of chairs in the shade of a tall magnolia, and Ed pulled out a Camel cigarette. Tom asked if that was the same brand he'd always smoked.

"Yep. Got started when I was in the Army. These were the same cigarettes we had in our C-rations."

Tom smiled, catching Ed's attention. He pulled out a Marlboro, lit it, and inhaled. "Same here. They put Marlboros in *our* C-rations and I didn't see a need to change. If it ain't broke, don't fix it."

Both men smiled and hung onto those words—it was a breakthrough moment.

Tom spoke next. "After I, um… left, I drifted around, picking up work here and there. You taught me to do most anything with my own two hands, so I worked a lot of odd jobs. Mostly, I worked on houses, both new and old, a little electrical work and plumbing, and some painting. I found more steady work as a painter, so that's the path I took. I'm my own boss, have my own place, and Chris lives with me."

"He seems like a great kid, Tom. Like you were, only a little more shy."

"He is, Ed. We get along all right, but he spends a lot of time on his computer. He's not into playing sports like I was, but he has good grades. He used to ask me to help with his homework, but sometime during middle school, I just couldn't keep up with the math. I never could."

Tom glanced over at Ed, who grinned broadly. "What's so funny?"

"You're watching yourself grow up, Tom. Back when you were in school, it got to where neither your mom nor I could help you with *your* homework. Heck, neither of us went to college, but we did all right."

The mere mention of his mother hung in the air.

"Are you married, Tom?"

"Not anymore." Tom wasn't prepared to open up his personal life yet.

"Where do you live now? I think I heard Ms. Myers mention Morgantown. Is that right?"

"Yep. I bought a small, three-bedroom, two-bath house, and that's where Chris and I live. It's about an hour and a half drive from here and interstate most of the way."

It was obvious both Ed and Tom were avoiding the elephant in the room—the fallout, and the reasons behind it. In the back of his mind, Tom wondered if his father remembered any of that. Or maybe his avoidance was merely another symptom of dementia.

After a few more minutes of silence, both snubbed out their cigarettes and grabbed another one. Tom lit his and offered to light Ed's. "Thanks."

"Do you still follow the Steelers?" Tom wanted to keep the conversation going.

"I do, but they're a different team these days. I miss the days of Terry Bradshaw, Franco Harris, and Lynn Swann. The seventies were the best."

"I don't disagree. I think the seventies were the best football teams of all time, not just the Steelers. These days, it's all about money. Football is just not like it used to be."

Tom decided to ask *the question.* "Ed, do you know what's happening?" That came out of nowhere, but Tom wasn't sure how else to ask.

"What do you mean?" Tom noticed Ed was trying to focus, like he knew something was amiss, but couldn't quite figure it out.

"Has anyone told you that you've been diagnosed with dementia?"

"The doctor may have told me something like that, but I don't remember." Ed smiled and winked at Tom. "I didn't believe her. I told her I thought she was full of it. I mean, *all* old folks get a little senile. So what if I forget to go to an appointment, or miss a class, or skip a workout? At this point in my life, I should be able to do *what* I want and *when* I want to do it."

Tom could see Ed was getting a little irritated, so he changed the subject. "Hell, Ed. I forget things, too. It's no big deal.

"Say, isn't it about time for lunch? How about we go to the dining room and grab something to eat?"

Both men snubbed out their cigarettes, stood and headed indoors. It was still cloudy and cool, but the rain had held off.

AFTER LUNCH, they leisurely strolled back to Ed's apartment, not saying much along the way. It was obvious Ed was a little tired and probably needed an afternoon nap. Tom had always heard the older people get, the more sleep they needed—like napping dogs and cats. But before he left, he had one more question.

"Ed. Chris is working on a history project about World War II and asked if he could interview you about the war. Would that be okay?"

"Of course," Ed replied with no hesitation. "I always enjoy talking to the younger generation. I often speak to middle school kids about the war, the Germans, and what little I know about the Japanese. They seem to enjoy my stories.

"I don't get too gruesome, but I want them to know that war is terrible. It also helps keep me young and sharp. So sure, I'd be happy to spend time with my grandson. Just let me know when and where."

"Thanks. I'll let Chris know. It'll be in a week or two. It's part of his final project for his history class. He needs to finish it before the end of the school year.

"I need to get on the road and head back. Thank you for today and for lunch. I'll call the next time I'm coming up. Please tell Ester I said goodbye."

"Will do, Tom. Thanks for coming. Have a safe drive back."

Tom thought his father wanted to add something, but after a few seconds, decided he wasn't going to.

Halfway to the exit, he swung by Michelle's office to let her know how the visit went, but she wasn't in her office. The receptionist said she was out on appointments for the rest of the day.

STARTING HIS CAR, Tom noticed it was low on gas. Before getting back onto the interstate, he pulled into a small mom and pop grocery store with a couple of old style gas pumps. The road sign read, "Cold coffee & stale sandwiches served with a smile."

After filling up Sunshine, he went inside the store to pay for gas and to buy a cup of coffee. Walking through the squeaky wooden screen door, Tom was hit with a wave of nostalgia. The shelves were made from old wood but neatly stocked with very few empty spaces. The wooden floors creaked as he walked toward the cashier. The smell inside reminded him of the old grocery his grandmother used to take him to—fresh baked bread and cookies, and brewing coffee.

Standing in line at the cash register, he spotted a rustic gentleman in faded khakis and a dark green, button down shirt behind the counter. His weathered face looked similar to his own father's and he sported a well-worn U.S. Army Veteran ball cap.

"Mornin'."

Tom felt the veteran looking him over as he reached in his back pocket for his wallet.

"You look like Army. Vietnam?"

"Yes sir. And you? When were you in 'Nam?"

The older man cracked a big smile. "I was in the Korean War. I just turned sixty-nine last week."

The veteran did not look anywhere close to sixty-nine.

"Well then, Happy Birthday. I was Second Battalion, 28th Infantry—Black Lions."

"No kidding. Big Red One, eh? I was First Battalion, 14th Infantry, 25th Division—Tropic Lightning. Small world, isn't it?"

"Yes, sir. It is a small world."

Tom picked up his coffee and smiled at the veteran as he shook his hand. He noticed a long, jagged scar along the length of his forearm.

"Thank you, Son. Both wars were hell."

"All wars are hell," Tom said out loud as he walked out the door.

Part II

FLASHBACKS

We could have won the Vietnam War,
but we weren't allowed to.
There was one big STOP sign at the border.

7 - World War II—Only Moves Forward

Tom lazily stumbled down the hallway, still half-asleep, and headed straight to the kitchen to make a pot of wake-me-up juice. He found Chris up and already dressed, eating a big bowl of Wheat Chex.

"Good morning, Dad," Chris said with a hint of enthusiasm.

"Mornin', Son."

Tom noticed his son watching him with an anxious look as he made his way around the kitchen.

"I'm excited to see Granddad again. Aren't you?"

"I am, actually." Tom thoughtfully glanced over at Chris as he measured the coffee grounds. "I think he's also looking forward to seeing us again."

Tom fixed his usual quick breakfast—a fried egg sandwich on wheat toast—and sat down next to Chris at the kitchen table. Both hurried to finish their meal and were soon on the road. A few minutes after Tom pulled onto the interstate, he told Chris about his recent visit.

"Ed was a little more with it when I saw him earlier. He didn't repeat any questions like before and seemed normal. I also learned Ester Mills really is just a friend. Her husband died last year, and both were good friends with Ed. They all moved into Sterling Oaks about the same time. Your grandfather was joking when he said she was his girlfriend.

"I think the older people get, their sense of humor dries up, though they may not realize it. At least, it seems that way with Ed." Tom smiled.

"Dad, last night I was on the computer and read more about Granddad's division. There's a lot about the 80th on the Internet."

"Really? Like what?" Tom was curious to learn what his son had discovered.

"Well, they landed in Normandy on Utah Beach in early August, about two months after D-Day. By the end of the war, they had been in combat for 277 days. Even though the war was over in May, they remained in Europe. They were mostly in Austria, Germany, and Czechoslovakia as an Occupation Force until they came home in January 1946."

Tom calculated that amount of time in-country—eighteen months, give-or-take. The 80th had spent a month in England before landing in Normandy. He compared that to his time in Vietnam— January '68 through April '69—about fifteen months.

"Dad, how long were you in Vietnam?"

This was the first time in a while Chris had asked his dad about the Vietnam War. The last few times weren't pleasant for either of them.

"I was just thinking about that. I went over in mid-January 1968 and was supposed to be there for a year. That was the standard tour of duty for most soldiers. But I came home in the middle of that tour for my mother's funeral—that was in June '68. After the funeral, I flew back and stayed until April '69. So all in all, I was in-country about fifteen months."

Tom glanced over at his son. "I'm impressed, Chris. You said you found all that on the computer?" Tom didn't know a thing about computers or the Internet and frankly, didn't give a damn. But now it sounded like there was more on the Internet than just games. He would have to ask Chris about that someday.

"Do you know what you want to ask your grandfather?"

"Yep. My history teacher gave me some questions. He said most veterans focus on only a few stories they've told over and over again."

Tom could certainly attest to that.

"He said to use these as a guideline and to let Granddad tell his story his way. He also suggested I bring my tape recorder to record the interview. It may help me later recall some of Granddad's answers."

"What sort of questions?"

"Let me get them." Chris smiled as he reached into the backseat to retrieve his backpack. It had been a long time since he and his dad had a conversation like this.

"Okay, the first part is background stuff, such as name, rank, and serial number, birthdate, and where he was born. Granddad said he was with the 80th Division, but I also want to know which company.

"I should also ask him about his Army job and where he fought in Europe. He told us a little, but Mr. Johnson said that veterans may go into more detail when asked specific questions."

Tom was both intrigued and impressed with his son. While Chris excitedly discussed the questions he would ask Ed, Tom mentally answered them about his own time in Vietnam.

"There are other things I want to ask, like where had basic training and any medals he received. Granddad said he got the Bronze Star and two Purple Hearts. Hopefully, he'll tell us how he got them."

Cruising up the interstate, Tom was looking forward to this visit, much more than he originally thought. His father might actually talk more about the war now than he did when Tom was growing up.

It was another gorgeous day in the middle of April. The trip to Sterling Oaks seemed to pass quickly. When they arrived and parked the car, Chris commented, "Dad, do you realize you didn't smoke a single cigarette this whole trip?"

"I didn't really think about it, but you're right. I guess I didn't feel a need."

He wasn't sure why, but Tom appreciated his son's observation. He was more relaxed now than he'd been in a while.

They walked straight to Ed's apartment and rang the doorbell. Ed opened the door with a surprised look on his face.

"Well, good morning." Ed smiled as he greeted his son and grandson. "And to what do I owe the pleasure of this visit?"

Tom and Chris exchanged quizzical looks.

"I called a few days ago and told you we were coming. Chris is going to interview you about World War II. Did you forget?"

"Was that today? It must have slipped my mind. But that's okay, come on in.

"Can I get you a coffee, water, or something else to drink?"

"If you have coffee ready, I'll take a cup," Tom replied, still confused.

"I'll take a Coke, Granddad, if you have one."

"I just put on a fresh pot and yes, I have Coke."

After serving his son and grandson, Ed sat in his big recliner and asked about their week. All three took turns catching up. Ed looked half interested. Tom couldn't tell if he was bored, unfocused, or if this was part of his dementia. He found himself more in an observation mode as Michelle had suggested, watching and listening for anything that may seem odd or out of place.

Chris turned on his recorder and placed it on the coffee table.

"Granddad, thanks for letting me interview you for my World War II project. My history teacher said while you can learn some things from a book, you can learn a lot more from someone who was actually there during the war."

Tom couldn't agree more.

"I'm happy to do this for my grandson. A lot of World War II veterans live here at Sterling Oaks. Now and then, I'll get into a conversation with one of them. It's fairly easy to tell who was on the front lines and who was in the rear. I try not to make a big deal out of it. In the long run, it doesn't matter. We all did what we needed to do to win the war."

Ed leaned forward toward Chris, his fingertips touching, like a church steeple, one eyebrow arched.

"Tell me, Chris. What do you know about the 80th Division?"

"Well, they also fought in World War I and were reactivated in 1942 to fight in World War II. They weren't part of the D-Day invasion, but landed in Normandy two months later, in August."

"That's right. I'm impressed. It's probably more than Tom knew. I didn't talk much about the war when he was growing up. You're pretty smart, though," Ed added with a smile and a wink, scooting back in his chair. "You must get that from your grandfather." Chris smiled as he glanced over at this father.

"Do you know their nickname is the 'Blue Ridge Division'?"

"I read that, but I'm not sure why."

"The 80th Division—the *Blue Ridge Division*—originally recruited men from Virginia, West Virginia, and Pennsylvania. All are states in the Blue Ridge Mountain range. During World War II, there were three regiments: the 317th, the 318th, and the 319th. I was with the 319th."

Chris jotted down a few notes in his spiral-bound notebook. Tom watched his father watch his son.

"Well, that makes sense. Okay. Where were you born?"

"I was born in Pittsburgh on August 18, 1920. I ended up with the 319th because that regiment originally recruited men from western Pennsylvania."

"Were you drafted or did you volunteer?"

"I was drafted, as most men were back then. After the Japanese attacked Pearl Harbor in 1941, a lot of us wanted to join and many did. But my father needed me to stay home to work with him and my mother on the farm. When the war escalated, I was drafted in July 1943. I was almost twenty-three years old."

That surprised Tom. He wasn't aware that his father had been drafted. It also dawned on him that he was *only* eighteen. And… he *volunteered.*

"Where did you do receive basic training?"

"Basic training was at Camp Forrest, Tennessee. That's where the 80th Infantry Division was reactivated in 1942. I got there in July 1943. After that, we transferred to Camp Phillips, Kansas for a short while, then to the California-Arizona Maneuver Area for desert training in the fall of 1943. At the time, the higher ups believed we might need to fight in the desert of North Africa.

"From California, we took a train to Fort Dix, New Jersey. On July 1, we sailed on the *Queen Mary* over to Scotland, then traveled by train to England. We were there, I guess, about a month before going over to Normandy.

"All that time, we were getting organized, training, and learning about the Germans first-hand from soldiers who had already fought in France. They were in England recovering from their wounds.

"While in England, I was assigned to Company F, a rifle company, in the Second Battalion of the 319th Infantry."

"What was your job in the Army?"

"My MOS—that's Military Occupational Specialty—was a Rifleman. All Army personnel train to be riflemen. Many receive additional training to be cooks, clerks, artillerymen, or medics. But all of us learned to fire a rifle.

"I was already a pretty good shot. My father taught me. We hunted a lot in the mountains when I was a young boy. I also taught your dad how to shoot when he was young."

Ed glanced over at Tom, both exchanged smiles.

"Our primary weapon was the M-1 Garand rifle. We also learned to use machine guns, mortars, grenades, and several different German rifles. When you're at war, you may not have your own weapons and equipment with you all the time. You need to learn how to fight with any weapon you can get your hands on."

Tom got up to get another cup of coffee. "Ed, do you want a refill?"

"Yes, please. Black, no sugar."

Ed looked at Chris. "I never drank coffee before the Army. Back in basic, we always had milk and sugar. But when we got over to Europe and on the battlefield, I started drinking it black. It was so cold on some mornings that coffee or any hot drink tasted good."

As he filled both cups—black, no sugar—Tom realized he was more like his father than he previously thought.

"What major battles did you fight in, Granddad?"

Ed briefly closed his eyes and quietly answered. "There were so many." He paused a few moments, then opened his eyes, focusing on Chris.

"I guess the history books only mention the big battles, like the Battle of the Bulge, the Siegfried Line, and crossing the Rhine River. To tell you the truth, Chris, most history books are written by people who've never been a part of history. I mean, how can you write about something you've never experienced?"

Tom watched his father and hung on every word. He had never revealed this much detail.

"Let me walk you through a few battles we faced. I'll do them in order. That will help me remember them. Stop me if I go too fast."

Tom was amazed at how much his father recalled, even after fifty-six years. *Dementia, my ass.*

"The first time I experienced fighting the Germans was a place called Angers, France. It wasn't what I would call a major battle, but for those of us who had never been shot at, believe me, it was major to us.

"As it turns out, it wasn't that big of a fight, but the Germans knew how to launch their artillery at us. And let me tell you, being caught in an artillery barrage is no picnic."

That comment momentarily took Tom back to Vietnam and the hundreds of mortar and rocket attacks he'd also experienced—even inside his unit's base camp at Lai Khe.

"Let's see, I remember that we had to cross a lot of rivers and we had to fight to cross every one. The first major battle of the 80th Division was crossing the Moselle River in France.

"If I remember correctly, we failed on our first attempt to cross it in early September '44. The Germans anticipated our crossing in that area and were well prepared with their artillery. Several companies made it across the river, but because the Germans beat back most of our battalion, we all pulled back.

"We lost a lot of men during that initial crossing attempt. Orders came down to wait until we had a better plan to cross. That happened a few days later. We crossed the Moselle at a different location and pushed the Germans back."

Chris was tempted to ask his grandfather if he had killed any Germans during that river crossing, but he remembered what his dad had said earlier: *"don't ask veterans if they killed anyone."*

"Once we crossed the Moselle, we kept moving forward, pushing the Germans back. There were lots of other battles—both small and not-so-small. Some were in cities and towns, others in wooded areas. The next big battle for the 80th was the Battle of the Ardennes. You probably know it as the Battle of the Bulge.

"But before I get to that, I need to make a pit stop."

Ed rose from his recliner, put his coffee cup down on the wooden end table, and walked down the hall to the bathroom.

"You're doing a great job, Chris," Tom whispered to his son.

"Thanks, Dad. This is really cool. Granddad remembers *everything*."

Tom wondered again about his father's memory loss—dementia… or was it Alzheimer's—and how that affected him. *He's able to recall details from a half century ago, yet he didn't remember they were coming today.*

When Ed returned, he asked if they were hungry. It was a little after noon. Tom hadn't realized how quickly the time had passed. Ed's stories intrigued him, and he didn't want to stop, but he sensed Ed was ready for a break. The three of them walked down the stairs for lunch in the main dining area.

AFTER ANOTHER PLEASANT and leisurely lunch, Ed suggested they go outside for a smoke. Even though Tom hadn't smoked at all on the drive up, he felt a need—or maybe a connection with his father—to smoke. They walked outside to the same courtyard where he and Ed had talked earlier. Both pulled out and lit a cigarette.

Ed asked Chris if he smoked. Chris glanced at his dad before answering.

"I tried a couple of times, but gagged. It didn't taste good, and I almost puked. So, no sir, I don't smoke."

Tom beamed at his son's response. He was honest and forthright. Most of all, he was respectful, something he had tried to teach him his entire life. His grandfather was bringing out the best in him.

As they sat in the shade, Ed looked at Chris. "What's next? What else do you have for your old Granddad?"

Chris examined his list of questions, then looked over at his grandfather. "You said earlier that you have two Purple Hearts. Can you tell us about them?"

"Of course." Ed didn't hesitate before responding, almost as if he was proud that he had been wounded.

"The first one, I got hit by shrapnel—that's a piece of metal from an artillery shell—during the Battle of the Bulge. We were in a place called Heiderscheid, Luxembourg. It was the coldest winter that town had seen in fifty years and boy, we felt it. There was snow all over the place—deep snow, too. In fact, the combat engineers gave us some C-4 explosive to blast a hole in the frozen ground so we could dig our foxholes. It was that cold.

"We didn't have the right cold weather clothes or shoes, either, and there weren't enough blankets to go around. I remember our First Sergeant issued one blanket for every two-man foxhole. That way, one of us would have to stay awake while the other slept with the blanket.

"Anyway, one night we were in our foxholes—it was a clear night and the moon was bright. We could see a good distance, even in the dark. We heard the artillery coming in. The German howitzer 105s make a distinctive sound, like a slowly moving *swoosh*. It gets louder as it gets closer. Most of the time, their firing wasn't accurate, but we could tell this one would be close.

"We stayed low in our foxholes to wait it out. After that first shell hit, it was a little too close. The Germans never launched just one artillery shell; we knew more would be on the way. So the two of us ran toward another foxhole a few yards away.

"We were lucky because the next one landed right in the foxhole we had just left. It exploded with a deafening sound and we both dove for the new foxhole. I got hit with a piece of shrapnel. I reached around and felt blood and what I thought were pieces of torn flesh. I was sure I had a terrible wound in my back. It turned out it wasn't too bad.

"I still have a piece in my butt. I'd show you the scar, but this is probably not the time or place," Ed said with a smile, shifting in his seat as he pointed to his rear.

"It doesn't hurt. It never really did, but that was my first Purple Heart. The medics at Battalion Aid patched me up, and I returned to my unit the next day. I wasn't going to let a little pain in *my* ass stop me."

Chris and Tom both laughed out loud.

The truth of that moment slammed into Tom right then. This was the first he'd heard this story—the first time his father had opened up about his war. Tom himself had two Purple Hearts, one also for shrapnel. Yet he and his father had *never* taken the moment to bond over their shared war experiences. He frowned, shaking away his past years of regret, and continued to listen.

"I got the second Purple Heart for doing something foolish. It was the same action where I was awarded the Bronze Star."

"What happened, Granddad?" Both Chris and Tom leaned a little closer—they didn't want to miss a thing.

"We were in Germany and had crossed the Prim River—early March I think. The German army morale was pretty low. We'd been beating them further back more and more every day. But there were still plenty of German fanatics out there. We had to be careful and not take too many risks. But in war, that's all there is… risks.

"We were getting close to the town of Kaiserslautern, Germany. Just as we approached the outskirts of the town, a Kraut machine gun opened up on my squad, hitting several men. Two were killed instantly. We were pinned down. Every time we'd poke our heads up to see where the fire was coming from, that damned machine gun would fire on us.

"I was on the far right of the squad, slightly hidden from the Krauts' view. I could peek over an embankment to see the machine gun. It seemed like it was only a few yards away. I learned later it was almost sixty yards. I'm sure glad I didn't know that at the time," Ed said with a curt laugh.

"While they were firing on my squad to my left, I started crawling, keeping close to the ground. They didn't see me. I guess I was about twenty yards away when I grabbed a couple of my grenades and charged them. I remember it precisely. I thought that may be the last time I would run… *ever*.

"It was almost like slow motion. I threw both grenades. About that same time, another Kraut saw me and shot me, clipping me in the arm. But my grenade found its way into the machine gun nest, taking out two Krauts. The rifle shot only grazed me;the bullet went through the fleshy part of my arm. The grenade blast also dazed the Kraut that shot me, but I finished him off with my M-1.

"I stumbled into their nest, falling face first into what was left of one of the blown up Krauts. I still can't forget that awful smell." Ed crinkled his nose and slightly shook his head. "But when I got up, I let my buddies know the machine gun was out of commission."

As the story unfolded, both Chris and Tom closely watched Ed. His eyes were focused on the distant hills, but with a blank stare, almost as if he were back in Germany again, reliving that very day. Neither spoke and waited for Ed to return.

Tom lit another cigarette and asked Ed if he wanted one. After a long pause, Ed quietly said, "Yes. Thank you."

As Tom lit his father's cigarette, he noticed his hands were shaking. "Ed, are you okay?"

"Yes, I'm fine. I haven't thought about that event for a long time. It brings back some not-so-good memories."

Tom also stared out toward the hills and asked in a quiet voice, "Why didn't you tell me any of this when I was growing up? I mean, I must have asked you a thousand times."

"I guess I wasn't ready, Tom. Back then, I did my job over there and came home. I lost a lot of buddies and I didn't want to dwell on their loss. I… I just needed to move on."

Tom looked at his dad with renewed admiration.

"Did you ever tell mom any of this?"

"No, not really. She'd ask, but you have to understand *our* generation, Tom. We grew up in the depression era. Men didn't share their feelings. When I got back from the war, your mother was overjoyed I had made it. But she had a lot of friends whose husbands or boyfriends didn't come back. We were just happy to be together again." Ed took a long puff of his cigarette and slowly blew out the smoke.

"She told me I'd wake up in the middle of the night, shaking with cold sweats. She asked if I'd had a nightmare, but I couldn't tell her. I didn't want her to worry. She worried enough about me when I was overseas. I just kept it to myself and moved on with my life. That's what I did… that's what we *all* did."

Tom also remembered when he had nightmares about *his* war—and that he still had them.

"Is that why mom told me never to slam doors in the house and never wake you up?"

"Yeah, I guess she did. It took me a long time to 'get home,' so to speak, but we managed."

After a long few minutes of silence, Ed turned to Chris with a crooked smile. "Are you going to interview your dad about Vietnam?"

That surprised both Tom and Chris. Neither expected it, but looked at each other for an answer. Tom paused for a moment, then sat up straight.

"Today is Ed's day. Let's finish his oral history first. Then we'll see if there's time for mine."

Tom was obviously stalling, but deep down, he knew his son had a lot of questions for him.

Ed asked his grandson if he had any more questions. Chris had a couple, but wasn't sure how to ask them.

"Granddad, you showed me a few of your medals when we were here last time. Is the Bronze Star your favorite? I mean, does it mean the most to you?"

"No, the Combat Infantry Badge means more to me than the Bronze Star."

"Why that one?"

That surprised Tom. He'd received a Bronze Star and two Purple Hearts—the same as his father—none of which meant anything to him. There was too much pain and anguish associated with them. He also had the CIB, but it lay in the bottom of the same drawer with all his other Vietnam crap.

"The CIB was awarded to soldiers who fought against an enemy. It's more than that, though. To me, it's special because for those of us with a Combat Infantry Badge, you can't get much closer than that."

"You mean, fighting the Germans—getting close to them to fight?"

"No, not really. I guess what I'm trying to say is that while, yes, you are close enough to fight the enemy, you're not fighting alone— you are *never* alone. You *always* have somebody with you, someone who watches your back.

"That means someone who would lay their life on the line with you *and* for you. We did that so many times during the war. You just can't get any closer than that—close to the enemy, sure. But also closer to your buddies and closer to God.

"It's a bond that a veteran will never forget."

Hearing those words from his father, Tom began to tear up. He had never thought of it that way. He, too, had lost buddies in Vietnam. But he wanted to run away from all those memories—those nightmares of the entire war.

He didn't have the same feelings about *his* war as his father did. Vietnam was much different. Yet, there were similarities that he was just now beginning to realize.

Chris brought him back to the present. "Granddad, that's all I have right now. Is there anything else you'd like to add? And if I have more questions, can I come back?"

"That covers it, Chris. I don't have anything else. And yes, please come anytime. I've enjoyed visiting with you and your dad."

AS THEY DROVE HOME, Tom and Chris reflected on the day's events. The interview had gone well—much better than Tom expected—and both learned about Ed's time in the war.

Tom wondered if he had made a mistake keeping Chris away from Ed. But the simple fact was he just couldn't bring himself to talk to his father over all those estranged years. That was, until now.

"Dad. Granddad said he was wounded a couple of times and he won the Bronze Star. Did you get any medals in Vietnam?"

Tom wasn't ready to answer *that* question. He took out a Marlboro, lit it, and continued driving, not answering Chris. He took a couple of deep puffs from his cigarette. His son had touched a sensitive nerve, but after a moment, Tom decided to answer.

"Yes, I was wounded. Twice, like your grandfather. It hurt me a lot more than it did him. I was also awarded the Bronze Star.

"I know you're curious, but I just don't want to talk about it right now. Maybe another time, but not now. I hope you can understand." Tom glanced over at Chris—his face frowned at his disappointing answer.

"Let's talk about your grandfather."

Tom again avoided his own war. He wasn't prepared to go there… yet.

"Okay, I guess.

"It was strange when we first got there, wasn't it? I mean, Granddad didn't seem to remember we were coming, almost like he forgot."

"Yeah, I thought that, too. But when he began to talk about the war, he was very clear. It's almost as if that's a trigger for him to regain his memory. I'll ask Michelle—Ms. Myers—about that the next time I see her."

Chris smiled at his father's mention of Ms. Myers. She was a nice lady and seemed very helpful. He was sure that Ms. Myers liked his dad.

He didn't remember much about his own mother. His dad rarely talked about her. In fact, his father rarely talked with him much over the past few years.

But during the past few weeks, they had talked more than they had in a long time. He wondered if it was because his grandfather had recently come into their lives or if it was something else.

8 - World War II—The End of the War

Chris had completed and turned in his history project. After reviewing it, Mr. Johnson suggested he spend a little more time with his grandfather, learning what he did at the end of the war. He explained that's when the Third Army discovered German concentration camps—a lot of them. His grandfather may elaborate on those events.

Chris learned from the Internet that these were more than Prisoner of War camps. Here, the Germans killed the prisoners, mostly Jews and political prisoners. It was difficult for him to read about how cruelly the Germans treated Jews. But considering his grandfather had been an eyewitness, Chris wanted to learn what he saw first-hand. He knew from his history class these camps were one of the most important reasons the United States fought in World War II.

It surprised Chris that the world did not know about these atrocities at the time. Mr. Johnson simply pointed out that during World War II, there was no Internet. And not many people in France, Germany, or Poland spoke out against the Germans for fear of being killed.

Mr. Johnson provided Chris with several specific questions to ask his grandfather. He also said that if he drifted off topic or didn't want to talk about a specific event, to ask him about the weather—was it cold or hot? Was it clear or cloudy? Sometimes by slightly changing the topic, his grandfather might focus on more detail.

"DAD?" "DAD?!"

Tom answered from down the hall. "What's up, Chris? Are you okay?"

"Can you come in here? I found something on the computer."

"Sure. Be there in a minute."

Tom walked in and briefly glanced around Chris' bedroom. He'd purposefully given his son a lot of space—both physical and mental. He didn't want to be nosy, so he made it a point not to enter his room unless invited. At fifteen, Chris was certainly old enough to know right from wrong. But he was still a teenager and subject to the social pressures of high school freshmen.

Tom spotted a couple of band posters on the wall, neither of whom he'd heard about. Then he noticed a dartboard and smiled, remembering a similar dartboard when he was that age.

In the background, he heard a group he'd come to know as NSYNC, one of Chris' favorites. Tom also appreciated that his son didn't blare the music loud like other kids his age.

While there were clothes piled in the chair and a few scattered about on the floor, it wasn't as messy as he thought it could have been. There was a slight stale odor, but thankfully, it didn't smell like a high school gym locker room.

"What's up?"

Chris momentarily tore his eyes away from the computer screen, glancing at his father with an excited look. Tom sat down on the bed, behind him so he could also see.

"I was reading a little more about the 80th Division and where Granddad was near the end of the war and found these articles about concentration camps. They were horrible, Dad. It's tough to read, but then I realized that Granddad was there and witnessed a lot of this. That may be one reason why he didn't talk about the war with you."

Tom leaned forward. The horrible black and white computer images of tortured men and battered women were beyond one's imagination. The lamp shades made of tattooed human skin made him wonder what kind of human animal could do such a thing.

"Dad. Did you know this was how the Germans treated prisoners?"

Tom had to turn his head. Some of the images brought back similar memories of his past in Vietnam. He took a deep breath.

"Yes, Chris. War is much different than what you see in the movies. I know your grandfather was there and I'm sure he witnessed many prisons like these.

"Tell you what… when we meet with him again, let's be careful when talk about these camps. Deal?"

"I think you're right, Dad. These are pictures I'm sure he'd rather forget."

Chris leaned back in his chair, then looked at his dad and changed gears with a renewed excitement in his voice.

"Oh, and I found something else… not related to World War II. I got distracted and wanted to learn more about Granddad's dementia and Alzheimer's disease."

Chris typed away on the keyboard with the confidence of a teenage computer hack. "I found this document. *Dementia in World War II Combat Veterans—Observations*, authored by Dr. Michelle Myers.

"Is this Ms. Myers at Sterling Oaks?"

Tom pulled a chair up next to his son to get a better look.

"It must be. I guess she was still at the University of Pittsburgh when she wrote this. Have you read it, or… can you read it?"

"It looks pretty technical, Dad, and it's really long. The first part describes that she interviewed over one hundred World War II veterans during her research. I guess she knows a lot about veterans." Chris sat back so that his father could get closer to the screen.

"Wow. I had no idea.

"I thought you were only reading about World War II. What made you look into dementia?" Tom sat back in his chair, crossed his arms over his chest, and looked at his son.

"I don't know, Dad. I originally wanted to learn more about Granddad's war. But the more I read, the more I wanted to know more about him. It's hard to describe but… I didn't have a grandfather growing up like most other kids. Now that I have one, I'm trying to learn more about him."

Chris looked up at his dad, a question in his eyes. "Does that make sense?"

Tom felt a twinge creeping up the back of his neck. He had a strong urge for a cigarette and a drink, but knew he needed to answer his son's question.

"Chris, I wish things were different, I honestly do. I know I lost a lot of years with your grandfather… and with you. I can't change the past, but I know we can make the most of the future. We've got plenty of time."

Tom reached over and put his hand on his son's shoulder. "I'm pleased you want to know more about your grandfather. So do I."

THE DRIVE TO STERLING OAKS was enjoyable and engaging, with Chris and Tom chatting away. Tom showed more interest, not only about his son's history project but also about his social life.

Chris didn't have many friends. But then neither did he. Since starting high school though, Chris seemed to be coming out of his shell and socializing more. Tom wasn't sure if it was because he was a freshman in a new school or if he was growing up and becoming a young man.

Tom boasted about his job, something he rarely did, especially with his son. But what can you say about house painting? Instead, Tom spoke of his work ethic. Because he gave every job his best, contractors always had work for him. Now and then, someone would call him for carpentry work or repair. Tom could do most any work with his hands, like his father.

They arrived at Sterling Oaks mid-morning. After parking Sunshine, they hustled straight to Ed's apartment. Tom rang the doorbell and waited—no response. He had called earlier in the week and told Ed they were coming again. He should be home. Tom glanced at Chris, raising his eyebrows in question.

Tom rang the doorbell again. A few moments later, his father opened the door, looking annoyed. "Who's there?" Ed had an angry growl in his voice and a sour look on his face.

"Chris and me."

"Who?"

"Your grandson, Chris, and your son, Tom."

They were confused. The man standing in front of them looked gruff and unkempt. He didn't look or sound like the same Ed Reilly they had visited just a week earlier.

His father obviously didn't recognize them. He had not yet shaved, something Tom noticed right away. He had always shaved every day, with no exception. *Could this be another sign of dementia?*

Chris spoke first, somewhat hesitantly with a little worry in his voice. "Granddad, you said we could come back to talk more about World War II. Are you okay?"

Ed stepped back, looked down at the floor with a frown, then slowly up at Chris, then Tom, his eyes widening.

"World War II? Yes, I was there. Now I remember. You're Chris and Tom. Please… please come in. I'm sorry I don't have any coffee ready, but I can make some."

They followed Ed into his apartment, glancing at each other, not knowing what to say. Tom spoke up, "Yes, Ed. I'd like coffee. I'll make it if you show me where it is."

"Coffee's here in the kitchen. I'll go get cleaned up. Please, sit down and take a load off your feet."

Tom and Chris realized what they had just witnessed. Ed must have been in a "memory loss" stage—*dementia*. But as soon as Chris mentioned World War II, he snapped back into the present. They saw it and they heard it, but couldn't believe it.

Tom knew he *had* to see Michelle and relay this new observation. That would have to wait, though. Right now, it was Ed's day, and he didn't want to miss out. He had missed too much over the years.

Ed returned about the time the coffee was ready, neatly dressed and clean shaven. Tom poured himself and Ed a cup and brought a Coke for Chris.

"Did your teacher like your report?" Ed settled in his recliner.

"Mr. Johnson said he enjoyed reading it and that I had done a great job. He suggested I ask you a few more questions to make it more complete. Is it okay if I record this again?"

"Certainly. Fire away. Thanks for the coffee, Tom. You make a mean cup of java."

Tom was tempted to ask Ed about the initial unrecognizable

greeting, but decided not to.

"Granddad, the last time we talked, you told us about your awards and how you were wounded. Mr. Johnson said I should ask what you did when the war ended.

"Specifically, where you were and if you remember anything about concentration camps? Did your division liberate any? What did you see? How many prisoners were there? What shape were they in? What… "

"Hold on, hold on. One question at a time. It was fifty-six years ago. My memory is not as sharp as it used to be. Let me think for a minute.

"I remember we came across several concentration camps. This would've been in April and May 1945. There had been rumors that the Nazis were killing prisoners and Jews *en masse*. We heard it from the local townspeople as well as several POWs who had escaped.

"What we didn't know at the time—I don't think anyone will ever understand the monstrosity we witnessed—was just how many hundreds of thousands of Jews were slaughtered in these camps. They were gassed, they were burned in incinerators, and they were tossed in mass graves." Ed put his hands over his face and rubbed his forehead. "I can't even begin to describe the horror."

He took a deep breath, his voice fading as he lowered his chin.

"The big concentration camp that my division discovered was Buchenwald, which was right outside Weimar, Germany. It was the first concentration camp the Allies stumbled upon with a large population of prisoners still living. To this day, it's something I'll never forget—not the sights, the sounds, nor the smells. My God, how could anyone do these things to other human beings?"

Ed paused for a moment to regain his composure. Both Tom and Chris saw him tearing up. Neither spoke. The only sound in the room was his labored breathing.

Ed took a deep breath and continued in a quieter, more somber voice. He was rubbing his hands together, staring at them.

"When we first approached Buchenwald, we had no idea what we were about to discover. I distinctly remember several dozen men in striped uniforms running toward us. We couldn't tell if they were prisoners, Krauts, or what. We held our fire and spread out, forming a skirmish line, just in case they were Germans.

"When they got closer, they were as thin as I've ever seen a man. Their striped uniforms were torn and tattered and their hollowed eyes spoke of volumes of monstrosities and inhumane treatment. It turned out they had overcome the guards the day before and were fleeing the camp when they stumbled upon us. Apparently, the German guards knew the Allies were approaching. Most of them took off before we got there.

"These men in front of us were in horrible shape. They badly needed food, water, and blankets. We gave them what we had. As bad a shape as they were in, we were astonished that they each shared what we gave them with one another.

"One of them spoke broken English. When we asked if there were any more prisoners, they led us back down the hill to the camp."

Ed shifted in his seat, his eyes focusing on Chris. He shook his head side to side as he spoke.

"We couldn't believe our eyes. There were thousands behind the wire fence. The men that led us down to the camp were in far better shape than those still in the enclosure. Most were in rags, had hollowed eyes and drooping faces, and were nothing but skin and bones. Hundreds lay about on the ground… dead."

Ed took a deep breath and strongly exhaled, rubbing the back of his neck with his hand.

"We called Battalion, and they called Regiment. Within a few hours, dozens of supply trucks with food, blankets, and medics arrived. There were so many men to care for, we didn't know where to begin."

Tom and Chris were glued to Ed's descriptions. Chris' research revealed a little about concentration camps, but nothing this detailed. And to think, his own grandfather had been there and witnessed these horrors.

"Well, I thought that was bad," Ed's voice started to crack. He took a deep breath, sat on the edge of his seat, and continued. With his elbows on his knees, he rubbed his hands and stared at the floor.

"We began to explore the camp. That's when we found the

incinerators, and bodies stacked like firewood outside the building. We knew right then that the rumors were true. There were hundreds of wagons piled four-to-five high with dead men…" Ed had to pause before continuing "waiting to be incinerated. It was sickening. To this day, I can't get the sight or the stench out of my mind."

A tear ran down Ed's cheek as he looked up, staring out the window. He reached around and massaged the back of his neck again, turning his head as if to rub out the memory.

Tom recalled his time in Vietnam, when he first saw the devastating results of what Napalm could do to a human being. The smell of burnt, decaying flesh is unforgettable to a combat veteran. He almost said something to let his father know he'd had similar experiences, but decided against it. He didn't want to make this gruesome type of comparison.

Glancing over at Chris, Ed wiped his moist eyes and continued. "That's why I didn't cook out on a grill when your dad was growing up. It brought back too many horrible memories. Don't get me wrong, I like a good steak. I just can't watch it cook."

Ed looked over at Tom. "I'm sure you saw some horrible things in Vietnam, too, Tom. I know you never talk about it, and I don't blame you. I'm not sure I've ever told anyone about this before. There were just too many painful memories.

"But I will tell you this is something we should never forget. Wouldn't you agree?" Ed looked over at Tom, providing him an opportunity to answer his question.

"You're right about that, Ed. We should never forget the horrors of war. The problem is, there's a war every generation. You had World War II. Your parents had World War I. I had Vietnam. I just hope that Chris' generation won't have to face a war."

After a few moments of silence, Chris asked, "Granddad? I know the Germans surrendered on May 7, 1945. Where were you when the war ended?"

"That's an easier question to answer." Ed scooted back in his recliner, chin up. "Our unit was in Austria, near a town called Wimsbach. I remember the day like it was yesterday. We were patrolling the area around a huge ammunition factory. That's where we were when we heard those long-awaited words, '*All hostilities would cease at 12:01 on May 9, 1945.*'

"It was about 9:30 in the morning on May 8, a beautiful, clear, crisp spring day—the type Louise used to call a 'Champagne Day.' Fortunately, we didn't encounter any enemy.

"It turns out the Germans had surrendered the day before on May 7, 1945. We were all jumping up and down, hugging each other and some, including me, were crying—all tears of joy. We had fought for so long and so hard. A lot of men died—many were my buddies I had trained and fought with. And now we knew we wouldn't have to fight any more. Sooner or later, we'd be going home.

"Of course, we didn't ship out right away. We still needed to maintain order in our areas—we were now an Occupation Force. But that was all right. We could finally sleep under a roof, eat three square meals of hot food a day, and we found lots of German Schnapps and champagne. In fact, we were getting so picky, we only drank pink champagne.

"The most terrifying *and* most exciting time of my life was now spent simply celebrating life. I couldn't wait to get home to Louise. I wrote to her almost every day those last few months. I still have those letters around here somewhere. She kept them all. I guess after she died, I just put them in a box. I'll try to find them for you."

"I'd like that, Granddad."

"So would I." Tom chimed in.

"Well, to finish the story… after the war officially ended, we were in several places as an Occupational Force, including Austria, Germany, and Czechoslovakia. We shipped home in January 1946."

No one spoke for a few minutes. Ed stared out the window. This interview had brought back a lot of memories.

Tom looked at Ed—*really* looked at him with a renewed sense of admiration. He noticed how much he had changed since Tom had abruptly walked out of his life years ago. Ed was still a strong man and kept up his physique working out at the gym. His clothes were well-pressed and while he wasn't wearing a tie, you could tell he'd prefer one. He would probably wear a tuxedo to breakfast if they'd let him. His father had always prided himself as being well-dressed.

Tom also watched Chris, busily writing notes from the interview. He was proud of his son—he hadn't told him as much and he made a mental note to let him know.

Chris had also been more talkative these past few weeks, the same as Tom. They shared more than they had over the past years. He knew it was because Ed had reentered his life. He pondered all these recent changes to his routine and wondered what might happen next.

"Tom, *you* should answer some of these same questions Chris asked me. What do you think? Chris, turn that recorder back on and let's hear your dad's war history."

Even though his father had just unveiled memories he'd kept locked up for years, Tom was *not* prepared for that. Then he thought, *what could be so bad about answering a few questions from my own son?*

After a few thoughtful moments, Tom leaned back in his seat and said, "Okay, fire away, Chris."

9 - Vietnam—The Change in Attitude

"What unit did you serve with during the war, Dad?"

That was easy. "Second Battalion, 28th Infantry, 3rd Brigade, 1st Infantry Division. I was in Charlie Company." Tom answered without hesitation.

"I joined the Army on August 15, 1967. After basic training and AIT—Advanced Individual Training—I spent Christmas at home. I landed in Vietnam on January 15, 1968. My division was based in an area called Lai Khe, about thirty-five miles north of Saigon."

"When you say 'join,' Dad, did you volunteer or were you drafted?"

"Oh, I volunteered, Chris. My draft number was low. I didn't want to wait to be drafted. I wanted to control my own destiny." Tom hung onto those words, *control my own destiny.*" Somehow, that had changed a long time ago.

Ed piped in, disrupting the flow of Chris' questions.

"Did the infantry school still have those silly posters in the hallways and classrooms?"

"What do you mean, Ed?" Tom's eyes narrowed with his father's interruption.

"You know, *If the enemy is in range, so are you.*"

Chris laughed out loud. "That was a good one, Granddad."

"How about, *Don't draw fire; it irritates the people around you.* Or, *If you see a bomb tech running, try to keep up with him.*"

All three were now laughing together.

"*We are not retreating. We are advancing in another direction.*" Tom almost burst out. *"Try to look unimportant; the enemy may be low on ammo."*

Chris was laughing so hard, it took a few minutes before he could begin again. He enjoyed watching his father and grandfather share the same humorous memories of basic training. It had been a long time since he'd seen his dad laugh like this. Deep down, he knew something magical was happening.

"Dad, were you a rifleman, like Granddad?"

Tom settled down and eased back in his seat, realizing his son's questions would continue.

"Yes, I was. In fact, when I was growing up, I wanted to be in the Army like your grandfather. He taught me how to shoot, and we hunted a lot when I was younger. My MOS was 11 Bravo, Army Infantryman.

"Like Ed"—Tom began to compare his Army experience with his father's—"we learned to use different weapons. Most of us were issued M-16s, which could fire a single shot or go fully automatic with the flip of a switch.

"We also had M-60 machine guns and someone usually carried an M-79 Grenade Launcher with our squad while out on patrol. Everyone knew how to set ambushes with Claymore mines and grenades. The Vietnam jungle was a lot thicker than what your grandfather fought in."

Ed jumped in again, smiling. "You probably enjoyed that nice, warm summer sunshine weather, too." It was obvious he wasn't going to be left out of this conversation.

Tom looked over at his father and just scoffed.

"So what's better to fight in," Chris asked, tossing out the first of several volleys, "the hot humid jungle or the bitter cold winter?"

"I can't speak for your father, Chris, but I grew up in western Pennsylvania and remember many frigid winters here. My mother kept it nice and toasty inside our small farm house. While it may have been freezing cold outside with two feet of snow, inside was always warm and cozy.

"I *thought* I knew about cold weather. That was… until the Battle of the Bulge."

Ed was again on the edge of his seat, leaning forward. But this time, he looked directly at Chris, gesturing with his hands as if to make a point.

"They said it was the coldest winter in Europe in fifty years. I can certainly attest to that. The major difference from the winters back home was that during the war we didn't have any place to go to get warm.

We were outside in that freezing weather for weeks at a time, day *and* night. We'd stomp our feet to stay warm, but so many guys were sent to the rear with frostbite. We didn't dare light any fires on the front lines; we knew it would draw immediate fire from the Germans.

"The platoon sergeant forced us to change our socks every day. We'd tie them in a knot and wrap them around our necks and under our arms to keep them dry and warm. They sure felt good when we first changed them. That warmth didn't last long, though, because we didn't have the new winter shoe-pacs. Come to think of it, we didn't have *any* proper winter clothes."

Tom knew it had been cold, but this was the first time he'd heard his father describe it in detail. Ed glanced over, raising his eyebrows with a "your turn" look.

"No, we didn't have cold weather like Ed. It was always hot and humid. During the monsoon season, it rained almost every day, *all* day. Nothing stayed dry. We used to joke there were only two seasons in Vietnam: hot and wet.

"We'd hang our wet clothes up at night to dry, but they were wetter the next morning than when we'd taken them off. We had mosquitoes around all the time. They were especially miserable at night and drove us crazy.

"We had 'bug juice'—that was our nickname for insect repellant. It was a grunt's best friend next to his M-16. But all that did was piss them off.

"We also had to deal with shit that crawled, like fire ants, scorpions, poisonous snakes, and leeches. Oooh." Tom shuttered. "We hated those blood-sucking bastards the most.

"Oh yeah. There was also a crazy lizard in the jungle that made a sound like, 'Fuck you. Fuck you.'."

Both Ed and Chris erupted into laughter. "Is that true, Dad?"

"If I'm lyin', I'm dyin'." Tom had completely forgotten about the Tokay lizard until now.

"We had to take these huge orange anti-malaria pills every week. If we were out on patrol, we'd take them every day. They gave us gas and the runs, which didn't help, especially with some of our C-rations. That's why I never eat beans and franks. Or as we used to call them, 'beans and baby dicks'."

Tom grinned with that last comment. He looked over at Chris who was enthralled and thought how rare this must be for a teenager—witnessing two combat war veterans comparing their personal experiences from two *different* wars.

"Were you in any major battles, Dad?"

Tom settled back on the couch, his hands nervously rubbing the tops his thighs, and spoke with a more somber tone. "You remember me telling you about Ed's Baptism of Fire at Angers, France? Well, *my* Baptism of Fire came about two weeks after I arrived in-country. We didn't know it at the time, but it's now known as the 'Tet Offensive.'

"I was sound asleep in my hooch when the first explosion went off, shortly after midnight, followed by rockets and mortars dropping inside the base camp. We all jumped up, grabbed our weapons and huddled behind a bunker. I was a FNG—that's short for a 'Fuckin' New Guy.'"

That term cracked up both Chris and Ed.

"I thought I was ready, but I was pretty scared. My squad leader hollered for me to follow him. That was the first time I'd been under fire. I was shaking and said to myself, '*If this is the way it's going to be, then I need to be ready—fight or die.*' I wasn't ready to die, but I *was* prepared to fight. You're trying to kill me, well I'm going to kill you first.

"That's when it hit me. This really is a war. After a few minutes, I got my confidence back, my training kicked in, and well… I made it through the night, through Tet, and through the war."

Chris and Ed listened carefully. Ed knew Tom had fought in the Tet Offensive—it was the first time network television broadcast the realities of the Vietnam War with no censorship. The brutal scenes from the battles in Hue and Saigon were shown on TV in living rooms throughout the U.S. What the world saw on television—the *real*

Vietnam War—was much different from what the government had been saying—*lying*—all along. It ultimately changed the public's perception of the war.

Ed and Louise watched the news every night, trying to understand what was really happening in Vietnam. It was much different to see a war on television than it was to read about it in the newspaper, like Ed's parents had done during World War II.

Louise became more upset and irritable. Ed knew she was worried—she'd been through one war with him and now she was watching *another* war with her own son. He wondered if that triggered her heart attack.

"Dad, Granddad said you were wounded, too. What happened?"

Tom took a deep breath. "Yes, Chris, I was wounded, like your grandfather. One wound was for a piece of shrapnel—mine wasn't in my butt like Ed's, but in my back. The medics removed it."

Tom squirmed in his chair. He was not comfortable talking about this and needed a cigarette. He also needed a drink, but it was too early in the day to start.

"What about being shot, Dad? Did that happen when you won the Bronze Star?"

"Won the Bronze Star…" How does someone *win* a medal during a war?

Tom blinked his eyes, trying to focus and think clearly. He found it difficult to continue. That question immediately took him back to that fateful day when he lost his closest friend in 'Nam… the one who saved his life.

Suddenly he stood up, excused himself, and said he needed to go outside for a smoke. Ed started to get up, but Tom said, "Ed, I… *I* need to be alone right now. Can you stay and talk with Chris?"

"SO… YOU'RE MY GRANDSON. I'm not really as bad as your dad makes me out to be. We just happened to not agree from time-to-time."

"Twenty-five years is not how I'd define *time-to-time*," Chris replied sarcastically. He wasn't sure whether to stay or leave. Before he could say anything more, his grandfather asked, "What does a teenager do these days? Are you a good student? Do you play sports? Do you have a girlfriend?"

"Stop with all these questions, Granddad." Chris stood up, almost shouting. "I just met you a few weeks ago. I don't know anything about you."

Ed wasn't trying, but he obviously struck a nerve. Was Chris being a typical teenager or was he protecting his own father?

"There's nothing much to know," Ed said in a calm, grandfatherly manner. "I'm an old man and hard of hearing. Now and then, I have trouble remembering things. I rarely get out of bed in the morning without pain. I can't even tell you what day it is or what I had for breakfast."

An awkward silence settled in as they both contemplated what next to talk about. Chris thought about leaving, but remembering his grandfather had fought in World War II, he sat back down and asked a simple question.

"Granddad, what was it like fighting the Germans? I mean, for real?"

Without hesitation, Ed easily recalled, "Throughout our training, Chris, we were told the Germans were the enemy. In our minds, they were not real people, they were just… *the enemy*. They trained us that the Germans wanted to kill us. So that's how we prepared. We fought them, and we killed them—a lot of them. But… we also lost a lot of men.

"I can't remember what I had for breakfast this morning, Chris, but I can tell you what I ate on Christmas Day 1944. We were just outside Kirbelf, a small town in Luxembourg. I was sitting in a foxhole in the middle of the coldest winter Europe had seen for years. While it was cold, the freshly fallen snow was breath-taking, almost like I remembered as a kid growing up in western Pennsylvania." Ed looked out the window, thinking back to a time long ago.

"We were supposed to get what they called a 'holiday meal,' a full Christmas dinner with turkey and gravy, dressing, and all the trimmings. We were looking forward to that—real food and a hot meal." Ed sighed, his voice softening. "I guess the guys in the rear got that. I didn't. I was dug in on the front line in an OP—an Observation Post.

"I distinctly remember opening up a box of C-rations. Spreading them out in my foxhole, everything tasted frozen. But it was Christmas. I wasn't going to let a little snow and ice get in the way of *my* Christmas dinner. My foxhole buddy and I shared some hard candy we'd received earlier from home. It wasn't the best, but it sure tasted good."

"Did the Germans attack on Christmas?"

"No, not our unit. Thankfully, it was quiet, but some of our guys up the line fought off an attack. Fortunately, none of them died. I couldn't imagine what it would be like today, knowing your husband or father or son died on Christmas Day. How could you celebrate Christmas with that event burned in your mind?"

A minute passed before Ed turned the tables on Chris. He leaned forward. "Does your dad ever talk about Vietnam?"

Chris looked at his grandfather and hesitated before answering. "No. I've asked him a few times. He either ignores it or tells me he doesn't want to talk about it. All I know is what I've read in history books and what he told us today."

"I can understand. His war was much different from mine. Vietnam was not a 'popular' war, Chris. Not that *any* war is popular, but World War II started when Japan attacked Pearl Harbor. I mean, another country attacked the United States.

"We knew to the exact minute when World War II started—7:55 a.m., Hawaii Time, December 7, 1941. *'A date that would live in infamy.'* Hell yeah, we're going to war to protect our country.

"When the Germans began to overrun Europe, and Hitler conquered entire nations in a matter of days, the United States decided enough was enough. We would help defend our Allies and keep the Nazis from taking over the world. The country would now fight a war on two different fronts: the Pacific and Europe. The Normandy D-Day invasion happened on June 6, 1944, and well, you know the rest is history."

Ed shifted in his recliner, leaning forward with his elbows on his knees and hands clasped together, fingers interlocking. "World War II was a 'righteous' war, Chris. For men and women, both over there and here at home who lived through it, there was absolutely no doubt it was the right thing to do.

"The government rationed gas and food, women went to work in factories, and lots of people bought war bonds. The entire country sacrificed and supported the war effort. There was every reason to fight and no reason not to.

"When we got home after the war, all we wanted to do was to live in peace and safely raise our children."

Chris was absorbed in his grandfather's comments. He had never heard any of this. It wasn't in any of his history books.

"Did you know in World War II, two-thirds of the soldiers were drafted? I was one of them. In Vietnam, though, it was just the opposite—almost two-thirds of the soldiers and sailors volunteered… like your dad.

"Vietnam did *not* attack the United States and they sure as hell weren't threatening world peace like the Krauts and the Japs did. We know exactly when World War II began. I even remember where I was when I heard the news."

Ed shifted again in his chair and looked directly at Chris. "However, we don't know when the Vietnam War started. The history books tell you it was the Gulf of Tonkin incident in early August 1964. But who knows?

"Hell, I'm not sure anyone really understands why we were over there in the first place, but we were. At the time, the big threat was the spread of communism. Your dad wanted to do his part to support our country." Ed looked at Chris with a father's smile. "That's how Louise and I raised him. I was really proud of him. He was as patriotic as they come."

"So what happened, Granddad? Why was Vietnam a different war?"

"I'll tell you why," Tom erupted, startling them both. Neither Ed nor Chris had seen him standing in the doorway.

"The government lied to us to *start* the war. And they kept lying to us *throughout* the fuckin' war!" Tom was shouting like an awakened beast.

"Now, Tom. It wasn't like that and you know it. You're overacting again. Settle down, Son."

Tom could feel himself growing angry again and realized this would turn into the same argument that drove him and his father apart. He stopped short of saying something he would regret. Instead, he grabbed a Coke from the refrigerator and opened it.

"Ed, in *your* war"—he called it 'Ed's war' now—"did you know why you were fighting? I mean, did you see *any* difference from the time you left for war until the time you came home? You *knew* the Japanese had attacked us. You *knew* the Germans were attacking all over Europe. You *knew* why you were fighting."

Tom took a deep breath and quickly exhaled, then a long swig of Coke and looked at his father in disbelief. Before Ed could respond, Tom continued in a less angry but firm tone.

"I never knew why we were in Vietnam. Yes, I *know* we were told we needed to help keep communism from spreading to other countries. *And* we were told the Vietnamese attacked our Navy ships in the Gulf of Tonkin. Like many Vietnam veterans who volunteered, I swallowed that shit, hook, line, and sinker. *Both*, by the way, turned out to be blatant lies.

"But once we were over there fighting, we never seemed to be able to gain ground or push the enemy back. We'd attack one hill, hold it for a few days and some guys would get wasted. Then they'd order us off that hill. A day later, the gooks just walked right in and occupied that same hill—they had been patiently waiting for us to leave. They knew from experience that we wouldn't stay.

"Why did we fight for it in the first place, only to walk away and give it up? *Your* objective was to advance and capture territory. *Ours* was simply to kill the enemy.

"Why did our officers always want to know how many enemy we killed and how many weapons we captured? They *had* to know our kill ratio and body counts." Tom used air quotes to emphasize his meaning. "That's what was important to the REMFs. Kill the VC so they can report the numbers up the chain of command. It was more important to those Rear Echelon Mother Fuckers that we document how many more of the enemy we killed than they killed of us.

"We lost a lot of guys to sniper fire and booby traps that went out *after* a firefight to count the number of dead enemy. I bet those REMFs never did analysis on *those* numbers. Yeah, we followed orders all right, just like the guys giving them to us. What I never saw were the REMFs who issued those fuckin' orders. All those guys did was look at some stupid map. The whole thing just didn't make sense."

Tom sat down hard on the couch. His voice softened, but stayed firm. "Westmoreland called it the 'War of Attrition.' We were ordered to kill as many enemy as we could, hoping that eventually their death toll would reach an 'unacceptable level to their leaders.'" Tom again used finger air quotes.

"That was the general plan. That was *the* goal for winning the war. Well, how'd that shit work out?"

"The Germans did the same thing," Ed snapped back. "We'd take a town, they'd fight and retake it—we called it a 'counterattack.' But the result was the same. And yes, we lost good men, too."

"Yeah, but you didn't just let them have the town, you *made* them fight for it and you eventually fought to take it back. We were ordered off the hill just so the enemy could walk in with no fight.

"And wasn't your division's motto, '*Only Moves Forward*'? You kept pushing the Germans back and moving forward. You never had to worry about *not* crossing any lines on some stupid map.

"We didn't have a front line to push back. Hell, we *never* had a front line. And to top that off, we couldn't cross the South Vietnam border, even though Charlie *leisurely* strolled back and forth across.

"We could have won the war, but we weren't allowed to. There was one big fuckin' STOP sign at the border."

Ed was on the edge of his seat, still in the middle of this battle with Tom.

"I don't think there's much difference between what you saw and what I saw, Tom. We were fighting Germans and chasing them all over Europe. It wasn't until we got to Buchenwald that I understood why we were fighting and what we were fighting for. I don't think anyone knew what the Germans were doing to those poor Jews."

"That's the big difference, Ed. You *knew* why you were fighting— I *never* did and I still don't know." Tom had calmed down a little. "I've tried to block so many of those memories. Most of the time, it's worked—until now."

Tom leaned forward, elbows on his knees and hands clasped, and stared out the window. "How can I tell you what I've seen and what I've done when I've been trying so hard to forget? The war changed me, Ed. I went over as one man, but returned as another. I'm sure your war changed you, too. War changes everybody.

"But something happened to me after mom's funeral. Something that caused me to hate the very reasons we were over there. And now, years later, I'm just beginning to understand. Deep down, it still hurts. It hurts like hell."

A tear formed in Tom's eye.

"How can I love a country that betrayed me and my buddies? All those guys died fighting for what we thought was right. We came home to a country that hated us because we were over there… fighting… *fighting* for what we were told was the right thing to do."

Ed saw his son close to the edge of losing it again. It was obvious Vietnam had left him bitter toward the war *and* toward the country that had sent him to it. Ed's voice softened to one of a father comforting an emotionally hurting son.

"I'm sorry, Tom. I didn't mean to stir up unpleasant memories. I know they're still there. Mine are too. Maybe we should talk about something else for a while. That okay with you, Chris?"

Chris reached over and turned the recorder off. His hands were slightly shaking, not knowing what he'd just witnessed.

After a few minutes, Ed suggested they go for a walk. It was getting late, and he invited them to dinner. All three appreciated—needed—the break. Walking outdoors, Tom and Ed both lit a cigarette. Ed jokingly offered Chris a smoke, but he politely declined.

"Good boy," Ed and Tom said simultaneously, as Ed tussled Chris' hair.

10 - The Meltdown

Dinner with Ed and Ester had been a pleasant distraction, something Tom badly needed after the afternoon's "visit." Ester was attractive, a great conversationalist, *and* a listener. She had three children, all married with kids. Unfortunately, they lived hours away, and she *"didn't see them nearly enough."*

She and her husband and Ed had all moved to Sterling Oaks about the same time and quickly became friends. They were "co-founders," attended many of the same cultural activities, and enjoyed each other's company.

There probably wasn't any romance in their relationship, though Tom could be wrong. But Ed enjoyed living at Sterling Oaks, and that's what was important. Seeing the two of them together presented mixed emotions for Tom: joy for Ed, but sadness that his own mother wasn't there.

Tom had lost track of Ed—well, *more* than "lost track." He wanted *nothing* to do with his father after their meltdown in 1975. He needed to get as far away as possible. And he had succeeded. That is, until recently. Now he was torn between going back to his standard routine of work and being a loner, and wanting to spend more time with his father.

Ed was ill—Tom knew that. Michelle couldn't tell him how much longer he had to live. That was an unfair question, but it was the only thing he could think to ask at the time.

AFTER DINNER, Tom and Chris said their goodbyes and headed home. Sunshine hummed along south toward Morgantown. Daylight was fading as Tom reflected on the day's events.

He also appreciated Chris' quiet solitude, though they had talked more on these recent long drives. His son was more in tune with the world's events than Tom had given him credit for. He would have to keep that in mind in the future.

Dinner at Sterling Oaks began early—five o'clock. That gave him and Chris plenty of time to calm down after the unpleasant confrontation—*is that what it was?* Or maybe Tom was the one who needed to cool down.

Hearing his father opine about the Vietnam War and compare it to World War II gave Tom a sense of renewed optimism. Ed seemed to understand the impact the Vietnam War had on him—more now than before. They *were* completely different wars. Not many people would dare compare the two.

Chris broke the long silence. "Dad, did you know Granddad did all that during the war?"

That's an innocent enough question. His father had only shared a few stories when Tom was younger, but they were *nothing* compared to what he'd heard earlier today.

"I'll be honest with you, Son. Your grandfather *never* talked about the war like he did today. What's more surprising is that he remembered all those specific details, even with his dementia.

"I'll call Ms. Myers tomorrow to see if I can learn anything more. Besides, she's mentioned several times I should try to keep her up-to-date."

Out of the corner of his eye, Tom saw Chris' smile. He suspected his son knew there might be more to it than simply "keeping her up-to-date."

As they passed the turnoff for Washington Township, Chris asked *the* question, something he had wanted to ask ever since they first visited his grandfather at Sterling Oaks.

"Dad, can I ask you a question?"

Tom sensed something was up, so he lit a Marlboro and cracked his window. "Sure, fire away."

"What happened between you and Granddad?"

While he was prepared for most anything—his father and the Army had taught him that—he didn't know how he could avoid *this* question. It wasn't because he was afraid of telling his son about what he did in Vietnam. It was because he was terrified the flood of memories and horrid nightmares would return with a vengeance.

Tom knew this day would eventually arrive, but he wasn't sure he was ready. However, his own father just opened up to him and Chris about *his* war. That made Tom realize what was previously impossible, may now be possible.

He took a long puff on his cigarette.

Chris sighed. "It's okay if you don't want to talk about it, Dad. I just thought…"

"No, you're old enough to know. And… I should be old enough to tell you." He blew smoke out the window.

Tom thought for a moment about how to start this conversation. He recalled Michelle's wise words when she first talked about Ed. *"Start at the beginning."*

"Did you know I went to college after graduating high school?"

Chris looked at his dad. "No, I didn't know that."

"I was seventeen—not much older than you are now—when I graduated from Carrick High School in 1966. Neither of your grandparents attended college, but they wanted me to go.

"While I maintained good grades in high school, I didn't do so well in college. Hell, now that I think about it, I wasn't even shaving back then." Tom chuckled.

"I had *always* wanted to be a soldier in the Army, like your grandfather. But when you're that young, you really don't know what you want to do with your life.

"Your grandfather bought this car for me when I left for the University of Pittsburgh in the fall of '66. He knew I might join the Army and thought buying it would help me decide to stay in college. Obviously, that didn't work," Tom said with a delayed chuckle.

"College didn't cut it for me. I tried, I *really* did. I just couldn't get motivated. It was too boring and not challenging at all to me. Something was missing, but I didn't know what.

"Then one day, I saw a group of Army soldiers on campus. They were decked out in their neat, crisp uniforms, all clean cut, and standing *loud and proud*. There was an air of confidence about them, like my father conveyed while I was growing up. I knew right then I couldn't get that from going to college, but I could by becoming a soldier."

Tom took another long puff from his cigarette and glanced over at his son. "I'm what they call a 'Baby Boomer.' You know what that is, right?"

"I think so. You were born after World War II. The soldiers came home and started families—something like that."

Tom smiled at that simple summary—Chris knew.

"That pretty much sums it up. When I was growing up, we were taught that our fathers fought a heroic war against the Germans and the Japanese. Back then, military service was considered patriotic. If the country needed you, you joined—no ifs, ands, or buts. We heard it from our parents, our neighbors, our teachers, our ministers, and our government.

"President John Kennedy once said, *'Ask not what your country can do for you, but what you can do for your country.'* Those were powerful words I wanted to live up to.

"The war in Vietnam was heating up, if you can call it that. Ed had been in the Army—that's the branch *I* wanted to join. My draft number was rather low. Even though I was in college, I knew I would probably be drafted. So I drove down to the local Army recruiter's office and signed up. I was eighteen years old and legally able to sign documents.

"With that simple gesture, I signed on the dotted line to *'defend the United States against all enemies, foreign and domestic.'* I was a volunteer in the United States Army."

Tom took another long drag from his cigarette and stubbed it out in the ashtray.

"Your grandparents weren't too happy, though. I later learned both were proud of my decision. It was the first big commitment I had made all on my own. Yes, there was a war going on, but we didn't think it would last long. Like Ed said earlier today, Vietnam didn't attack us, and they sure as hell didn't pose a threat to world peace. So there wasn't much to worry about.

"I was at the top of my class in basic training." Tom glanced over at Chris—he was bragging now. "I took basic at Fort Dix, New Jersey and AIT at Fort Polk, Louisiana. I wanted to be the best I could be, like my father. I made it a point to study and train harder than anyone else. It was much more interesting and motivating than college.

"Since I'd already had a year of college, I joined as an E-2 and made Private First Class right out of basic. I was promoted to Specialist when I got to Vietnam.

"When I first arrived, I wanted to fight the hardest I could, and help my country win the war, like your grandfather did in World War II. I thought war was glamorous and glorious. At least, that's what the movies portrayed."

Tom paused for a moment, his tone changing. "It wasn't like the movies, though. Things were much different, both there *and* back here at home.

"When my mother died unexpectedly, I'd already been in-country for six months. I was a hardened and experienced combat soldier. I'd been on dozens of patrols, and even led a patrol squad a few times. While we were always hunting Charlie, we knew from experience he was also hunting us. I was shot at plenty of times, but never hit. At least, not back then."

Tom took a moment to light another cigarette.

"I flew home for my mother's funeral. I went from the jungle to my front porch in less than four days. Her service was the following day. I was hurting inside—my mom had just died. I didn't get a chance to say goodbye. She didn't go with me and Ed to the airport when I left for Vietnam.

"After her service, I looked up several of my old high school friends. They asked how it was over in 'Nam. When I tried to tell them what war was really like, well… they didn't want to hear what I had to say. They either changed the subject or said something stupid or ignorant. So I eventually dropped it."

Tom paused for a moment, drumming his fingers on the steering wheel.

"I also went to another funeral while I was home. One of my best friends, Jerry Jones, joined about the same time I did. He was a Marine, stationed up in Eye Corps (I Corps) in the northern part of South Vietnam. He was killed at Khe Sanh, just doing his job, same as me.

"Back before 'Nam, we used to drive around Friday and Saturday nights, shooting the shit, eating at the local drive-in restaurants, looking for girls, and enjoying being young and dumb." Tom added nostalgically, "Gas was less than twenty-five cents a gallon back then."

Tom was deep in thought, eyes focused on the road. Nevertheless, he reminisced about better days *before* Vietnam.

"Jerry had a full military funeral, complete with a color guard. I don't know why, but it was awkward for me. I attended his funeral in the same dress uniform I'd worn earlier to my mother's funeral.

"Deep down, I asked myself, *'Why did Jerry have to die?'* His family only knew that his squad had been ambushed while on patrol, somewhere near the DMZ. He'd been the point man and the first one down. Nobody could reach him for a while. By the time the medic got to him, Jerry was dead.

"No one was there to hold his hand. Nobody to tell him everything would be all right. He died alone. That was always my biggest fear in 'Nam—that I would die alone. Nobody knows if he died instantly or not. He had a closed casket funeral, so I figured it was pretty quick. At least, I hoped it was.

"I didn't hang around too long after his service. I spoke to his sister, Jennifer, though. She was a year younger. There wasn't really anything I could say; nothing would bring him back. I told her that Jerry was a brave Marine and well-trusted by his unit, because he was walking point. That's a job for only experienced and sharp men, since they are out in front, leading the patrol. What I didn't tell her was the point man was almost always the first one shot."

Tom realized he was telling his son things he had not spoken of… *ever.* "Are you okay with this, Chris?"

"You bet, Dad. I'm the one who asked. You've *never* talked about the war before. Are *you* okay talking about this?"

Tom's heart warmed and his face softened. He appreciated his son's understanding. *He's looking out for me.*

"I got off track. You asked why Ed and I argued.

"After I went back to Vietnam, it was… *different*. Or maybe *I* was different. It didn't matter. When I first went over, I was all gung ho and patriotic. But something changed. I don't know if it was my mother's death, Jerry's death, or what. I just didn't have that same desire to fight like I did before. I had lost my sense of purpose.

"Jerry was the first person I knew from home that died over in 'Nam. He was my best friend." Tom's eyes began to water.

"It became a different war for me. I started to be more cautious. At least, as careful as one could be in war. I didn't volunteer as much as I did before. A lot of guys saw that change in me, too. At that point, all I wanted was to survive and not get killed, finish my tour, and come back home. I was more scared then than when I first got over there.

"After I came home from Vietnam, I burned all my uniforms. I never wanted to be seen in them again. I had been spit on, sworn and cussed at, and called a 'Baby Killer' by protesters—by *Americans*. I couldn't for the life of me figure out why.

"I had served—*proudly*. But when I returned home, I didn't feel welcomed in my own country. I also began to read more about the war and hearing different perspectives, especially Johnson's and Nixon's continuous cover-ups, and it made me sick to my stomach.

"Your grandfather and I argued more and more. On a patriotic scale, he was at the top where I *used* to be. I was at the very bottom. I wanted to put the war as far behind me and as quickly as I could. But he *always* had to make his point and told me time and time again that we were right to be in Vietnam, fighting communism. He didn't want to listen to what I had to say. Hell, *I* was the one over there, *not* him.

"To top that off, he kept after me to make something out of my life. He had made a career for himself, and I should be able to do the same. I didn't want to go back to school, so I tried working at his appliance business.

"But I didn't like being around people. Several months later, I moved out of the house and got my own apartment. Eventually, I found lots of work doing odd jobs here and there.

"Looking back now, I realize not all of this was Ed's fault. In fact, most of it was probably mine. I just couldn't bring myself to swallow my stupid pride and let him know that. I think, too, we both missed mom. Without her there to keep us all together, the war had driven us further and further apart.

"The last straw came one night after I'd had too much to drink. I told Ed that I felt betrayed by my government, my president, my country, *and* my own father. That's when he told me to get the hell out of his house and he never wanted to see me again.

"So I did. We hadn't seen nor spoken to each other since then. That is, until a few weeks ago."

Tom had been so engrossed in conversation with Chris, he realized he'd missed his turnoff to Morgantown. He just passed the exit sign for Fairmont, West Virginia. He didn't know where the time had gone.

He turned off the Fairmont exit, crossed over, and got back on the interstate heading north. He took his eyes off the road for a second and looked over at Chris, worried he may have said too much.

In the background, Edwin Starr's version of *War* played on the Oldies station. The words to that song meant more today than before.

War, huh, good god
What is it good for
Absolutely nothing, listen to me

Normally, Tom couldn't stand Vietnam War protest songs, but the more he thought about it—especially the past few weeks—the more they made sense. Not at the time *during* the war, but *now*.

Neither Tom nor Chris said anything more until they arrived home. Tom didn't know if his son was avoiding any more talk. It had been a heavy conversation, one he couldn't have anticipated.

He asked Chris if he wanted to get a snack and talk more. Chris declined, but he gave his dad an enormous hug—something he hadn't done in a long while.

Chris began to walk away. After a few steps, he turned around and looked at his father, his eyes moist.

"Dad, I know I'm growing up and I still have a lot to learn. Sometime in the future, I know that I will leave home. But I want to make sure when I leave, you and I won't be angry at each other, like you and Granddad were. I want to be able to come home."

"I promise you, Chris. That will *not* happen." That struck a nerve and Tom knew exactly why. This was a promise he knew he would keep.

"I love you, Dad."

"I love you, too, Son."

Both had tears in their eyes. Chris headed to his room, and Tom headed to the kitchen. He couldn't remember the last time he'd told his son he loved him, let alone hearing it from him. He needed a drink—a strong one. This had been a hell of a day, one he would never forget.

11 - Michelle Myers

"Good afternoon, Sterling Oaks Retirement Community. This is Michelle Myers. How may I help you?"

"Michelle?"

"Yes?"

"This is Tom Reilly."

"Oh hi, Tom. How are you today?"

"I'm fine, Michelle. I hate to bother you, but I was wondering if you had a few minutes to meet sometime this week. I've visited Ed a few times and I'm still trying to figure out what's going on."

"What do you mean, Tom? We periodically check on him and he seems fine."

"I'm not sure. I'd rather meet in person than to discuss this over the phone. It's... sort of... *difficult* for me."

"I understand, Tom. Yes, of course. Just let me know when you're up this way. I'll make time."

"Is tomorrow morning too soon?"

"No, not at all. I assume you'll be here mid-morning? I should be in my office. Feel free to stop by when you get here."

"Thank you, Michelle. I appreciate it. If you haven't guessed, I'm pretty confused and I'm trying to sort things out."

"Not a problem, Tom. I'll look for you tomorrow morning. Goodbye."

"Bye."

TOM DIDN'T SLEEP MUCH that night. Maybe it was because he drank a little more than usual, though that was never a problem before. Maybe it was Ed's situation. Maybe it was the anticipation of seeing Michelle again. Or maybe it was the recent inner rumblings of his own haunted past.

He was confused. His world had been up-ended the past few weeks. While he enjoyed this improving relationship with his father *and* his own son, he knew *he* still had problems. Problems he thought he'd put behind him long ago.

He would make this trip alone. He told Chris he would see Ed again, but didn't mention Michelle. Chris was beginning to study for his end of the year exams. It wasn't long before school would be out for the summer. This was his first year in high school and as far as Tom had observed, he'd adapted well.

During the past several years, he hadn't felt close to Chris. He often wondered if it was him, or did all fathers feel this way about their teenage kids. But Chris was his only son. After his wife died and *after that one night*, Tom swore to himself he would take good care of Chris. Sometimes, though, he wondered if his son was taking care of him.

TOM WAS OUT THE DOOR before Chris left for school, but said he'd be back in time for supper. They'd order out again, whatever Chris wanted.

He was glad that he could take another long drive to Sterling Oaks. Sunshine was his safe place—more so these days. It also gave him time alone with his thoughts.

Pulling up to the guard gate, Earl came out with a big smile. "Good morning, Mr. Reilly. How are you today?" He was still gushing over Tom's GTO.

"I'm fine, Earl. Thank you for asking. I'm here to see my father and Ms. Myers."

Earl raised his eyebrow and smiled. Tom noticed, but was not offended.

"Ms. Myers has been with Sterling Oaks since before we opened. She's one of the top mental health specialists in this part of the country. I think she left a rather cushy job at the university medical center to come here."

"I didn't know that, Earl."

"Yep, she's a beaut… I'm talking about your car, Mr. Reilly," Earl belted out with a grin.

"Thanks, Earl. She's very special to me."

"Every man's got a name for his car, *especially* one like this. What do you call her?" Earl not only knew his cars, but he was also familiar with the culture.

"I named her 'Sunshine'."

"Sunshine? Nice. Mind if I ask why, 'Sunshine'?"

"Well, I spent some time in 'Nam and it rained a lot. But when the sun came out, well… sunshine was always a welcomed sight."

"That's a great story. I didn't realize you were a veteran—like your father. He must be proud of you."

Tom wasn't ready for that comment, but he liked the sound of it: *"like your father."*

"I'd like to think so, Earl. There were times, though, when we disagreed, but most of the time we got along. At least, when I was growing up."

Tom didn't want to carry this conversation any further. Sensing that, Earl responded, "Well, we all have things we would have done differently had we known better. If we could only go back in time. Anyway, thanks for chatting. Here's your pass. You know the way."

"Thanks, Earl. I'll see you around."

Tom eased Sunshine through the gate. He was beginning to like this place. Everyone has been so friendly. He understood why Ed had chosen Sterling Oaks.

"KNOCK, KNOCK," Tom said while knocking on Michelle's office door.

"Good morning, Tom. I trust you had a pleasant drive up?"

"Yes, I did. I love this time of year, especially after the long winter. We had about two feet of snow down in Morgantown. I was ready for spring."

Tom sat down in one of the two chairs facing Michelle's desk.

"Me too. Can I get you a cup of coffee or something else to drink?

"Coffee would be nice. Black, no sugar. Thank you."

"I'll be right back."

Michelle stood and walked down the hall. Tom wondered if he should have followed, but she returned within a minute. "Here you go."

Tom noticed Michelle's slim, athletic build. She was wearing dark slacks and a flowery blouse that showed off her physique. Her shoulder-length chestnut hair was wavy and flowing. Tom guessed she was in her late forties, just a few years younger than he. She was attractive and carried herself well. It was obvious she took care of herself, something Tom thought he needed to do better for his own health.

"Now, what questions can I answer for you?" Michelle sat in the chair next to Tom, crossed her shapely legs, and sipped her coffee. He noticed that she was watching him.

"I've seen Ed several times since I first learned he was here. I can honestly tell you I've enjoyed our visits… well, *almost* all of them." He flashed a quick smile.

Michelle seemed to listen for more than the spoken words. He recalled what Earl had said earlier about her being a top mental health specialist.

"Anyway, my son, Chris, is working on a school project. He interviewed Ed a couple of times about World War II—he's really into history. Ed was delighted to help and was very specific about details. He remembered almost everything, even whether certain days were cloudy or sunny."

Tom paused a moment. "I'm a little confused about this dementia. Or… is it Alzheimer's?"

Michelle took a moment, carefully weighing her answer. "Your father has Alzheimer's disease, Tom. There's no doubt about that, but it is in the early stages. While he may drift in and out of a conversation, he is still mentally with us."

"Still mentally with us." Those words hung in the air for a bit before Tom spoke again.

"Michelle. When we last visited Ed, he didn't recognize us at first and seemed angry and confused when he first opened the door. We had just seen him the weekend before. But when Chris asked him if it was still okay to talk about the war, he snapped right back into his old pleasant self after a few moments. I mean, we walked in, got coffee and a soda, and Ed talked for over two hours. At first, Chris and I were confused. But after a few minutes, everything returned to normal.

"Is that a symptom of Alzheimer's?"

"Unfortunately, yes. When you and I first met, I probably threw too much information at you."

Michelle took a deep breath and shifted in her seat.

"I've worked in the health profession for many years. While I observe these resident interactions almost daily, I can tell you that Alzheimer's affects everyone differently. I wish I had a magic formula for you, Tom. But everyone has to learn how to deal with this condition in their own way. It's not an exact science.

"When you visit your father, does he seem more 'with it' in the morning or in the afternoon?" Michelle used air finger quotes.

"I haven't noticed. Is there a difference?"

"You may hear the term 'sundowning.' It means the Alzheimer's patient's memory loss or symptoms appear to get worse as the day goes on.

"The best advice I can give you is to realize your father's memory *is* fading. Ed told me you've met several times. He enjoys your visits and always looks forward to the next one.

"He knows there's a history between the two of you. I don't know what that is—it's not my place to ask, unless someone wants to tell me. But your father wants to make up for lost time. He's told me that several times over the past month."

Michelle let that sink in. She asked Tom if he wanted a refill on coffee. He did. Both stood, their eyes locking for a moment. Michelle smiled with soft eyes. Tom felt a little awkward. Following her down to the break room, he noticed she walked with graceful elegance.

After they both refilled their cups, Michelle suggested they go outside. That surprised Tom, but he welcomed the invitation. They walked down a familiar hallway and out to their courtyard. Tom pulled out a Marlboro and offered one to Michelle, who politely declined. He lit his cigarette as they sat on the bench. Over to the side, he spotted a cardinal and heard several robins chattering in a magnolia.

"When I met with Ed yesterday, he told me you talked a little about Vietnam. He didn't go into detail, but he mentioned there were things that still bothered you about the war.

"Ed is a smart man, Tom, regardless of whatever happened between you. I know it had something to do with the war. I assume it was the Vietnam War and *not* World War II. But that was a long time ago."

Tom stared out toward the distant hills. It was a gorgeous day. He was here with a beautiful woman—someone who showed a little interest in him. At least, from a professional standpoint. He was hesitant to bring up those old feelings again. Yet with Michelle...

"Yes, I was in Vietnam. It was a war that we should never have fought. We never should have gone over there, but we did. I did a lot of things I'm not proud of. I also think—I *hope*—I did some good.

"The problem over there was sometimes you didn't know if you were doing the right thing or the wrong thing—you were just doing it. I lost a lot of friends, some hurt more than others."

Tom paused for a moment and sat up straight. "I guess in some ways, I feel like I'm still there."

"Tom. Can I ask you a question?"

"Sure."

"Have you ever talked with anyone at the VA about Vietnam? I don't mean to pry, but it sounds like you still have issues that need to come out. Could you be suppressing them?"

Tom looked over at Michelle, then glanced away.

"I'm not sure I know what you're talking about," Tom lied.

"Well, in my experience, I've seen a lot of men and women who have served in the military. When they come back from war, they are a different person."

"*A different person.*" Yep, Tom could easily relate to that.

"Most guys who went over to Vietnam—hell, *any* war—came back completely changed. War does that to a man. In most cases, not necessarily for the good. Everyone became a little nutty over there—

it was one way of saving your own sanity.”

It wasn't Tom's intention, but the more he watched Michelle, the more she reminded him of his deceased wife, Barbara—a striking face, wide round eyes, a perfect delicate nose, and shapely lips. Tom lit another cigarette before continuing.

“Michelle, I appreciate what you're saying. I really do. But right now, I'm just trying to understand my father's condition. I know I've got a few problems, but I'm working them out.”

Yeah, sure. Been working on them for thirty years.

Tom's answer was absolute; that was all he would say about the war. At least for now.

After a few moments, Michelle spoke, using her professional matter-of-fact voice. “As far as we know, Tom, your father's Alzheimer's symptoms are normal. We've observed nothing out of the ordinary, except he spends a little more time in his apartment than he used to. I know some of his friends stop by to visit. We haven't heard of anything unusual. Like I said, we are monitoring him, as we do with all residents here.”

Michelle shifted her position, looking directly at Tom. “I will tell you this, Tom. There *will* come a time when Ed will need to move into the Memory Support Neighborhood. I don't know when that will be, but he won't be able to stay in his apartment. He will need additional specialized care, both mental and physical, at some point. You need to keep that in mind.”

“I will, Michelle.” Tom stood up. “I think I'll go visit Ed now, if that's okay.”

“Of course.” Michelle also stood and shook Tom's hand. “If you have questions, please call me. You have both my office and mobile numbers.”

TOM DECIDED TO STROLL around the grounds to clear his mind before going to see his father. Michelle's comments forced him to think about his own well-being. He knew he had nightmares and he also had trigger points that caused flashbacks. Hell, *all* war veterans have them. That was one thing that drove him to drink more.

When he first returned home from Vietnam, Tom worked in his father's appliance business. After a while, that didn't pan out. He enjoyed the repair work—he was good at it. He just didn't like interacting with people. But he found plenty of work that didn't require him to be around people. He was his own boss and could work his own hours.

He married later than most men his age; he was thirty-four. He found the girl of his dreams, Barbara Davis, who was twenty-five. They met at a Steelers football game victory party. After the first few dates, things quickly blossomed. She had a degree in Nursing and worked in the Intensive Care Unit at the University of Pittsburgh Medical Center.

Barbara was vibrant and exciting. She was a well-educated woman, both in college and in life. What attracted Tom the most was that Barbara was just plain down-to-earth and easy to talk to. He loved the way her dark brown hair flowed off her shoulders. Her honey brown eyes spoke of exciting things to come in their lives.

They fell in love and were married in a simple private ceremony by a Notary. Two years later, Chris was born, and he became the center of their lives. Both cherished every minute they had with their son.

Barbara was aware that Tom had fought in Vietnam. The few times they tried to talk about the war, Tom eventually made it clear that was a subject to avoid. She knew his father was still alive, but he also made it known he didn't want to have anything to do with him.

Both worked hard, and they spent all their free time with Chris. That didn't leave much time for each other, though they tried their best to make the most of what they had.

But ever since Chris had been born, they seemed to drift apart. It didn't help that Tom had nightmares and that he refused to share them with Barbara. It didn't help that he drank too much, but that never came between them. At least, not that Tom was aware.

He still couldn't grasp why Barbara's life tragically ended one night. She was driving home from work after a late night shift. It had been snowing, but the roads were supposed to be clear. Somehow, her car slid off the road, crashing into an embankment. She had been wearing a seatbelt, but the impact crushed her.

Just like his own mother, Barbara's life was cut far too short. Tom was devastated… *again.* He couldn't grieve. He didn't even have a chance to say goodbye—not the way he wanted. Years later, he was still very much in love with Barbara.

And now, he's here with Ed—his own father—at the end of his life. *Is that what they call this stage of life?* Ed was eighty-one years old and physically healthy. But his mind was slowly deteriorating. He had not been a part of Tom's life for the past twenty-five years. That was Tom's choice, *not* Ed's. But now, things were different.

Now—*this time*—Tom had the chance to say goodbye, something he hadn't been able to do with his mother *or* his wife. Tom had an opportunity to make up for lost time, something not many people were given: a second chance.

The more Tom thought about that—*a second chance*—the more he was determined to make this right, no matter what. He put out his cigarette and headed toward Ed's apartment. He hoped he could mend things with his father before it was too late.

"You can't control how Ed reacts. You can only control how you react." Michelle is one smart lady, Tom thought with a smile.

12 - First Ride

"Good morning, Ed. I hope you don't mind my stopping by. I should've called, but I was up this way and figured I'd drop in for a visit."

"Hi, Tom. No, not at all. Come on in. I was just having some coffee. Can I pour you a cup?"

"Yes, please."

His father seemed to be "with it" this time—no confusion and no anger; just his old self, whatever that may be these days. Both sat down on the couch with coffee.

"Did Chris get what he needed for his project?"

"Yes. He asked me to thank you and to let you know he received an A-plus. His history teacher was impressed with the report. I think he went beyond the call of duty," Tom replied with a proud smile.

"Good. I was hoping he did well. It's funny how I can remember details that happened more than fifty-six years ago, yet every so often I forget what day it is." Ed chuckled as he sipped his coffee. He settled back on the couch.

"What brings you up this way?"

"To be honest, I needed to talk with Ms. Myers."

"Oh? Business or pleasure?" Ed looked at Tom with a raised eyebrow and a twinkle in his eye.

"I think… both." Tom smiled, too.

"She's a charming young lady, Tom. She understands older people, especially us veterans. She comes to visit me a little more than she did in the past.

"At first, I thought she checked on everyone around the campus. But I guess she's concerned about my well-being. She's told me several times I have dementia, but I just don't know. Oh, sure, I forget things now and then. A lot of people around here do. It happens when you get older. You'll see. Anyway, I'm glad you stopped by."

Tom decided not to pursue that any further. Michelle periodically checks on him. He's in good hands and in a safe place.

"Tom, whatever happened to that old Pontiac GTO?"

That surprised Tom. He didn't think Ed would remember his car, it had been so long.

Tom's face lit up. "I still have it, Ed. She's become a part of me. I just couldn't bear to part with her. Besides, she's paid for. In fact, I drove her up here today," Tom stated proudly.

"Really? Any chance we can go for a ride? I'd like to get out for a bit if you have time. Ms. Myers also suggested I should stop driving. I told her I'd think about it."

"I'm up for it. Any place you'd like to go?"

"Let's just see where she takes us." Ed stood, heading toward the front door.

After walking down the stairs to the first floor, they stopped at the reception desk. Margie looked up. "Good morning, Mr. Reilly."

"Good morning." Ed and Tom replied almost simultaneously, both smiling.

"This is my son, Tom. We're going out for a little while, Margie. I'm not sure when we'll be back, but don't wait up for us," Ed added with a smile and a wink.

"Have fun, you two. Don't do anything I wouldn't do."

"Margie is always a kidder," Ed said on the way out the door. "She keeps tabs on all us inmates. I try to let her know when I leave. Normally, we have a shuttle bus that takes us out, whether it's shopping or to a Steelers' game. There are a lot of Pittsburgh fans here. I don't follow the Pirates or the Penguins as much as the Steelers, but others do."

Tom had a smile a mile wide. It had been years since he and his father had taken a car ride together. As soon as they got to the parking lot, Ed stopped dead in his tracks.

"Are you okay, Ed? What's wrong?" Tom rushed to his father's side. *Is he having a heart attack, or is dementia setting in?*

"Wow. You don't know how this takes me back, Tom. I halfway expected a beat-up old clunker. But here she is in pristine condition, almost… almost like you just drove her off the dealer lot. My God, Son. You really have taken great care of her."

Tom beamed with pride at hearing his father's comments. "You taught me to take care of my stuff, Ed. I've always done that, believe it or not."

After they both got in and buckled their seat belts, Tom cranked up Sunshine, revving the engine and letting her purr. His father was in a state of euphoria.

"Have you done anything to her?" Ed's hands reached out to gently rub the dashboard.

"Just routine maintenance. I've rebuilt the engine twice and the transmission once. I added headers a while back and had a few dings taken out. Other than the usual, she's still the same GTO you bought me before college. I named her 'Sunshine.'"

College. That was so long ago. When was it? 1967 when I dropped out to join the Army? Thirty-four years ago?

"Where to?"

"How 'bout we head toward the old homestead? I haven't been back there in ages. That okay with you?"

"Sure, I think I can find my way."

With the destination set, Tom put Sunshine in reverse and backed out of his parking spot. He slowly drove down the paved road, and waited for the security gate to lift. He waved at Earl as he and his father set out a new adventure.

Cruising north on I-79 Ed asked, "Mind if I smoke?"

"Go right ahead. I'll join you."

Both cracked their windows and lit their cigarettes.

"Sure is a beautiful day for a drive."

Tom thought his father wanted to say something more, but simply answered, "Gorgeous."

Out of the blue, Ed asked, "Tom, you mentioned that you used to be married. If you don't mind me asking, what happened?"

Tom had realized earlier with Chris these kinds of conversations were easier while driving—you could avoid direct eye contact. He pondered the question as Sunshine made it way up the interstate.

"I married a beautiful girl, Ed. Her name was Barbara Davis. We met at a Steelers' victory party of all places. Can you believe it?

"She was a nurse at the University of Pittsburgh Medical Center and worked in Intensive Care. We were very much in love. After Chris was born, well… he kept us both busy. We were a family, like you, mom, and me. You would have really liked her, Ed."

Tom took a deep breath and slowly exhaled.

"One night Barbara was driving home after working a late shift and hit a patch of black ice. She skidded off the road and was killed. She was gone in an instant."

Ed's expression changed to sadness as he looked at Tom. "I'm sorry, Son. I… I truly am. I *know* how difficult it is to lose someone you love. Your mother died quickly, too. It's hard on both you *and* me. Believe me… I know." Ed's voice trailed off.

Neither Tom nor Ed realized it, but they made another father and son connection. *A hard one*, but nonetheless, an emotional connection.

A few minutes later, Ed spoke up. "Tom. I've been thinking."

Tom sensed his father may want to talk about something important. He wanted to make sure he heard every word.

"I'm eighty-one now and I'm very comfortable at Sterling Oaks. I'm not moving anywhere else. I sold our house a while back and I don't travel anymore. I've got a car I don't drive and I'd like Chris to have it. I mean, if you're okay with that and if he wants it. It's not anything like this car, but it's only a few years old. It's got low miles, runs well, and best of all, it's paid for. Would that be all right?"

Tom was surprised. "Chris would be thrilled to have his grandfather's car, Ed. That's a wonderful gesture. He's learning to drive and should get his permit this year. I'm sure he would love it. Thank you."

"I'm glad to do that." Ed looked at his son who noticed the stare, but Tom kept his eyes straight ahead, focused on the road.

A few miles further down the road, Ed asked, "Do you remember the time we drove up to the courthouse to register you for the draft?"

Tom shot a look at Ed, but it was not returned.

"Vaguely. I recall you were more nervous than me."

"I was." Ed replied matter-of-factly. "I had been through a war. I wasn't looking forward to my son going through another one. That's why your mother and I were thrilled when you left for college. It's also one reason I bought you this car. I hoped you could avoid the war.

"I understand why you volunteered and why you wanted to go. But just because I fought in World War II didn't mean you needed to fight in another war."

Tom hesitated before responding. "It wasn't that, Ed. Growing up, *you* were my hero. Not only because of fighting and helping to win the war, but you came back and made something of your life. I always looked up to you, whether or not you knew it."

Ed lit another cigarette.

"You remember when I drove you to the airport? Your mother said she couldn't bear to watch you fly out. She made up an excuse to be away."

Tom glanced over at his father and responded solemnly. "I never knew that. I thought her sister was ill, and she needed to stay with her."

"That's what she wanted you to believe. The truth was that a lot of young men were going to Vietnam. She knew many would not come back. Your mother experienced that same fear during World War II with me and many of her friends. She didn't want to face that again, so she said her goodbyes a few days before you left.

"I never told you this, but we were extremely proud when you joined the Army to serve your country, despite the growing anti-war sentiment.

"Do you remember what you said at the airport when we last shook hands?" Ed glanced over at his son.

"I told you I would make it back home in one piece." Tom spoke softly, remembering his exact words. "I was confident I would."

"I know you were. That was one of the proudest moments in my life, seeing you exude that confidence. But I wasn't as confident. I remember watching you get on that plane in Pittsburgh. It had been a long, hard day for me, but I kept my feelings inside. I kept telling myself, 'I need to be strong for you.'

"When you were at the top of the stairs, you looked back and waved. You couldn't see me in the crowd. Deep down, I had the same sinking feeling I had when *I* left for Europe to fight in World War II. *He's not going to make it back home.*

"I had been to a war. I knew the dangers you would face. When you waved, I thought that might have been the last time I would see you alive—*ever*. I cried on the drive home. It would be a while before I realized that you, like me, would make it home alive. I couldn't tell that to your mother, but I talked to God and prayed every day— *EVERY DAY.*"

Tom was close to tears. Hearing these words from his father after twenty-five years of anger was heartwarming, something he hadn't felt in quite a long time. Not sure how to respond, he lit another cigarette.

Sunshine continued to cruise down the interstate. Traffic was light this time of day.

After a few more minutes of silence, Tom took a deep breath. He needed to get something off his chest—bottled up emotions that had been weighing on him for a long time. He bit his lip, holding back years of anger.

"I'm sorry for walking out on you, Ed. I know it was hard on you. But I didn't believe in the same things as you. All you and I did when we were together was argue. It just got old after a while. I needed to find my own way. I couldn't do that when you were around.

"I should have reached out to find you. I know that now. But after those awful things you said, I didn't think you ever wanted to see me again. After a while, I quit thinking about it."

"I never understood why you left," Ed jumped in, his voice strong and bitter. "Yeah, we had a squabble now and then, but all fathers and sons do. You didn't write, you didn't call. I didn't know if you were dead or alive. It's like you dropped off the face of the planet."

Ed was getting riled. Tom sensed it, but he would not back down… not this time.

"I'm sorry I've been such a fuckin' disappointment to you all these years, Ed. I just couldn't live up to your damn expectations. I had to find my way out of this crap hole. You made a life for yourself after the war. I needed to do the same. But I'm not you."

Ed forced himself to keep his mouth shut and lit another cigarette.

"Here's the turnoff to Pittsburgh," he said matter-of-factly as Tom steered the car toward the off ramp. He was calming down, although still a little irritated.

They rode in silence for a few miles, both wanting to avoid another heated confrontation. Tom drove down familiar streets to his old neighborhood in west Pittsburgh—Westwood. It had been years since he had driven this route. But he had no problem driving straight to their old home on Hyde Street.

The house had changed little from Tom's memories of growing up. Still standing tall, the two-story structure had a fresh coat of light gray paint with a dark blue front door and trim, and it maintained that 'welcome' look. The yard looked as immaculate as when he'd lived there.

He pulled up alongside the curb across from the house, cut the engine, and asked his father if he wanted to get out to walk around.

"No, not really. I just wanted to see if it was in as great a shape as I left it. Looks like a young family has moved in. There are a few toys in the front yard. I always liked this neighborhood. It was a safe place for us."

"I remember wonderful times here. Mom loved this place, too. I remember the last time we were together. She had cooked a sumptuous meal. Even though I know she wasn't pleased that I had joined the Army, she kept that to herself.

"I miss mom."

"I do too, Son. I talk to her every day."

Both men realized they had made another step in mending their relationship—*is that what this was?*

Tom recalled the last time he was here, at this very house—the same house he grew up in—parked on this same curb. It was a few days after Barbara had died. He was as depressed as he'd ever been. Chris was staying with Barbara's sister, who had been so supportive during that difficult time.

Even though he had walked out of his father's life and had not spoken to him since the meltdown, Tom needed his father. But he wasn't sure his father needed him, or even wanted to see him. Ed didn't even know about Barbara. Or Chris.

He'd had a few drinks, trying to get up the courage to face his father. He drove his GTO and parked on the street across from the house at this same spot. But as soon as he turned off the ignition, that argument—that old fight—weighed in, keeping him from opening the door of his car. He waited a few more minutes, fighting the rising rage within him.

Then, with a *"fuck it, it don't mean nuthin',"* he cranked up his car and sped off, stopping at a bar before going home. Only, he didn't make it home that night. He woke up the next morning in his car… in a ditch.

Ed broke Tom's train of thought, keeping him from going down that slippery slope again.

"Tom, are you okay? You look like you've seen a ghost."

"No, I'm fine. I was just recalling… some old memories. I'm okay," Tom lied.

"Well, thank you, Son. Thank you for bringing us back to our home. That was very special."

"Me too, Dad. Me too."

Tom realized this was the first time he had called Ed—his father—'Dad.' It was a warm and wonderful feeling, and he felt his body relax into the seat.

"Where to next?" Tom looked over at his dad.

"I could use a drink. How about you?"

"It's only one o'clock in the afternoon, Dad. Isn't it a little early?" Tom smiled.

"I don't know. What time is 'drinking time'?" Ed smiled, too.

"Tell you what. Let's drive around the old haunts a little more, then we'll head back to Sterling Oaks and I'll buy you a drink there. How about that?"

"Works for me."

13 - Rebuilding Relationships

After the trip down memory lane to the old Pittsburgh homestead, Ed and Tom—father and son—returned to Sterling Oaks, both filled with the enthusiasm of a renewing relationship. They both wondered why it had taken so long. And yet, neither wanted to admit foolish pride had anything to do with the separation.

These were two *stubborn* U.S. Army combat veterans who had served their country in different wars. Yet, in some ways, they were still fighting their own personal battles.

Tom left early that afternoon after only one drink, even though Ed was buying. He made up an excuse that he had a full week of work and needed to get home to have supper with Chris. Ed asked if he'd bring Chris to visit again soon. Getting to know him *and* his dad was good for his soul.

That was a no-brainer.

TOM WASTED NO TIME returning to Sterling Oaks. While it had only been a few days since his last visit, it seemed longer. He wanted to see his dad again. He wanted to have that father and son relationship that he remembered from before.

After the recent trip—complete with a ride in Sunshine to the old house where he grew up—he needed to learn more about what his father had done since they had "parted" ways.

It was a weekday. Chris was still in school, but that was okay. He was excited about finishing his freshman year. There would be plenty of opportunities to spend time with his grandfather over the summer.

Tom had called the day before. His plan was to visit Ed in the morning, then Michelle in the afternoon. Fortunately, she didn't have any meetings that afternoon and "should be available." He wasn't sure what she meant by that, but he liked the idea that Michelle might be… *available.*

"Good morning, Dad." Ed slowly opened his front door. Tom wasn't sure what mood he'd be in, so he was prepared for anything.

Ed was dressed, but his hair was disheveled. He didn't have the sparkle in his eyes and didn't seem to recognize his own son.

"Who are you?"

Tom suspected he might be in a 'memory loss' stage.

"Hi Ed. I'm your son, Tom. We went for a ride earlier this week in my old '67 Pontiac GTO. We talked about World War II, the Battle of the Bulge, and the 80th Division. Does any of that ring a bell?" As previously suggested by Michelle, Tom pulled out all the stops.

Ed backed up a little, stared down at the floor, peered at his watch, and then back at Tom—a completely changed state of mind. "Good morning. Yes, of course I remember. That was a great trip. We should do that again soon. Come on in."

With that simple exchange, Tom knew he must've hit at least one trigger that jogged his father's memory. Michelle had suggested he note these triggers and Ed's reactions to them, not only for his own recollection but also to share with her. She was working on another mental health article and this would help her research. He was elated *and* eager to assist.

Tom noticed a few more Post-it Notes stuck around Ed's apartment, but didn't look too closely at the details. He didn't want his father to think he was being nosy.

Ed was dressed for the day and had finished his breakfast. He suggested they go outside. They both liked nature and being outdoors. Ed liked to walk—he always did. At least, when there wasn't a foot of snow on the ground.

There were several things Tom wanted to talk about with his dad. It worried him, though, that any of them might set Ed off, even though Tom was usually the one who lost his temper first.

"Ed? Can I ask you a personal question?"

"Sure. Okay if I smoke?"

Both men lit cigarettes. *"Can I ask a personal question?"* was a lead-in to a potentially sensitive conversation. Tom wasn't sure how else to start.

"After mom died and after... well, after I left... did you ever find... um... someone else?"

Ed stopped walking and looked at Tom. "You mean like 'to date'?"

"Something like that." Tom avoided eye contact with his father. They started walking again.

Ed took his time to respond, searching for the right words. "Several years passed after your mother died before I even thought about asking another woman out. I was still very much in love with her. There was a great big emptiness in my life. She and I shared everything in our lives. Frankly, I just wasn't interested, and the business kept me busy. Or maybe that was just an excuse. I don't know."

Tom recalled when Barbara died. His father's words were *exactly* as he'd felt.

"There were a few women in our church that I dated off and on, if that's what you want to call it. This was a few years after you'd left. Those were friends and companions, though—really just someone to spend time with.

"To be honest, while I found several ladies to spend the night with, I never found anyone I wanted to spend the rest of my life with. As time passed, I had plenty of friends to keep me company. I found I just wasn't interested in dating anymore."

Ed stopped to put out his cigarette. "What about you? Did you find someone else?" Ed again turned the tables on his son.

"Same as you, I guess. I dated around a bit. But when you're a loner—or at least, trying to be alone—there are not many choices.

"After Barbara died, my life became a long series of non-lasting relationships. Don't get me wrong, I liked the ladies, but as soon as a relationship got close, I'd high tail it and haul ass. I don't know if it was because I'd lost Barbara or I'd lost buddies in 'Nam. I just didn't want to get close enough to lose someone I loved… again."

Tom briefly looked up toward the sun, shielding his eyes with his hand. "Besides, I was raising Chris and didn't want to share him with anyone else. I made a promise to myself one night that I'd raise him the way Barbara would want him raised."

Tom lit another cigarette and continued walking.

"I've made a few mistakes—I guess all dads do—but we managed. He's not in jail and he doesn't do drugs, I'm fairly certain of that," Tom said with a big grin. "Overall, I think I've done a decent job. At least, so far.

"What about Ester? Are you seeing her?" Tom wasn't sure if that was the right question to ask, but he was curious.

"Do you think it's wrong? I mean, your mother's been gone for over thirty years."

"No, not at all, Dad. To be honest, when I first met Ester—she is lovely, by the way—I *was* a little uncomfortable. I mean, seeing my father with another woman was unnerving. I know you told me you were all good friends, but it was just a little weird for me."

"I'd tell you it gets better as you get older, Son, but I'd be lying." Ed smiled. "I've learned over the past few years, since living here in a community with a lot of 'old' folks—myself included—that life is for the living. People come, and people go. Those that remain become long-time friends. You should learn that.

"It's funny in a way. I'm eighty-one and I've been told I have dementia. To tell you the truth, I still feel young. Sure, I'm a little sore when I first get up, especially on chilly mornings. But I've got a good routine here. I work out in the gym several times a week, I swim, I go to exercise classes, and I love to walk outside, even in the winter.

"What's changed? I'm still young at heart. I just never thought this would happen to me."

"What, getting dementia?" Tom shot his dad a worried look. He seemed to have forgotten all anguish for the moment.

"No, getting old." Ed grinned.

"Someone put up a list of ten 'Perks of being 80' in the Common Room. When they first put them up, it pissed me off. I didn't want to be lumped into that 'old person' category. After a while, though, it kinda grew on me. Ester's husband, Richard, pointed out that most of them pertain to us. Some were spot on. I can't remember them all, but they are funny:

Kidnappers are not interested in you.
No one expects you to run—anywhere.
People call at eight at night and ask, 'Did I wake you?'
There's nothing left to learn the hard way.

"There's more, but you get the idea. I guess what I'm trying to tell you, Tom, is don't let life slip by. Yes, you need to make sure Chris is safe and healthy, and finishes school. But don't let all that get in the way of your own health and well-being.

"I'm not trying to tell you what to do, Son. Hell, I've made some not-so-good decisions myself. What I'm saying is that there's an entire world out there waiting for you. Don't stay boxed in and let it pass you by."

Tom realized that this father-to-son talk—*is that what you call this?*—made him truly feel like a son. *Why did I waste all those years?*

"I appreciate that advice, Dad. I really do. I'm still trying to figure out what I want to do when *I* grow up." Tom was smiling now, too.

AFTER LUNCH, they leisurely strolled back to Ed's apartment, making small talk along the way. Tom couldn't stay long. He had an appointment to meet with Michelle.

Ed arched his eyebrow. Tom thought he may say something. He sensed his dad knew this was more than a professional meeting with Ms. Myers. But after a pleasant walk and another superb meal, his dad probably wanted to lie down for an afternoon nap.

Tom was walking in the clouds. He couldn't remember the last time he and his father talked about something so deep and so personal and so... *normal.*

He wished Ed had known his wife, Barbara. But Tom also realized *he* was the reason they never met. While the memories of long ago fights were still there, they somehow didn't seem as bad now.

He floated down to Michelle's office and found her at her desk, typing away on her computer. When Tom gently knocked, Michelle smiled and invited him in. "I'm just finishing up a document. I'll be right with you."

"Can I buy you a cup of coffee?" Tom asked with a wide, hopeful smile.

"Yes. Thank you. I would appreciate that." Michelle smiled, then returned to her computer, deep in concentration.

"Be right back."

Tom walked down the hall to the break room and poured two cups of coffee. Michelle liked hers with cream. Walking back to her office, he was on a high—a great visit with his father and now, Michelle. Life was good.

"Good afternoon. Do you still have a few minutes for me?"

"I always have time for you, Tom." Michelle stood to come around to the chairs in front of her desk. "Thank you for the coffee."

She had a bright, Pepsodent smile and a natural beauty. She didn't wear lipstick and barely any noticeable makeup. He also noticed when Michelle talked about her work—*her love of her work*—her hazel eyes sparkled.

"My pleasure."

"How is Ed today?"

"It's amazing, Michelle," Tom blurted out, excited to share details of his visit.

"It's almost as if there's no sign of dementia. Well… there was when I first arrived. But like you suggested, I mentioned a few things that helped him snap out of his memory loss. You told me it won't always work, but it sure did today."

Michelle took a sip of her coffee before responding. "I'm glad you are enjoying visits with your father."

There was that professional tone in her voice again. Tom wished she'd pay more attention to *him*. But he wouldn't push any buttons… yet. He just enjoyed spending time with her.

"We had a pleasant stroll around the campus this morning and talked like a real father and son."

"That's great, Tom. What did the two of you talk about?"

"Well, I wanted to know if he'd had any female relationships since… since my mother died. I wasn't trying to pry. Well, maybe a little." Tom nervously fumbled for words. "I was curious why, after all these years, he didn't remarry."

"What did he tell you?"

"He told me that while he dated a little, he didn't find anyone to spend the rest of his life with. I think I understand. He loved my mother so much. When she died, he just lost interest in other women."

"Was there anything else?"

Tom glanced at Michelle, then quickly looked away. He wasn't sure he wanted to answer that question, but she seemed interested.

"Well, yes. I believe I mentioned we had a falling out several years after I got back from Vietnam. I… I sort of walked out of his life."

"Walked out of his life." Those words hung in the air for a few moments before Michelle spoke again.

"Yes, you mentioned there was a falling out, but you didn't go into detail."

Tom hesitated. *Should he tell her the whole story, part of the story, or just skip it altogether?*

"Tom, do you want to go outside?"

Damn, this woman is good.

"Yes. I would. Thanks. Here, let me take your cup back to the dining area."

"Thank you. I need to walk down the hall. I'll meet you in the courtyard."

Tom met Michelle at the doorway to the courtyard.

"It is a gorgeous day."

They walked toward "their" bench under the shade tree.

"Michelle? Mind if I ask you a personal question?" Tom wasn't sure how to ask if she was married or not, but he was going for it.

"Not at all. But just because you ask doesn't mean I'll answer."

"Fair enough.

"Earl told me you left the University Medical Center to come work here. I'm not sure what it is you do, but you are kind, professional and knowledgeable, and so helpful to me. Do you always spend this much time with family members? I mean, I appreciate your helping me understand my father's condition and what to expect, but do you do this with everyone?" Tom wrestled to get the right words out.

Michelle also struggled. While she *was* a professional, Tom sensed she was on the verge of sharing something personal with him.

"Tom, I left the University Medical Center when Sterling Oaks first opened. The CEO recruited me because of my research with veterans and their unique mental health issues. It was an excellent career move for me.

"I spend as much time as I can with family members. As much schooling and training as I've had and all the research I've done, I'm still learning new methods that can be applied toward future patient care."

Michelle shifted in her seat, turning slightly toward Tom.

"To answer your question, *some* family members are easier to talk with than others. *Most* would rather be somewhere other than here, especially those dealing with Alzheimer's parents.

"But you, Tom… you *genuinely* want to be with your father. I can tell it is making a difference for both of you. After so many years apart, it is amazing to watch your relationship redevelop."

Tom hesitated for a moment. He hoped Michelle would let on that there might be an additional personal interest, but he heard nothing.

He lit another cigarette, taking his time before continuing. He took a deep breath and exhaled smoke in a long, billowed stream.

"When I first got home from Vietnam, I moved back in with Ed. We both thought that was a good idea, but I was struggling, trying to 'get home.' I had bad—*terrible*—memories that wouldn't go away. I drank a lot, probably more than most guys. Drinking seemed to help, but the memories always seemed to resurface after a few days.

"I went back to work for my father. He owned an appliance business. I loved working with my hands and was always good at it. If I didn't know how to fix something, I'd tinker with it until I either figured it out, or I broke it and had to order a new part."

Tom cracked a slight smile, but only momentarily.

"I didn't enjoy working with customers, which was a big part of the business. Dad always said, *'the money is in sales.'* He was right, but money wasn't that important to me. I just didn't want to be around people."

I still don't, Tom almost added.

"We'd argue about the littlest of things. It always came back to him asking, *What are you going to do with your life?'* After a while, I got tired of hearing it and moved out of his house into my own place. I continued to work at his store, but he kept reminding me I should do something better. He even suggested I go back to school and become a lawyer—I was good at arguing." Tom chuckled.

"One night, I had been drinking too much and Ed had too much to drink and, well… we had another falling out. I said things I've since regretted and I'm sure he was the same. But I left, never wanting to see him again. I didn't care if he lived or died, I was done with him. I was *that* angry."

Tom hadn't told that to anyone in quite a while. He wasn't even sure if Barbara knew that much detail. He didn't know why he told Michelle. It wasn't because she was a mental health specialist. She was just easy to talk to.

"Tom, mind if I ask you a personal question?"

That brought him back to the present. "Sure, fire away."

"I know you have a son, Chris. He seems like a wonderful young man. I can see that he and Ed have developed a great relationship." Michelle paused for a moment and looked at Tom. "May I ask you about Chris' mother?"

She beat me to the question. Was she being polite or was she interested?

"I married a wonderful woman, Michelle. Her name was Barbara. It was several years after I had walked out on Ed. I wasn't looking, but there she was and we hit it off well. We got married, and two years later, Chris was born. We were a real family."

Tom took a deep breath and lit another cigarette. He wiped his brow, not from sweat, but because he was apprehensive.

"Barbara was an ICU nurse. She was killed one night in a terrible automobile accident coming home late one night from a shift. The roads weren't too bad, but she hit an icy patch and smashed into an embankment. She died on impact. At least, that's what the paramedics told me."

Michelle's face dropped and she covered her mouth with her hand as she gasped out loud.

"I am so sorry, Tom. I didn't mean to pry."

"That's okay, Michelle. It's been thirteen years. Most days are tolerable. But every so often… well, I'm sure you understand."

Tom sat up straighter, shifting mental gears again.

"Anyway, it's me and Chris now. We get along most of the time. But now and then, we are at each other's throats." Tom smiled.

"Since I've reconnected with Ed, things are… *better*. And besides, I've met you." Tom looked over at Michelle, who appeared to be deep in thought.

Michelle's face darkened slightly as she momentarily glanced at Tom, then away. She cleared her throat. "I was married once. No children, thank goodness."

Now it was Michelle's turn. She had that thousand-yard stare out into the distance. Even though she had not been in combat, Tom could tell she personally knew what war could do to a person.

"He was a good man. At least, when we first married. We did all those things young couples did. Like you and Barbara, we were deeply in love. But something changed after a few years. I was still in college working on my doctorate. That took a lot of personal time, both at school and at home.

"I wasn't sure what would set him off. There were a few nights when he would wake up from a nightmare in a cold sweat screaming, *'Kill him. Kill him.'* It scared me. His pajamas would be soaking wet. Sometimes, he would remember the dream the next morning and sometimes, he wouldn't.

"Even though I was still in school, I knew a little about PTSD— did I mention that Bill was a Vietnam veteran? No, I guess I didn't. I knew I could help him, if only… if only he'd let me. But he would *never* talk to me about Vietnam."

Tom took all of this in, recalling similar heated conversations with Barbara.

"Anyway, between the drinking, the staying out late, the nightmares, and the yelling and screaming—it just seemed like everything I did was wrong. I felt like I was always walking on egg shells. He shut me out of everything. When he was away, I was always anxious, wondering if he'd come back and if so, what mood he'd be in.

"We tried counseling, but that was marriage counseling. I knew Bill could use more specialized therapy, something he denied he needed. Every time we tried to talk about it, it turned into one big ugly screaming match. Thank goodness there was never anything physical."

Michelle gazed up moodily at the cloudless sky.

"Finally, after one night of drinking and screaming and me throwing and breaking dishes in fits of anger, we decided to call it quits. Neither of us enjoyed each other's company. We both knew we didn't belong together anymore. So we divorced. He moved to the other side of the country, and I don't hear from him."

Michelle looked at Tom. Her eyes softened with grateful relief to be able to share such a personal story.

"That's probably more than you wanted to hear, Tom. I haven't talked about it in a while, and I'm not sure why now and why with you. But there's something about you that seems, well… *genuine*."

Both leaned back on the courtyard bench, far enough apart to not be physically touching, but close enough to feel each other's thoughts. Their shoulders were rounded, casual and easy. Neither spoke for a long time.

14 - Charles Smith

Ed had called earlier in the week—*that* was a first—and asked Tom and Chris to drive up on Sunday. Their normal weekend visiting day was Saturday, but he wanted them to meet a special friend. He mentioned they would be attending the church service at Sterling Oaks. He didn't want them to be surprised. Besides, it was Mother's Day, and he thought it would be special if all three were together.

The weather was overcast and rainy. Tom and Chris talked a little on the drive up, but nothing heavy. Lately, Ed had more normal days than not, and that was a good sign. The last couple of visits felt... *normal*. Something that grandsons, fathers, and grandfathers did all the time.

Life was good... today. Tom had reconnected with his father and they were rebuilding a relationship destroyed by a war. He and Chris were getting along better than ever like a father and son should. He had some sort of connection with Michelle. She wasn't married and seemed *genuinely* interested. He tried not to read too much into her comments, but he sensed something was there. These things took time, and he didn't want to blow it.

Chris had several exams to take the following week. One of them was history. He told his dad he was confident he'd aced the class with his report, *A World War II Account by Chris Reilly and Ed Reilly*. His paper had impressed his high school teacher, earning him an A-plus.

Chris mentioned he'd also interviewed his own father and thought he had talked about the Vietnam War because his grandfather talked about what he'd done during World War II. Mr. Johnson encouraged him to continue his conversations with his grandfather. It would help him understand more about the war and how it affected all veterans. He might also better understand his *own* father's experience.

Mr. Johnson had fought in Vietnam in an artillery unit and was keenly aware of the issues Vietnam veterans faced when they returned home.

Sunshine cruised up the interstate.

"Dad?"

"Yes?"

"Are you going to see Ms. Myers again?"

That was an innocent enough question. "Not this trip. When I called earlier this week, she said she'd be out of town at a conference." Tom glanced over at his son. "Why do you ask?"

"Just curious. I know she looks after Granddad, but she seems to like you."

"What makes you think that?"

"I guess it's kind of like in the movies. You can tell by the way people look at each other. I've seen her watching you, especially when you and Granddad are together. Trust me, Dad. She likes you."

"I think she's just being polite and professional." Tom tried to avoid having *this* conversation with his son. But it was almost like he needed—*wanted*—Chris' permission to date another woman. It *had* been more than a dozen years since Barbara died—*geez, it seems like it was only yesterday.*

"It's okay, Dad. I may only be fifteen and I know you still miss mom. It's alright if you like somebody else."

Was this kid reading my mind?

"How did you get to be so smart at such a young age?"

"I don't know, Dad. You seem… *happier.*" Chris looked out the front window, watching the sunlight glint off a small pond alongside the highway.

"You're not as depressed as you've been in the past."

Tom couldn't recall a conversation like this with his son—ever. *Has he really grown up? Or was it that he just hadn't paid attention to him like a normal father? Was he having a father-son conversation like he and his dad recently had?*

He often wondered what their lives would be like had Barbara still been alive. And the big question *now* was whether Barbara would have convinced him to reconnect with his father.

THEY ARRIVED about a half hour before the Sunday service began and went straight to Ed's apartment.

"Good morning. It's nice to see you again. Come on in."

And so the visit began, cordial, as all visits with family should be. Ed didn't have any memory issues today. Michelle had warned Tom that an Alzheimer's patient may sometimes slip into a memory loss with little warning. You would just have to watch for it.

How do you watch a person's memory? That was a question he wanted to ask, but then realized it was just a tongue-in-cheek comment. He didn't want to embarrass himself—he'd already done that at least a dozen times.

A few minutes before eleven, they arrived at the church service, which was held in an alcove in one of the larger reception areas. It included a small, light wooden pulpit which matched the nearby woodwork, an upright Baldwin ebony piano, and rows of neatly lined cushioned chairs. There were more, larger windows in this area than in other areas. The design was such that it helped keep the area well lit.

A number of residents were already seated, a few in wheelchairs. Ed beamed as he introduced his son and grandson to everyone.

After sitting down, Ed leaned over and asked Chris if he'd been to a church like this before.

"No, Granddad. We don't go to church."

Ed's lips pressed tightly and his eyes focused inward. Tom sensed his dad now had a new challenge ahead of him—seeing to it that his grandson *and* his own son begin attending church.

"Good morning." A deep, booming baritone voice brought everyone's attention to the front of the room. A handsome African-American, with a square jaw and a wide grin, stood tall at the pulpit. Tom could tell he could handle himself by the way he filled out his suit.

"I pray everyone is doing well this morning. It is truly a glorious day in God's world. Happy Mother's Day, too. Can I get an Amen?"

Tom wondered if he'd made a mistake coming on a Sunday for this service. His mother and father had raised him as a strict Presbyterian. They attended Sunday school and church almost every week, but he had not been in years.

He had steered clear of any religion since the war. But he was here for Ed, and Chris seemed interested—whether it was the pastor, the surroundings, or he was placating to his father and grandfather. It was only an hour service. How bad could it be?

WHEN THE SERVICE ENDED, Ed made his way toward the pulpit, making sure Tom and Chris were next to him.

"Good morning, Charles. I'd like you to meet my son, Tom, and my grandson, Chris."

"Good morning. It's nice to see you this morning. Ed's told me a little about you."

There it was again. *"Ed's told me about you." What was he telling people? Was it that they hadn't spoken in years? Or was it something else?*

"Nice to meet you, sir." Chris was the first to speak.

"I enjoyed your message, Charles. Thank you." Tom thought that was the appropriate response to make, though his mind had drifted out of the sermon more than he listened.

"My pleasure. Always a joy to spread the Lord's word." Charles had a broad, welcoming smile.

"Ed tells me you are a Vietnam veteran. So am I—2nd Battalion, 5th Marines."

Tom noticed when Charles spoke about being a former Marine, he stood a little taller.

"I was there in '69-'70. You?"

Tom hadn't talked to another Vietnam veteran in a long time—something he purposefully avoided. He was always anxious about sharing anything personal with a stranger. He quietly replied, "Army, 2nd Battalion, 28th Infantry, '68-'69. We were based down in Lai Khe, Tri Corps."

"Lot of tough fighting down there." Charles' comment caught Tom's attention. He mumbled something under his breath that no one heard. Charles sensed his uneasiness and changed the subject.

"Ed is one of our regulars," he said with a broad smile, his big perfect white teeth gleaming.

"*All* of us are regulars. At least, those of us still here, and willing and able to come." Ed grinned, sharing a common conversation.

After a few awkward moments, Charles stuck out his hand. "Very nice to meet you both. Maybe we can grab a cup of coffee someday, Tom. I work over in the memory unit—we call it the 'Memory Support Neighborhood.' But that sounds too much like 'Mr. Rodgers' Neighborhood' to me, so I just refer to it as the memory unit."

"Thank you. I'm sure I'll see you around." Tom shook his big, calloused hand. He didn't know if Charles was aware his father had memory problems and would move to the memory unit sooner rather than later.

After the service, Ed invited them to "hang the feed bag." They walked down the hall to the main dining room. "Table for three, please."

When asked if Ester would join them, Ed replied she was out of town, visiting one of her children for a few days.

After ordering lunch, Tom asked, "How often do you attend church, Dad?"

"Every Sunday, good Lord willing and the creeks don't rise," Ed replied with a wide smile. "I've only missed a couple of Sundays since your mother passed away. I feel so much closer to her when I'm in church.

"Do you go to church?"

"Are you asking me or Dad?" Chris asked, taking a sip of his water.

"Both."

"No, Granddad. We don't go to church."

"Such a shame." Ed gazed lovingly upon his grandson. "There's a lot you can learn at church, Chris. Not just the Lord's word, mind you, but also the people and their life's experiences. I always enjoy the Sunday service.

"The sad thing is there comes a time when a regular doesn't show up. That usually means something not-so-good happened. When you reach our age, though, you realize life on this earth is not for eternity.

"That's one reason I stay close to God—I *know* I'll be with Louise again." Ed looked up at the ceiling, slowly blinked his eyes, and smiled—a ritual he had followed for years.

Tom thought he ought to say something and just when he was about to, lunch arrived. He decided to keep his thoughts to himself.

AS USUAL, lunch was exceptional. Ed glanced around the dining area, looking for any new faces. He always introduced himself to newcomers as a "co-founder"—like someone who was important. Everyone appreciated his friendly gesture.

"When I first moved here, I served on several committees. Since Sterling Oaks was brand new, there weren't that many of us. The CEO asked us to help shape the various functions and activities as we grew. It was fun… for a while. Then with more new folks moving in, it was time to let the younger whippersnappers take over."

"Granddad, how many people live here?"

"I think we are at ninety-five percent capacity, Chris—about 375 residents. I've heard rumors they were adding two more wings to the skilled nursing and memory unit. Probably just in time for me to move in," Ed smiled and winked.

Chris curiously looked around the dining area.

"What are you looking at?" Tom wondered if his son saw something he may have missed.

"I don't know, Dad. It seems like everyone takes their time."

"We call this the 'slow zone'," Ed quipped with a wide smile. "When people get older, they tend to slow down. Some people walk slower, some talk slower, and some eat slower."

Chris laughed out loud.

They finished their lunch and walked back to the apartment. Ed wasn't tired like before, so they sat down for a longer visit.

"Chris."

"Yes, sir?"

"See that shoe box over there on the desk? Can you bring it to me?"

"What's in it?"

"Bring it over here and I'll show you."

Chris' eyes opened wide. "Are these the letters you wrote home during the war?"

Now Tom leaned forward, equally excited, his eyes bulging.

"Yes. At least, most of them. I read them again over the past few days. They brought back a lot of memories. I thought you and your dad might like to have them. My only request is you keep them as safe as I have."

"Awesome, Granddad. Thanks. I'll take care of them, I promise."

Tom was dumbfounded. He knew Ed had kept the letters he wrote home during *his* war but had never seen them. Now he wondered if his father had the letters *he* had written. He would have to wait to ask that question. Right now, his focus was on Chris' excitement—his own, too.

"It's been years since I read them. I can remember the days when I wrote many of them. The weather was a factor, of course, especially during the winter. That's why some are shorter than others. I tried to write Louise and my mother and father as often as I could.

"You can tell a lot from reading these letters and how much I'd changed, even though I tried not to let on how awful things were. They were like your letters, Tom. I know things were far worse than you let on. I tried not to dwell on it too much. I didn't want your mother to worry. Lord knows she worried enough during *my* war."

After another walk outside, Tom mentioned they should leave soon to get on the road. They turned down Ed's dinner invitation, but promised a rain check. There would be many more visits in the future.

15 - The Event

"Tom?"

"Yes. Who's calling?"

"Tom, this is Michelle Myers at Sterling Oaks."

"Oh hi, Michelle. To what do I owe this pleasure?"

Tom stepped down off his six-foot step ladder. He was working—the weather in mid-May was perfect for painting—when his phone rang. He didn't recognize the number, but it was a welcomed voice.

"Tom. Your father's had an event. He had a mild stroke yesterday and is in the hospital. He's going to be all right, and should be back at Sterling Oaks in a few days. I stopped by to see him this morning on my way into work. He asked me to call and let you know he's fine. He also said there's no need for you to come up yet."

Tom wasn't sure how to respond and began to ask questions. "Michelle, what does this mean? What exactly is a stroke? Is he flat on his back? How will he get around?"

"Tom, it's okay. He's only suffered"—Michelle stopped mid-sentence when she realized that wasn't the right word—"he's experienced a mild stroke. We don't know the full extent at this time. The doctor is monitoring him and will need to run additional tests. He should be able to return to Sterling Oaks in the next day or two.

"It would help if you came up when Ed returns." Michelle paused.

"There are also several documents his lawyer wants you to look over."

Tom's eyes narrowed. "Ed has a lawyer? For what?"

"Relax, Tom. Most people Ed's age have at least one lawyer. He helped him get all the legal paperwork together when he sold his business and when he moved to Sterling Oaks. He's been Ed's lawyer and close friend for years."

"All right." Tom calmed down. "Should I come up tomorrow, or should I wait until Ed is back in his apartment?"

"Let me call you when he returns. He will likely be confused. Most people who have a mild stroke are a little uneasy when they first get back to their surroundings. Part of it is that his body may not function the way it used to. That's one thing the doctor wants to determine before releasing Ed from the hospital.

"The second, and perhaps more important in Ed's case, is his Alzheimer's. We're not sure if the stroke affected his mind or not. We'll evaluate that further when he returns to Sterling Oaks. He'll be in the Memory Support Neighborhood for a few days. I'm sure he would appreciate seeing a familiar face."

"I'll be there when you need me, Michelle. Is there anything else I can do right now?"

"No, I don't think so, Tom. I know you and Ed were getting along well. You should continue to visit as often as you can. He also enjoys spending time with Chris."

"Thank you, Michelle. I appreciate your call."

Tom added, "I'd like to buy you a cup of coffee the next time I'm up your way." He wasn't sure why he said that at this moment; it just blurted out. Something about her reassuring voice, though, was comforting.

"I'd like that. Thank you. I'll call you when Ed returns or if anything changes."

"Thanks again."

"Goodbye."

Tom ended the call as he stepped outside to fire up a cigarette. It was spotty overcast, but no rain in sight. He looked off into the distant, cloud-covered hills. He was painting the inside of a two-story house in a new residential development on Cheat Lake.

He loved what he did—being part of something new. He was not only helping the surrounding community grow but knew that a new family would move in soon and would appreciate his handiwork. This was much different from the "Pacification" program, helping the local Vietnamese in the small hamlets around Lai Khe. Though, those were some of the few good memories of *his* war.

He cherished his time alone with his thoughts when he painted. Lately though, his father weighed heavily on his mind. He was building a new relationship and wondered—sometimes out loud to no one in particular—why he had walked away in the first place. It wasn't just pride. It was stubbornness, something he definitely got from his father. But at the time, he just had to leave.

And Ed has a lawyer?

He wasn't sure what Michelle meant by "legal documents," but that was the least of his concerns. He couldn't do anything about his dad right now but worry, so he turned back to his work. He needed to finish this job as soon as he could.

TOM WAS PREPARING an easy supper. His kitchen wasn't large, but it suited him and Chris. He'd made only a few changes when he first bought the house, adding a small island in the middle to give him ample room for cutting and serving. He'd also installed the new energy-efficient CFL ceiling lights to compensate for the minimal lighting coming through the single window which looked out to the small backyard.

While cooking was therapy for him, he wasn't always up for it. But it was something he and Chris could do together. And lately, his son wanted to help more. *That was a good thing, wasn't it?*

"Is Granddad going to be okay?" Chris sat on a bar stool at the counter watching his dad expertly wield the cutting knife.

"Michelle thinks so. I don't know much about strokes, but it affects the brain. That, in turn, may affect other functions, both physical and mental."

"Are you worried, Dad?"

Tom stopped cutting carrots and laid the chef's knife down. There was genuine concern in his son's eyes and voice. He needed to be strong for Chris. Or was it he needed to be strong… period?

"Yes, I'm worried. I'm also confused."

"About what?"

"Visiting your grandfather has been good for me, Chris. I mean, until several months ago, I rarely thought about him. There were just too many painful memories. Since that first visit though, I've enjoyed getting to know him better. He's a *much* different man than I remember. But then, so am I."

Tom took a deep breath and slowly exhaled, feeling that all too familiar surge of guilt once again.

"I'm struggling because I went so long without trying to find him. I'm struggling because I was stubborn to keep him out of my life for so long."

Tom paused, then looked directly at Chris. "But the hardest part? The hardest part for me is the simple fact that I kept you and him apart all these years. That was pure selfishness. That's what is so confusing to me right now. Does any of this make sense to you?"

"I think so, Dad. I know we've had our differences—probably similar to you and Granddad. But we've always been able to work through them. I'm only fifteen, but I've grown up a lot this past year. Watching you and Granddad together has been… *enlightening*."

Tom realized his son was right. He *was* his father's son. Was he thinking about Chris or his *own* father? It didn't matter. He felt closer to his son than he had in a long time and that was a wonderful feeling.

Tom picked up the knife and continued cutting vegetables. He looked up with a slight grin. "Did I tell you that your grandfather wants you to have his car?"

"What? No way. When?" Chris' face lit up.

"Settle down." He knew his son would be excited. "You're not old enough to drive yet. He says he's no longer driving it and it stays parked in the garage. Dad thought you might like to have it."

"Awesome. What kind of car is it?"

"I haven't seen it yet, but he said it's a Chevy Malibu. He *always* bought American-made cars. I imagine it's a four-door and I'm sure it's in tip-top shape. He always took great care of his cars. That's how *I* learned how to work on my car. Dad did about everything himself. I just hung around, learning what I could."

Tom wished he'd done the same for his son. But this was a different generation. They didn't work on cars—they worked on computers.

"When do I—I mean *we*—get it?" Chris' eyes bulged.

"Well. There's a slight problem. We have to let Dad make that decision. Since he's had this stroke, he should first get settled back in his place. Michelle said it's essential I meet with his lawyer. And I'm sure there's a bunch of other things. We just need to be patient.

"One thing we can do soon is to get you behind the wheel of my truck."

"Can't I learn to drive the GTO? That would be awesome."

"No, that's not going to happen. At least not yet. The GTO is a manual, stick-shift transmission. I want you to learn to drive the truck first. It's automatic and easier to drive."

It was obvious that Chris' high hopes were quickly dampened. Tom knew that question would eventually surface. He had other reasons for not letting him drive Sunshine.

"Okay. When can I start?"

"Why not this weekend? We can go to one of the mall parking lots and I'll teach you the basics. When you get more comfortable driving, we'll try other places. You also need to study for your learner's permit. I'm sure that will take a little time, too."

Tom enjoyed seeing Chris' enthusiasm. It reminded him of his younger self when he first got his GTO. He was excited for his son, but he was also worried about his father. Tom *was* on an emotional rollercoaster.

He thought about Michelle and her soothing voice.

"Buy you a cup of coffee..." Tom's comment was *so* lame. But the fact she said she *"looked forward to it"* was, in a word, exciting. Or was Tom making too much of her response?

Whatever. He had a great deal on his mind right now and wondered what may lie in the near future.

16 - The Lawyer

Tom and Sunshine were on the road bright and early the day after Michelle called. Ed had returned to Sterling Oaks the day before. Tom made arrangements to miss work—something he rarely did. As he pulled onto the interstate, the Eagles *Desperado* played on the radio, but he wasn't paying attention. He had too much on his mind.

And freedom, oh freedom, well that's just some people talkin'
Your prison is walking through this world all alone.

Michelle had also mentioned Mr. Jones, Ed's lawyer, would like to meet and discuss several legal documents. Tom wasn't sure what that meant, but he would find out soon enough.

He knew lawyers charged an arm and a leg for their "so-called" professional services. Fortunately, he hadn't needed one for a long time. He didn't even know how much it cost to live at Sterling Oaks, much less how Ed paid for it. *He must be doing all right after selling his business.*

He replayed his recent trips to Sterling Oaks and how his dad— and he—had changed. During the initial visit, Ed blew up, but Michelle calmly talked Tom into returning. He was grateful for that— both to visit his dad again *and* to see Michelle.

Was he attracted to her? What was it that made him feel comfortable around her? He couldn't quite put his finger on it, but she seemed interested. Or was she that way with every family member? Yet, she seemed to understand Vietnam veterans and the issues they faced after the war.

Earl had mentioned she was one of the top health care professionals in the area. Maybe it was just her way to help everyone feel comfortable at Sterling Oaks. It was difficult to tell; it had been a long time since he'd been in a relationship.

His mind drifted back to his father. Over the past few days, he thought Ed may be at the end of his life. That was because he knew nothing about strokes. Chris had researched the Internet and learned Ed most likely had a "mini-stroke." Tom made a mental note to learn more about computers. Chris told him the medical term—Transient ischemic attack—but neither of them could pronounce it. He only remembered the initials, "TIA." That was much easier.

From what they read, it sounded like it was temporary. The fact that his father had returned to Sterling Oaks was a good sign. Michelle said nothing about his needing help to get around—another good sign.

TOM ROUNDED THE TURN and eased Sunshine up to the guard gate. A familiar face appeared, but Earl wasn't smiling.

"Good morning, Mr. Reilly. I heard about your father. I'm sorry, but I understand he's back now. Is there anything I can do for you?" Earl's voice and face expressed genuine concern.

"Do you have any jokes this morning?" Tom frowned, showing a worried look.

Earl smiled and raised his eyebrows. "I've got a million of 'em. What did the dyslexic, agnostic, insomniac do?"

"Tell me, Earl."

"He stayed up all night wondering if there really was a dog."

A moment passed, then Tom got it and cracked a smile. "Thanks, Earl. I needed that."

"My pleasure, Mr. Reilly. If you need more, I'll be here."

"Thank you." Tom gunned his engine and winked at Earl, still drooling over Sunshine.

After pulling into his usual parking spot, he quickly walked inside. Margie looked up from her computer and weakly smiled, pointing down the hall. "He's in room 1967."

"Thank you, Margie."

What happened to her usual cheerful, "Good morning…" greeting. Was there something she didn't want to tell me?

He hustled down the hallway and found Ed's room. The door was closed, but he quietly knocked. Michelle opened the door.

"Good morning, Tom. Come in, please."

"Hi, Michelle. Is… is everything all right?"

Walking in, Tom spotted his dad lying in bed, still in his pajamas. He sensed something was not right. Michelle quietly closed the door behind him. Ed noticed, but didn't recognize him. Tom caught Michelle's eye with a puzzled expression.

"Ed's memory has slipped," Michelle said matter-of-factly. "The aide reported he woke up this morning, confused—that's not unusual—and called me. I had just walked into my office. I knew you were coming this morning, so I wanted to assess his condition and meet with you before you arrived. But you're here now, and I've done what I can.

"Your father is confused. He's not sure what day it is or where he is. This is similar to what the security guard reported two months ago, when I first contacted you."

"Is there anything we—*I*—can do?" Tom was visibly anxious, fidgeting and shifting his gaze between Michelle and Ed. *Was he going to lose his dad before he knew who he was?*

"The best thing right now is to sit and talk with him. He may remember something that helps jog his memory. This is one of those transitions we are still learning about."

"Okay. I understand. Would you mind staying, Michelle? I'm not sure what to do or say."

"Of course. I've got time before my next appointment. I'll sit over here, out of the way."

"Thanks. I feel better when you're nearby." Tom wasn't sure what that meant—it just came out. He was trying to focus on his father.

He walked over and stood beside the bed, looking down at a man who he hoped would soon return as his father. "Hi Dad. I'm glad to see you are back home again."

Ed looked up. There was a glazed and confused look in his eyes. "Who are you?" His father's voice was weak.

"I'm your son, Tom. Don't you remember?" As soon as he said that, Tom realized that was *not* the question to ask. He quietly cursed to himself.

"I'm Tom Reilly, and my son—your grandson—is Chris. He interviewed you for a school project on World War II a few weeks ago. He got an A-plus on his report."

"World War II? Chris?" Ed lowered his gaze toward the end of the bed and blinked several times. It almost looked as if he was blinking himself back to reality.

"Oh, Chris. My grandson. Yes, of course I remember. We talked about World War II and a little about Vietnam. How is Chris?" Ed lifted his head off the pillow and looked around the room. "Did he come with you today?"

Tom glanced over at Michelle, a tear in his eye. She was equally surprised. Her watery eyes told him, *"Keep talking, don't stop now."*

"Not today, Dad, but he'll come with me next time. I promise."

Tom choked up, witnessing his father's transition. *His dad was back.*

"Okay. I'm a little confused. But then, I'm eighty years old, right? No, wait—eighty-one. A little senile at times, but I'm okay." Ed cracked a slight smile as he slowly sat up in his bed.

"I know I'm not in my apartment, but I am at Sterling Oaks. Isn't that right, Ms. Myers?"

Michelle quickly stood and walked over, standing close to Tom, arms touching.

"Yes, Mr. Reilly. You are in the Memory Support Neighborhood. You had a mini-stroke a few days ago, and we took you to the hospital. I'm sure you don't remember, but that's okay. In a few more days, we'll get you back to your own apartment."

Ed was ready to get dressed and get the day going. He asked the whereabouts of his clothes. Michelle said she'd ask an aide to come in and help.

"I don't need no fuckin' aide, Ms. Myers. I'm perfectly capable of getting dressed myself," Ed argued loudly while standing up.

Luckily, Tom and Michelle were there to catch him before he tumbled over. He sat back down on the bed.

"On second thought, maybe I do." Ed smiled weakly, winking at his son. Neither Michelle nor Tom could tell if Ed's wobbliness was because of his recent stroke, but they didn't want to take any chances.

After the aide came in, Michelle and Tom left the room. She asked if he wanted to join her for a cup of coffee. "You mean, like a date?" As soon as he said that, Tom's face turned red, and he wanted to hide.

"I'm sorry, Michelle. I didn't mean to say that. I was out of line."

"No, that's okay, Tom. No offense taken. But yes, we can get a cup of coffee. After all, you did offer to buy me a cup, right?" Michelle smiled, revealing a charming set of dimples. She was definitely flirting. It took his mind off his father and he immediately felt at ease.

Both settled in the smaller dining area down the hall from the memory unit.

"Michelle, do you remember me telling you that when Chris and I visited Ed in the past, a couple times he was confused when we first arrived? But as soon as we started talking about World War II, he snapped right back into the present. He not only recognized us, but he remembered specific details about the war."

"Yes, I remember. I saw that just now. While I've experienced a lot of different triggers for memory recall, this is the first time I've witnessed one like this."

"Not only that, Michelle, but he was also knowledgeable and specific about the Vietnam War. He told me things I'd never heard from him before. It almost seems that once he regains his memory, he not only recalls World War II, but also more recent events. He still can't tell me what he did yesterday or the day before, but I'm guessing that's part of this memory puzzle. Is that correct?"

"Yes, Tom. It is. I should mention *this* is a unique situation. Most people with Alzheimer's steadily decline in their memory loss, recalling fewer and fewer events. Ed, however, seems to recall *more* events *and* recalls them more frequently.

"From what you've told me and from what I just observed, you are one of the luckiest family members I've met here. I mean, you can relive some of your childhood *and* adult memories with your father. Not everybody gets to do that at this stage in life."

A second chance. Yes, Tom knew he was lucky.

Michelle finished her cup of coffee and excused herself for her next appointment. Tom stood to shake her hand, holding it longer than normal. Her hand was soft and reminded him of Barbara. She smiled, gazing into his eyes, and didn't seem to mind.

"Good morning, Michelle."

Both dropped the handshake and turned to see an older, gray-haired gentleman wearing a suit and tie, and holding a briefcase standing a few feet away.

"Margie said you were down this way."

"Good morning, Mr. Jones." Michelle stepped away from Tom toward the stranger—*intruder*—to shake his hand.

Mr. Jones? That must be the lawyer.

"Mr. Jones. I'd like to introduce Tom Reilly, Ed's son."

"Good morning, Tom. It is a pleasure to *finally* meet you."

He wasn't sure how to take that, but Tom assumed Mr. Jones was just being courteous.

"Good morning, Mr. Jones."

"Tony. Please call me Tony."

"Tony it is, then. Nice to meet you, too."

"If it's okay with the two of you, I'll check on Ed, then I've got an appointment to meet." Michelle resumed her professional tone of voice.

"Certainly. I'll speak with you later."

Tom narrowed his eyes and gave the lawyer a hard look. He was getting… a… little… *jealous?*

"Tom, do you mind if I call you Tom?"

"Not at all. That *is* my name."

"Good. Mind if we meet in the conference room? Your father will be fine. They are probably helping him shower before he gets dressed. I have several legal documents that Ed wanted me to discuss with you."

"Okay. Lead the way."

Tom was slightly confused and anxious. *Why would his father need a lawyer? But then, why does anyone need one?* Michelle had told him that Mr. Jones—Tony—was his father's lawyer and his friend. That thought made him feel a little less uncomfortable.

The conference room was outside the memory unit, right around the corner from the dining area. Tony closed the door and motioned Tom to sit at the round table across from him. His mannerisms indicated he liked to be in control. He set his briefcase down on the floor beside him. When he put on his glasses, Tom noticed his weathered expression showed years of legal experience. Yet something was missing…

Tony Jones looked directly at Tom and without hesitation, spoke. "I guess I should get right to the business at hand. Ed told me about your little argument years ago. It didn't seem that big a deal to me. I can understand why *he* was upset, but I can't understand *your* attitude."

Nice way to start a conversation, asshole. Tom hadn't dealt with many lawyers, but this one pissed him off.

"Mr. Jones…"

"Tony, please call me Tony."

"Mr. Jones." Tom spoke with the determined confidence of a combat veteran. "Were you in Vietnam?"

"No."

"Korea?"

"No."

"World War II?"

"No, I wasn't in the military."

"Then you don't know shit about what I feel, what I saw, what we *all* did over there, do you?" Tom caustically replied, slammed his fist on the table, then quickly stood and turned to walk toward the door, shaking his head in frustration.

Mr. Jones' expression changed dramatically as he sat back in his chair. Tom heard him take a deep breath and exhale.

Tony Jones spoke softly, after a few moments of silence. "My son was killed in Khe Sanh in 1968. You probably didn't know that." Tom stopped dead in his tracks.

As soon as he mentioned his son's death out loud, Tony's eyes changed from a combatant lawyer to a soulful father. A father who had lost his son in a long ago war. Tears welled up in the attorney's eyes as he spoke. He removed his glasses and wiped away a tear.

"I can't imagine what you and he had to do while you were over there. I only know he was fighting for his country and that he believed in what he was fighting for."

Tom slowly turned and walked back toward the table. "I'm sorry. No, I didn't know."

As Tom started to speak, he sighed like most people do when remembering something intense. Not wanting to look directly at Mr. Jones, he stared at an old unfamiliar painting on the wall and spoke in a quiet monotone, almost in a matter-of-fact voice.

"When I first got over there, I *was* like your son. I was fighting for something *I* believed in, too. But when I returned to Vietnam after my mother's funeral, there was a difference—a *major* difference—in what I believed. It's difficult to describe that change. I saw so many of my buddies needlessly wounded and killed, I started not to make any more friends. My attitude changed from killing the enemy to keeping myself and my buddies alive. It was almost that simple.

"What was your son's name, Tony?"

"Jerry. He was a Marine."

Now Tom sat down hard, staring out the window. His hands trembled as he pulled out a cigarette. He didn't care if he was breaking the rules. A long silence followed.

"I knew your son, Tony. Jerry was one of my best friends in high school. He enlisted a little before I did."

Tom took a deep breath. "When I came home for my mother's funeral, I also went to Jerry's. He was an outstanding soldier and a great football player. And... he was my friend." Tom's eyes began to tear up. "I was heartbroken when I found out Jerry died. I lost a lot of friends over there. In more ways than I can count, I don't think I ever came home. Part of me is still over there."

A few moments passed.

"It was a Saturday morning when they came to tell us." Now Tony was staring out the window, his fingers massaging his temple, remembering that dreadful day.

"My wife and I were enjoying a leisurely breakfast when the doorbell rang. We weren't expecting anyone, but we both looked at each other with the same anxious thought, 'something happened to Jerry.' Even though he wrote often, we always worried about him.

"When I opened the door and saw a Marine officer and a Marine chaplain, both in uniform… I knew. I could hear my wife sobbing in the background—she knew. They said Jerry died a hero. All they could tell us was that he was on point when his unit got caught in an ambush while out on patrol.

"He came home a few days later." Tony took a deep breath, then slowly exhaled. "That same day, we received the last letter he had written to us." Tony looked at Tom, his eyes watering. "There was *nothing* in his letter about being afraid or worrying about death. He was a *proud* Marine… and *proud* to be serving his country."

Tears streamed down Tony's cheeks. A tear rolled down Tom's face as he fought to keep from crying.

"The hardest thing I had to do was to wake my daughter, Jennifer—Jerry's only sibling—to tell her that her brother had been killed in Vietnam."

They sat in silence for a while, both reflecting about a terrible time in their lives.

Tom still wasn't sure why he was meeting with Tony. Michelle said it was important and that he had Ed's legal papers he needed him to look over.

After a few more respectful and quiet minutes, Tony turned, his voice changing from that of a grieving father back to a professional lawyer. He wiped his eyes with a clean handkerchief. "Tom, I've been your father's attorney and friend for a long time.

"As you know, Ed is a proud man. Until recently, he didn't want to have any contact with you. Now he has this terrible disease. He asked me to prepare several legal documents for you to read and, if you think it's appropriate, to sign them. He wants you to take over his finances and help make decisions for him—become his 'Guardian,' so to speak."

Tom knew nothing about the law. While he was a little wild in his younger years, he stayed out of trouble, except for a couple of speeding tickets in his GTO soon after returning from Vietnam.

"I'm not sure I understand, Tony."

Tony leaned forward, elbows on the table, wanting to make sure Tom heard every word.

"Tom, you are Ed's only living relative—you and Chris. He doesn't have a lot of money. What he has, he wants to leave to the two of you. He's already set up a trust fund for Chris so he can go to a good university, if he so desires. The rest is helping manage Ed's end of life."

"End of life." Those words sent shivers up Tom's spine. "What do you mean, 'end of life'? How much longer does he have?"

"It is not a question of how much time your father has to *live.*"

"Then what is it?" Tom's eyes narrowed.

"It's how much time he has before he completely loses his memory. As I'm sure you've witnessed over the past two months, Ed has mostly been 'with it,' so to speak." Mr. Jones tried to speak Tom's language as he explained complicated legal details.

"He and I have met several times over the past few weeks. Ed had a very successful business. When it came time to retire, he didn't know where you were. I tried to convince him to let me find you, but he flatly refused. Something about 'foolish pride,' I believe, were his exact words. To be honest, I wasn't sure if he was talking about you or himself. So, I let it go.

"I've been helping manage Ed's finances for the past few years, ever since he moved to Sterling Oaks. We have an account set up so all of his expenses from Sterling Oaks are automatically withdrawn— with oversight, of course.

"I can continue to manage his assets, if you so desire. But he wanted me to ask if you would take them over, which is detailed in these documents."

Tony sat back in his chair, his voice changing to a softer tone.

"Ed is still of sound mind and body in the legal sense. But as you are aware, Alzheimer's takes that memory away, bit by bit. He thought the sooner the better, and I couldn't agree more."

Tom took a deep breath and sat back. "What do I need to do?"

"First, let me review his basic finances with you. He has plenty of money to last the rest of his life and there will be some left over. Chris' trust fund is already set up and accounted for.

"The Durable Power of Attorney allows you to act on Ed's behalf in his legal and financial matters. That means you can make all legal decisions for him and, if you so desire, also make financial decisions. The Medical Power of Attorney is another document that allows you to make health decisions for Ed.

"There are additional documents called Medical Directives, but let's hold off on those until you understand what all these other documents mean."

Tom slowly stood and moved his chair back to its place. He needed to step outside for a smoke, and invited Mr. Jones to go with him. Tony didn't smoke, but he welcomed the opportunity to walk outside to the courtyard for some fresh air.

They walked in revered silence over to a shaded area, under a large oak tree, and sat in separate chairs, facing the magnificent view of the green foothills. Neither spoke for a few minutes. Several nearby bird feeders provided songbirds the opportunity to feast, then fly to a nearby tree, singing to their heart's delight.

Tom lit a cigarette as he contemplated what next to say to his best friend's father.

"I'm sorry about Jerry. I know it must still be hard for you and your wife and Jennifer.

"Jerry and I hung out a lot during high school. I didn't think we'd *both* join the military." Tom chuckled under his breath. "After we graduated, we sort of lost touch with each other."

"Jerry always wanted to be a Marine," Tony replied after a couple of moments. "The day he graduated from basic training was the proudest moment in his life. Even though he knew he was going to Vietnam, I honestly think he was looking forward to it. He was proud to serve his country. And…" Tony looked up and closed his eyes. "I know he still is."

Tony looked at Tom with renewed admiration.

"Tom, I know you and your father had a falling out and from what I could tell, he was angry at the world, not you. I think at the time, he wanted you to stay close to home because the only thing he hadn't lost control of was his business. Louise had died and he was afraid of losing you to the war, even *after* you came home.

"I didn't know Ed back then—we first met when he wanted to sell his business. We quickly became good friends—*best* friends.

"I think the thing that hurt Ed the most was that you left him alone… again, even though he was probably part of the problem. He didn't have anyone else and his pride kept him from trying to find you. He can be a stubborn old geezer, like many of us when we reach a certain age."

Tom smiled at that comment. He wasn't of "that age," but he certainly knew about being stubborn.

Tony's eyes darted between Tom and the far hills, like he had something on his mind. "Do you mind if I ask you a question, Tom? I don't mean to bring up the past, but can you tell me a little about what you experienced in Vietnam? Did you ever walk point for your unit? I'm just trying to understand a little about what Jerry did while he was in the jungle."

Tom took out another cigarette, lit it, and took a deep breath. He glanced over at Tony, then turned away, staring at the blooming blue bell flowers and tulips in the courtyard. He leaned forward, elbows on his knees.

"I guess it's different for everyone, Tony. Yet there's probably a lot of similarities. After I first arrived in-country and after my week-long orientation, I couldn't wait to go out on patrol. I'd never shot a man before and while I wasn't looking to kill, I wanted to be out in the jungle and not in base camp.

"I've always loved the outdoors. Besides, that's what I'd signed up for.

"I was out on patrol the first week, but not in front, even though that's where I wanted to be. I was ready, willing, and able. But the more seasoned grunts dampened my enthusiasm—for good reason, I might add. They kept telling me that my turn would come and I needed more experience. I understood, but I was like a sponge. I wanted to learn anything and everything I could. Even back in base camp, I'd spend time asking questions.

"Then, my first time out front—on point—I had another experienced point man right behind me. Together, we probed our way through the trails. I was high on adrenaline. While we found a few booby traps on that first patrol, no one got hurt. I imagine it was very much the same as Jerry experienced."

Tom glanced over at Tony who was staring out at the foothills, listening intently. "Are you okay, Tony?"

"Yes. Please… continue."

"Well, I really liked walking point, so much that I volunteered every patrol I went on. I was good at it, too. Everybody thought I was nuts, but they were happy to oblige.

"Dad and I spent a lot of time in the woods around here when I was growing up and he taught me a lot about how to read the forest. I seemed to hear and see things before others did, and managed to keep everyone safe. It only takes a quick moment of hesitation to get into a life and death situation.

"I never really worried about dying or getting shot. I was more worried about *not* spotting something that would eventually kill members of my squad. I'm sure Jerry was pretty much the same."

Tom took a moment before continuing. He realized this conversation was not only helping Tony, but also gave himself a sense of relief—sharing an experience that few people could relate. He spoke again with a renewed sense of pride and confidence.

"I don't know what happened. I don't think anyone does. But I can tell you this, Tony. Marines wouldn't let just *anybody* walk point. Jerry *had* to earn that privilege and by doing so, had the admiration and respect of *everyone* in his unit. He was a solid Marine, through and through."

Tom let that last statement hang in the air. While he was trying his best to offer support to Tony—someone who'd lost a son to a war—he realized that his own father had lost a son *because* of a war.

After a few more minutes, they walked back inside to the conference room. Tom didn't stay long. His father was still weary from his hospital ordeal and needed rest. He did, however, spend a little more time with Tony and signed all the legal documents.

Ed wasn't wealthy by any means but had enough money to comfortably live the rest of his life at Sterling Oaks. Tony assured him there would also be a small inheritance. However, Tom didn't care that much about money—it just wasn't important to him.

17 - Vietnam—Mom's Funeral

Tom sat alone in Sunshine and stared out beyond the green-capped hills. The engine was off, windows rolled down, and he was smoking a much-needed cigarette. This had been a busy and confusing day.

He was glad his dad was back home. *Is that what Ed calls Sterling Oaks now?* He would have to get used to that.

The realization that his dad was going to die—not soon, he hoped—set in. He never thought of death this way. It was much different in Vietnam—you faced death *every* day. You got used to the fact that somebody was going to die. You hoped it wouldn't be you or any of your buddies. That guilt *never* left him, even after thirty years.

An air ambulance helicopter flew low overhead toward Pittsburgh. He glanced up and followed its flight path, pushing his thoughts deeper into Vietnam.

THE FIRST TIME he'd ridden in a chopper, his unit was flying to a recently cleared landing zone (LZ), close to the Cambodian border, near the Ho Chi Minh Trail. His squad leader had instructed them to be ready for North Vietnamese Army (NVA) and Viet Cong (VC). Both had been spotted in the area.

He didn't know if they were headed into a hot LZ for a world of hurt, or if it was free and clear. For Tom, on his first combat venture deep into the boonies, it didn't matter. He experienced that all-too-familiar adrenaline rush.

Green smoke appeared above the tree line, popped from a smoke grenade by the grunts on the ground—that was a good sign. It was *not* a hot LZ, and the enemy was not firing at the landing grunts.

As soon as his helo touched down, all eight men in his squad jumped out on cue. It took off within a matter of a few seconds, making room for the next slick to drop off its load of grunts. Thank God, there were no bodies or wounded to load for the return trip.

As soon as Tom's feet hit the ground, he felt the additional sixty-pound weight of his supplies and ammo. Tom wasn't a big man and weighed only a hundred and sixty pounds. Like most grunts, though, he was tough and wasn't going to complain about carrying extra weight. Following his squad leader, he chambered a round in his M-16, his finger on the safety, ready to release at first contact.

HIS MIND SNAPPED BACK to the present. He hadn't thought about that event in a while. Normally, the sound of helicopters didn't faze him. In all the choppers he'd ridden in during the war, he recalled only a few times landing in a hot LZ. That didn't bother him.

The thing that bothered him the most was having to load bodies on the returning helo. *That* was hard, especially if one of them was a buddy.

Tom shook his head, clearing his thoughts and wondered if that 'Nam flashback was triggered by his recent meeting with Tony Jones.

He'd also stopped by to see Michelle, but she was busy in afternoon meetings. She ducked out to briefly speak with him and ask about Ed. Tom wished he could have spent more time with her. He needed someone to talk to after learning Tony had lost his only son in Vietnam—Tom's closest friend in high school.

He cranked up Sunshine. It amazed him she always spoke softly to him, something not many people understood. His dad's wise words were always, *"You take care of her and she'll take care of you."*

When he first heard that phrase, he thought it meant if he took care of his car, it would drive well. He learned years ago, though, it was much more than that. She takes care of *me*. Sunshine is my safe place and always has been.

Driving past the guard gate, he realized he was low on gas. He stopped by the old mom and pop grocery store to fill up. He also wanted to grab a cup of coffee for the trip home, so he went inside to pay. A familiar face, the old Korean War veteran, sat behind the counter, still wearing his U.S. Army Veteran ball cap.

"Afternoon, Army." He remembered Tom. "How're things today?"

"Okay, I suppose."

"You look like a man with a load on his mind."

He was keenly observant. Tom sensed a welcomed comradery he hadn't known since his days in Vietnam with his brothers-in-arms.

He smiled, acknowledging the vet's comment. "I guess I do. My dad is at Sterling Oaks. That's why I've been coming up this way."

"Nice place. Lots of old folks there."

"Yeah, there are." Tom quickly got the joke and cracked a wider, warmer smile.

"My father is also an Army veteran. He fought in World War II with the 80th Division in Europe."

"The 80th was part of Patton's Third Army, wasn't it?"

"Yep. He was part of the original company that went over." Tom stated proudly. "He made it through the war in one piece."

"Stay right here, Army. I've got something I'd like to give your dad." The old vet disappeared into a back office with a slight limp as he walked.

Tom sipped his steaming coffee—just the way he liked it. He'd decided long ago not to talk about his Vietnam past, especially with strangers. Most people just didn't care. He'd also learned that guys who had been in combat had a unique way of explaining things—they won't say anything unless specifically asked. Others—the ones who *never* saw action—well… they'd volunteer their entire military career.

This guy—*this* Korean War veteran—had *definitely* seen combat.

"Give one of these to your dad." The vet returned and handed him two new U.S. Army Veteran ball caps. "Keep one for yourself. And the coffee's on me today."

Tom was stunned. He didn't know this guy from Adam, but something about the brotherhood of Army veterans…

"Thank you, sir. By the way, what is your name?"

"Most people call me 'Pop.' It's much easier than my real name, James Bartholomew Williams the Third," he said with a smile.

Tom returned the smile. "Thank you, Pop. I really appreciate this. I'll give it to my dad the next time I see him. I know he'll be appreciative, too."

"My pleasure. Us Army vets have to stick together. Have a blessed day, Son."

Tom brushed his hair back with his hand and proudly put on his new Army Veteran ball cap. It fit perfectly. Smiling at Pop, he walked out the door, standing a little taller. He wasn't sure what to think of that exchange. There was, however, something to what Pop said, *"Us Army vets have to stick together."*

With a full tank of gas and the windows rolled down, he smoked a Marlboro. Listening to oldies while driving Sunshine, life didn't get much better. The Byrds' *Turn, Turn, Turn* played on the radio. Tom reached to change the station—another protest song—but stopped to listen.

A time to kill, a time to heal
A time to laugh, a time to weep

It sounded—*felt*—different this time. He wasn't sure why, but he liked the tune better today. He was aware the words came from the Bible, but couldn't recall which verse.

His thoughts returned to Mr. Jones—Tony—and his son, Jerry. He recalled the back-to-back funerals. *That* was one hell of a week, one he'd never forget.

He tried to remember where he was when his CO first contacted him about his mother. He was in the boonies on patrol, somewhere east of Lai Khe. His unit had just completed a successful night ambush, killing several Viet Cong, and capturing weapons and ammo.

The grunts used to call them "Search-and-Destroy" missions. But they had been instructed to start calling them, "Reconnaissance in Force" (RIF)—a bullshit political change of wording. It didn't matter, the mission was still the same: hunt down and kill the enemy.

He'd been in-country for six months, had his *Baptism of Fire* during the Tet Offensive, and been on dozens of patrols. He'd been shot at multiple times and narrowly escaped a few enemy ambushes. But he hadn't yet been wounded.

He was a solid and seasoned point man. Most of the time, he didn't worry about dying. Although anxious during his first few patrols, he quickly picked up the jungle fighting tactics from the experienced grunts in his unit.

Several of his squad members jokingly asked multiple times if he had a sixth sense. He seemed to spot enemy snipers, trip wires, and booby traps before anyone else. In all his time—at least, during that *first* six months in Vietnam—he never experienced the "point man's paranoia," that sensation a grunt gets when he's been on point too long and expected to be shot.

He'd been in a heavily wooded area, about ten klicks (kilometers) from the main base camp at Lai Khe. His platoon leader called for him to come up front and quietly relayed the Red Cross message about his mother. Tom was devastated. They were already returning to base camp. Instead of humping it back, his CO let him hitch a ride on that day's re-supply chopper.

The Army worked hard to get young soldiers home in times of need, especially in this situation. Once back at base camp, he cleaned up, dressed in his Khaki uniform, and caught a chopper to Tan Son Nhut Air Base at Saigon. He then flew military flights to Okinawa, Guam, Hawaii, and San Francisco. And finally, a commercial flight to Pittsburgh. Tom was back home in less than forty-eight hours from the time he'd learned of his mother's death.

The World was much different from when he'd left six months earlier. He was so focused on getting home, he didn't pay attention to the protesters at the Oakland airport. He witnessed several of them yelling and spitting on soldiers. It didn't seem to matter if they were Army, Navy, Air Force, or Marines. The only commonality was that they all wore a military uniform.

He watched as one young couple stood in the way of an Army soldier, poked their fingers in his chest, and demanded to know how many innocent people he had killed. They were angry about the war.

Hell, who wasn't? The cause of the war seemed just. But being run by politicians who continuously fed the country ongoing deceptions was *not* justifiable. *"We were there to fight the spread of communism."* At least, that's what the government wanted us to believe.

So, Jerry Jones' dad is an attorney? He wasn't aware of that during high school. All he knew was that his sister, Jennifer, was a year younger. He had only briefly spoken to her at the funeral.

Something about Tony Jones stuck with him, though. He wasn't sure what. When he told Tom his son had died in Khe Sanh, he didn't make a connection until he learned his name. And… he was Tony's son. Jerry Jones had been Tom's best friend in high school.

That hurt—*bad.* He'd known many soldiers who died in Vietnam. Some he'd held in his arms as they screamed their dying breath in pain and agony.

He felt sorry for Tony, one of over fifty thousand Vietnam War Gold Star families. Maybe "sorry" wasn't the right word. While there were a lot of soldiers who died in 'Nam, there were just as many families who were also affected. They lost, too. Tony was one of them.

This was the first time Tom recalled meeting the father of a soldier that had died in the war. Someone he had personally known. Someone who was a hometown friend.

His guilt began to return—*why was he spared and not…*

Tom shook his head side to side. He didn't want to head down that destructive path. He thought he had buried that memory long ago.

On his return trip back to 'Nam, he also faced the outrage of the protesters. He traveled as military standby in his Khaki uniform, the Army uniform-of-the-day.

There were a few protesters at the airport and, like it or not, he had to walk right past them. He didn't recognize anyone and wondered if any were from Pittsburgh or recruited from out-of-town. They didn't care if he had come home for his mother's funeral. Hell, they didn't care about anything except their fucking protest.

He thought to himself, *these idiots have no idea what war is like. The loudest explosions they'd ever heard was a cherry bomb going off on New Year's Eve. They've never experienced an incoming mortar round or watched as another grunt got blown apart.*

Several spat at him. All of them yelled at him and called him a *'baby killer.' That* shocked him. He couldn't understand how someone could be that judgmental just because he wore a uniform. Why were they angry at him? He was serving *their* country and protecting *their* freedoms. Instead of confronting them, he just ignored them and quickly made his way through the crowd.

Funny that none of those chicken-shit bastards got close enough to get in his face. While only five-foot-ten, Tom wasn't a big man, but he had enough combat experience and that same air of confidence his father had shown all his life. He was returning to a world where problems were solved by shooting them. Hell, he had faced death every day for six months—and he carried that look of *try me, asshole. I'll kick your ass to kingdom come. Bunch of fuckin' cowards.*

Listen to her tachin' up now
Listen to her whine
C'mon and turn it on, wind it up, blow it out, GTO

Ronnie & the Daytonas' *Little GTO* played on the radio, snapping Tom out of his funk. He reached over to turn up the volume and loudly sang along.

18 - Comparing Wars

Tom and Chris were preparing dinner in the kitchen. Lately, they cooked more at home and ordered out less. Chris was helping tonight, something that made Tom proud and feel like life might be returning to some semblance of normalcy. Tom *knew* it was because his own father had reentered their lives.

"Dad? Can I ask you something?"

"Sure. Ask me anything."

"I've been thinking about Granddad and what he told us about the war." Chris stopped chopping the salad lettuce and looked up at his dad. "I've also been thinking about you and Vietnam."

Whoa. Tom looked up at his son, a question in his eyes.

"I spoke with my history teacher, Mr. Johnson. He's a Vietnam veteran, too. He really liked my report. I also told him I had interviewed you after Granddad talked about World War II."

An awkward silence filled the room. Tom wasn't sure where this conversation was headed.

"Anyway, after he graded my report, he told me it might be pretty cool to interview you *and* Granddad at the same time to compare World War II and the Vietnam War."

Chris hesitated for a moment, his gaze more focused on his dad.

"I know you don't like to talk about the war, Dad. But since you *did* talk about a few things, I was hoping you would help. What do you think?"

Tom paused before responding. He took a deep breath, pursed his lips and let out a slow breath, then replied with a crooked but enthusiastic smile. "That's a great idea, Chris. I don't know why I didn't think of it before. You're right. It would be interesting to compare the two wars. We've done a little of that already. This might be..." Tom raised his eyebrows, "*easier* than before.

"I'll call Dad tomorrow. I think he'd appreciate another visit from us. He seems to enjoy talking about World War II these days."

"Awesome!"

AS SUNSHINE HUMMED along I-79, Tom and Chris chatted away at nothing in particular. They had become best friends—like a father and son *should* be—sharing more with each other. It was like they, too, were making up for lost time.

Jefferson Airplane's *White Rabbit* played on the radio. Chris reached over to turn up the volume.

One pill makes you larger, and one pill makes you small
And the ones that mother gives you, don't do anything at all

"What is this song about, Dad? The words are... *weird.*"

Tom laughed out loud. "I was thinking the same thing. It's a fantasy from the book, 'Alice in Wonderland.' Grace Slick was the lead singer for the band, Jefferson Airplane. She was probably high when she wrote it. This was a popular song in the late 60s and early 70s.

"A lot of guys in 'Nam did drugs. Hell, they probably still do," Tom added with a chuckle. "That is, if they're still alive. The stoners would sometimes play this song while smoking marijuana or tripping out in base camp. I think it helped them realize there was another world outside Vietnam. That's how they coped with the war."

Tom glanced over at his son.

"I'm thankful I never got into drugs, Chris. I hope you never do, either."

"Don't worry about me, Dad. I don't plan to. There are a few people at school that do—or *say* they do. They hang out together. To tell you the truth, they kinda scare me. They're *weird.*"

Tom proudly smiled at his son's comment.

Pulling up to the guard gate, the ever-present Earl walked up to greet them, still smiling and still admiring Sunshine. Tom decided it was time.

"Mornin' Earl. Got a few minutes?"

"Sure, Mr. Reilly. What can I do for you?"

"Okay if I pull over for a minute? I've got something to show you."

"Absolutely."

Earl raised the security gate and Tom slowly drove through, gunning the engine. Pulling off the road, he switched off the ignition. He and Chris got out and walked around to the front of the car. "Want to see what's under the hood?"

Earl quickly joined them. Tom watched as Earl's eyes opened wider than ever.

"Holy Toledo, Tom. This engine sparkles like a moon beam across Walden Pond. It looks like she's still stock. Is that right?"

"Yes sir." Tom winked at his son with a slight grin. "She's got a little over 280,000 miles on her. I've rebuilt the engine twice and the transmission once. I added a set of headers when I first got her. Other than that, she's all original. My dad bought her for a little under $3,000 back in the fall of '66.

"Four hundred cubic inches of pure 335 horsepower muscle with a four-barrel Rochester Quadrajet carburetor and a four-speed Hurst 'dual gate' shifter." As Tom spit out the specs, Chris noticed his father beamed like a tomato on the front of a seed catalog.

"You just made my day, Tom. Hell, made my year. I really appreciate you taking time to show me your car. Sunshine, isn't it? I still can't get over how pristine you've kept her. She looks brand new.

"Well, thank you. I know you want to see your dad. But wow… thanks again."

Tom gently lowered the hood as Earl floated back to the guard shack. He liked Earl. In fact, he liked everybody at Sterling Oaks. He understood why his father had chosen this place to retire. Hopefully, he would be here for a long time.

LIKE EVERY VISIT to Sterling Oaks, Tom hoped his father was "with it" today. But he'd grown accustomed to the on-again and off-again mental stability issues that dementia brings. He'd seen the anger and the angst. But during the same visit, he'd seen his father swing back into a pleasant mood, full of himself, and laughing away at the "good ol' days," as he liked to call them.

Tom knocked as he slowly opened the apartment door. Ed was still in bed, snoring loudly. He smiled as he recalled his father's earlier comment about Louise's snoring. *"She snored so loud it woke the dog."*

Chris walked over to the window and opened the blinds to let in the morning sun.

"Who's there?" Ed growled.

"It's me and Chris, Dad."

"Oh, good morning. Is it daylight already? I must have dozed off again."

His dad slept more these days. No one could tell Tom if it was because of his dementia, the mini-stroke, or just old age. It didn't matter. His father recognized him. This would be an exceptional day.

"Hi, Granddad. It's ten o'clock. We thought you'd be awake."

"That's okay. I'm glad you're here. Give me a few minutes to get dressed and brush my teeth."

"Okay, Dad. We'll be down the hall in the dining area."

"Thanks. I won't be long."

TOM AND CHRIS were sitting at a table when Ed walked up, cleanly shaven, wearing a pair of pressed khaki slacks, a light blue button-down shirt, and a navy blue sports jacket. His hair was neat and he wore a big grin. "Where to today, gentlemen?"

"It's gorgeous outside, Dad. Want to head to the courtyard?"

"Sounds like a plan. Let me grab a cup of coffee."

Ed was "with it" and raring to go. Tom wondered if his father remembered they were going to compare war experiences. He was in a pleasant mood and that's what was important. Three generations of Reillys would spend more time together today. Tom realized how lucky he was.

"Chris, did you bring your recorder?"

He remembered.

"Yes, Granddad. I'm ready when you are."

"Fire away."

"Well, my history teacher suggested I record the two of you talking about several aspects of your wars. I want to compare World War II with the Vietnam War, in your own words."

"Are there any rules?" Tom asked smugly, knowing this could turn into a friendly competition between father and son.

"No rules, Dad." Chris smiled, getting the joke.

"So here's the first question. Granddad, I know your division trained together for months, then landed in Europe to fight the Germans. Dad, you went over as a replacement. What were your personal experiences when you first arrived?"

"Do you want to go first, Tom?"

"Sure. I'll tackle this one.

"When I first walked out of the plane in Vietnam, I felt like I'd walked into a sauna. It was hot and humid, even in mid-January. It would get worse, though—a lot worse. That was my initial impression. That and seeing stacks of rectangular boxes in a hangar, which I later learned were caskets on their way back to the U.S.

"I didn't know anybody in my unit when I first arrived. People wouldn't buddy up with me, but I learned why later. I was assigned to a squad of six guys—seven when the walking wounded returned."

Tom smiled at Ed, knowing his father understood what he meant.

"It wasn't that they were unfriendly, but we weren't close friends by any means. After my one-week orientation to Vietnam—we called it 'CIC,' or Combat Indoctrination Course—my squad leader and another guy took me under their wings and showed me the tricks of jungle fighting. It must have stuck, because I'm still here today."

"Unlike your dad," Ed picked up when Tom finished, "we trained as a division; about 15,000 troops. We all shipped overseas to England at the same time. Then over to France. We had been together as a complete division for almost two years. I had already made several good friends." Ed's face momentarily fell. "Unfortunately, a lot of them didn't make it back.

"The major difference between your dad's initial experience and mine is that he had not trained with the soldiers he fought with in Vietnam. I did."

Ed shifted his position in his recliner and began to gesture using his hands. "You see, Chris. There's a certain trust you develop with fellow soldiers. It doesn't happen overnight. We had been training and fighting together as a unit for a while. It takes time for a fresh recruit to earn that trust. We had the same experience as your dad when replacements came into our company. We already knew how *we* would react in combat—we didn't know how *they* would."

"Your dad learned on-the-job. I can't even imagine what that would be like, fighting day after day in thick jungle. I mean, at least, we could see the surrounding area and the enemy most of the time.

"I read somewhere, that in Vietnam, GIs saw an average of about 240 days of combat during their one-year tour of duty. During World War II, I think the average was around forty days in roughly the same amount of time. It sure seemed like more to me. But that's because Vietnam was a different war."

Ed looked at Tom, raising his eyebrows with a "your turn" look.

"That's about it, Chris. Your grandfather hit the nail on the head. You won't get a better comparison between a division that trained together versus replacements. And we were *all* replacements in Vietnam.

"We rotated out after a year of service unless you wanted to extend your tour. And who in their right mind would be that stupid," Tom said, mumbling something else under his breath.

After a few moments of awkward silence, Ed turned to Chris. "What's next?"

"I know you both fought in different parts of the world. I also heard you say sometimes you found the people were friendly. What did you think of the local people, their cultures, and the food?"

"Dad, you want to take this one first?"

"Certainly, Son.

"I was in several countries in Europe including England, France, Luxembourg, Germany, Belgium, Czechoslovakia, and Austria. I can tell you *everyone* was overjoyed that we were there. They had put up with the Krauts—both before *and* during the war—for much too long. They *loved* us.

"When we liberated a town from the Germans or marched through one that had recently been liberated, the citizens almost always lined the streets, like it was a parade. Men came out to shake our hands, children saluted us, and the women—*some* of them—threw their arms around us and planted a big kiss." Ed smiled at that long ago cherished memory.

"Everybody would sing and dance in the streets. Many would give us food, even if we were just passing through. I spoke a little French and German, but only enough to get by. I couldn't carry on a conversation. Between their broken English and my attempt at butchering their language, we managed to communicate.

"We didn't spend much time in these small towns, though. At least, not at the beginning. Most of the time, especially in France, we would bivouac outside the town. We weren't sure if there were Germans holed up in the towns or not. Even though the underground fighters helped us estimate enemy counts and locations, we were still wary of the French.

"When we finally reached Germany, though, we often stayed in hotels we commandeered. Hot water? Well, that was a luxury we took advantage of whenever we could. Now and then, we'd take over the local town bar. Most of the time, the citizens didn't mind. In fact, several even offered their homes. They'd fix meals for us and sometimes provide beer or wine if they had it. It became much easier toward the end of the war.

"I can tell you while there were similarities between the countries, there were also differences, mostly the language and the food. But everybody loved us."

Ed turned his attention from Chris to Tom with a crooked smile. "What about you, Tom? Did you get a chance to sample the local cuisine?"

Tom knew there was *no* comparison between the food and accommodations. His father was baiting him, and he knew it.

"You mean, other than alcohol?" Tom chuckled at his answer. He knew his dad thought the same thing.

"You need to understand, Chris. During World War II, most of the enemy wore uniforms, whether they were Germans or Japanese. You could almost always tell who the enemy was, right, Dad?"

"That's right. There were times, though, we wondered if any of the civilians were in cahoots with the Germans. That's why we were always on guard."

"In Vietnam, we had two different enemies. The NVA—North Vietnamese Army—wore uniforms most of the time and were usually easy to identify. The Viet Cong, well… that was different. The VC were often locals who had been 'recruited' to fight for the NVA." Tom used air finger quotes.

"They didn't wear uniforms. Most of them wore the same black pajamas—that's what we called their everyday dress—as civilians. Many lived in the same village. Looking at them side-by-side, you couldn't tell the difference between a local villager and a VC, unless one had a weapon.

"Our daily mantra for the VC was, 'farmer by day, soldier by night.'

"The experienced grunts told us that if children were around, most likely there weren't any VC or NVA in the area. But then I've also watched local village children lob grenades at troops. So I tried not to get too close to them.

"*Pacification* was a term coined by politicians. In my opinion, it was strictly for political reasons. Johnson, followed by Nixon, wanted the American public to believe we did more than just *kill* people in Vietnam. The idea was that we—U.S. soldiers—would 'win over the hearts and minds of the locals and lessen their desire to revolt.'

"The official word from the REMFs was that Pacification was 'designed to repel the Communist threat to the South Vietnamese through economic development initiatives and a military counter insurgency strategy.'

"It was pure bullshit! It may have looked good on paper, but in reality, it was hit or miss. We'd periodically go out to local hamlets— those were tiny villages in Vietnam districts. Many were close to base camps like Lai Khe. We'd be in a twenty-man platoon or a smaller eight-man squad and our task was to aid the local civilians.

"Sometimes, we'd bring them rice we had captured from an enemy cache. Sometimes, our medics would give checkups to the local children. Other times, we'd help rebuild their hooches that may have been destroyed by our artillery or the enemy's; it was difficult to tell."

Tom leaned forward, elbows on his knees, tapping his fingertips together, his eyes cast downward.

"I heard stories of people in some local villages, though, where kids would come around selling beer and Cokes to anybody and everybody. Then they'd run back to their village and tell the VC how many soldiers there were and report on our positions.

"Some of the villagers appreciated what we did, but they were wary. They had put up with shit for years from the communists, the NVA, the French, and *now* the Americans. I don't blame them for not trusting us—not one bit.

"Obviously, many of the Vietnamese didn't want us there. You could see it in their eyes. Even little kids on the side of the road would yell, *'Fuck you, GI.'* I asked myself all the time, *'Why are we even here?'*"

Tom leaned back and shifted in his seat, his chin resting on his clasped hands.

"I never witnessed any of this myself, but several guys in my battalion reported finding murdered and maimed locals—women and children included—in villages they'd just visited a few days earlier. How can you try to help someone knowing the enemy may retaliate against them? And *they're all the same countrymen.*

"I complain now, but I can honestly tell you that doing some of those things for the locals… well… it made it a little easier to be over there.

"While your grandfather enjoyed hospitality in several countries, I was only in one: South Vietnam. And like Dad said, many of the villagers offered us food. Most of the time, it was edible and sometimes it was a nice change from our C-rations we had when out on patrol. But I much preferred the meals back in base camp, even though that may have been a day or two away."

Chris observed that both his father and his grandfather were staring blankly at a blank wall, thinking about what they just shared.

"Dad? You told me a tour of duty in Vietnam was a year, right?"

"Yep. The enlisted men had a year-long tour. Marines were there for thirteen months. Army officers also had a tour for a year, but they spent only six of those months in a troop command."

"What? That's nuts, Tom. I never heard that. How in the hell did the Army think they'd get anywhere? It takes *months* of experience to learn how to lead men through combat."

"No shit, Dad. It was a revolving door. There were a lot of officers wanting combat experience—you know, *lifer* career officers. Vietnam was not a huge theater like Europe or the Pacific. The higher-ups limited an officer to six months command of a combat unit. It was pure bullshit. Those decisions were made by upper-level assholes who obviously didn't have any boots-on-the-ground experience.

"We had three different COs rotate through Charlie Company while I was there. And only one of them was worth a shit."

Tom took a moment before continuing, his eyes cast downward studying his feet, searching for the memory.

"There was this one green lieutenant who came into our unit, replacing our best platoon leader who had to rotate out. He had dark hair with a lifer crew cut and was probably less than a year out of college. Son-of-a-bitch couldn't even read a simple map.

"Most of us had seen shit like this before with new officers that thought too much of themselves. We learned to dodge their petty bullshit orders.

"This dumb shit brought a mortar barrage down on our own position one night while we were out on patrol. The senior squad leaders tried to warn him the coordinates he fed to the FDC—Fire Direction Controller—were on top of us, but that arrogant prick just ignored them.

"I trusted *these* noncoms with my life. They were trying to keep us alive, but they couldn't convince this son-of-a-bitch *louie* he was wrong. They ran back and told everyone to 'get down, get down—incoming.' Well, needless to say, several of our guys got wasted.

"That was a turning point for me, Dad. I lost *all* confidence in the officers in our company. I had more trust in our noncoms."

Tom scooched back in his seat, his eyes staring at a blank wall. "Fortunately for us, that fuck got transferred to a rear supply unit."

"Chris, if you haven't heard it before," Ed added, "that's what they call 'friendly fire.' We had that, too, but not like *that*. Maybe an accident by our own forces miles away, but never by our own commander."

"And before you ask…" Tom jumped back into the conversation, not wanting to leave this memory unfinished. "That is *the* reason I never liked to work for anybody but myself. I tried when I got back, Dad. I really did. But I was still trying to sort things out. I simply didn't like to be around people. And…" Tom lowered his gaze, "I found I couldn't work for you. I'm sorry, I tried. I just had to learn to survive on my own."

"I understand, Son, more than you'll ever know."

Tom's face softened. He appreciated hearing that from his father, though it wasn't exactly an apology for his hateful words years ago. It was more of a confession that he knows more now than he did then. Tom felt the same, but said nothing. He didn't want to spoil the moment.

"This one's a hard question. What was your toughest experience in war? I mean, was it being away from home, having to shoot people… what?"

"The hardest thing for me was losing my buddies." Ed spoke first, without hesitation. "I lost a lot of friends, men I proudly called my brothers. I would have given my life for them, as they did for me. Why I wasn't killed during the war, I'll never know. I guess it just wasn't my time. But I am glad I'm here now." Ed smiled at Chris, then at Tom.

"Your grandfather nailed it, Chris. After a while, the blood and guts and smells didn't bother me anymore. Well, I say that—they really did. I guess I just got used to it.

"I reached a point where every time we'd go out on patrol, I expected somebody to die. It didn't always happen, but when it did, it was usually at night. There were so many firefights—we'd call them a 'mad minute.' That's where everyone in the patrol would shoot and lob anything and everything for a full minute, trying to kill whoever was shooting at us.

"But like Dad said, the hardest thing was losing a buddy. Even though I came in as a replacement, so did everybody else. I found a few guys to hang out with. We drank and played cards while in base camp during stand down and got to know each other.

"You learn what these guys are made of during combat. You're all out there just trying to stay alive, watching each other's back. But after losing a few buddies, I just didn't want to experience that gutting pain of losing another close friend.

"That may also be the reason I don't have any friends now… other than you and Dad." Tom glanced at his son and his father with a weak smile.

Ed sat up and looked at Chris, rubbing his hands together. "The war experience is something *everybody* should know about and something *nobody* should go through. Old men start the wars and young men die in them."

"I couldn't have said it better, Dad. The government, in all its wisdom, spends billions and billions of dollars on the military for weapons and training, but only pennies for veterans recovering from war. Why? Because there is no profit to be made *after* a war.

"Maybe if these politicians had the balls to serve in the military themselves, then they'd have compassion to understand the problems veterans face. In fact, it should be the law that if the U.S. starts another war, then the politicians' kids should be the first ones drafted."

"I couldn't have said it better, Son."

It was clear both father and son were on the same page.

"Tom, I told you I went back to Europe one time to visit several of the old places we fought in France and Luxembourg. It was very rewarding and helped bring closure. Have you ever thought about going back to Vietnam?"

Tom's initial reaction was one of surprise. But after a moment, he regained his composure, leaned forward, glaring at his father, and dropped his voice, enunciating each word clearly. "Believe me, Dad, when I tell you. I'm in Vietnam every… fuckin'… night."

He sat back and took a deep breath, sighed, and then looked at his son to see if he had more questions.

"I've got one more question."

"Fire away," both Reillys responded simultaneously, winking at each other.

"Granddad. When the war was over, you stayed in Europe for a while, right?"

"Yep. The war in Europe officially ended on May 8, 1945—that's called 'VE Day' for 'Victory in Europe' Day. After that, we had to stay and maintain order for several months as an 'Occupation Force.' Most of my division returned to the states in January 1946."

"What was it like coming home? I mean, I know you sailed back on a ship. When you got home, were there any parades? Did your parents come pick you up?"

"No, there weren't any parades when we returned. There were later, but all we wanted to do was get home. The Army was helping us the best they could.

"After we tied up at the pier and disembarked, we walked over to the main personnel office. There were thousands of us, but there were plenty of personnel folks, too. They processed us out of the Army as quickly as they could. Most of us boarded buses for the trip home. I took one from New York to Pittsburgh. It took almost a full day.

"My mother and father and Louise were all waiting at the bus terminal. I was so happy to see them, and to hold them and hug them. It had been eighteen months. I spent the next few days just sleeping and eating and visiting with family and a few friends.

"Oh yeah… I completely forgot about this until now. When I first got home, none of my old clothes fit. I had lost so much weight during the war. My mother took me to the local department store to buy several pairs of pants and shirts. I felt like a brand new man. The only problem was, my mother was an excellent cook. She insisted I needed to eat more. Within a few weeks, my new clothes didn't fit at all."

Both Tom and Chris erupted into laughter.

"Didn't they have a point system, Dad? I mean, some guys came home earlier, didn't they?"

"They did, but I didn't have enough points. Besides, there were men who deserved it more than me."

That surprised Tom. All soldiers deserved to come home after a war. His father had two Purple Hearts and had been awarded the Bronze Star Medal. *That wasn't enough to come home early?* Maybe that's why his father had been so strict during Tom's early years.

"While I wanted to go home earlier, the fact that we were no longer at war in Europe made it easier. Keep in mind, however, we were still at war with Japan on the other side of the world.

"A few of our guys wanted to fight the Japs, but not me. No, I'd had enough. I just followed orders and kept my head low. They promoted me to Sergeant, though, toward the end of our stay. I got a little more money and a half a cup of coffee on Sundays," Ed added with a smile.

"We didn't have any point system in 'Nam." Tom resumed the conversation. "Our DEROS—that means Date Eligible Return from Overseas—was one year after we arrived in-country, almost to the day. Unlike Dad's war, I left *before* the war was over. In fact, the Vietnam War didn't officially end until April 30, 1975—six years *after* I'd left.

"Some veterans say we fought a ten-year war. But I've heard arguments that because the troop rotation period was only a year, we fought ten, one-year wars.

"Dad's entire division returned to the U.S. with many of the same men he had trained and fought with in Europe. I flew home on a 'Freedom Bird'—that's what we called our flight back to *The World*— with strangers. Of course, we were all overjoyed to leave. But many of us—me included—worried about the guys we left behind. They were still fighting. No one knew at that time that the Vietnam War would be the longest war the United States would fight.

"We went over alone, we came back alone, and I stayed alone." Tom sighed again with a deep and distant look.

"See, Chris," Ed picked up the conversation, "your dad fought with men he didn't know from Adam. When he finished his tour, he flew back with strangers.

"In fact—correct me if I'm wrong, Tom—when soldiers returned and processed out, the personnel officers told them they should change out of their uniforms into civilian clothes before traveling on a commercial flight or train. That right?"

Tom shot a hard look at his father. *How did he know that?* The U.S. government was more concerned about pissing off the protesters— *voters*—than they were in welcoming back the soldiers who fought and died for their very freedom to protest.

"I wasn't aware you knew that, Dad, but you're right. It was almost like the government wanted me to hide the fact that I was a soldier and *now* a Vietnam War veteran. I had fought and bled for a country that didn't seem to care anymore. When I came home and walked off the plane, I felt like my uniform went from a badge of honor to a mark of shame.

"And yes, I changed out of my uniform. There were some guys, though, that stayed in uniform, and they faced the protesters. I saw a lot of fights, but I just didn't care anymore. I had survived an enemy in the jungle, fighting almost every day. Now, I needed to learn how to survive a different war back here—a war of indifference.

"I always thought protesters were just plain assholes. The funny thing was, they never really knew what they were protesting—*we did.*

"It wasn't long before I burned my uniforms. Part of that was to bury a memory. Part was my own protest. I know that pissed you off, Dad, but I just needed to let go of some frustrations.

"I spent the first five years back home in survivor mode. You were too busy to notice. When someone asked me about Vietnam, at first, I tried to tell them what is was really like over there. But most of them just didn't want to hear. After a while, I just kept to myself.

"They taught us well how to be killers and we were good at it. After we killed—and we killed a lot—we came home. They expected us to act like a normal person again. How can you do that? They don't teach you how to forget."

Tom was a little riled, but he didn't feel the same animosity as before. It was as if this conversation with his father and his son was much needed therapy—for both him *and* his father.

"I understand, Son. I really do. I only wish I'd known back then. I'm sorry for all those things you had to go through. I never had to experience any of that. I'm sorry for all those terrible things I said, especially when you came home. Most of all, I'm sorry I wasn't there for you when you needed me the most."

Chris knew his grandfather and his father had finally reached a truce. *I guess this is how a father and son apologize to each other after twenty-five years.* After a few more moments, he spoke up. "That's all the questions I have. Is there anything else we should talk about?"

"I'd like to add something," Ed said without hesitation. "I never talked with your dad about *my* war… until now. These past few months of getting to know you and him have been… *enlightening*."

Chris and Tom smiled at Ed using that particular word.

"I'm not sure why I didn't talk with him about any of this. I wish the hell I had. But the past is the past. Your dad still has a lot of memories buried inside. Believe me, I know, because *I* do. I hope someday in the near future, he will share *his* Vietnam War with you."

Ed looked Tom directly in the eye and said with a softened, fatherly voice, "Don't wait until you're old like me, Tom. Chris deserves to know these things so he will *never forget* what you and I sacrificed to preserve the freedoms of this great country of ours."

Part III

REDEMPTION and FORGIVENESS

I feel like my faith in God died on the battlefield.

19 - The Move

It was early June. Tom was up high on an extension ladder, painting the outside of a modest, two-story house in a new development in southwest Morgantown. He always enjoyed this time of year—warm and sunny. Being able to work outside in the fresh air on such a beautiful day helped keep his mind clear and sharp.

His phone rang. Recognizing the number, he answered promptly.

"Good morning, Michelle."

"Hi, Tom. I hate to bother you. You're probably working. Do you have a few minutes?"

"Sure. Hang on a sec while I climb down; I'm on a ladder.

"Okay. What's up?"

"Tom, your father's had another event. It's not a stroke like before, but he experienced several memory loss episodes the last few days. I don't think it has anything to do with his earlier stroke. I wanted to personally call and let you know."

"Thank you, Michelle, I appreciate that. But... it sounds like there's something else you want to tell me." Tom's old combat instincts were on target.

"There is. Tom, we need to move Ed from his apartment to the memory unit..."

"You mean the Memory Support Neighborhood, don't you?" Tom's interrupted response sounded sarcastic.

"Yes, that's correct."

"Why now? I thought you said earlier you have a Care Team monitoring him. Can't he stay in his own place with someone who periodically checks on him?”

“Unfortunately, that’s not possible. Sterling Oaks has strict policies when it comes to dementia and Alzheimer’s. They are meant to protect the patient. This is the reason we have the special memory unit—the Memory Support Neighborhood. Professionals are there around the clock to assist residents when they need specialized care, like your father.

“A security guard found Ed wandering around the grounds again. This time, the guard couldn’t reach his *realm of reality*. He was, however, able to escort him back to his apartment without an incident, and then he called me. I spent a lot of time with Ed determining the extent of his memory loss.

“Tom? Are you still there?”

“Yes. I’m trying to process this new information.”

“I understand. It would help if you—and Chris, if he can—meet with me and your father. We can discuss what it will take to move him to the memory unit. I’d like to establish some timelines this week. Any chance you can drive up in the next few days?”

Before he could answer, Michelle continued in her compassionate voice. “I’m sorry to bring this on you so suddenly, Tom. I know you and your father have made great headway on rebuilding your relationship. I know we talked about this possibility in the past, but I didn’t expect him to be at this point so soon.”

Michelle chose her words carefully. She needed to convey the urgency about his father’s worsening condition. “Tom, the sooner we can move Ed to the Memory Support Neighborhood, the better. If he remains stable over the next few days, then you and he can pick out furniture and personal items he may want to take.

“Does this make sense?”

Tom struggled with this sudden turn of events.

“I think so. My father needs to move while he still remembers things, right?”

“Tom, you have a way to simplify complicated situations. Yes, that is correct.”

“It comes from trying to live a simple life in complex times, Michelle. When should I come up?”

"I know you are busy, but sooner is better than later."

"Let me call you back later today. I need to talk with Chris and make arrangements with my work. That okay with you?"

"That works for me. I realize this is difficult for you, but it *will* be for the best. I look forward to seeing you again soon. And this time, Tom… I'll buy *you* a cup of coffee. Bye."

"Goodbye. And thank you."

That emotional rollercoaster resurfaced. With the sudden dismal news about his father, Tom was speeding downhill at breakneck speed. But when Michelle mentioned buying coffee, he perked up again.

Something was there, he could sense it, but he was still wary. He just wasn't sure what to make of it. He was, in a word… *confused.* It's not like he had nothing else to do, but he was looking forward to seeing both his father and Michelle again.

TOM AND CHRIS drove up to Sterling Oaks early Saturday morning. It was the middle of June on a sweltering summer day. Today was *the* big day—the day Ed would move from the apartment he had lived in since 1997 when Sterling Oaks first opened to the Memory Support Neighborhood. His new home, if you could call it that, was a "parking space," according to Chris.

How were they going to get all of Ed's possessions from a 950 square foot apartment to a room that was barely 120 square feet? *That* was the big question. Fortunately, most of it was empty space that they could fill as they wanted.

The Memory Support Neighborhood didn't allow residents to have alcohol in their rooms. That ruled out a built-in bar, something Ed said would be a welcomed addition. Chris chuckled at that suggestion.

Easier, smeasier, my ass—somebody still has to move all his crap. Apparently, Sterling Oaks Retirement Community, *Aging with Dignity*—didn't allow a garage sale on premises, not even a "sale with dignity." Tom assumed his dad would let him know what he wanted to take with him, *if* he was "with it" today. Then, they'd determine what to do with the rest of his possessions.

Tom didn't want any of Ed's furniture, but Chris may find one or two pieces. They would either haul it back to Morgantown or call a moving company. *Easy, peasy.* They had a plan.

A pot of coffee was ready when they arrived. That was a good sign.

They'd already had the *"Why do I have to leave my home?"* discussion a week earlier. Ed was initially distraught and shed a few tears because he had to leave his home. But both were resigned that Ed *would* move.

After realizing several of his friends had already made a similar move to assisted living, he seemed to accept this new destiny. At least, for the time being. He stated several times, *"I moved to Sterling Oaks for this very reason. I can stay and progressively move as I need to. After all, this is what 'Aging with Dignity' means, isn't it?"*

Chris seemed much more comfortable these days with the two of them. He mentioned several times that he looked forward to these visits, even this one "move day," as he called it. He had grown closer to his grandfather he had not known prior to a few months ago. Tom also realized it had improved *his* relationship with both of them.

Chris was learning to drive Ed's Chevy Malibu, which they had driven back to Morgantown a few weeks earlier. It was a midnight blue, two-door sport coupe—albeit only six cylinders. He'd been driving it more and more—with his dad quietly advising him in the car. Several times, he asked his dad's advice about taking care of his new car. *"Take care of her and she'll take care of you."* Like father, like son.

This trip would be an overnighter. They planned to stay in the apartment. Ed would sleep in his new room in the memory unit to make sure the bed was comfortable enough for him.

Michelle had given Tom a cheat sheet of ideas on how to "downsize"—that's what they called this type of move. There were three boxes marked, "Take," "Toss," and "Donate." But before going through the minutiae, she suggested they first pick out the big items. They needed to make sure the selected furniture would fit in Ed's new "home."

Ed was adamant he wanted his big recliner, his end table—built by his father, Tom's grandfather—and the light blue porcelain table lamp, a wedding gift to him and Louise from his favorite uncle.

In addition, he wanted the small, round wooden kitchen table with two chairs. His four-drawer oak dresser and matching mirror were small and would also fit. Those pieces would take up most of the available floor space.

After walking through the apartment one more time, they decided that was enough furniture. Ed didn't want to keep anything else, either in storage or at Tom's house in Morgantown. Chris asked about his antique desk, which delighted his grandfather. "Something to remember your old Granddad."

Ed asked if there was enough space to hang the pictures and citations on the "Me Wall." Tom assured him there was. He made a mental note to remember how they were arranged. According to Michelle, it was important to keep Ed's things as familiar as possible. The move itself would be disruptive enough. If he was in familiar surroundings with his favorite furniture and pictures, it would make it much easier and less depressing.

Chris looked through his "new" desk and pulled out an old family scrapbook.

"Granddad. Is it okay if I look through this?"

"Bring it over here, Chris. Let me see what kind of trouble I used to get into."

The three sat on the couch, Ed in the middle. Tom beamed.

"What are you so happy about? *I'm* the one that's moving."

"Dad, I'm just happy that we—three generations of Reillys—can be together."

All three smiled. It was a tender moment for the Reilly clan, one that was long in coming. One they would never forget.

Ed opened the weathered scrapbook and flipped through the yellowed pages, sharing pictures and stories of various family members. They were in chronological order, so Chris "met" several generations of Reillys, even before his grandfather was born.

There were also plenty of photos of Tom growing up. A picture of a gushing six-year-old riding a bike for the first time without training wheels. A picture of him and his dad, huddled together under a blanket, at a snowy Pittsburgh Steelers football game. And a few photos playing baseball with his father in the front yard.

"Is this Grandma?" Chris pointed to a black and white photo of a lovely young lady with long, wavy black hair, wearing a dark knee-length skirt and high heels. She had a bright smile from ear to ear.

"Yes, that's Louise. I took this right after I got back from the war. She was so beautiful and full of life. This is one of those special memories I always have of her."

"Is this you, Granddad?" Chris pointed to another black-and-white photo of a soldier in uniform.

"Yep. I was home after basic training before shipping overseas. I was a handsome young devil, don't you think?"

"I do, Granddad. You *still* have a lot of hair."

"Thank you, Chris." Ed exchanged smiles with his grandson. "That's one reason your grandmother married me. That and the fact that I was a man in uniform. Women back then couldn't resist a good-looking man in a uniform.

"Here's a photo of your dad with his brand new Pontiac GTO. We took this photo in the driveway the day he drove it home from the dealership."

"It still looks like that now, Granddad."

"I know. We took a ride a few weeks ago. I was stunned at how well your dad has taken care of her all these years. She's just like brand new."

Tom leaned back a bit and smiled, loving this exchange between his father and his son.

"Is this you, Dad?" Chris' eyes widened as he saw a color photo of his father in his Army uniform, standing next to his mother.

"Yep, that's your dad. I took this a few days before he shipped off to Vietnam. Do you remember that?"

"I do. Mom sure was a beautiful lady. I can see why the two of you were so happy together."

Ed stared at the photos, engaging memories of long ago. Tom got up to get another cup of coffee.

"After you left for Vietnam, we tried to get back into our daily routine," Ed began to reminisce. "It worked… at least for a few days. We read the paper and watched the news, trying to see what was going on over there.

"We tuned in to watch Walter Cronkite every night on the news. When the Tet Offensive started—that was right after you got over there—the Vietnam War got a lot more TV coverage than before. It was a stark contrast to what was covered during World War II.

"Your mother was almost beside herself. She got so worked up every day, she had problems sleeping at night. I tried to tell her you were well-trained, and the Army knew what they were doing, and you'd be all right. I don't think that helped, though.

"We always looked forward to the letters you wrote home; they were always comforting to us. I mean, you *never* said how terrible things really were over there. At least, those you wrote *before* you came home for her funeral. They reminded me of the letters *I* wrote home during the war. I didn't want my parents to worry, either.

"That may be the reason she had a heart attack," Ed said quietly. "She had survived one war with me. She worried through another one with you."

Ed leaned back, staring at nothing but old memories.

"She was in downtown Pittsburgh, shopping for clothes with friends. I was at work, like always. I got a frantic call from the hospital saying Louise had suffered a massive heart attack. They tried to revive her, but she just couldn't come back."

As Ed said these things out loud, his voice began to break. But in some semblance, he was certain he would see her again someday. And it was apparent that thought comforted him.

"I miss her, Son. I've missed her every day. I tried to keep going. Work kept me busy most of the time. After you left, I was… well, angry. Angry at you, angry at Louise for dying, angry at the war, and angry at the world. I realize now it was foolish pride.

"I'm sorry for the things I said that drove you away. I never meant those things, but I was too proud to apologize. I now know the Vietnam War was completely different from World War II. My problem was I didn't realize it back then."

Ed was in tears, as was Tom. Neither spoke for a few minutes.

"I'm kinda tired right now. Do you mind if I lay down for a bit?"

"That's fine, Dad. We can go through these other things. We'll be quiet."

"Wake me when it's time for lunch." Ed headed down the hall to his bedroom and closed the door.

TOM AND CHRIS quietly looked through drawers and closets, trying to determine what to take, what to toss, and what to recycle.

Rummaging through the hall closet, Tom decided his dad still needed coats, both a sports jacket and a winter coat. He saw a few familiar things—things he recalled from his childhood—but nothing he wanted to keep. They were Ed's and had no personal meaning for him.

Then, he spotted a shoe box on the top shelf, pulled it down, and opened it. He took a deep breath, brought it over, and sat down on the couch.

His dad *had* kept all of Tom's letters. There were dozens of them, all in chronological order from basic training at Fort Dix all the way through the last letter he wrote home from Lai Khe, telling Ed he was getting out of the Army. *"I'm required to stay in Army Reserve for two more years."*

Inside the same box was an old faded National Geographic map of Vietnam. When he unfolded it and laid it out on the coffee table, Chris came over and sat down beside him. This was the first time Tom had seen any of this—both the letters and the map. Several locations with corresponding dates were clearly marked on the map.

"Is this where you were in Vietnam, Dad?"

"Pretty much," Tom said quietly, still recovering from the shock of his discovery. "I had no idea your grandfather kept my letters and made this map. He really did follow me through the war."

"Are you going to read them? They must be over thirty years old."

"I'll read them later. Right now, I'm trying to get Dad moved. These will have to wait."

Chris got up and began searching through the drawers of his new desk, hoping to find the World War II letters Ed had shown them earlier. He spotted an old, weathered file folder, pulled it out, and carefully opened it. Inside was a certificate. At the top was a picture of a military medal with a red and blue ribbon and a bronze colored star.

The certificate title read, "The Bronze Star Medal," and below it, "SP4 Thomas J. Reilly, 2nd Battalion, 28th Infantry." At the bottom were the words, "For Heroism in Ground Combat in Vietnam on 26 October 1968." Attached to the other side of the folder was a citation for the medal.

It was his father's Bronze Star Medal Citation.

Bronze Star Citation for Specialist Four Thomas J. Reilly

Specialist Four Thomas J. Reilly, 2nd Battalion, 28th Infantry, while serving as a rifleman in Charlie Company, took part in a search-and-destroy operation near the village of Tay Ninh on 26 October 1968. As his unit was moving in dense jungle, they were suddenly subjected to intensive enemy fire from automatic weapons, small arms, and RPGs from a numerically superior Viet Cong force. Several men in his squad were wounded in the first moments of the firefight.

SP4 Reilly, who had been out front of the unit serving on point, quickly returned, and disregarding the intense hostile fire coming from the VC positions, began to provide sufficient suppressive fire to cover the evacuation of the wounded. Only when the intensity of the hostile fire had diminished did he then move to assist in carrying other wounded men back to the unit's secondary defensive perimeter. It was at this point with all the wounded having been evacuated, that he and another soldier returned to set up a defensive position to keep any of the enemy from approaching his unit from behind. The two soldiers were once again engaged in an intense fire fight with the enemy. Both were wounded by the enemy attack on their covering position. After delaying the enemy advance, both men began to move back to the main body of their unit. SP4 Reilly, slightly wounded in the leg, picked up the other soldier who had been wounded in the secondary attack, and was able to carry him back to the safety of the unit.

With complete disregard for his own personal safety, SP4 Reilly was instrumental in insuring the speedy evacuation of the wounded and contributed significantly in his unit's repelling of the Viet Cong attack. His personal bravery, aggressiveness, and devotion to duty are in keeping with the highest traditions of the military service and reflect great credit upon himself, his unit, the 1st Infantry Division, and the United States Army, and he has been awarded the Bronze Star Medal with "V" device for valor.

By direction of the President under the provisions of Executive Order 11046, 24 August 1962, AR 672-5-1, and USARV Reg 672-1.

"Dad? Is this yours?"

Tom looked up at his son, saw the citation he was holding, and quietly replied, "Yes."

"I've never seen this."

Tom tried to suppress that rising feeling—that long forgotten memory of what happened *that* day. He had done that so many times over the years. But today was different. He took a deep breath, heaved a big sigh, and asked his son to sit down.

Sitting down beside his father, Chris looked much older than fifteen.

"I know you have a Bronze Star, Dad. But whenever I ask about Vietnam, you always change the subject. You never want to talk about it."

"I didn't want to talk about it because I simply didn't want to remember. I've tried to forget that day, though for lots of reasons, I couldn't. Maybe it *is* time I finally told you."

Tom closed his eyes for a moment and took another deep breath. For the first time in over thirty years, he let the memories of that fateful day flow freely.

"We were out humping the boonies on a search-and-destroy mission. My squad got ambushed. I was on point, but for whatever reason the gooks didn't shoot me first. Instead, they shot the 'slack man'—the guy ten feet behind me—and he went down. He was dead before he hit the ground. A bullet went right through the middle of his helmet and blew out the back of his head.

"We all hit the ground and started shooting—fully auto, *rock 'n roll, and let it go.* But Charlie had us surrounded—the wood line lit up. We killed a few of them, but not before a few more of our guys were hit, including me. It wasn't bad, I caught a piece of shrapnel in my arm. It hurt like hell, but I could still fight. I bandaged myself up. Then, they seemed to disappear into thin air.

"We got everybody's wounds dressed, ready to move out and withdraw. Then, Charlie opened up on us again. I couldn't tell if it was the same group or another. It didn't matter. I could still fight, as did the other guys—even those who had been wounded. But Charlie wouldn't stop.

"We scampered back down the trail and got the hell outta there. But someone needed to keep Charlie off our ass. Here's the stupid part: two of us volunteered.

"The rest of the squad withdrew and my buddy and I kept firing at the enemy as they appeared. We needed to cover our ass before heading back to join everyone else. We set an ambush using a couple of grenades and a trip wire, hoping that would finish off anyone coming our way. Our luck ran out, though, and my buddy was hit again. He couldn't move.

"I dropped my rucksack, picked him up, and threw him over my shoulder. Grabbing my M-16, I started back, but got hit again in the leg with a round from an AK-47. I stumbled along the trail. My buddy was cranking out shots while I ran with him. About that time, the grenade ambush we'd set went off. The enemy stopped firing. Who knows how many were killed, but somebody else would have to venture out to get that body count.

"We caught up with the squad—it must've been a hundred meters or so—and just fell down, totally exhausted. But… my buddy was dead. He had been hit again while I was carrying him out. He never had a chance.

"They awarded me the Bronze Star a few days later. *It don't mean nuthin'*, 'cause a lot of guys died that day. For some reason, I was spared. Yeah, I was shot, got a Purple Heart and the BSM, and a few days off. For the life of me, though, I don't know why *I* wasn't the one killed that day.

Chris was completely absorbed in his dad's recollection and sat stunned with a look of bewilderment. "You are a hero, Dad."

Before his son could continue, Tom bluntly interrupted. "Don't ever call me a hero, Chris. The heroes are the ones who didn't come back. All I could think about was saving my buddies. It was pure reaction and adrenaline, something I had faced a hundred times before. Only this time my luck ran out. All I did was try to keep myself and my buddies alive. That was it, plain and simple.

"I'm not the hero, Chris. My buddy is the hero. That last bullet that killed him should've hit *me* instead…"

Tom let that last statement hang in the air.

"I've felt guilty every day since that happened. That was supposed to be *my* bullet, not his. I shouldn't even be here."

A tear ran down Tom's cheek.

"You never told me that."

Both Tom and Chris were startled and turned to see Ed standing in the hallway. Neither had heard him get up.

"*Now* I understand the guilt you've been carrying all these years, Son. I'm sorry you lost your friend. It was one of the hardest things for me, too. I still live with those memories every day. I'll never forget them.

"What was your buddy's name, Tom?"

"Wayne… Wayne Johnson. We called him 'Sunshine.' He lit up the room with his big smile and sunny disposition." Tom cracked a slight grin.

"He always had good things to say about anyone and everyone. Never a bad word, no matter how crappy a day it may have been. His demeanor, his coolness—even under fire—kept us all calm. Nothing ever rattled him. Sunshine died protecting me, Dad… keeping me safe. I did everything I could to save him, but it just wasn't enough."

Tom fought the tears rolling down his cheeks.

Without hesitation, Chris commented, "Geez, Dad. You and Granddad were both awarded the Bronze Star for risking your lives to save others. It's clear to me you put your lives on the line for your buddies."

Both Tom and Ed looked at each other, then at Chris. He appeared much older than his fifteen years.

Ed sat down hard in his recliner. "I could use a drink. How about you?"

THE DOORBELL RANG. Tom glanced at the clock, it was two in the morning. "What the fuck?" He was a little discombobulated, then remembered he was sleeping on a couch in his father's apartment. He got up to answer the door, not knowing who it was. In the back of his mind, he wondered if something had happened to his father. They had just moved him to the memory unit earlier that day.

"Who's there?"

"It's me. Open the fuckin' door."

Tom opened the door to his father's big shit-eating grin.

"Dad, are you okay? I thought you were in your new room."

Ed walked right past him, looking over his shoulder. "I didn't like that fuckin' place. *This* is my home and I want to stay *here* and sleep in my own bed."

Tom wasn't prepared for this.

Chris slowly sat up, rubbing his sleepy eyes. "Everything okay, Dad?"

"Your grandfather decided to come back to his apartment. Everything's fine.

"Did you let anyone know you were leaving?"

"Fuck no. If they want me, they can come and get me."

Tom could tell that Ed was having fun. He had escaped the memory unit and evaded Security.

"I'll call the memory unit to let them know you're over here and that I'm with you. I think we should do that, don't you?"

"If you say so. Say… do you want a drink? I've got some gin around here somewhere."

"No. I'm good."

"Chris, you want to join your grandfather for a drink? It may be the last time for a while."

"No, Granddad. I'm not old enough to drink."

"Good boy. On second thought, I'll just go to bed. That okay with you?" Ed stated as he marched down the hallway to *his* bed.

As he called Security to let them know his father was back in his apartment, Tom began to giggle. Despite what anyone else would ever think, this *was* hilarious. He wasn't sure what else to do, but he would share this with Michelle and Charles; both would get a kick out of it. They would probably need to review the security. Somehow, he didn't think his father posed any threats. After all, this was his apartment.

Tom laid down with one eye open and one eye shut—just like back in 'Nam. Only this time, the "incoming" was not mortar or rocket fire. It was only his dad. He smiled at that comforting thought and nodded off.

20 - Vietnam—Managing Memories

Tom found himself mentally at Sterling Oaks more than physically. Although he loved his work—helping to build homes for new families—his dad was constantly at the forefront of his mind. With his father's progressive Alzheimer's disease, Tom wondered how much longer before his dad would no longer recognize him.

He spent at least one day every weekend at Sterling Oaks. Some weeks, he'd also visit on a weekday, taking time off from work. Even though his trips were primarily to visit his dad, he would always try to stop by to see Michelle.

His father's furniture fit comfortably in his new room, but it just wasn't the same as his old apartment. The memory unit was smaller and much less homey. Ed was initially frustrated, but over the past few weeks, he'd grown more accepting of his new accommodations. Tom wasn't sure if his dad was resigned that this was now his home, or if his acceptance was simply a part of his Alzheimer's.

There were no more episodes of Ed escaping the memory unit. Michelle and Charles helped modify the security protocols. They did, however, enjoy Tom's humorous recollection of the episode. It was a special bond all three would always share.

IT WAS JULY 4TH, Independence Day. Tom pulled into the parking lot at Sterling Oaks, got out of his car, and looked around. He noticed there were more cars than usual. Chris had decided to stay at home to hang out with his friend, Rachel.

Tom didn't mind. These drives alone gave him an opportunity to sort things out. There were still some old Vietnam War haunts stuck deep down inside. Though his focus was on his father these days, those memories crept up periodically.

Michelle suggested at one point he ought to speak with a VA counselor—a PTSD specialist. Something had changed over the past few months, though. His nightmares weren't as bad now as they had been right after Chris was born. He wondered if it was because of his renewed relationship with his father *and* his opening up about the Vietnam War, or if it was simply because Michelle made that suggestion.

Even though those buried memories resurfaced, he continually found a way to suppress them, like he'd done many times before. *Only Moves Forward*—that was his dad's Army division's motto. He had adapted that attitude. It was his new defensive mechanism.

TOM WALKED STRAIGHT to the memory unit, hoping his dad was "with it" today. Unfortunately, Ed didn't recognize him, but was pleasant and invited him in to sit and chat.

His dad sat across the table from him and just stared. Tom wondered how he should start this conversation. He decided he would try *the* trigger.

"Good morning, Ed. Nice to see you up and around. I know you don't recognize me, but I'm your son, Tom. We've talked several times about the time you spent in the Army with the 80th Infantry Division during World War II. Does that ring a bell?"

His father smiled and acknowledged Tom with a slight nod, but still didn't recognize him. "That's nice."

He tried a different tactic. "I drove up in the old '67 Pontiac GTO this morning. She still purrs like a kitten and looks brand new, just like it did when we brought her home."

"That's nice. Did your mother come with you today?"

Michelle had mentioned patients with Alzheimer's disease often remember things from long past, such as their spouse, but may not remember that person is no longer living. Tom was prepared for that, but hearing his father ask about his mother again was still unnerving. His face fell with a heavy sigh.

"No, Louise died a long time ago. I came home from Vietnam for her funeral. After that, I had to go back."

Tom didn't want to have this conversation again, not with someone who wasn't aware of who he was. He excused himself, saying he would return in a few minutes.

"Nice of you to visit. Please come again soon." Ed stood to shake his son's hand. "What was your name again?"

"Tom. Tom Reilly."

He needed a cigarette. What he really needed was a drink, but that would not happen anytime soon. Stepping out into the hallway, Tom almost ran into someone—a familiar face.

"Excuse me. I should watch where I'm going. Oh… Mr. Reilly, isn't it?"

"Yes, it is. Good morning, Charles. I didn't expect to see you here."

"Not a problem, Tom. I'm filling in for a friend today. I normally work the night shift and have taken care of your father several times. He's such a wonderful gentleman, with incredible stories, I might add. How is he today?"

"Not too well. He doesn't recognize me. He just asked again about my mother. She died years ago."

"I'm sorry to hear that. It's common for Alzheimer's patients to remember people and places and events from years past, but not realize time has passed.

"I'm on my break and going for a cup of coffee. Would you care to join me?"

Tom needed to talk to someone, but when he checked earlier, Michelle wasn't in her office. He didn't know anyone else at Sterling Oaks.

"Sure, I could use some company."

They quietly walked down the hall, out the memory unit secure door, and into the dining area. Charles poured two cups of coffee and added cream and sugar to his own. He asked Tom how he liked his.

"Black, no sugar, please."

"Here ya go." They both sat down at an empty table. Tom warily glanced around, noticing they were alone in the dining area.

"I heard your father recently moved over here. That must have been hard."

"For him or for me?" Tom asked, not expecting any answer, staring out to nowhere as he sipped his coffee.

"For both. You may not realize this, Tom, but there aren't many people who get a second chance to reconnect with their fathers, especially after twenty-five years."

Charles knows their history.

"I've been working at Sterling Oaks since they first opened. I've met plenty of people who come and go, so to speak. I like working here in the memory unit. I float around to other units when needed, but I like it over here the best."

"Charles? Or should I call you Charlie?" Tom wanted to be polite.

"Charles... always. *Never* Charlie.

"I had a smartass jarhead Private call me Charlie one time in the boonies. He thought he was hot stuff. I pointed out to him—gently, but firmly—Charlie was the enemy. *I'm* not the enemy. I am 'Charles.' After a little more... *persuasion*... he got the point and never asked again.

"Most guys in 'Nam had nicknames, but I always insisted my name was Charles. The guys in my unit respected that."

It was obvious to Tom that Charles enjoyed sharing this story. That impressed him. He was a confident man. With his broad shoulders and thick forearms, Tom could tell he meant business.

"Mind if I ask you a personal question?"

"Not at all, Tom. Lay it on me."

"How did you get from Vietnam to, um... well... *here?*"

Without hesitating, Charles replied, almost as if he'd been asked this type of question many times.

"I was one of those 'volunteer draftees,' Tom. I grew up on the streets of Detroit and in '68, there was a lot of... how should I say... *tension* in the country.

"I was a little punk kid with a lot of rage—like a lot of kids from my neighborhood. Being from the Black east side of Detroit with several brothers and sisters, I learned early in life how to take care of myself. I had to… to survive.

"I was good at boxing. My dad told me more than once, I should go pro, but I was also good at getting into trouble. One night, I hit a cop. Wrong place, wrong time, *wrong* guy. I was pretty street savvy, and most of the time, I could talk my way out of predicaments. Not this time, though. The judge threw the book at me and basically said, 'Jail or 'Nam?'.

"I didn't want jail time, so I took what I thought was the easy way out. I 'volunteered' and joined the Marines."

Charles eyed Tom while taking a sip of coffee, making sure he was listening.

"When I got over to 'Nam, I kept my head low. But like most Marines, I wouldn't let my buddies down. I took whatever they threw my way—got hit a few times and have three Purple Hearts, a Bronze Star, and the CAR—the Combat Action Ribbon.

"Up in Eye Corps, we were close to the DMZ and, well… let's just say the fighting up that way was *always* intense. Funny how our side was the only one that respected the boundaries of the DMZ."

Charles shifted in his seat and gently set his cup down on the table.

"I know you faced some tough shit down your way, too. Hell, I don't think any fighting unit—Marine *or* Army—had it easy over there. I guess I didn't realize being such a big guy would get me shot so many times. But I survived and made it back home alive."

Tom sensed Charles was proud of his accomplishments in Vietnam, something he himself didn't feel.

"Stop me if I'm telling you too much, Tom. Part of me thinks you're still trying to get home from 'Nam."

Tom was and Charles sensed it. He drained the rest of his coffee, then looked away.

"Unfortunately, I got hooked on drugs and drank a lot—both over there and here, when I got back. There was just too much shit I couldn't get out of my head. I'm sure you experienced similar things when you tried to 'come home'."

Charles glanced briefly over at Tom, who was listening intently.

"I tried talking to some of my friends about 'Nam, but they didn't want to hear what I had to say. They all thought the Vietnam War was wrong. All of us lost a lot of friends over there. I still don't know why we were over there.

"I came to live with the simple fact that I could have died on the streets of Detroit almost as easily as in 'Nam."

Charles' descriptions of both 'Nam and "coming home" were spot on. Tom had many similar experiences. Fortunately, he never got into drugs.

"I grew up in a stereotyped world, Tom. I was black. Over in 'Nam, it didn't seem to matter as much—we all bled red. When I came home, though, I found myself in another, completely different stereotyped world: I was a Vietnam veteran."

Charles shifted in his seat, carefully twirling his empty coffee cup with his hands.

"After stumbling around in the streets for a while, I watched several of my friends… die. Both from the old neighborhood and from 'Nam. Some OD'd, some killed themselves, and others just got shot in the streets. I knew I needed to clean up my act. Otherwise, I'd end up either in a big world of hurt or worse… dead. Although it took time, I got clean and found the Lord with the help of a good friend."

Tom took in every word. Charles preached without sounding preachy. He had that "been there, done that" attitude, but pushed nothing on you. He simply spoke from his own personal experience *and* from his heart.

Tom took a deep breath and studied his new friend. He had a lot of questions, but only asked one.

"How were you able to leave all that shit behind you? I mean, it's like my own being—my *soul*—is still stuck in Vietnam."

Charles carefully chose his words. Tom needed guidance, just like so many other veterans he had counseled over the years.

"If you mean 'leaving' Vietnam, Tom, I didn't. There are some days I make it through most of the day without the war in the very forefront of my thoughts. It's never more than a heartbeat away.

"Life is a reflection of attitude, Tom. If you want to change your life, you need to change your attitude. I learned a while back that the rear-view mirror is much smaller than the front windshield. Don't keep looking behind you, because it is so limited. Where you are headed is more important than what you've left behind. There is so much more to do and see.

"The worst thing a veteran can do is to refight a war he's already fought. It won't change the outcome… *ever*. And besides, what was your father's division motto? *Only Moves Forward*."

Charles hesitated, but only for a moment. He knew Tom was processing what he'd just said.

"I found the Lord, Tom—or maybe the Lord never left me. I just needed reassurance he was still around. While I think *everyone* needs Christ in their life, I realize not everyone knows that."

After a few more moments of silence, Charles asked *the* question.

"Tom, do you believe in God?"

"I used to," Tom's gaze slowly fell to the floor, as he hung his head.

"That's not what I asked."

"I *know* what you asked." Tom looked up and quietly answered. "I'm trying to avoid the question. I just don't know anymore…"

Tom was struggling—*had been struggling*—with this very question for a long time. It's not that he didn't want to believe in God. It was as if he needed permission to believe, after all the things he had seen and done in Vietnam.

"I was raised in a Presbyterian household, Charles. Over in 'Nam, I was on a constant seesaw. On one end, I sent up multiple prayers, multiple times a day—mostly to keep my sorry ass alive. On the other end, I was on the far side of atheism. I mean, how can a kind and loving God—*the God I grew up with*—let something like that war happen? To this day, I still have the same questions."

Tom stared down at the floor, elbows on his knees, and took a deep breath. "I feel like my faith in God died on the battlefield."

"So did mine, Tom. But once I returned to *The World*, I found my faith again. This time, it became much stronger.

"I know you're hurting, Tom. I've been there—many times. I've been on that rollercoaster of emotions almost all us war veterans continuously ride. Even your father has been there, though in his day, it was a different ride than ours. We can't change the choices we made back then. The best we can do is to learn from them, keep moving forward, and try to do better.

"No matter how far away you wander from Christ, He is always with you, Tom. *He always has been.*"

Charles let that last statement sink in for a moment. He sat up straight and looked directly at Tom, his voice changing from that of a soulful pastor to one of a proud Vietnam veteran.

"You know I'm a part-time pastor, right? Well, I also get together with a small group of Vietnam veterans a couple of times a month. We've been meeting for a few years. While most vets are hesitant at first to talk about Vietnam, *all* will tell you they look forward to our meetings. Without fail, almost everyone in our little group shows up every month.

"Why don't you to come to our next meeting, Tom? No promises, no commitments, no guarantees. Just a chance to meet some great guys who have been on that same ride you're on. I'm sure you'll get something out of it."

Charles made sense. He had figured out a way to leave Vietnam behind. At least, the terrible stuff. Or maybe he just learned to manage it. It couldn't hurt to meet other veterans. Who knows, he might even see someone he served with.

"I'd like that. Thank you."

"You asked me earlier how I got here, Tom. I've learned those who hurt the most often have the greatest ability to heal. That's why I do what I do.

"I hope to see you in a few weeks. Well, I'm sure I'll see you around here when you visit your father, but I look forward to seeing you at our next veteran meeting."

"Thanks, Charles. I think I'll go back and check on my dad. Have a great day."

"You too, Tom."

Both men—both seasoned Vietnam combat veterans—stood, firmly shook hands, and realized a new bond had been made. Where it would lead was now up to a greater being.

21 - Vietnam—Differing Perspectives

Tom decided to walk outside before returning to visit his dad. He needed to clear his mind, grab a smoke, and reflect on his recent conversation with Charles. His new friend had shared several personal thoughts and feelings—something Tom had needed for a while. Someone who'd been there and seen what he had seen, felt what he had felt—another combat Vietnam veteran.

After a few minutes of quiet solitude and solemn reflection, he walked back inside to the Memory Support Neighborhood. Along the way, he observed the décor was different here than in the main residential apartment area where Ed used to live, something he hadn't noticed before. Here, it was plainer with fewer colors and patterns—less confusing. Tom wondered if it was designed that way, specifically for residents who experienced memory loss.

Just inside the unit, he stopped to read a framed poster on the wall he hadn't noticed before.

<u>Alzheimer's Disease – Tips for Communication</u>
  1. *Never argue; instead agree.*
  2. *Never reason; instead divert.*
  3. *Never shame; instead distract.*
  4. *Never lecture; instead reassure.*
  5. *Never say "remember;" instead reminisce.*
  6. *Never say "I told you;" instead repeat.*
  7. *Never say "You can't;" instead say what they can do.*
  8. *Never demand; instead ask.*

9. Never condescend; instead encourage.
10. Never force; instead reinforce.

Reading through the list, Tom recalled the many arguments he'd had with his dad before he walked out of his life. *I wish I'd known this shit back then. I would've acted differently. Or maybe Dad would have. You can't go back there, Tom. You have to keep moving forward.*

Quietly opening the door, he found his dad had fallen asleep in his recliner. That seemed to happen more frequently since the move.

Taking a moment to look around the pitifully small, plain room, Tom's eyes focused on the "Me Wall." It looked the same here as it did in Ed's old apartment. He hoped his dad had smoothly transitioned to his new room, both physically and mentally.

Tom walked over to take a closer look at the photos hanging on the wall. He must've stared at them a hundred times when he was a kid, trying to imagine what his father had experienced during the Battle of the Bulge. He closed his eyes, visualizing what it must have been like when the Germans first broke through the Allied lines.

His dad had said their regiment was somewhere in northwestern France when they received orders to quickly move north, not knowing what they were about to face. Over a period of twenty-four hours, they traveled 150 miles in open trucks through freezing, cold rain and snow, rushing to get to Luxembourg. Their orders were to protect Luxembourg City, the capital of Luxembourg, and defend Radio Luxembourg.

Ed's stories and pictures detailed how cold it actually was. Even though his father had endured many frigid winters in western Pennsylvania, he'd said it was no comparison to the weather he faced that winter in '44 and '45. The big difference between the winters in Pennsylvania and the Battle of the Bulge, was that no one in Pennsylvania had tried to kill him.

Tom himself was thrown into one of the toughest Vietnam War battles not long after he first arrived in-country. He had barely checked in through the 90th Replacement Battalion at Long Binh and assigned to the 2nd Battalion, 28th Infantry Regiment, 1st Division. His orders were to report to Lai Khe, headquarters for the 2/28th, about a three-hour drive north of Saigon.

Lai Khe was strategically located in an unused section of the Michelin rubber plantation on a direct line between Cambodia and Saigon. Miles and miles of single, double, and triple canopy jungle nearly surrounded it—jungle so dense, visibility from above was impossible.

The First Infantry Division's main Area of Operations (AO) comprised an extensive area in Tri Corps (III Corps), stretching north from Saigon to the Cambodian border. Sometimes, a *little* beyond to include some NVA sanctuaries, though that tidbit of information wasn't widely "publicized." A main NVA infiltration route ran right through their AO, straight to the heart of South Vietnam—the Ho Chi Minh Trail.

He was assigned to Charlie Company, a rifle company, and ended up in 1st Platoon, a group of about twenty-five hardened grunts. The company's welcoming sign greeted him: "Charlie Company, 2nd Battalion, 28th Infantry, 1st Infantry Division, The Black Lions: *Duty First, No Mission Too Difficult, No Sacrifice Too Great.*"

The Tet Offensive was so named because the initial attacks began the early morning hours of January 30, 1968, on the eve of the Lunar New Year. It was the "Year of the Monkey." According to the locals, Tet was *the* most sacred of all Vietnamese holidays. Both sides had agreed to, and both sides were *supposed* to observe a two-day cease-fire of peaceful celebrations—just like previous years. Everyone expected to take a few hours of much needed rest. Many of the South Vietnamese soldiers had already left to celebrate the New Year at home.

Who the hell would attack on this, of all days?

Over 85,000 NVA troops, VC, and guerillas simultaneously attacked more than a hundred cities and hamlets. Tet was the largest military operation conducted by either side up to that point in the war.

Tom's attack came early in the morning on January 31, 1968, two weeks after arriving as a brand-new recruit. *And…* it was Tom's *Baptism of Fire.*

He closed his eyes as the memory of that first battle came to light—almost as if he was reliving it once again.

Charlie Company had been out on patrols for several days and were on their normal stand-down at Lai Khe Base Camp. Tom was new in-country and had spent his initial indoctrination week in camp learning the basics of jungle fighting, the enemy, and what to expect. He'd been on perimeter watch, but there had been minimal activity.

There had been rumors the VC were planning a big offensive and the entire camp was placed on yellow alert, meaning a potential enemy attack. They were *always* on alert, but something about these new rumors made most of the "old" grunts usually more nervous.

After the normal day's routines and the night's activities, Tom settled down on his air mattress in his hooch for the night. Soon after midnight, he heard the first blast in the middle of the base camp. Most everyone assumed the noise and the light show was part of the New Year's celebration. Within a few minutes, the sound of additional incoming mortars and rockets hastened everyone's departure from their bunks.

Since he was a FNG and newly assigned to the unit, he was to stick with his squad leader. Both ran to their assigned bunker close to their hooches, about twenty yards away.

Tom *thought* he was mentally prepared for this attack. But between the incoming mortars and rockets, he was terrified. The one training piece he remembered was that during a mortar or rocket attack, you stay low.

He didn't have to worry about finding his way around in the dark. The exploding mortars and rockets lit the sky bright enough to see almost beyond the perimeter where he had been on watch just a few hours earlier. The air was also full of crisscrossing red (USA) and green (NVA) tracers, and the pungent smell of cordite. It didn't take long to realize he was in the middle of a war. He decided then and there, he was not going to die—*not* today.

"What was it like for you at night? I mean, when you were in Vietnam?"

Tom spun on his heel. His dad was standing right behind him. He had been so entrenched in thought, he didn't hear Ed wake up and get out of his chair. One thing was for sure, though—his dad was back. At least, for now… for today.

"It depends on where we were and what we were doing, Dad. When we were in base camp after a patrol, I would probably have been drinking beer, playing cards, writing letters, or watching a movie. That's how we blew off steam after coming in from a patrol.

"When we were out in the jungle, well… it was different—*much* different."

Tom shifted his stance, placing both hands in his pockets.

"There were times though, when I'd be lying on the ground on my poncho, looking up at the night sky. I loved those peaceful times. While I was looking up at those stars and moon that seemed so close, I knew that someone back in *The World*… back here at home…" Tom turned to look at his dad. "Maybe even you and mom would be looking up at the sky, too. It was mesmerizing and peaceful.

"But most nights belonged to the VC. They often targeted our NDP (Night Defensive Position) by dropping mortars on us, no matter where we were. Our base camp's nickname was 'Rocket City.'" Tom cracked a slight smile. "I always slept with one eye open."

Tom shifted his weight. His voice changed to a monotone.

"I went camping once with Barbara over in the Blackwater Falls area, about a year after we were married. It was early fall, and the leaves were beginning to turn color. It was a gorgeous time of year. We called it, 'God's paintbrush.'

"That trip didn't go too well, though. Even though I knew—*I knew*—I was *not* in Vietnam, I couldn't sleep. It reminded me too much of those nights sleeping in the jungle. I tossed and turned and woke up in a sweat. I couldn't tell if the sounds I heard were coming from the forest or if it was the enemy creeping up on us. I finally crawled outside and sat, leaning against a tree in front of our little tent, my Buck knife in my hand, at the ready." Tom smiled with a slight chuckle. "Needless to say, we didn't camp anymore.

"What about you, Dad? What was it like for you?"

"Not much different. A lot colder, of course, but we were in foxholes most of the time. I loved the freshly fallen snow, though. It reminded me so much of the beauty of Pennsylvania in the winter. It was beautiful and peaceful, especially when the moon and stars were brightly shining.

"When we were out in an LP (Listening Post) it was different though. On dark and cloudy nights, where there was no moon or stars, I'd strain to see out in front. Everything I'd hear a noise or every time I thought I'd see movement, I thought there was a Kraut out there, waiting for me to move and then shoot me. That was the worst."

Both stared at the pictures on the wall. After a few moments of collective silence and reverent thoughts—*another* father and son connection—Ed asked about joining him for lunch. "Absolutely."

Tom slouched when his dad picked up the remote television controller and started punching buttons. "I'll call Ester to see if she can join us."

He realized his dad's memory may be slipping again, so he picked up the phone and handed it to Ed, who returned a confused look.

"I'll call her, Dad. What's her number? Oh, I see. Here it is.

"She said she'd be delighted to join us. Do you want to eat over here in the memory unit?"

"Oh, let's eat in the main dining room. The food is much better and there's more variety. Let me get my coat."

After gently hanging up the phone, Tom realized this must be what a caretaker does, or at least, a family member, for their mom or dad afflicted with Alzheimer's. He felt like he was being a parent to a parent. He didn't mind. Then again, he wasn't a full-time caretaker.

It suddenly dawned on him that this was the primary reason Michelle said Ed needed to be in the memory unit. It's a much more controlled environment with more nurses, aides, and assistants to help care for the elderly, somewhat forgetful residents. He was grateful for all these people and that his father was at Sterling Oaks, in excellent hands.

ESTER ARRIVED AT THE SAME TIME they walked up to the dining room. Ed smiled and gently kissed her on the cheek. She smiled and reached out to take Tom's hand.

"Good afternoon, Ester. It's a pleasure to see you again."

"Hello, Tom. It's good to see you, too. I'm glad you came to see your father. It's not as easy for me to visit him in the memory unit as it was when he was in his apartment."

The head waiter led them to a small table near the far side of the dining room. They were looking through their menus, deciding what to order for lunch, when a boisterous voice bellowed from across the room. Tom looked up to see a short, balding, pot-bellied older man meandering toward their table. His demure and grand entrance reminded him of the old comic, W.C. Fields.

"Ed Reilly. You old dog, you. Hi Ester. You look quite lovely today."

"Oh drat. It's that awful Hank Ennis," Ester whispered to Tom under her breath.

"I hope he doesn't stir up any trouble. Never you mind him, he's just another Texan braggart with a big mouth, that's all. Worst of all, he's a blithering Cowboys fan."

Tom tried earnestly not to grin at Ester's laughable remarks about a fellow inmate.

"Hi Ed, Ester. Glad to see you out and about today. And who is this joining you, may I ask? He's much too young to be living here."

The man spoke so loud, his thundering voice almost burst Tom's eardrums.

Ester spoke up in a quiet tone, almost defensively. "Hank, this is Tom, Ed's son."

Hank stuck his hand out and Tom stood to shake it.

"Tom Reilly. Nice to meet you."

"Your dad is a real card. He's told me some great war stories. I also fought in World War II. Unlike your dad, though, I was in supply. But I was up there right with them. Right, Ed?

"Were you in the Army, too?" Hank barked, not giving Ed a chance to reply.

"Yes, sir. I served in Vietnam."

Hank continued to dominate the conversation with his obnoxiously loud tone. Tom wondered if people in the next county over could hear.

"Well, I've got six kids, all in the military. Three are in the Army and two in the Navy. My youngest daughter, though, decided to join the Air Force—pissed me off big time." Hank chuckled out loud. "But

I'm just as proud of her as all the others.

"Well, nice to see you again. Enjoy your lunch."

And with that, Hank Ennis quickly walked off looking for his next victim, allowing no one else to get a word in edgewise. All three were grateful that the dining room suddenly became much quieter. Ed nonchalantly mumbled Hank was one of those veterans who made mountains out of molehills.

Tom had seen this type of braggadocio many times before. While Hank may have fought—*been there*—during World War II, it was obvious he wasn't on the front lines. He had probably never fired a round from his rifle after completing basic training.

Men like Hank needed to brag about themselves alongside men who had been in actual combat. It didn't matter if it was World War II, Korea, or Vietnam. Tom never understood why. They all fought for what they believed in. And they all had jobs to do—jobs that relied on each other's support. Maybe it was an inferiority complex or worse, *guilt*.

Ed was still mostly "with it" and enjoyed visiting while they took their time eating lunch. No one talked about war, just a casual time to catch up with old friends. Ester did, however, share that one of her sons spent time in the Navy.

"My son, David, was on an aircraft carrier in the early seventies. I'm not sure what he did, but he said he worked on the flight deck and wore a yellow shirt, if that means anything to you. From what he described, they worked long hours. He was always moving around with planes taking off and landing around the clock. He told me some had a lot of bullet holes in them when they landed.

"He was only in the Navy for three years, but he made two cruises over to Vietnam. He's a computer engineer now. I still don't know what he does," Ester smiled proudly. "He and his family live in San Diego. I don't get out as often as I'd like, but I do see them a few times a year."

Tom didn't personally know many Navy men while in Vietnam, but he had the utmost respect for them. He had met a few Navy Corpsmen, most of whom were assigned to Marine combat units. Corpsmen and medics were a grunt's best friend, next to their M-16.

Most medics volunteered to serve their country. Instead of killing people, though, they wanted to help. *And…* they were fearless. If someone screamed, "medic!" they would race to the wounded, regardless of the god-awful circumstances. All GIs took care of their medics, no matter what branch of service.

He was also familiar with many of the Navy fast movers. He had called in a few strike aircraft himself to take care of attacking Viet Cong. They not only came to the rescue when called, but they took off from an aircraft carrier and, after completing their missions, returned to land on them. Those guys had balls.

AFTER LUNCH, the three leisurely strolled around the campus enjoying the sunshine and warm day. Ed was at ease with Ester, her arm threaded through his as they walked together.

Tom had concluded earlier that whatever was between them, it was between them and none of his business. He was grateful his father had found a companion—*is that what they call a relationship at this stage of their lives?* He just enjoyed spending time with him and thought again about those lost years.

Ester parted ways in the courtyard and said her goodbyes, giving them both a quick hug. "Thank you for joining us for lunch. I hope we can do it again sometime."

"My pleasure, Tom. It was lovely to see you again. Bye, Ed. Call me soon, okay?"

"I will. I promise."

Tom wondered if his father would remember this day *and* remember to call Ester. He thought about writing a reminder note, but decided not to. It would probably just get lost in his room.

Walking back toward the memory unit, they bumped into Charles.

"Good afternoon, Mr. Reilly."

"Good afternoon, Charles," both responded simultaneously.

"It's another glorious day on God's green earth, don't you agree?"

"Indeed it is. I thought you worked the night shift?"

"Normally I do, Tom, but I'm helping another aide this week, so I switched to the day shift," Charles offered with no further detail.

"Is there anything I can do for either of you?"

"No, but thanks. I'll see you next week."

Ed didn't pick up on that last part of the conversation, which was fine by Tom. He wasn't sure he wanted to let his dad know he planned to go to a Vietnam veterans' meeting. At least, not yet.

"Charles is a great guy. Did you know he's a Vietnam veteran?"

"I do, Dad. We've talked a few times since you moved over to your new room."

"He's also a pastor—always has a great message when he's here. He knows how to reach people." Ed added, "We never fought alongside any blacks when I was in the war. From what I can tell, though, Charles could fight with the best of us. Did you know he used to be a boxer?"

Tom's unit was integrated, as most were in the Vietnam War. There were a few skirmishes between some of the racists and the brothers. But as far as Tom was concerned, everybody bled red.

He had several black buddies in his squad. They sometimes got wild on their own while on stand-down in base camp. But like all the guys in his squad, they were simply blowing off steam. In the boonies though, everyone—black, white, Hispanic—were all just grunts, all watching each other's back.

"He told me, Dad. He grew up in Detroit and boxing was his way of surviving in the streets. It probably also helped him during the war—he's got quick reflexes and a remarkable instinct. He told me he'd been wounded several times, but always returned to his unit. He didn't want to let his buddies down."

As they continued walking toward his room, Ed asked, "Did I tell you that Charles fought in the Vietnam War?"

Tom sighed deeply. It was tough watching his father slip away. He'd seen this before and had learned, with Michelle's help, the best thing to do was to just go with the flow.

"You can't control what Ed says or does, you can only control how you react."

Over the past couple of months, both Chris and Michelle had helped him learn more about Alzheimer's disease. Chris had grown closer to his grandfather. Like his dad, he wanted to learn what he could, not only about his time in the war but also about Alzheimer's.

He'd read a lot about the disease on the computer and shared what he'd learned. It amazed Tom that a high school freshman could learn so much on his own by doing research on the Internet.

Michelle not only translated technical medical jargon into a language Tom easily understood, but she also provided comfort and encouragement, helping him better cope with his emotions. He liked Michelle and wanted to spend more time with her. During the past few weeks, though, his focus had been on his father.

As he understood it, Alzheimer's disease slowly progresses in the brain but is different for each patient. Only the final outcome remains the same, and there is no cure. Eventually, the Alzheimer's patient's brain dies, causing not only memory loss but also basic, physical motor controls. Tom had noticed this a few times when he tried to help his father re-button his shirt and when he asked about Louise.

Ed still had pleasant days, but they were fewer than before his stroke. Sometimes he would snap back into the present when they talked about the war—*both* WWII and Vietnam—but not always. Lately, though, his dad seemed to have more frequent memory lapses. Tom wondered if there was a connection between a stroke and Alzheimer's, but Michelle told him it was still being studied.

Tom helped Ed ease into his recliner. It looked like he was almost asleep and asked if he wanted to get into bed, but he declined. "Can you turn the TV on for me? Let's see who's playing today."

As soon as Tom switched on the television, his father began to snore. He left the TV on for background noise and went outside for some fresh air. He needed a break from the small room and time to gather his thoughts. Once out in the courtyard, he pulled out a cigarette. But before he could settle down and light it, he heard a familiar, warm greeting from behind.

"Hi, Tom. I thought I might find you out here."

Tom turned toward the lovely voice and faintly smiled. "Hi Michelle. Ed's taking a nap and I wasn't ready to leave. I came outside to clear my head."

"Tough visit?"

Was it that "tough" to visit your own father? Was it really "tough" to try to mend a relationship that fell apart years ago?

"Actually… today is a good day."

Michelle sat down beside him on the shady bench, crossing one leg over the other. Tom noticed her shapely legs.

"I understand you met Charles Smith."

Tom glanced over and wondered how she knew these things. *Was she keeping tabs on him?*

"Charles is one of my favorite people here. He's a veteran like you and he picked himself up from the lowest place one could ever be. He's made a remarkable comeback."

Michelle settled back on the bench, looking out toward the hills. She seemed at ease with Tom. "I think I mentioned before that I was once married to a Vietnam veteran.

"Well, at the time we divorced, I knew Bill still had problems from the war. But he refused to talk about them to me. Or anyone, for that matter. Sometimes we'd go out to dinner or to a movie, and it seemed he just wasn't comfortable in strange places, especially if they were dimly lit. He'd sit with his back to a wall and was always wary of anyone near us. It was like he was ready to fend off an attack or make a quick exit. As time went on, he talked a little less and drank a little more."

Tom easily related to that, but kept listening. Everything Michelle described—*everything*—he had experienced, some of which he still did.

"We now know it as PTSD—Post-Traumatic Stress Disorder." Michelle shifted position on the bench and switched to her professional role, trying to explain—*confess*—her own personal experience. "It's had other names, including 'shell shock' and 'battle fatigue.' Even during the Civil War, it was called 'Soldier's Heart.'

"The name is new—it wasn't officially called PTSD until 1980— but the experience is not. About a third of all Vietnam veterans have been or will be diagnosed with PTSD. The research is still in the early stages, but we are learning quite a bit."

Michelle's voice changed from a professional tone to a softer, defensive tone.

"Denial is a strong psychological tool. But eventually, denial breaks down. I knew something was going on with Bill, but I was deeply involved in my research and school. He was so distant at times, I guess I didn't put two and two together and realize what he was going through. Or perhaps it was easier to ignore him. Sometimes it was difficult to tell."

Her gaze turned to Tom with a slight upbeat tone in her voice.

"Anyway, Charles has helped me better understand how PTSD affects a veteran. He's also helped me better understand my own feelings, having been married to a veteran. I just wish I had known earlier. Perhaps I could have salvaged…"

That unfinished statement hung in the air for a few moments before she stated matter-of-factly, "But the past is past and I needed to move on with my life."

Michelle again shifted her posture on the bench. "My principal area of research focuses on dementia and how it affects combat veterans. My father was also in World War II. He never talked about the war. As a kid, I guess that was normal for us—we didn't know any different. I'm sure you felt the same. But as I got older, I noticed things bothered my dad that didn't seem to bother other World War II veterans."

Tom listened to a very familiar narrative. Michelle was telling *his* story as a young boy growing up with *his* dad. She wasn't just relaying professional guidance. She was talking to him as a close friend and confidant, someone she could easily talk to. He liked this new role.

Michelle took a deep breath. Tom sensed she was about to confess something deep and personal.

"When I was having my marital problems, my father *never* understood why I couldn't work things out with my husband. They were both veterans. My father overcame his problems and worked through most of his issues with my mother. At least, I think he did.

"We tried to talk about it, but my father's stubbornness always got in the way of logic. He didn't want to hear about what I knew, either from my research or from my marriage. He became more defensive of my Vietnam veteran husband than me—*his own daughter.*"

Tom recalled when his father seemed to always side with everyone but him—that argument that eventually led to their parting ways. He knew *exactly* what that alienation felt like.

"Is your dad still around? Does he better understand now?"

Tom looked at Michelle, who looked away.

As she spoke, her face fell, her eyes cast downward. "No, Dad died in 1989. He was only sixty-nine when cancer took him. We were able to reconcile and come to terms, though it was probably too late. I forgave him and told him I loved and appreciated him. Still…" Michelle breathed out a heavy sigh.

"That's one reason I'm intrigued with you and your father, Tom." Michelle sat up straight and looked at Tom with a serious grin. "Perhaps 'intrigued' isn't the right word, but there's something about you that wants me to get to know you better."

Tom took this all in, hearing every word, but hardly believing it. That is until he looked into Michelle's sparkling hazel eyes—eyes that spoke more to him than any words he could possibly hear. He reached out to touch her hand, but Michelle flinched, backing off a little with a soft smile.

"I need to be careful, Tom. I've been through this drinking, self-destruction, and depression once before," Michelle said with the same weariness of a soldier talking about war. "I don't want to go through that again. And besides… I work here. People may question my professionalism if I get involved with a family member of one of my patients while I'm here on the campus.

"Does any of this make sense?"

When Michelle spoke in that soft, reassuring voice, Tom searched her eyes for sincerity, something to hang onto.

"Of course it does, Michelle. It's just that it's been such a long time since I've been in a relationship. I've almost forgotten how to act."

"I don't think so, Tom," Michelle laughed in her appealing way, all white teeth and cute laugh lines. "You are quite the gentleman."

"When I'm here, I'm torn between spending time with my dad and wanting to be with you. It's hard to explain." He looked up to see if she understood his point.

"I'm also aware that I have issues I need to work out. I know they are still there. I've been able to bury them over the years, yet they creep up now and then. More so, lately."

Shifting her position, Michelle sat up and focused on Tom. His eyes told the story of having seen the horrors of war. "What are you afraid of, Tom? What scares you the most? It's okay if you'd rather not answer. Believe me, I understand how painful it can be to talk about these things."

He took another deep breath and quickly exhaled. This time he didn't hesitate to answer.

"I went over to Vietnam as an eighteen-year-old kid, Michelle, full of innocence. Over in 'Nam, I was in combat almost every day in one way or another. *Nothing* scares me anymore. I've been shot at and missed and shit at and hit. I've been under mortar and rocket fire for hours at a time and hit multiple times by shrapnel. I've watched guys vaporize before my very eyes and…" Tom hesitated a moment with a deep breath. "I've had friends die in my arms."

Tom's hands shook as he lit a cigarette. "What's left to be afraid of, Michelle? I *had* to bury those memories. If I thought about them, I'd get depressed. If I talked about them, I'd get angry. If I argued with someone about them—especially someone who hadn't been there— I'd get into a fight."

Tom took another deep breath and exhaled, slightly shaking his head, letting some weight fall from his shoulders.

"Memories, Tom. That's what bothers you—having to relive those memories."

Tom took a deep drag of his cigarette then slowly blew out smoke.

"I still have nightmares. Lately, they seem to be more frequent than before." He paused. "I can't for the life of me figure out why they've suddenly returned."

"Tell me about them." Michelle's brow furrowed as she shifted back into her professional mode. She seemed to accept there may be more than one nightmare. But he didn't mind. This is what he needed.

"I have a recurring nightmare." Tom had a slight tremble in his voice. He was again staring out to nowhere with an emotionless, blank look on his face.

"I'm back in the boonies, under attack from the VC and NVA, just like *that one time* with my squad. I relive that dreadful day over and over.

"Only instead of being able to save a few guys, I can't run fast enough or jump high enough to reach any of them. Every time I get close, they slip farther away. I try to scream to warn them, but I can't utter a single word. It's as if my voice has been silenced. I watch them die over and over and over again. And then, I wake up in a cold sweat.

"Sometimes I can get back to sleep. Most of the time, though, I get up, turn the light on, sit in my chair, and stare into a blank space, hoping those memories fade away. I'm afraid to go back to sleep, because I'm afraid the dream will start over again if I doze off. Then, after a while, the day starts."

Tom swallowed hard and shook his head as if he could shake off the emotions his nightmare always seemed to bring.

"Have you ever talked to anyone about these nightmares? I mean, other than me?"

"Barbara asked me once about my nightmares." Tom's tone was again sober. He sighed, turning to face Michelle.

"I didn't want to talk to her about them, but she insisted. I probably had too much to drink one night and let my guard down. I gave in and told her some of the horrible things I saw—*things I did.*

"I shouldn't have, I know that now. She was only trying to help. I must have terrified her. She told me later my eyes spoke of the unspeakable horrors I had witnessed. I think she was also scared I'd wake up, thinking she was the enemy about to attack. She was worried for both her and Chris. I vowed never again to say anything to her about Vietnam—*ever.*"

Michelle listened carefully… listening to a Vietnam combat veteran, like her ex-husband, who was pouring out his soul and exorcising some of his demons. She *never* had the opportunity to hear these confessions from her own husband. Perhaps this was why her marriage may have failed. Like her ex-husband, she sensed Tom had been emotionally scarred for many years.

"I tried to talk with my father once, but he didn't seem to have time to listen. He kept telling me they would go away one day and to quit bitching and moaning. Just *'get over it,'* were his words. I guess he got over his war. I couldn't."

Tom sat up straight, but still avoided eye contact.

"I wasn't ashamed of what I did over there, Michelle. I was only trying to survive—keep myself and my buddies alive. When I came home, though, people I didn't even know made me feel like I should be ashamed. I just shut down and quit talking about it.

"There were times though, right before my meltdown, when my father made me feel like I was a fuckin' loser." Tom clinched both his fists tightly.

"You're not a loser, Tom. You never have been. You are just lost."

Lost. Is that what this feeling has been all these years? Lost?

He looked up, tears welling in his eyes. He had needed someone to talk to, someone to listen, someone who cared… for a long time.

Michelle reached out and gently held his hand, like his mother used to do. She told him that everything would be all right, like his mother used to say when he got hurt.

"When Barbara and I were having our problems, soon after Chris was born, I found it was easier to be outside, working in the yard or working on my car, rather than confronting them. It's like what you said earlier about your marriage.

"I could never tell Barbara what I just told you, Michelle." Tom's voice started to crack. "I don't know why. She was my wife. I loved her so much. But after Chris was born, there was so much for both of us to do. We began to drift apart.

"She started working night shifts at the hospital. She said the shift differential would help pay for some of the bills. I was certain we were both making enough money to keep up the household.

"Since the night she died, I've blamed myself for her death. I mean, did she really need to work the night shift? Did I drive her to it? I ask myself that question all… the… time. I'll never know, will I?" Tears were flowing down Tom's cheeks.

"You can't blame yourself for that, Tom. It wasn't your fault, and it wasn't Barbara's. You were both lucky to have so much love in your family and to have a son that will continue that love.

"There's a term used in the health profession, Tom. It's called 'Survivor's Guilt.' I'm sure you've heard it before. Maybe, just maybe, it affected you."

Michelle was wearing her professional hat again, but he realized she was right.

"Tom, you survived the Vietnam War. You came back home to a country that didn't appreciate what you had done. You married a wonderful woman and made a family, only to lose her in a tragic accident. None of that is your fault, but you blame yourself for it."

Michelle reached over, firmly grasping Tom's hands in both of hers. "Look at me, Tom. One thing Charles has helped me to better understand is you can't refight these battles and you can't blame yourself for the past.

"Did he ever share with you his philosophy about the rear-view mirror and the front windshield? It is a wonderful explanation of looking toward the future instead of focusing on the past. Some say, *'It's okay to look at the past, but don't stare at it.'* It looks like you've spent most of the last thirty years staring at your past."

Tom let go, pulled out another cigarette and lit it. His hands shook as he recalled his past and *now* his present. His heart beat faster being close to Michelle.

A few quiet minutes passed. "Michelle, would you have dinner with me?" That came out of nowhere, but Tom took his best shot.

Michelle answered without hesitation, "I would like that. Yes."

Both sat on the bench gazing out beyond the lush green slopes and open countryside. The sun was high overhead against a pastel blue sky as they held hands in the warm sunshine. A great weight fell from Tom's shoulders. Today was a splendid day—for both of them.

22 - Vietnam Veterans

In Vietnam, Tom had quickly learned that you wanted to be buddies with everyone—you needed them to watch your back. But you didn't want any close friends—it hurt too much when one died. Thirty years later, he was still wary of strangers, even other veterans.

He wasn't sure what to expect from this Vietnam veteran meeting, but he trusted Charles. Something about him seemed right. And what did Pop say? *"Us Army vets have to stick together."*

According to Charles, the meeting would be informal, more of a social get together. It was *"an opportunity to spend time with some great guys—Vietnam vets. Nothing heavy and no expectations. There are no rules."*

They were meeting at the local American Legion Hall, not far from Sterling Oaks. Tom had put in a full day of work. He left Chris to fend for himself, knowing he would order delivery pizza and would be fine. He simply told him, "I'm meeting with some other veterans," and left it at that. Chris didn't mind, nor did he have any questions. That made it easier since Tom didn't have any answers… yet.

He hadn't been to an American Legion Hall or a VFW in decades. When he finished his tour of duty and first returned to the states, he wasn't even old enough to drink. He'd spent more than a year in Vietnam, legally able *and* willing to kill, and he'd certainly drank his share of beer in base camp. He'd risked his ass for "freedom." Yet he couldn't drink legally in the United States when he was discharged. *What kind of fucked up world was this?*

His last visit to a VFW was disastrous, and he vowed never to step foot in one again. He had tried to find a friendly face, but he'd been chased out by the older World War II and Korean War vets. They didn't take kindly to Vietnam veterans.

Tom bitterly recalled the last time he'd gone to a VFW. He had punched out a Korean War vet who had told him, *"Guys like you lost the war for us."* Once again, he had reached a dead end—another disappointment in how Americans, even the older vets who *had* seen combat, treated returning Vietnam veterans.

HE HOPED he wouldn't have to fight tonight. In the back of his mind, though, he knew that most of the WWII and Korean War veterans were either dead or too old to attend. That thought put his mind somewhat at ease.

As soon as he walked through the front door of the American Legion Hall, he spotted several World War I posters on the walls directly in front of him. There were a few pool tables and a bar off to the side with a grill to order food. The smell of grilled hamburgers and greasy fries reached his nostrils.

A dozen or so patrons sat at the bar, all chatting away, and paid no attention to the stranger who had just walked in. Even though smoking was no longer allowed in the Hall, the smell from years of stale smoke still lingered.

Every wall had different sized framed photos of veterans from the surrounding area who had been killed in different wars. He studied their faces and noticed most were young but all had that distinct look of honor—honor to serve their country.

Most included a series of ribbons, the soldier's rank insignia, and other memorabilia that he assumed were personal items donated by the families of the deceased soldiers. Several included a folded American flag. It was a virtual smorgasbord of war memories to remind patrons they should never forget what war does to a community.

Tom spotted Charles, who smiled and waved, immediately getting up from his table, and walked over. "Glad you could make it, Tom. We've got a good turnout tonight. Most of the regulars are here. They're aware that you're coming, so don't feel like you're a FNG."

Charles grinned. He liked to welcome new visitors just so he could use that throwback term, "Fuckin' New Guy."

Instead of sitting at Charles' table, they walked to a back meeting room. "It's a little quieter back here." Tom spotted a table in the back with trays of cookies, bowls of chips and pretzels, and a coffee urn.

Charles spoke loudly, using his deep, commanding baritone voice, getting everyone's attention, something he proudly took advantage of. "I'd like to introduce Tom Reilly. He's the new guy."

Before Tom could utter a single word, one of the sitting vets shouted out, "Did you bring any *ba mui ba?*" That was the "33" local Vietnamese beer all 'Nam vets knew about—rumored to contain formaldehyde. The others in the room all laughed out loud. *Just like back in 'Nam.*

"*No biêt*—I don't understand. Not this time. I didn't get the orders." Tom spoke without hesitation, knowingly taking the bait. "But I was wondering if any of you could help me find a bucket of prop wash?" Everyone roared at that old FNG joke. *Just like back in 'Nam.*

"No, but I found where they keep the left-handed screwdrivers and the metric crescent wrenches," another veteran shouted out, again causing everyone in the room to explode in laughter. *Just like back in 'Nam.*

Several vets responded in unison, "There it is."

With that simple exchange, Tom found something he'd lost years ago—a comradery, *a brotherhood*—a welcome like no other. It transported him back to a time when he served with men whom he didn't know personally, but he admired each one because of their past shared experiences.

"Welcome to our monthly local Vietnam veterans meeting, Tom," Charles said. "Glad to have you visit. When we have a new visitor, we normally take turns introducing ourselves. We always start with the FNG. What unit did you serve with and when were you in 'Nam?"

Tom spoke up loud and proud. "My name is Tom Reilly. I fought with the 2/28th Infantry, based in Lai Khe, down in Tri Corps, from '68-'69."

"Where do you live now?"

"I'm down in Morgantown."

"Welcome aboard, Tom. I'm George Davis. I was a Navy Corpsman, serving with the 3rd Marines, '70-'71. I'm up in Pittsburgh."

"Frank Kaplan here. I was an Army Huey pilot with the 173rd Airborne, and in 'Nam '69-'70. I live here in Canonsburg."

"Joe Boyle. 26th Marines '66-'69. I couldn't get enough of it, so I made two tours. Ooh-rah." Joe beamed. "I live in Pittsburgh."

"Howdy. Lee Fisher. I was with the 13th Marines, '67-'68. I live in Pittsburgh."

"José Rivera. I was with the Americal Division in Tri Corps, '67-'68. I live in the hills."

That comment brought a few chuckles from the other vets.

"Bill Baker. I was with the 2/8th Infantry in Two Corps, '66-'69. Like my friend, Joe, I made a couple of tours. I live in Pittsburgh."

"Gilberto Montemayor, formerly with the 173rd Airborne Brigade in Two Corps, '68-'69. I live in Pittsburgh."

As Tom listened to each veteran introduce himself, he observed several carried physical wounds of the war. A couple were in wheelchairs. Another carried a pair of crutches, missing his left leg. One wore an eyepatch.

He wondered what kind of additional obstacles these courageous, wounded warriors had faced over the past thirty years. The remarkable thing was that no one complained about their physical condition. All seemed to be elated to have survived the war and be among friends— other Vietnam veterans.

"Tony Alvarez. Former Marine with the 1st Marines in Eye Corps, '65-'66. I live in Canonsburg."

"Jim Johnson, also a former Marine with the 1st Marines in Eye Corps, '65-'66. Tony & I served together. I live in Pittsburgh."

"I'm Ron Smith, Army Special Ops down in Two Corps, '65-'66, currently residing in Pittsburgh."

"Ray Connor. I'm the only Air Force guy here tonight. I was in 'Nam '70-'71. I live in Pittsburgh."

"Vernon Driggers."

Tom waited for the rest of Vernon's introduction. Charles pointed out Vernon didn't share much, but he was one of us. "Always has been, always will be, right?"

"Right you are, Sarge."

"I'd like to open with a prayer," Charles said. "Please bow your heads.

"Dear Lord, we thank you for keeping this humble group of warriors together, keeping them safe and watching out for them and their loved ones. We thank you for bringing Tom Reilly to our meeting tonight. We ask you also continue to help us heal from our individual wounds as well as our collective wounds. Please continue to watch over our comrades who are no longer with us—those that died in Vietnam and those that died afterward, here at home. May we never forget them. In Jesus' name we pray, Amen."

Tom noticed not everyone bowed their heads, including himself. However, like Tom, they were respectful of others who did.

"Please stand, if you can, uncover, and face the flag for the Pledge of Allegiance."

The last time Tom recited the Pledge of Allegiance was at a Steelers football game, years ago with his dad. These continued traditions of this veteran group emotionally moved him. As he removed his ball cap and placed his hand over his heart, reciting the pledge, he remembered how much he liked military traditions carried over from multiple generations.

Charles was obviously in charge of the meeting. He made a few business and general announcements before asking, "Does anyone have anything they'd like to share? Anything that's happened this past month?"

Tom sensed an uneasiness in the room. This was his first encounter with this group. In fact, while he had known a few vets off and on through the years, this was the first time he'd been with a group of veterans—*ever*—since the end of the Vietnam War.

Several shared a few stories. A new job here and there, and a job recently lost. A few shared about their families, some with kids in high school, like Tom. One veteran was going through a divorce. He didn't know how many were married, or perhaps like him, widowed.

Another veteran announced his parents had just moved into a retirement community. When Tom asked, it wasn't Sterling Oaks, but he noticed Vernon Driggers took an interest in the discussion. Several mentioned an assortment of ailments or medical problems, but didn't go into detail.

It was almost as if he'd been transported to a time when Vietnam veterans were together—not over *here*, but over *there*. Not under combat conditions, but in base camp, relaxing. Combat soldiers, engineers, artillery, medics, clerks, pilots, support, officers *and* enlisted—it made no difference. Not here, not now, not anymore. They *all* had been over there.

And like Tom, they all experienced those ever-shifting emotions upon returning home. Several had found their way. Others, like him, still struggled. It didn't matter anymore. At least, for the present time. Here… tonight… he was welcomed.

Tom recalled something his father had said earlier when he was describing the CIB to Chris. *"You're not fighting alone—you're never alone. You always have somebody with you, someone that watches your back, somebody that would lay their life on the line with you and for you. You just can't get much closer than that."*

"If there are no other announcements or questions, I think we're about done. Let's close with a prayer. Please bow your heads.

"Dear Lord, we thank you again for bringing us together and helping us stay fit and healthy. For those experiencing loss or health problems, please be with them and help them through their transition. All of us veterans are individuals, each with a service particular to him. It may be hard to find any of us that are in total agreement about the war, but one thing we all agree on is we all came home different men than when we left. We don't ask to return to being that former self, just that you help us be the best we can be.

"God, grant us the serenity to accept the things we cannot change, courage to change the things we can, and wisdom to know the difference.

"We know you are there for all of us. In Jesus' name, Amen."

"Amen."

"Thank you for coming to join our brotherhood." Charles made his way over, making sure Tom felt welcomed. "We hope to see you again. Meanwhile, I'm sure I'll see you the next time you visit your father."

After the official meeting broke up, a few vets left the Hall. Others stayed around and continued to chat. It was obvious several of the older veterans had hearing issues—they talked loud. It reminded Tom of the residents at Sterling Oaks.

"By the way." Charles caught up with Tom before he left. "Several of us combat vets get together periodically at a local restaurant, usually for lunch. Sometimes, it's easier to share *our* unique perspectives with a smaller group. If you're interested, I'll call you the next time we get together."

"Thanks, Charles. I really enjoyed this. And yes, I would like to get together for lunch. To be honest, I wasn't sure what to expect, but I'm so glad I came. I felt... welcomed."

"That you are, Tom. *Welcome home!*"

23 - The Date

Tom looked at the three button-down and two pullover shirts, and two slacks laid out on his queen-size bed. Other than jeans and t-shirts, his wardrobe was pitiful, but he'd never seen the need for fancy clothes.

His only dress slacks were a pair of khaki pants he'd worn once before with his one dark blue sports coat. He wondered if he should wear the coat which led to whether he should wear a tie which led to which pair of shoes to wear. He shook his head. Too many choices.

Tom made a command decision: keep it simple. Khakis, the dark blue button-down shirt with the sleeves rolled up, and his one pair of semi-dress shoes—brown loafers. Blue was Barbara's favorite color. He felt comfortable she would approve.

Earlier in the day, he'd trimmed his goatee and now smiled widely as he slowly turned his head side-to-side, making sure he hadn't missed anything. He thought about wearing a spritz of Old Spice, but decided against that. He hadn't worn any cologne for years; why start now?

He spotted Chris in the mirror behind him, leaning on the door frame with his arms crossed.

"How do I look?"

"You look fine, Dad. Believe me, Ms. Myers will be impressed." Chris sported a proud grin.

"I can't remember the last time I've been out on a date. Maybe that's why I'm a little nervous."

"I wouldn't worry about it, Dad. It's like riding a bicycle—once you get back on, it all comes back to you."

This back-and-forth banter between father and son reminded Tom of his recent ride with his father in Sunshine. Both Chris and Ed suggested, in their own unique ways, not to screw things up with Michelle. That thought relaxed him and he smiled to himself.

"Where are you taking her?"

"A little restaurant called *Stefano's*. It's not too far from here."

"Are you going to pick her up or meet her there?"

"What's with the twenty questions?" Tom cracked a smile. "We're going to meet there."

"I don't know, Dad. I'm just trying to pick up a few pointers. It won't be too long before I start to date."

Tom smiled lovingly at his son. They had come a long way—bonded—now that Ed and Michelle had entered their lives.

SUNSHINE WEAVED ITS WAY through the late afternoon rush hour in Morgantown. Summer was winding down, but students had yet to return to West Virginia University. Traffic wasn't bad, and Tom arrived at *Stefano's* fifteen minutes early. He wanted a cigarette, but passed, not wanting to smell like stale smoke.

As soon as Michelle drove up—Tom spotted her from his car—he stepped out of Sunshine and walked toward her. He wanted to be "the gentleman" he remembered from a previous life. He was still anxious about this first date, but Chris had reassured him that his mother would approve.

"You can't remain a loner your entire life, Dad." How did this kid get to be so smart at such a young age?

"You look amazing, Michelle."

"Thank you, Tom. You're quite handsome yourself."

Tom began to relax as he and Michelle made their way into the quaint, out-of-the-way restaurant. He'd made a six o'clock reservation earlier in the week, and the hostess promptly seated them in a corner booth. It was mid-week and they were part of the early evening dinner guests—not too crowded, making Tom feel a little more at ease. She carefully lit the candle in the center of their table. Tom's nose slightly twitched as he picked up on Michelle's perfume, something familiar…

Michelle glanced around and immediately noticed the "water theme" ambience. Fish nets gently drooped from the ceiling and several large aquariums were strategically placed around the room, each filled with a variety of fish and underwater plants. Huge wooden framed paintings of seascapes hung on the walls. A twinkling starburst over the rectangular bar and strategically lit stacked stone walls cast a flattering light over everything.

"Very nice, Tom. Have you been here before?"

"No. This is my first time. A work buddy recommended it. He said besides excellent food, it had a warm, cozy atmosphere. So far, I'm impressed."

"Me, too." Michelle's dazzling smile was warm and unassuming and her wavy brown hair fell angelically to her shoulders.

Their waitress immediately walked over to take their drink orders. Michelle ordered a glass of Italian Pinot Grigio; Tom asked for his usual Kentucky bourbon and soda.

"How was work today?" Both Tom and Michelle laughed out loud as they simultaneously asked the same question.

"You first." Michelle smiled with her sparkling eyes. She seemed at ease.

"What can I tell you about house painting?" Tom was purposefully being sarcastic. "Actually, I really enjoy what I do. Being my own boss, I get to pick and choose what jobs I want. And I get to work outside, at least during most of the year. It helps keep me sane in this crazy world. Today was a gorgeous day.

"How about you?"

"Oh, same-oh, same-oh."

Tom could tell she enjoyed this initial banter by the way her mouth curled up a bit as she spoke. "I didn't visit with Ed today, but when I checked on him yesterday, he was doing well. I'm sure I would've heard if something urgent came up.

"Besides my regular visits with other residents, I worked on another research paper, and I attended a couple of *boring* administrative meetings. Sometimes I think they're a waste of time. Then again, *I'm* the one who scheduled them." Michelle's smile was relaxed, helping put Tom more at ease.

The waitress quickly returned with their drinks. It was almost as if she knew exactly when to step in, without interrupting their conversation. He understood why his work buddy, Jim, had suggested *Stefano's*.

"What can I get for the two of you this evening? Ladies first."

Michelle glanced through the two-page old-style menu and, without looking up, asked, "What would you recommend for tonight?"

The waitress responded without hesitation. "*Stefano's* is well-known for our fresh water trout, pan-seared in a brown-butter sauce. We serve it with oven-baked, herb-crusted fingerling potatoes, roasted carrots in a mild sweet bourbon sauce, and a side mixed-green salad drizzled in our own light Champagne-flavored dressing."

"Oh, that sounds wonderful. I'll have that." Michelle closed her menu and handed it back to the waitress.

"And for you, sir?"

Tom hadn't looked through the menu. He initially thought he'd order the standard Delmonico steak and baked potato with a salad, but after listening to the waitress describe the mouth-watering meal, he opted to have the same.

"Perfect. I'll bring you a basket of our famous *Stefano's* butter rolls right away, but I'll give you a little more time before placing the order. It looks like this is your first time… here."

Tom shot the waitress a sharp glance, but softened his glare when he noticed her soft smile and wink. He wondered how she knew this was their first date.

Taking a sip of his drink, he looked over at Michelle—her eyes danced in the candlelight.

"Michelle, I really appreciate you looking after my dad. I'm not sure what I would have done had I not met you. But… I'm just really glad to be here with you."

Michelle took a small sip of her Pinot. He watched. She blushed.

"Thank you, Tom. I'm glad we met, too, even under the circumstances. I don't usually date a patient's family member. Actually, I think this is a first. There's a certain level of professionalism that I need to maintain, not only to Sterling Oaks but also to myself.

"I hope you understand, but to tell you the truth, I'm glad you asked. In a way, I was hoping you would."

Tom's mind raced back and forth between his first few dates with Barbara and now this first date with Michelle, not knowing where this relationship would end up. For now, though, he focused on the present.

"Did I hear you grew up in Pittsburgh? I remember seeing that on your father's chart."

"I did. Born and raised and never left the state until... Vietnam." Tom hesitated, dropping his eyes when he mentioned the war. He didn't want to talk about it, especially on a special night like this. He changed gears.

"You already know so much about me, but I don't know a thing about you. Where did you grow up?" Tom asked, sipping his bourbon.

"I'm from a small town just outside Madison, Wisconsin, called Belleville.

"When my dad came home from the war—he was originally from Chicago—he wanted to settle down in a small town, one far away from the big city that offered peace and quiet. My mom was from Belleville, so that was a natural choice for him. Just the two of them for a while, until I came along."

Tom noticed Michelle was fidgeting with her napkin and recalled her previous confession about her dad. He decided to change the subject.

"How did you end up in Pennsylvania? I mean, I know you have a Ph.D. in Psychology, but from where?"

Michelle paused for a moment, swirling her glass of wine, almost as if she was hesitant about revealing too much.

"Well... I went to the University of Wisconsin-Madison for my Bachelor's and Master's degrees. But after six years in the same place, it was time for a change, so I moved to Pittsburgh to work on my Ph.D. *That* took another six years, but was well worth it. I'm very passionate about my work, especially working with veterans."

Michelle finished her Pinot and looked around for the waitress.

She promptly appeared. "Would you like another Pinot Grigio?" Tom's glass was still half full.

"Yes, please."

The waitress took Michelle's empty glass and asked, "Are you ready for me to put your order in?"

Michelle looked at Tom, raising her eyebrows and giving him the opportunity to make the decision.

"Yes, thank you." Tom answered.

Michelle seemed to avoid looking at Tom, but he wasn't sure why. After a few moments of silence, Tom asked her, "Are you okay, Michelle? You seem a little... distant."

"I'm fine, Tom. Now and then I think about my dad, what he went through during the war, and how it affected him. I based my dissertation on both research *and* my own childhood. Don't get me wrong. Dad showed a lot of love and affection for both me and my mother, but there were times when I was a teenager that he seemed distant. As I got older, that distance seemed to increase. I don't know why."

Tom could relate, but he didn't want to continue down this path.

The waitress returned with Michelle's drink. "Can I refill yours, sir?"

"No, thank you. I'm good for now."

Tom's voice had a distinct "one and done" tone that Michelle seemed to pick up.

After a few more minutes of casual conversation, a different waiter brought their meals, which both Tom and Michelle could smell before they arrived. "Wow, this looks fantastic," Michelle said, stating the obvious. "Thank you."

They looked at each other and clinked their glasses, "*Bon appétit,*" each savoring that first bite. Tom watched Michelle and noticed she had many mannerisms similar to Barbara. He smiled to himself as he took another bite.

All during the casual meal, Tom and Michelle talked about life growing up in different parts of the country, focusing more on the fun times when they were younger. Tom was at ease around Michelle and enjoyed hearing her talk about her life and her work. It was almost... *normal.*

After finishing their meals, the waitress cleared the table. Michelle asked Tom if he was going to have another drink. "I'm not prying, Tom, but I don't want to overdo it myself."

Tom chuckled at that remark. "No problem. I learned a long time ago that when I'm out on the town—which is rare, by the way—I'll only have one drink, especially if I'm driving." Michelle's eyebrows slightly raised. Tom noticed, but offered no further explanation.

When the waitress returned Tom ordered a black coffee. "Anything for you, ma'am?"

"I'll have a decaf cappuccino, please."

Michelle looked at Tom with a wide grin. Their hands were on the table, almost touching. Tom noticed. His eyes shifted left to right, and he decided it was time to confess.

"Michelle. There's something I want to say, but I'm not sure where to start."

Michelle leaned forward with her eyes on Tom and gently placed her hand on top of his. With a slight smile, she softly said, "I've always found the best place to start is at the beginning."

Tom glanced down at her hand resting on his; it was warm to the touch and soft, very much like Barbara's.

"We've only known each other for a few months, yet… I feel like I've known you a long time. It's hard to explain, but I'm also very wary about moving too fast. There's something here, I can sense it, and I believe you can too."

Michelle slowly sat back in her seat, releasing Tom's hand, but still keeping it on the table.

"What is it, Tom? Are you worried about getting too close?"

How did she know that?

Tom looked up, then away.

"It's been more than thirteen years since Barbara died, Michelle. I know I need to—want to—move on, but I still have this nagging feeling. It's hard to shake. I look at you and I see her. You have a beauty and a warmness that reminds me so much of her."

Michelle sat back a little more and gave him a thoughtful look. "Is that a bad thing, Tom?"

He picked up on her defense. "No… no, not at all. It's one of those things I need to work on, Michelle. It's me, not you."

Michelle looked around, then announced she needed to go to the restroom. Tom stood as she backed her chair up. He was still trying to be the perfect gentleman, but reminded himself, *I may have just blown it.*

When Michelle returned, she sat back down with a renewed sense of confidence. However, Tom felt the emotional distance between them had increased.

"Tom. Do you have a picture of Barbara? I don't want to pry, but I'd like to meet her. That is… if you're okay with that."

Tom smiled, partly because it flattered him that this beautiful woman having dinner with him wanted to see a picture of his wife, partly because she assumed he carried a photo of her with him, but mostly because she seemed genuinely interested. He reached into his back pocket and pulled out his weathered leather wallet, carefully extracting the photo he'd cherished for years.

Michelle took the photo and glanced at it, then her eyes hardened as she looked closer, leaning toward the candlelight.

She then looked up at Tom with a puzzled gaze. "This… this is Barbara?"

Tom wasn't sure how to react. "Yes, that's Barbara."

Michelle kept looking at the photo, then sat back in her seat.

"I know her. I mean, I… I knew her." Michelle's eyes focused on Tom. "She worked at the University of Pittsburgh Medical Center in the Intensive Care Unit, didn't she?"

Tom's surprised look did not go unnoticed. "Yes. How did you know?"

Michelle carefully handed the photo back to Tom. Her eyes had a blank stare, searching for a long forgotten memory.

"After I completed my research and began working on my dissertation, the hospital called me in to consult on a case—a Vietnam veteran had attempted suicide. He had just come out of the ICU and was transferred to the mental health unit. Barbara was the one who introduced me to him."

Tom leaned forward, arms on the table, tapping his fingers together anxiously. He was all ears, hearing for the first time from someone who had worked with his wife. Someone who cared. Someone who cared for him.

"I didn't remember her name until now. But I vividly remember her giving me the medical background of this patient—the Vietnam veteran—and explaining what treatment he'd had and what she'd experienced. She was extremely detailed, like she knew more about the patient's mental state than his physical state.

"I thought it odd at the time, but didn't think twice about it. I've studied veteran patients in many capacities, but this was the first one that had tried to kill himself."

Tom's clasped his hands tightly on the table, his thumbs tapping each other. He nervously shifted in his chair.

"What was so strange, Michelle?" Tom wanted—*needed*—to know.

Michelle looked around for the waitress. She needed another decaf. She took her time to answer.

"I'd worked with many veterans during my research. Most were World War II veterans, since at the time that was my focus. Because word spread about my research with combat veterans, I also periodically worked with Korean War and Vietnam War veterans. It was not unusual to find them in various states of mind, primarily because of PTSD.

"Barbara made a comment that I'll never forget. And I'm somewhat hesitant to bring it up now."

Tom was on the edge of his seat. "Please, Michelle. Tell me. I… I need to know."

Michelle took a sip of her decaf, carefully weighing her response. Tom couldn't take his eyes off her.

"We started to talk a little about our husbands—both were Vietnam veterans. I was in the middle of a divorce, so she listened while I talked. It was therapeutic for me to share some deep thoughts with the wife of a Vietnam veteran. She understood… she *knew*."

Tom leaned in closer. "Did she… did she talk about me?"

Michelle's gaze turned to the side, deciding whether she should confess.

"Yes, a little. What I remember was that she worried about you, Tom. She didn't go into detail, but because both of us had married war veterans, well… we sort of already knew the ups and downs."

Michelle leaned in closer, putting her hand on Tom's, then cradling it with both hers.

"Your wife loved you, Tom. She truly did. She was as confused about the war as I was, but I know for a fact that she worried about you like I did for Bill. This particular patient was not the first that had tried to commit suicide, but it was the first Vietnam veteran she had encountered. She was worried about you... *for you.*"

Tom's eyes welled up with tears. Hearing these soft words from Michelle about Barbara helped him realize just what he had... *and* what he'd lost. He couldn't return to that previous life. But he could continue forward with this one. That's *another* second chance he'd been given.

He took Michelle's hands and wrapped both his around them. "Thank you, Michelle. That means more to me than you'll ever know."

24 - Last Ride

Ed was in his room, sleeping. He seemed to nap more these days. Tom wasn't sure if it was the Alzheimer's, the stroke, or the fact that his dad was just… *old*. His health had been declining over the last few visits with more labored breathing when they walked. Tom also noticed his eyes didn't have as the same sparkle as before.

Charles poked his head in to see if everything was all right. Tom nodded, "Yes," but followed him outside into the hallway.

"I wanted to thank you for hooking me up with the veteran's group, Charles. It helps to realize there are other men—other Vietnam vets—who experience these same struggles I have. While I've tried to bury them, I now know I need to learn to manage them."

"No problem, Tom. I've been around vets a long time, including veterans like your father. While I *think* I know a lot, I'm still learning. And to be honest, that's okay. I know this is God's way to help *me* heal—by helping others.

"Is there anything I can do for you or your father?"

Tom took a moment, then glanced up and smiled. "Actually, there is. I want to take him for another ride in my GTO. It has special meaning to us both. He'd enjoy it once we got him up. Can you help me get him ready?"

"Of course. Be happy to."

Over the past month, there was no consistency whether his father would wake up "with it" or "out of it." While it had bothered him in the past, Tom realized that this is the way Ed's life—*and* his life—was right now. This time, though, his father didn't recognize him.

"Hi Ed. It's Tom. Are you up for a ride in the car?"

"Yes, I'd like that," Ed said sleepily, though his eyes were wide open. "I feel I've been sleeping my entire life. Let's get some fresh air."

After helping him dress, they deliberately walked slowly outside to a lovely summer day. His dad didn't use a walker like many others in the memory unit, but Tom knew it wouldn't be much longer. He slouched a little more and wasn't as stable as he'd been a few weeks earlier.

Ed stopped for a moment and looked up at the clear, blue sky. "Looks like another gorgeous day. Louise calls this a 'Champagne Day.' Is she coming?"

"No, she's not coming with us this time, Dad." He'd gotten used to his father asking about his mother.

"What a shame. She'd enjoy a ride in the country, especially on a day like today."

Tom opened the passenger door of his GTO and reached in. "I've got something for you, Dad." Handing him a U.S. Army Veteran ball cap, Tom added, "I thought you might want to wear this on our ride."

Ed stared at the cap in his hand and cocked his head a bit, his eyes narrowing. Then he looked up toward the sky, squinting in the bright sun. He seemed to smile his way back to the present.

"World War II. That was a long time ago, but it seems like yesterday. Thank you, Tom. Where did you get it?"

Reaching into the car again, he pulled out *his* ball cap. "Same place I got this one. Right down the road from another Army veteran."

"Well, next time you see him, tell him thanks. I've always wanted one of these." Ed slicked his hair back with his hand and slipped on his new hat. "Thanks for helping me, Charles. Want to go for a spin with us?" Ed grinned with that certain spark back in his eyes.

"I'd love to Mr. Reilly, but I'm still working. Perhaps another day?" Charles helped him ease into the car.

"I'll make sure. See you later."

Tom looked across the roof of the car and smiled. "Thank you," he said just loud enough for Charles to hear.

"Let's blow this popsicle stand." Tom slid into his seat, buckled his seatbelt, and cranked up Sunshine. "Where to today?"

"Oh I don't care, Son. Let's just point the car down the road."

"Deal." Tom happily agreed as he slowly backed out of the parking space.

He decided to drive north again, not knowing if they would stop in Pittsburgh or continue to drive further toward Meadville and Erie. Sunshine was full of gas.

"I'm glad you wanted to go for a ride, Dad. It's been a while. I figured you'd like to get out of your room."

"You're right about that. Okay if I smoke?"

"I'll join you." Tom pulled out a cigarette, and they both cracked their windows.

"Chris out of school yet?"

"Yep. He finished his freshman year a few weeks ago and did quite well. He matured a lot in his first year of high school."

"It's probably because he wants to do well in high school so he can go to college."

"I think it's also because you've been a good solid influence on him, Dad. I only wish…"

"Me too, Son. Me too." Ed finished their same thought.

"We've lost so much time, Dad. I wish things had been different. Do you know what I mean?"

"I do, Son, but let's not dwell on the past. Let's talk about today and what the future may bring."

"What do you mean?" Tom shot his father a curious glance.

Ed took a deep drag on his cigarette and blew the smoke out the window.

"Tom, you may not realize it, but I probably won't be around much longer. I don't dwell on it, though. Over the past few months, between this Alzheimer's shit and my stroke, well… I know my days are numbered.

"There's no sense in getting teary-eyed, it's simply life. It took me a while, but after Louise died, I learned you have to live every day like it's your last. Death is just the next step in life's journey.

"I'm delighted that you and I—and Chris, too—have been able to spend time together. While I wish I'd swallowed that stubborn, foolish pride of mine years ago, I can't change that." Ed paused a moment. "So goes life."

They rode along for a little while before Ed broke the silence.

"I need your help with something, Tom."

"Anything, Dad. Just name it."

"I want you to help me plan my memorial service."

Shit. Tom was *not* expecting that. He momentarily glared at his father, then refocused on the road.

"Nothing fancy, just a simple memorial service at Sterling Oaks. I've already written out most of what I want. I'd like you and Chris to share a couple of stories. Can you do that for me?"

"I'll try."

"Don't try, Son—*do!*" Ed used his demanding fatherly voice.

"Okay, Dad. I'll do it. What else?"

Tom wasn't sure he wanted to continue *this* conversation. But since his dad was still in present mind, he was determined not to leave any unfinished business. He didn't know if they would have another opportunity to talk like this again.

"I asked Tony Jones to say a few things, too. I've known him longer than anyone else. He's my best friend.

"I also asked Charles to read a couple of Bible verses and lead everyone in a couple of my favorite hymns. He said he would. I like Charles very much. While I didn't serve with black soldiers during the war, I told him I'd proudly serve with him in the afterlife. He's a great man who's helped other veterans through some of their toughest days."

"I know, Dad. I've met with his veteran's group a few times. It's helped me better understand the emotions and feelings I've kept bottled up all these years."

Both took time to light another cigarette.

"You and I, Son… our wars were not really that different. At least, from our personal battles. We both fought for what we believed in. We were both shot, and we saved a few lives. Believe it or not, we did do some good things in our wars.

"The biggest difference is when *I* came home, I was welcomed home as a returning soldier *should* have been welcomed. I'm not just talking about my mom and dad and Louise. I'm talking about the fact that America welcomed us all home.

"You *never* got that homecoming. To this day, I still don't understand. You deserved to come home to a country that was proud of what you did. Every soldier deserves that respect. Things are changing, but I'm not sure the best way for you to accept that change."

Ed's voice changed to a more somber tone—not as a father, but as a friend.

"There's one thing that will help you, Tom, but you'll probably tell me to go to hell." Ed paused, briefly looking over at his son.

"You need to go to *The Wall.*' Go visit Sunshine. Talk to Wayne. Tell him how much you love him. Tell him you are living the life you both fought for and both deserve. You need to do that, Son. If you don't do it for yourself or for Sunshine, do it for me."

Tom was in tears hearing his father speak softly to him. All of this made sense—*now.* He'd known about the Vietnam War Memorial. He just never wanted to visit it. He wanted to leave all that shit behind him. Perhaps his dad was right. Like Charles said, you can *never forget* Vietnam.

"You may be right, Dad."

"Damn right I am." Ed looked at Tom with a wide grin. "Damn right."

In the background, the radio played Sgt. Barry Sadler's *The Ballad of the Green Berets.* Ed reached over to turn up the volume. "I always liked this song."

Put Silver Wings on my son's chest
Make him one of America's best

"Dad, can I ask you a question?"

"Sure. Fire away."

"Do you believe in Heaven? I mean, do you believe you'll be with mom again after you… you know… pass away?"

"I do, Son. I've been thinking about that a lot lately. I guess it's because I'm getting closer to the end of my life. I don't have a clue when that will be, but I'm closer today than I was yesterday." Ed grinned.

"I've also been dreaming more about her. Sometimes I wake up in the middle of the night and I swear she's in the room with me. It just seems so real.

"I honestly believe I'll see lots of folks again when I get to Heaven. At least, those who aren't in hell." His dad smiled at that comment. Tom understood *exactly* what he meant.

"I'm not sure I've ever told this to anybody, considering it's very personal. I know you're struggling with your own beliefs in God and I hope and pray you'll find Christ again… soon.

"There's no doubt in my mind I *will* go to Heaven. When I get there, I *know* I'll be with Louise again—for eternity. There is no such thing as time, as we understand it, in Heaven. I'm sure I'll also see my parents, my dogs, my friends, my fellow soldiers… pretty much everybody and anybody. And, in the same sense, they'll 'see' me in their own version, in their own time.

"What they'll 'look like' I have no idea. Here on earth, we only think in terms of two and three dimensions. In Heaven, I truly believe there are an infinite number of dimensions. At least, as best as we understand 'dimensions' here on earth."

Ed closed his eyes and continued.

"When I see Louise, she'll be just like the days when we were together, not old and not young, just me and Louise. When I see my own parents, it'll be like when I was a kid, or perhaps as a young man, or even a soldier or maybe, all the above."

Ed looked over at Tom. "Ha! Multiple copies of me in Heaven. Can you imagine?

"When I meet the men I fought with in the war, there won't be any blood, or any hurt, or any weapons. We'll simply be good ol' Army buddies, sharing a beer at a local English pub or an outdoor Austrian bar.

"Does any of this make sense to you?"

"I think so, Dad. You believe Heaven has no hurt and no worry. Whatever we think we know—or want to know—about Heaven will be unimaginable once we're there."

Ed smiled. "You have the ability to simplify complicated things. It comes from being a war veteran. Believe me, I know."

Sunshine crossed the Ohio River as they left Pittsburgh behind. Neither wanted to turn off, so they kept cruising north on I-79.

"How are things between you and Michelle?"

Damn. Another question he wasn't prepared to answer. It's like he was back in high school, talking to his father about his first girlfriend.

"I like her, Dad. I really do, but I'm just not sure."

"Oh, she's interested, Son."

"What makes you think that?"

"Besides her telling me?"

Tom glanced over at his dad's broad smile.

"It's obvious to me. I may not have my wits about me all the time, but when I see her and the way she looks at you and hear the tone in her voice when she talks about you, well... I know these things."

Tom was grinning now. He had wanted to tell his father about their budding relationship, but there was too much happening in his life right now.

Even though they'd been on a first date, he still had mixed feelings. In one sense, he felt he was betraying Barbara, even though he knows she would be all right with him in a relationship. They had talked about "what if something happens." But he still had that nagging guilt.

"I don't know, Dad. She was married before to a Vietnam veteran and divorced a while back. She said it was because of his PTSD.

"Over the past month, she's also helped me realize I have PTSD symptoms. But I'm working through them. At least, I don't keep those old feelings bottled up inside anymore. I'm able to think about them without getting depressed. Better yet, I'm *now* able to talk about them."

"Like I said, although we went through many of the same struggles in our own wars, yours were different. But you're getting through them. It just takes time.

"And as far as Michelle is concerned... she likes you, Tom. Just don't fuck it up." Ed chuckled, causing his son to smile.

"Thanks, Dad. I'll try."

"Don't try—*do!*"

"One more thing I want to pass along to you.

"When you were young, your mother and I had you baptized. You were always active in church when you were younger. I know you drifted in and out of church during high school. I get that—lots of your generation at that age did.

"But I do know this. You need to find a way to get Christ back in your heart. The war changed a lot of your beliefs. Believe me, when I was under an artillery barrage, I prayed to God to get me through and He did. There were times, though, when I questioned God.

"Most combat soldiers have had those deep spiritual questions. I'm sure you have for quite some time now. I wish I could take away your hurt, Tom, but I can't. I can only tell you if Christ is in your heart, He *will* help you. *That* is a fact."

Ed took a deep breath and pursing his lips, let it out slowly. His voice lowered and softened.

"I lost my faith twice—once during the war, and once again when Louise died. How could *my* God let these things happen? But I found a way—with the help of my friends *and* my church—to live my life the best I could.

"I think I have… well, except for that foolish pride shit that drove us apart." Ed looked over at Tom with a wide grin. Tom returned it with a big smile.

"If you haven't figured it out yet Tom, Charles is a *beacon deacon*."

Realizing what he just said, Ed snorted. "I should've been a poet. But Charles *is* a beacon that can help you find Christ. I've seen it happen on several occasions."

Tom struggled with the words he had wanted to say for a while.

"Dad, I can't take back the hurt I caused when I left. We may have lost twenty-five years, but I *honestly* feel that the past few months, we've been able to make up for a lot of that lost time."

Glancing over at his dad, his heart skipped a beat. Ed's head was leaning on the window and for a moment, Tom worried he had passed away. But he watched his chest rise and fall with each breath—still strong. He was sure Ed was at peace with the world, something Tom longed for. He must be tired from the drive and the deep and personal conversation.

"I love you, Dad. I always have, though I never told you enough," Tom said softly.

"I love you too, Son." Ed's eyes were still closed, but the words floated about. "Your mother and I always have and always will. They called *us* 'The Greatest Generation.' But to me, *yours* is the Greatest Generation—you are *my* hero." Ed's voice trailed off as he gently slipped back into his dream state.

With tears flowing freely down his cheeks, Tom got off the next exit, drove over the interstate, and headed back toward Sterling Oaks. He and his dad had reached another major milestone—possibly the final one. He wondered if anyone was keeping count.

In the background, the radio quietly played *What a Wonderful World* by Louis Armstrong. Tom reached over to turn the volume up.

> *I see trees of green, red roses too*
> *I see them bloom for me and you*
> *And I think to myself what a wonderful world*

25 - The Last Goodbye

Tom couldn't remember the last time he'd worn a coat and tie. Chris also wore a long-sleeve, button-down dress shirt and tie, even though it was a hot summer day. Today's drive in Sunshine seemed to take longer than before. Both realized this may be their last trip to Sterling Oaks. They were on the way to say a final goodbye to a father, a grandfather, and a World War II veteran—Ed Reilly.

TOM HAD RECEIVED an urgent phone call from Michelle just a few days earlier. Ed had taken a turn for the worse. She urged him to come as soon as he could.

He'd spent a day with his dad the previous weekend, recalling some pleasant childhood memories, even though Ed wasn't totally with it the whole visit. That wasn't uncommon, according to Michelle. But because of the combination of his stroke—and perhaps other undetected TIAs—and the quickening progression of his Alzheimer's disease, the staff noticed Ed's daily routine and demeanor *dramatically* changed. He was quickly going downhill.

They made record time in Sunshine. Earl waved them through the security gate. Tom swore he saw him salute out of the corner of his eye as he quickly drove by.

Wasting no time getting to Ed's room, they gently knocked and walked in. His father was sleeping, but his breathing was noticeably labored. Charles was on duty as his aide. He didn't know how much longer Ed had to live. But he was calm and reassuring there was time.

Charles slowly closed the door on his way out so they could have some quiet time alone with Ed.

Tom looked down at his sleeping father with soft, worried eyes. Ed was cleanly shaven and freshly bathed. He looked peaceful and... *ready*.

It was hard to describe his feelings, but during the past few months, Tom's outlook on life had significantly improved. He had learned more about his father—both before the war and after. He had also grown much closer to Chris since Ed had reentered his life. Most of all, he learned it was okay to let go of old, buried memories. "Manage them" was the term used by several of his new Vietnam veteran friends. And it wasn't just the war memories.

"You can't change what happened; you can only change how you deal with what happened." Michelle had taught him that.

After a few minutes of respectful and emotional silence, Chris excused himself to get a soda and some fresh air. He did not know it would be the last time he'd see his grandfather alive.

A few more minutes passed. As hard as he tried, Tom couldn't take his eyes off his father. He watched Ed's breathing change—change to what he had witnessed many times before in Vietnam—the breath of a dying man. This was different, though. There was no pain, no agony, and no anger. This was his father—his hero. This time, he'd been able to say goodbye to a loved one—something he hadn't been able to do with either his mother or his wife.

He wondered out loud if his father would soon be with Louise. "Is there really a Heaven?" For the first time in longer than Tom could remember, he hoped—*he prayed*—there was a Heaven and... there was a God. A kind and gentle God—one he remembered from before... Vietnam.

With one last gentle breath, Ed Reilly passed quietly into the next realm. It was as if his dad needed to finish mending his relationship with Tom before he could leave to be with Louise again.

Tom spent a few cherished, tearful minutes alone, quietly talking to his father before leaving. He was at peace, something he had not felt in a long time. He had forgiven his father. More importantly, he *knew* his father had forgiven him.

Charles was patiently waiting outside in the hallway, praying to himself. He had a soulful and calm look about him. "I'm sorry, Tom. I prayed you would get here in time and that your father would pass peacefully. Not everyone gets that chance." A tear rolled down Charles' cheek as he spoke.

"He was one of my all-time favorite residents. I know that sounds strange, coming from an old veteran like me. He always had a big heart. Not everyone I take care of—especially those with Alzheimer's—show that type of compassion. But your father *always* did. That's something *I'll* never forget."

Tom leaned with his back against the wall in the hallway.

"I don't understand, Charles. Why did he go so quickly?" Tom was emotionally drained. "We were together only a few days ago. We were just getting to know each other again."

"I think it's because he closed this chapter here on earth. He made amends with you and Chris. He helped you get started with your own healing. And… I think he was ready to be with Louise again, he missed her so much. It's what he wanted and what he believed."

Tom stuck his hand out to shake, but instead, Charles embraced him in a brotherly hug.

"Thank you, Charles. I appreciate all you've done for my dad… *and* for me. I need to find Chris."

"He's in the dining area. I think he knows, but you'll need time with him. I'll call the funeral home. They should have someone here soon. I also need some time to get your father ready.

"It's our policy to close all the doors in the hallway when someone passes away so we don't disturb the other residents and family members when we move Ed. I'll keep the door closed until we're ready to transport your father. It won't be that long."

"Thank you. My dad really liked you. He told me you were his favorite. I'll go find Chris. We'll be here when you're ready."

Tom wasn't sure how to tell his son that his grandfather—the grandfather he had only recently met—was dead. When he sat down, Chris simply asked, "Did Granddad die?"

"Yes. He did. He knew we were here with him, though. After you left, he opened his eyes, but didn't move or say anything. I walked over beside him and he followed me with his eyes. I held his hand. It wasn't as strong as before. I knew it wouldn't be long. And then… he just… passed, letting out one last breath. It was the most peaceful death I have ever witnessed. I am thankful I was there with him. Dad did not die alone."

"Do you think he's with Grandma?" A tear rolled down Chris' cheek and he wiped it away with the back of his hand.

"I *know* he is. He believed it. No matter what I believed before, I believe it now."

Both sat in silence.

After a few minutes, Charles came in and quietly told them he was ready. They walked down the hall to Ed's room and stood outside his door. Tom wondered what the next few minutes would bring.

Charles slowly opened the door. The transporter wheeled his father out on a gurney. He was in a black body bag, similar to the ones Tom was all too familiar with from Vietnam. This was much different, though. He knew this was the right time and the right place and all was right in the world.

Tom stood straight as an arrow at full attention and did something he hadn't done since leaving Vietnam. He saluted his father—his hero—for the final goodbye. Chris saw that and, like his dad, stood and saluted his grandfather.

They followed Ed down the hallway.

Suddenly, Tom stopped dead in his tracks. Chris turned and saw his father like he'd never seen him before. His face was turning ashen as he dropped to his knees and started shaking almost uncontrollably.

"Charles. Charles. Help!"

Charles turned and saw Tom on the ground with his hands clasped over his head. He double-timed it back to where Tom had collapsed. It only took a few moments before Charles realized Tom was having a major panic attack. His veteran combat instincts took over.

"Chris. Go get me a can of soda—quickly."

Chris sprinted down the hall to the break room.

"Tom. It's okay. You're safe. You are *not* in Vietnam. Look at me, Tom. Look at me." Charles' voice was stern, but confident.

Tom glanced up with terrified eyes, something Charles had witnessed many times.

"What is it, Tom? Talk to me."

"It's the body bag, Charles. I knew my dad was in a body bag. I just freaked. I'm sorry. I'm so sorry," Tom was sobbing.

Chris returned with the soda.

"Here take this. Chris got you a Coke. Take it, buddy. Hold it." Charles gently grabbed Tom's arm and handed him the can, wrapping both his hands around it. "Look at it, Tom. Look at the Coke can. Feel it. You're back in *The World*. You're safe. You're with buddies. It's all right."

Charles looked up at Chris with reassuring eyes.

"Chris, can you find Ms. Myers? I think she's in her office. Your dad will be all right. He just needs a little time to decompress. He is having a panic attack brought on by a flashback to Vietnam. It's probably the first one you've seen. He'll be all right, I promise."

Chris ran to find Michelle. Charles turned his attention back to his friend.

"Talk to me, Tom. What do you see?"

"I'm sorry, Charles. I had a flashback of an ambush. There were a couple of guys who didn't make it. They were good buddies. When we went back to search for them, they had been blown to pieces. We had to find them and… put them into body bags. The only thing was, we didn't know whose body parts went into which bag. It was… a mess."

Tom took a deep breath and exhaled, shaking his head side to side trying to remove that gruesome memory. "Whew."

"Is Chris okay? I'm sure I scared the hell out of him." Tom's breathing slowed and his color began to return to normal.

"He's fine. He got you the Coke, and he's gone to find Ms. Myers."

"Oh no. I don't want her to see me like this."

"It's okay, Tom. She works with veterans all the time. She knows that veterans, especially Vietnam vets, experience panic attacks. You'll be fine, I promise.

"Your heart rate is already starting to drop. Come on, let's get you up so we can walk down to the break room. You'll be okay. The worst has passed."

"Thank you, Charles. I appreciate your help… and for helping Chris cope with this. I can't remember the last time I had a flashback like that. And how did you know a can of Coke would help?"

"Unfortunately, there are a lot of veterans who have triggered flashbacks and panic attacks. I've found that if I can give them something familiar to hold on to—see, touch, smell, and taste—it helps calm them down. It doesn't always work, but it's one thing I've learned over the years."

"Tom. It's Michelle. I'm here." She had followed Chris back, almost running in her heels.

"I'm sorry you have to see me like this, Michelle." Tom's voice was weak as he buried his head in his hands. "I guess I had a panic attack after seeing Dad wheeled down the hallway. But now that Chris and Charles—and now you—are here, I'll be okay. I… I just need a few minutes."

Michelle flashed a worried look at Charles, who nodded with a "Yes, he'll be fine" look.

She was grateful for his calming effect. She'd witnessed his uncanny ability to work with veterans time and time again. She knew this was *the* reason he was so well-loved by all the residents and staff.

Michelle asked Tom if he wanted to go outside for a smoke. "No, I'll be okay."

That shocked all three of them. But having both Charles and Michelle there alongside his son, Tom knew this was what he needed more than anything right now—close friends and family that understood what he had been through.

TOM AND CHRIS walked into the Oak Room, the massive main auditorium at Sterling Oaks. Every seat was filled. A few of the "younger," eighty-year-old residents stood in the back. *Ed must have touched a lot of people.*

Charles and Michelle met them at the entrance and walked with them down to the front center row. Tom acknowledged Tony Jones with a nod and a weak smile, who also sat in the front.

As soon as they took their seats, Charles strolled up to the front of the auditorium. This was the first funeral—memorial service—Tom had attended since Barbara died.

Charles was a big man. Today, though, he appeared much larger and sharply dressed as a pastor in a dark gray suit and tie, not an aide wearing scrubs in the memory unit. He was tall and handsome and carried that air of confidence of a seasoned combat veteran. Confidence that Tom recently rediscovered within himself.

"Good morning. Thank you for coming. This is a most blessed day the Lord has given us. Can I get an Amen?

"We're here today to celebrate and honor a friend to all, a veteran of World War II, a father to Tom, and a grandfather to Chris… Mr. Ed Reilly. Please bow your heads for a prayer.

"O God, we gather today to honor one of your soldiers who fought the good fight for his country and for his family. While we mourn the loss of Ed Reilly today, we are grateful he is with Louise again, who left him so early in life. We know he will now be with her eternally. We thank you for bringing his son and his grandson together to form a never-ending, all-loving bond."

Tom struggled as he listened to the opening prayer. Charles had a wonderful delivery, pausing at the right moment to make a point, his voice full of passion for both Ed and the Lord.

But Tom's heart was heavy with thoughts of his father and why he had been so stubborn when he was young. Why he was stubborn when Tom came home from Vietnam. And why he was stubborn when Tom walked out of his life. *Foolish pride? Or was it something else?*

"Grant that through the passion, the death, and the resurrection of your Son, that they may share in the joy of your Heavenly kingdom and will rejoice in you forever. We ask this through Jesus Christ, our Lord and Savior, Amen."

Charles' prayer suddenly made sense. Ed's stubbornness was one reason he'd survived his war. *And* the reason he was who he was. That stubbornness brought them together again, after twenty-five years. A second chance, as Charles so succinctly put it.

That was God laying his hand on Tom's heart to accept his father the way he was, *and* to accept himself.

"I'm sure many of you knew that Ed was a deeply spiritual man. It should not surprise you he planned this memorial service. That was his nature, taking care of things himself, so there was less for others to do. He left us far too early in life. But as you'll soon hear, he left several lasting legacies.

"Ed had several favorite passages in the Bible and wanted me to read a couple of these to you. They were important to him. He hoped they would speak to you. "I'm reading from the New International Version Bible. Our first passages are from the book of Romans, Chapter Eight, verse 18 and verse 38.

"Verse 18 tells us, *I consider that our present sufferings are not worth comparing with the glory that will be revealed in us.*

"And from Verse 38, *For I am convinced that neither death nor life, neither angels nor demons, neither the present nor the future, nor any powers, neither height nor depth, nor anything else in all creation, will be able to separate us from the love of God that is in Christ Jesus our Lord.*"

Was his father still speaking to him… through Charles? Is there life after death? His dad believed it. Tom was convinced—maybe he knew all along—that his mother and father were now together in Heaven for all eternity.

"Our second passage comes from Second Timothy, Chapter Four, verses 7 and 8."

Tom's eyes narrowed as he looked up at Charles. He knew this verse all too well. It was a common passage spoken at memorial services in Vietnam. It was also the one read for his friend, Wayne Johnson—Sunshine.

"I have fought the good fight, I have finished the race, I have kept the faith. Now there is in store for me the crown of righteousness, which the Lord, the righteous Judge, will award me on that day—and not only to me, but also to all who have longed for his appearing."

Charles paused as he glanced out at the guests attending the memorial service. All eyes were on him as he spoke solemnly.

"I've been working here at Sterling Oaks since we first opened in 1997. Ed was one of our co-founders, moving in about a month after we opened. I only knew him from afar, since I work primarily in the

Memory Support Neighborhood. I've always made it a point to get to know as many residents as I can. I know most everyone, but I know *all* the veterans."

Charles took a deep breath. He was beginning to choke up a little.

"Let me share with you one story I think you'll appreciate. It was one of Ed's favorites.

"As most of you know, Ed fought in Europe during World War II. Like most World War II veterans coming home, he got busy with life, started a family, and a business. Time flew by fast, as we all know. The older we get, the faster it slips by, doesn't it?" Charles glanced out at the attendees, many nodding their heads at his comment.

"He finally had the opportunity to go back to visit France and Luxembourg to help celebrate the fiftieth anniversary of the end of World War II. As you can imagine, there were plenty of celebrations and thousands of people from all over the world attending. Ed didn't think he'd run into anyone he had served with.

"Imagine his surprise when he saw a familiar face—his old platoon sergeant. The last time they had seen each other was toward the end of the Battle of the Bulge. His platoon sergeant had been wounded and captured. Ed assumed he had been killed.

"But the Lord works in mysterious ways. They ran into each other in Luxembourg while visiting one of the many towns they helped liberate. Both immediately recognized each other, but neither could recall the other's name—it *had* been fifty years.

"As they curiously walked toward each other—like a sign from God—both recalled each other's nicknames. It shouldn't surprise you that Ed's nickname was, 'Steeler'. The sergeant's was simply, "Sarge." That's all they could remember. Neither knew the other's actual name, but shouted out their nicknames from the war, instantly recognizing one another."

Charles paused for a moment with a slight chuckle.

"It's funny the things you remember from years past. You can almost transport yourself back to that specific time and specific place. We all know there's a reason for that. While we often call these events 'coincidences,' I'm convinced it is God's way of remaining anonymous."

Several attendees nodded, agreeing with Charles' comments.

"That was one of Ed's favorites and he wanted me to share that with you today. He had a knack for telling a story, then spinning the Lord into the meaning of that particular story. I don't know how he did it, but he just did."

Charles took a deep breath. "Tony Jones, I believe you wanted to say a few things."

Tony slowly walked up to the podium, pulled out a sheet of paper from his inside coat pocket, and slipped on his reading glasses. His eyes were tired and red. He spoke for a few minutes about the time they first met, when Ed's business took off and he needed legal advice. Both had sons who had fought in the Vietnam War. Unfortunately, Tony's son had been killed. Ed Reilly became the brother Tony never had, creating a unique bond and friendship.

Tom was concerned that he might bring up the history between him and his father, but was grateful when he didn't. Instead, Tony spoke of how Ed had found new life getting to know his son and grandson over the past few months. He also joked about his affection for the Pittsburgh Steelers and his return trip to visit France and Luxembourg. It was a fitting tribute by Ed's closest friend.

When Tony finished, Charles strolled up to the podium. "Chris, I know you have a few words to say about your grandfather."

Chris was anxious as he stood, a slight tremble in his hands. But after looking at his dad, who urged him on with a "you can do this" nod, he found his confidence.

He read from a document he'd prepared himself with only a little input from his dad. He wanted to let everyone know how proud he was of his grandfather *and* his own father. Chris spoke about how the three of them connected after so many years. While he wished he'd known his grandfather longer, he was grateful for the brief time he had with him.

"He was a warrior—before, during, and after the war. He always stood for what he thought was right. After his wife Louise died, he found the necessary strength to carry on. His old Army division's motto was, '*Only Moves Forward*'. That was the motto he followed until his dying breath."

Tom was proud of his son. When he turned to face his grandfather's picture, stood at attention, and delivered a perfect hand salute, Tom lost it. He knew his father would be proud of his grandson.

Chris sat down next to his father, who gave him a big hug. Michelle wrapped her arms around both and hugged them tightly.

Charles stood, slowly walked over to the podium, pulled out his handkerchief, and dabbed away a few tears. He spoke softly into the microphone. "Tom, Ed wanted me to let you know, he saved the best for last."

Tom stood, slightly trembling as he straightened his sports coat. He glanced at Michelle and Chris, and finally at his dad's Army portrait on the easel next to the podium. The closer he moved toward the podium, the stronger and more confident he felt. He had been given this second chance, and he wasn't going to blow it.

He wasn't sure what he was going to say at his father's memorial service. When he thought about it earlier, part of him wanted to share his anger and angst in the hopes it would help *him* heal. But that anger had disappeared over the past few months.

Part of him wanted to share that he had kept his wife and his son from meeting his father—something no one should ever do. But there was no need. His father had spent time with Chris, and Tom *knew* that Barbara and Ed had met in Heaven, along with Louise.

Instead, Tom focused on what his father had meant to him while growing up, and what he meant to him when he was in Vietnam—a rock, like his mother. A rock that helped him overcome and conquer his fears during the war and helped him to survive.

Those same feelings helped him to come home—*really* come home. And he was blessed for that chance to be with him before he died.

Tom got through his entire tribute without shedding a tear. Ed would have been—*was*—proud of him. He'd lost twenty-five years with his father and thirty years buried within himself.

What was it that Charles said? *"I know I'll live in Vietnam the rest of my life. But it won't stop me from living the best life I can."* It was time to catch up and get things right with *The World—His* World.

After Tom finished his praise for his father and sat down, Charles walked back to the podium. "Ed attended church service here at Sterling Oaks every Sunday. He told me more than once, he had only missed two Sunday services since his wife, Louise, passed away. That is amazing. Ed was an outstanding leader and a gentlemen's man.

"He knew all the mainstream hymns. If it was up to him, we'd sing all 373 hymns in the book, from start to finish." That brought a chuckle from the attendees. "However, in the interest of time, we'll only sing two of his favorites. Please turn to page 124 in your hymnal to sing *It Is Well With My Soul.*"

Tom didn't know the words to this hymn, though he remembered it from his early youth. He mouthed the words as he recalled attending Sunday school and church every Sunday with his parents. Times were much simpler back then.

> *Whatever my lot, thou hast taught me to say*
> *It is well, it is well, with my soul*

"Now please turn to page 225 for our closing hymn *Amazing Grace.*"

Tom knew this hymn. He'd sung it many times in church when he was growing up. He also heard it at almost every memorial service he attended for a fallen soldier. It was the closest he felt to God, when he was *over there.*

> *Through many dangers, toils and snares*
> *We have already come.*
> *T'was grace that brought us safe thus far*
> *And grace will lead us home*

There were so many memorial services in Vietnam, Tom had lost count not long after he arrived. While he wasn't required to attend them all, he said goodbye and paid respect to *all* of his buddies who were killed in action. It was such an important tradition of the Black Lions—of *all* military branches. Some services were harder than others—Sunshine's the hardest, by far.

There was no body nor casket at an in-country memorial service. The body was already on its way home. The "spirit" of the soldier who died was represented with a pair of boots and a rifle, stuck in the ground by its bayonet between the boots. A set of dog tags hung from the pistol grip of the rifle and a helmet rested atop the rifle butt.

Tom only spoke at one memorial service—Sunshine's. Even then, he struggled, trying to express how much he loved his brother—*all* of his combat brothers. *What do you say about someone you tried to save who gave their life to save you?*

Somehow today, at his own father's memorial service, the words rang truer than ever before. Tom reached for and held Michelle's soft hand. He blinked back tears he'd held for a long time, but they flowed freely. Chris grabbed his other hand and whispered, "It'll be okay, Dad. Granddad is with Louise now."

"One last thing I'd like to share, and this comes from Ed's son, Tom. During World War II, the Army issued soldiers a small pocket Bible. Ed's father had written a note inside the front cover: *'Read Psalm 91 every day and you will come home.'* Ed said he read that passage every day or night. In Ed's own words, *'I did… and I did.'*

"Tom shared that story with me a few days ago. He also asked me to make sure I place this same pocket Bible in Ed's breast pocket. He told me, *'My father carried this Bible through hell. I want him to have it when he's in Heaven.'*" Charles held the Bible up for everyone to see. "Tom, your will *will* be done. Amen."

Charles closed the memorial service with a solemn prayer. Tom knew that he'd seen death come many times and in many ways—both in Vietnam *and* at Sterling Oaks—each person meant something special to him. He realized the truth in Charles' words. *"Those who have been hurt the most often have the greatest ability to heal."*

After the memorial service, a few people walked over to offer their condolences.

Ester was still teary-eyed, dabbing her eyes with a soft handkerchief, but gave both Tom and Chris a strong hug and said a few comforting words about his father. Tom knew she had lost a companion. But he also knew that Ester *knew* Ed was now with Louise. That thought seemed to comfort her.

Earl was there, too. He was the first person Tom had met at Sterling Oaks. He would never forget Earl and the love of old cars they shared. He recently learned Earl was the security guard who first found his father wandering around the campus—that first time when Michelle had contacted him. *This really is a small world.*

In the background, Tom noticed a man slowly walking toward him that he'd met—and judged—earlier, Hank Ennis.

"Hello, Tom," Hank said quietly and respectfully. "And you must be Chris. I'm so sorry about your father. Ed was a gracious and honorable man, well-respected around here, and a great friend to everyone. I will truly miss him."

Was this the same awful Hank Ennis he'd met a few weeks ago? The same loud and obnoxious Hank Ennis that interrupted their lunch with Ester?

"I tend to brag about my own children," Hank offered with a faint smile. "To tell you the truth, they are too busy to come visit me. I only see one or two of them a year. I wish they were closer. But I am *so* pleased you could visit your father so many times. I know you two reconnected and made up for lost time."

Made up for lost time? Were Tom and Ed finally able to do that?

"Well… I know you've got others to talk with, so I'll say goodbye for now. I hope if you're up this way again, you'll stop by."

"Thank you, Hank. I appreciate your kind words."

Tom watched in astonishment as Hank strolled out the door, dabbing away tears with his handkerchief. This was *not* the same man that he'd met a few weeks earlier. *Did Hank's attitude change because he observed Ed and Tom's relationship grow?* He appreciated seeing a softer, less harsh side of Hank. *This* Hank appeared to be more genuine than the one he had previously met.

Michelle held Tom's hand and had her arm around Chris. Even though he had just lost his father, for the first time in a long, long time, Tom was at peace and… *almost* normal.

26 - Vietnam—Letting Go

A few days following his father's memorial service, Tom decided it was time… time to unveil his Vietnam memories. Like his father said, Chris deserved to know.

Tom realized in many ways, he was much like his father. But he didn't want to keep *his* war from Chris like Ed had kept his from him. His father had finally lowered his barriers after all those years. Tom wasn't going to wait that long. He wanted to make sure his son would never forget what he—*they*—had sacrificed to serve their country.

Despite the recent flood of miserable memories, he still loved his country—he *always* had. He just needed his father to remind him.

"CHRIS. Can you come into the living room, please?"

"Sure, Dad. Be right there."

It had been an emotional struggle for Tom to get to this point. But between Michelle, Charles, several Vietnam veterans he recently befriended, *and* his father, he had summoned up the necessary courage to share this buried part of his life. He was tired of hiding from these memories—memories that had created an abyss between him and his father. He wasn't going to let that happen with his son.

He'd spent quite a bit of time rummaging through his Vietnam graveyard that had been buried in the bottom of his desk drawer and pulled out everything. At first, he struggled with these painful reminders, but now he was prepared to show everything to Chris. He needed to tell his son what war does to a man.

"What's up? Wow, what is…? Is this your Vietnam stuff, Dad? Holy shit." Chris' eyes bulged. The marble-topped coffee table was covered with photos, medals, and letters. It was obvious that his father had been up most of the night sorting through his past.

"It's time you knew a little more about my war," Tom said solemnly. "The things on this table won't tell you everything, but it may give you an idea of what I had to do to survive. Maybe now you'll understand why I am the way I am."

Chris walked over and sat down next to his dad on the couch. Tom took a deep breath and slowly exhaled through pursed lips, letting go more of his demons.

"I was a much different person in 'Nam than I am now. Over there, I had to kill to survive. Over here, I'm still fighting these memories to survive.

"During the past few months, your grandfather talked more about his service in World War II—stories I'd never heard. It made me realize I shouldn't keep this part of my life from you, like he did from me."

Tom looked at his son, who was still in a state of shock, his eyes shifting from memory to memory. "I'm not proud of everything I did, Chris. But I am proud—*finally*—that I can share this with you.

"Last night, I read through the letters I wrote home to your grandparents. They brought back a flood of memories and made me realize how much I'd changed since then. You should read them when you have time, but only if you want to." Tom set the box of letters off to the side on the end table. Next, he pulled out his medals.

"I told you before I had been wounded—this is my Purple Heart. See this small oak leaf cluster in the middle?" Tom tapped the oak leaf a few times, remembering the day when he was shot, trying to save Sunshine. "That means I was awarded two Purple Hearts. I was actually hit a few more times, but they were only small pieces of shrapnel I pulled out myself."

Tom carefully laid the Purple Heart back in its case and picked up the next medal.

"This is my Bronze Star; you remember my story. The 'V' in the middle stands for Valor. Your grandfather also has one."

"I remember both stories."

Tom grinned with pride and looked at his son. "I'll be honest with you, Chris. After Dad told us how *he* rushed that German machine gun nest, I'm not so sure I deserve this for what *I* did.

"This is my Combat Infantry Badge. I didn't realize how important it really was to me until Dad talked about the closeness of soldiers. He was absolutely right. It means more to me now, thanks to him.

"You know what these are, don't you?"

"They're dog tags, right?"

"Yep. I wore these every day. Fortunately, I came home with both. Do you know why there are two?

"No."

"If a soldier is killed in action, one dog tag stays with him, usually on a long chain around his neck. The platoon sergeant takes the other and gives it to the unit commander to start the process of notifying the next of kin.

"A lot of grunts kept the second dog tag in their shoelace—that's what I did. Because they're made of metal, they make too much noise while you are humping through the jungle. Another reason is if you got blown up, your boot would most likely still be intact."

"Dad, didn't soldiers have names on their uniforms, even when they were on patrol?"

"Yeah, they did. But it was common for soldiers to give other grunts their clean uniforms if they were wounded or flew out early. So, you couldn't rely on just the nametag.

"There are several other medals. This is the Vietnam Service Medal. All soldiers who fought in Vietnam have one. This is the Republic of Vietnam Campaign Medal. Like the Vietnam Service Medal, all soldiers received one—at least, those who were there for six months, or if they were wounded.

"This is the National Defense Service Medal. All U.S. military personnel received this medal whether they were in the war or not."

Tom placed all the medals back into their cases, and laid them side by side on the table.

"I was in the Second Battalion of the 28th Infantry Regiment. We had a special shoulder patch. Our nickname was the 'Black Lions of Cantigny.' The Black Lions have been around since before World War I and have quite a military lineage. There were a lot of great guys in that battalion and in my unit, Charlie Company. I'm sure you can read more about them on the computer.

"This is the Big Red One patch—the First Infantry Division. It was rumored that during World War I, a general decided the soldiers in his division needed to be identified with a shoulder insignia. He cut a red numeral '1' from his red flannel underwear and someone sewed it onto a piece of gray cloth from the uniform of a captured German soldier. It's just a rumor, but I think a good one, don't you?"

"I like it, Dad. What are these?" Chris pulled out two lighters, both with inscriptions.

"These are called Zippos. We used these to light cigarettes and whatever else we needed to burn. They're not used as much today. Most everyone these days uses disposable butane lighters. But during the war, these were quite popular. Most grunts had them engraved by the locals."

"What do the inscriptions mean?"

Tom was prepared to answer *that* question. In a way, it described precisely how his attitude changed from the time he first arrived until he left. He took a deep breath.

"When I first got to Vietnam, I was all gung ho. I wanted to be the best soldier I could be. At the time, this was a popular inscription, *'Death Is My Business and Business Has Been Good.'* That basically meant I was there to kill the enemy, no matter if they were NVA or VC.

"They taught us that the enemy was a target and *not* a human being. Either I shoot him or he shoots me. It was that simple. Or so I thought. There was no time to figure out if it was right or wrong. It was just necessary to survive. You either got good, or you got dead.

"I can honestly tell you, Chris, I was only trying to keep myself and my buddies alive. I wasn't trying to see how many of the enemy I could kill.

"Besides, most firefights took place at night. When everyone is shooting in the dark at moving enemy targets, you have no clue how many enemy you may have personally killed."

Holding the second lighter in his hand, Tom took an extra moment, shifting his weight on the couch. He tapped the lighter with his index finger.

"I had this second Zippo engraved not long after I returned from my mother's funeral. My attitude toward the war had completely changed. It's difficult to explain, but I didn't have the same sense of purpose as when I first got over there. The war just didn't make sense to me.

"We were fighting for people that didn't want us there and killing people that didn't want us in their country. Back here in the states, people didn't want us to be over there. So why were we in Vietnam in the first place?

"That's when I got the second Zippo engraved, *"NAM 68-69. We the Unwilling, Led by the Unqualified, to Kill the Unfortunate & Die for the Ungrateful."*

Chris thought about that for a minute.

"Dad. I know you volunteered for the Army. I understand that was the patriotic thing to do. Granddad was drafted, though he said he wanted to join the Army after Japan attacked Pearl Harbor. Like he mentioned earlier, World War II was a different war.

"Like both you and Granddad said, wars change people. From what little I've learned about the Vietnam War, it changed a lot of people, both who were there and those who weren't. I *do* understand why the war changed you.

"You told me not to say this, Dad, but you really are *my* hero." Chris reached to hug his father. They shared a few quiet moments—father and son.

Tom glanced at the photographs on the coffee table. There were a few of him and other soldiers in his unit. He picked up each photo and after pausing a moment, told his son who was in the photo. He didn't forget names. These were men with whom he had proudly served. Many fought the same fights he did, both in Vietnam and at home. These were men—*brothers*—he would never forget.

Tom picked up another photo and sucked in a deep breath. It had been a long time since he'd looked at this particular photo. He spoke without looking up.

"This man next to me, Chris… this… this is Wayne Johnson. We nicknamed him 'Sunshine.' He and I became close after my mother's funeral.

"He was from Boston, a good kid from a good family *like me*. He joined the Army, *like me,* and came in as a replacement, *like me,* soon after I got back. When he first arrived in-country, he was only nineteen years old, *like me*. We took this photo while on stand-down in Lai Khe. We had just returned from a patrol and were trying to enjoy life. At least, as best we could while in the middle of a war.

"We hung out a lot together. There was something about Wayne that made everybody like him. He always had a kind word to say about everything—never negative. In fact, when he first arrived, we used to kid him because he didn't cuss. I took him under my wing to teach him the fine art of the Army language."

Tom smiled, cherishing those long forgotten memories of a man who saved his life—a man he called *his* own hero.

"Is that why you named your car, 'Sunshine'?"

"Yes, it is." Tom carefully placed the photo down. "Sunshine always brings me back to a safe place. I think Wayne would like my GTO, don't you?"

"Absolutely. I *know* he would."

"Dad. There's something I don't understand."

"What, Chris?"

"You told me earlier that a normal tour of duty in Vietnam was only one year, right?"

"That's right."

"If you went over in January 1968, you should have been home in January 1969. But you didn't get back until April 1969. Why did they keep you longer? Was it because you came back for grandma's funeral?"

"Not really. When I first enlisted, I joined for two years. At one point, I even thought I might make the Army a career." Tom chuckled.

"I spent several months in basic and infantry training. Normally, I would have spent a year in Vietnam, then transfer to another post for the rest of my enlistment term. Most likely, that would have been somewhere in the United States.

"But considering what I experienced—both in 'Nam and here in the states—I didn't want to wear a uniform any longer than I had to. The Army let you extend your tour to get an early discharge, if that makes sense. I would've had almost six months left of my enlistment if I rotated out. I just couldn't stand the thought of coming home to a country that didn't appreciate what we were doing over there.

"It's hard to explain, Chris, but I felt safer and more welcomed in the Vietnam boonies, fighting the enemy alongside my buddies, than I did back here in *The World*. That's why I extended my tour for three months—to get out early.

"Believe it or not, I still think that was the right decision. While I regret some things I did, *that* is not one of them. In fact, when it came time to leave, it was harder to leave my buddies in Vietnam than it was to leave home the first time. In some ways, I feel like part of me is still over there."

Tom had that look, that thousand-yard stare again. Chris finally understood what it meant.

"I'm glad you made it back, Dad." He reached over and put his hand on his dad's shoulder and looked him straight in the eye. "I hope someday, you'll finally be able to leave Vietnam behind and *really* come home."

TOM HAD ATTENDED several veteran meetings and each one left him wanting more. As Charles reported, almost everyone showed up every month. He was getting to know several. They all had things in common: honor, love of country, sacrifice, and brotherhood. They all still fought a war here at home—much different from combat. A war that only Vietnam War veterans understood—*a war of indifference*.

Most Americans didn't give a rat's ass about the war when he first returned home—even through the eighties. Like Tom, many of these men continued to fight their own individual battles. Most made it, but several couldn't and gave up. Because these vets met regularly and shared their lives with others who had been *over there*, they were able to live somewhat normal lives in *The World*. And that was what he cherished the most—a *normal* life.

Tom had grown closer to Charles. He was more than just an aide who worked in the Memory Support Neighborhood. He was, as his father had succinctly put it, a *"beacon deacon."* His father's disease also helped create this special friendship—a bond between two Vietnam combat veterans.

Almost every time they met for coffee or at the veteran's meetings, Charles was full of life, never down, and always joyful. He reminded Tom of Sunshine—never a negative thing to say about anyone and *always* positive.

"Life is too short to hang out with angry people." Charles was right. He talked a lot about his life before finding the Lord—mostly his drinking and drug addiction. While he shared *that* painful past, he never spoke about any of his experiences in Vietnam—good or bad.

IT WAS TOM'S TURN TO SHARE, something he'd previously talked about with Charles. He stood at the front of the room, looking out over the two dozen plus Vietnam veterans, all respectfully quiet.

"I buried my father a few weeks ago. He was also a war veteran. Until a few months ago, I wasn't sure he was still alive. We sort of... 'parted ways'..." Tom stated, using air finger quotes, "after I got back from 'Nam. We hadn't seen each other for over twenty-five years. I had tried to bury my memories of him, as well as my own Vietnam memories, but I just couldn't."

Tom shifted his weight and stood a little taller.

"Earlier this year, he found me and asked that I visit him at a retirement home. He had been diagnosed with Alzheimer's disease. How could I *not* go?

"I consider myself extremely fortunate to have been able to reconnect with him, especially after all those years." Tom glanced over at Charles and smiled. "Charles would use the term 'blessed.' You see, when I was growing up, he was my hero. In fact, I wanted so much to be like him, I volunteered to join the Army. I wanted to serve my country, like he did, for what I believed was right; just like so many of you.

"I wish the hell I hadn't turned my back on him all those years.

But I feel like during the past few months, I'd been given a second chance to know who he truly was. And I'll tell you… I found out he was *still* the hero I grew up admiring."

Tom wasn't sure if anyone was listening, but no one spoke as all eyes were on him. All he wanted to do was to share his recent personal struggle with his new found brotherhood. He wanted to convey the fact that no one should let the Vietnam War destroy their lives, their relationships, or their families.

"War changes men. It changed my father. It changed me. It changed all of us. My dad's death put things in perspective. Second chances don't always come around. I wanted to—*needed to*—make things right with my dad before he died. I can honestly say I was able to do that. I also intend to make things right before *I* die."

When Tom finished, not a soul spoke. Many were in deep thought—not the thousand-yard stare looking back on their *past* lives, but more of a hopeful look at their own *future*.

Charles walked over and firmly shook his hand.

"Welcome home, Tom. Welcome home."

AFTER THE MEETING wound down, Vernon Driggers, the quiet veteran, slowly made his way over. He walked with a slight limp, one leg shorter than the other. Tom had noticed him listening intently when he spoke about his father and rebuilding their relationship.

"Hi, Vernon."

Vernon was a little taller than Tom, but still had that somewhat distant, wary look. He wore jeans and a plain dark green polo shirt, and he had a noticeable beer belly. Tom assumed he, like himself, had trouble trusting people. When he was young, he trusted almost everyone, until they proved different. *After* the war, he trusted no one, *until* they proved they could be trusted.

"I heard what you said, Tom. It brought back memories of my dad. He died a long time ago. We never could see eye-to-eye. Even though we both served, he didn't think I did enough. I was wounded twice and got shipped home before my tour was up. I was tired, I'd seen and done too much, and I just wanted to get the hell out of there.

I hoped he would understand, but he didn't seem to. My dad died before I could talk with him about Vietnam.

"Hearing your story tonight helped me better understand my own father. When he died, I tried to tell him how I felt, but I'm not sure he heard me from the grave."

Vernon moved a little closer. "Do you mind if I ask you a personal question?"

Tom wasn't sure he was ready to answer any questions that may dwell on his past. He almost replied with Michelle's stock answer, *"Just because you ask doesn't mean I'll answer,"* but stopped short, and simply said, "Sure, fire away."

"You mentioned at one time you had a drinking problem. But now, it looks like you're able to manage it."

"And you want to know how?"

"Yeah," Vernon said quietly, but loud enough for Tom to hear.

"Actually, it was my deceased wife and 'Nam buddy that pulled me out of that gutter," Tom stated clearly, with newly found confidence.

"After my wife, Barbara, died, I slipped into a deep depression and drank a lot more than I should have. Our son was only two years old at the time.

"One night, I was driving home and stopped for a drink. I stayed a little too long and had a little—well, *a lot*—to drink. But I managed to stumble back to my car and started driving. The next thing I remember, I was in a ditch, out of sight from anyone passing by on the road. I was there almost all night.

"I woke up from a dream—one of those dreams that, you know, seems so real. Suddenly, Barbara appeared in my dream, alongside my 'Nam buddy, Sunshine. That was strange enough. They had never met, and I *never* told Barbara about him, but the message was crystal clear.

"I vividly remember Barbara telling me, *'You can't go on living like this, Tom. You've got a son who needs you. I need you to take care of him, love him, and raise him like I was there.'* Sunshine spoke up next and said to me—clear as day, I swear it—*'I didn't die protecting your sorry ass for you to waste your life away on alcohol. You've got to get your shit together, Tom. Clean it up and make something of yourself. Make me proud.'*

"The next day, I stopped drinking—cold turkey. It wasn't hard. All I had to do was to look at my son and I saw Barbara's sparkling eyes speaking to me. I'd look in my bathroom mirror and see Sunshine standing behind me with that big ol' grin. He *always* had my back.

"There was so much love in our little family, I knew from then on what I needed to do. And that was to take care of Chris like Barbara and Sunshine were still here with me."

He had previously shared his dream with Charles, who said with a broad acknowledging smile, *"That was the Lord talking to you, Tom."*

"Don't get me wrong, Vernon. While I stopped drinking back then when I needed to, I find now I'm able to drink responsibly—I *manage* it. For sure, I don't drink when I drive. I learned that lesson the hard way," Tom added with a smile.

Tom had noticed Charles glancing over in their direction, but waiting out of earshot. A few minutes passed before Charles made his way over.

"Tom, Vernon. Glad you guys hooked up. Vernon's been coming to our meetings for what say, three years now?"

"That's right, Sarge."

"This is the first time I've seen him speak up—glad to see that, Vernon. I'm sure you both have some things in common to share. Anything I can do to help, just give me a call."

"Thanks, Sarge," both replied simultaneously as Charles turned to talk to others.

"Thanks, Tom. I still struggle, and drinking is part of it. But I haven't had to deal with what you've been through."

"I'm glad you haven't had to either, Vernon. But we all have to find our way back home, don't we?"

"Yeah. Charles always tells us we will never forget Vietnam, or what we did over there—good or bad. I'm not looking for closure. I know that won't happen until after I die. I just want to be a normal person, like I was… *before* 'Nam."

Vernon had avoided direct eye contact with Tom. But then he looked Tom straight in the eye. "What I want, more than anything right now, is peace—peace with my family and peace with myself."

"I know where you're at, Vernon. I'm there, too. Thanks to my dad and thanks to this veterans group, I think I'm on the road to healing. Like Charles said, if there's anything I can do to help, I'm a phone call away."

"I will, Tom. Maybe we can get together for lunch sometime?"

"That sounds good to me. Let's plan on it."

"Thanks. Have a great night. I'll see you next month."

27 - The Wall

Tom didn't sleep a wink in the D.C. hotel. He knew exactly why. Even though he'd been planning this trip to the Vietnam War Memorial—*The Wall*—for several weeks, he *thought* he was prepared. A few of his new veteran friends had made the trip in the past, but expressed mixed emotions. Several said it helped bring closure. Others stated, *"too little, too late."*

Charles had been multiple times. He convinced Tom it would do him good to visit *The Wall*. Tom was apprehensive, but he hoped this trip would help him better cope with his Vietnam nightmares.

"You are not that different from your father," Charles had told Tom a few weeks earlier. "You've both been to war, fought for what you believed in, and done things you regretted. But you both made it back home in one piece.

"I know you don't want to hear this, Tom, but your father got over his anxieties. While the wars were different, they made you into the men you are today.

"What bothers you the most?"

"Over there or over here?"

"Both."

Tom pondered over the question.

"Over there, the hardest thing was losing my buddies. Over here… *over here*, it's the simple fact that we"—Tom used *we* more than *I* these days—"never felt welcomed home after fighting for the very freedoms our country sent us over to defend."

That was one of the most difficult statements Tom had ever said out loud. While simplistic, it stated *exactly* what he, and many Vietnam War veterans, experienced.

The last few months had been quite dramatic—a major change in his life. Tom had been given a second chance. No, he'd been given *several* second chances. He was grateful for that. He *knew* there was some sort of divine intervention, but he wasn't sure what. However, he was convinced these events were not merely coincidences.

He had reconnected with his father and made amends. He had seen him change from a confident and proud man to one who was literally losing his mind. Most of all, he was thankful to have been able to spend the last few months with him. His father had forgiven him for walking out of his life. And he had forgiven his father for the angry words he had spoken so many years ago.

More importantly, Tom had forgiven himself.

He understood how the war changed his dad. Their renewed relationship also helped him better understand his *own* war and internal struggles. With his father's help, he exorcised many of his Vietnam demons. He realized he still needed more time, but knew he was on the right path.

Both Michelle and Charles had helped Tom accept the fact that he would never forget Vietnam—he would carry those memories with him to the grave. There would be triggers that would set off flashbacks and memories. He had to learn to accept them and deal with them. They would always be a part of his life.

While he had carried the burden of haunted and guilty memories around for thirty years, he found it really wasn't that difficult to let go. Instead of sliding down that dangerous path, they taught him to focus on the positive things he had done, both in 'Nam *and* what he was doing now. *"You have to talk about your past so you can look forward to your future."*

Michelle had helped him better understand PTSD and how to anticipate and overcome the ongoing episodes. He now counted her as one of his few friends. His father's disease had brought them together. They had bonded because of their mutual friends, family, and similar Vietnam War experiences. Tom was not alone—not anymore.

She had suggested the next time he had a nightmare, to not only journal the nightmare, but also to "rewrite" the ending in his *own* words on *his* terms. Doing so might help rewire his brain and thought process. *"When you have that nightmare again, force your thoughts to finish the dream the way you want—your ending."* That was an interesting conversation they had a few weeks earlier.

"Tom, do you ever dream about sex?" Michelle asked, seemingly out of the blue.

He cautiously answered, "Yes," as he perked up, not knowing what she was *really* asking.

"Do you wake up in the middle of that dream, only wanting to close your eyes and 'finish' the dream, *your* way?"

He swore she was flirting with him. Or was she just being professional and trying to help?

"Yes," this time with a little less caution.

"So, you can rewrite the ending of *that* dream about sex… in your mind… half asleep. Am I correct?"

"Yes."

That hit Tom like a hammer—he realized Michelle's simple analogy. She just handed him a key to help "manage" his nightmares.

"It may not work all the time, but it's a proven technique that works not only for combat veterans but also others who may also experience PTSD."

He had done that a few times as she'd suggested, and found that it helped. *"It's not an exact science, but it's worth a try."*

They had been on several dates and enjoyed each other's company. However, both were wary of quick romances and wanted this relationship to grow. They agreed not to rush into anything. Even though she didn't say it out loud, Tom knew Michelle was cautious about becoming involved with another Vietnam veteran.

She was the first woman that he had strong feelings for since Barbara had died. He worried his nightmares and flashbacks would return and drive her away like he thought they did Barbara. Michelle kept reassuring him he was not responsible for Barbara's death. While he *knew* that, he still carried some guilt.

Chris seemed to be all right with their growing relationship. He even told his dad several times that he thought his mother would have liked Michelle. *Was his son giving him permission to love another woman?*

Tom had also struck up another friendship with Vernon Driggers, a fellow combat veteran. He was still quiet as a mouse at the monthly veteran meetings, but they had also met several times for lunch. They continued to talk about their fathers and their shared past Vietnam experiences. Both had lost their fathers. Tom had reconciled with his. Vernon didn't get that chance.

They were veteran buddies, and each shared their cell number. *"Call me if you need me. Anytime, day or night."* Neither had called other than to get together, though they agreed the lifeline would help, if needed. Both had experienced that deep emotional valley many veterans felt where life may not be worth living.

Vernon had been a Specialist in the 25th Infantry Division, also known as the "Tropic Lightning" Division. The 25th was headquartered in the Cu Chi area in Tri-Corps, known for miles of underground tunnels used by the Viet Cong and NVA for sneaking around and to store caches of food and weapons. He had seen more than his share of combat and had at one time been a "tunnel rat," crawling through underground tunnels with nothing but a flashlight and a .45 pistol.

He harbored more internal struggles than Tom. He mentioned he'd been involved in several incidents where civilians had been "accidentally" killed when their hooches burned. Vernon didn't go into details, but said it happened soon after witnessing several buddies blown up—*vaporized*—in an ambush, only a few feet away. He obviously wasn't proud of what he'd done.

Tom himself had "accidentally" executed a prisoner.

A VC sniper had just killed several grunts in Tom's squad. He'd been captured when he ran out of ammo. His platoon leader told him to load the sniper on the same chopper that was carrying his dead buddies—the same soldiers the VC had killed earlier—back to base camp to be "interrogated." It was a little hike down a narrow trail from where the prisoner was captured to the waiting helo. Tom didn't think twice about it—he made sure *that* prisoner didn't make it to the chopper alive.

Tom knew *exactly* how Vernon felt.

From what little he talked about his relationship with his father, Vernon had tried to make him proud. He had come home early because of his injuries. But his father told him he should have stayed to finish his tour.

Tom didn't have any idea what happened. The important thing was they could open up and share similar experiences—*memories*—of their past, both good and bad. Sometimes Charles met with them and, *just like back in 'Nam*, the three veterans were like brothers, always watching each other's back.

Tom appreciated sharing experiences with another combat veteran, something he didn't feel comfortable doing while meeting with non-combat veterans. He still met with them regularly, but it was more of a social get together.

He also realized that had he not gone to that first meeting with Charles at the American Legion, he would not have been able to get more involved with this smaller group of combat veterans. What was it that Pop said? *"Us vets have to stick together."*

IT WAS STILL DARK OUTSIDE. Chris slowly woke up, rubbing his sleepy eyes. "Are you okay, Dad?"

"I'm fine, Chris. I'm just a little anxious, that's all. There's no need to rush. *The Wall* isn't going anywhere."

"That's okay, Dad. I'm ready to get up and get the day going."

Tom smiled at that comment. His son sounded more like him *and* his grandfather—*ready to get the day going*.

After a quick bite at the hotel breakfast buffet, they walked out into a warm and humid D.C. summer day. It was late August. The sun was barely up, but Tom wanted to get to memorial as soon as possible, hoping to avoid any crowds. He still didn't enjoy being around people.

He wasn't sure how he would react, but he was on a critical mission. The mission today was to find Sunshine.

Tom wasn't sure what he would feel or say, but he was glad Chris was with him. Not because he worried he may have another panic attack, but because their relationship was like a father-son relationship *should* be—loving, interesting, and just being together, even during challenging times. The fact that Chris insisted on accompanying his dad made it more special.

The Vietnam Veterans Memorial was dedicated on Veterans Day, 1982 and inscribed over 58,000 names. The names were arranged in chronological order on seventy separate panels—the two end panels contained no names. Tom knew where he wanted to look first.

He had directions from the hotel. After crossing Virginia Avenue, they walked in silence another couple of blocks to the intersection at Constitution Avenue. Both looked at each other. Neither could see the memorial from the street.

How can you not find a 250 foot wall in plain daylight? Were they even in the right place?

Chris spotted several other men wearing old Army fatigues. He pointed in their direction. "It must be over there, Dad."

As they walked around the corner, *The Wall* was almost hidden from view from the street. *Sort of how the government tried to hide the real Vietnam War from the American people.* While that thought initially crept into Tom's mind, he would not let it belay his real mission.

The memorial looked just like the photos Chris had shown him on his computer. What the computer couldn't display, though, were the feelings Tom experienced as soon as he saw the almost endless lines of names. There were so many, as far as the eye could see.

As they walked closer, Tom felt his heart beat faster and harder, almost jumping out of his chest. Michelle had given him a small good luck token—a talisman—to hold when he felt anxiety setting in. He took a deep breath and rubbed it between his fingers. Tom recalled that conversation.

"When you were under fire, I imagine your adrenaline was running rather high, wasn't it? What did you do to settle down? I mean physically, not spiritually." Michelle's mental health specialty was working with veterans. He trusted her judgement *and* her question.

"The first few times, I was scared shitless. But after a while, I guess I got used to it. The thing that helped me the most was to slow my breathing by taking deep breaths."

"Did that work?"

"Most of the time, yeah."

"Then when you feel anxious or panicky, grab your token to have something to hold. Then force yourself to take deep breaths. Hopefully, that will help dampen your anxiety."

That simple exercise calmed him. He didn't know if it was the breathing, the token itself, or that Michelle had given it to him. It didn't matter, because it worked. Tom walked closer to *The Wall* and began looking for the name, Wayne Johnson—his 'Nam hero, *Sunshine.*

They were early, but not the first ones. There were veterans roaming the sidewalk in front of the memorial, several with family members. Only a few were by themselves. A few older men and women milled about, apparently looking for specific names. Tom assumed they were parents of veterans who had died in the war, and were here to pay their respects.

They slowly walked down the sidewalk in front of the memorial, but Tom wasn't sure where to look. Then… after a few steps, Tom *felt* something gently guide his thoughts, almost speaking his name.

He slowed and stopped in front of a panel, turned his gaze to focus on a particular section, and reached out to touch a name. He closed his eyes.

Chris knew he had found Sunshine. The sun peeked out from behind a cloud and he saw his father's reflection stand out against the smooth black granite surface. He was looking eye-to-eye at the name, Wayne Johnson.

"I didn't know what to expect today, Sunshine. I know I should have come visit you sooner, but I just couldn't. Why am I standing here… looking at your name? Why aren't *you* here instead, looking at *mine?* I've tried to forgive myself for years. I've asked God so many times 'Why?' But I never got an answer.

"You came to me in a dream one night telling me to get my shit together—that was real. I *know* it was you. I've tried to live up to that promise I made to you then. Some days are easier than others. I still struggle with those doubts. Could I have done anything different to save you, to save the others? A huge part of me died with you, Wayne."

A tear rolled down his cheek. As Tom spoke to Sunshine, he remembered another Bible verse, one he often heard in 'Nam at memorial services.

"Greater love has no one than this, that he lay down his life for his friends."

That was from the book of John, Chapter 15, verse 13. *Why did it speak to him right then? Was this more than a coincidence? Was that his father speaking to him from Heaven?*

He knew Sunshine was listening, and that thought comforted him. Tears flowed down his cheeks. After a few more quiet minutes of solitude, Tom stepped back, stood at full attention, and saluted PFC Wayne Johnson—his brother in arms—one last time.

Tom wiped the tears away and looked around. He spotted several other familiar names of men he had fought alongside with, who were also part of the Black Lions division.

He looked for more names. Recognizing a few, he realized he had more friends that died in Vietnam than he had here at home—buddies he had forgotten. He reminded himself he was just a kid—*we were all just kids back then*—fighting a war we shouldn't have. But we went over there believing in what we were fighting for.

As Tom started to walk alongside *The Wall*, he glanced through the almost limitless list of chiseled names against the black surface. He felt guilty for not reading every name and paying homage to the men who fought and died alongside his own buddies.

Each of these soldiers was more than just a name. Every one of them had family and loved ones left behind—lives that would forever be changed. He had witnessed that first hand, when he first met Tony Jones, his best friend's father, and his own father's best friend.

Tom asked where to look on *The Wall* for the time when he was in 'Nam, '68-'69. Chris walked over to the main registry and after a few minutes, came back, "I found them." They located Jerry Jones' name listed on a panel.

Tom spent a little time with Jerry. He needed to tell Jerry that his father was proud of him and that he was an honorable man. Tony

Jones was also a friend to *his* father, helping take care of him during those last few months. He *knew* Jerry heard him.

After an hour of pacing back and forth between panels 34E and 27W, it was time to leave. Chris asked if they had time to wander over to the Smithsonian. Tom was already walking in that direction. "Of course, I think we should. There's a lot more to see and do. Let's take advantage of D.C. while we're here."

As soon as they reached the end of the Vietnam Memorial sidewalk, a young teenage boy with curly blond hair and fair complexion, similar in size and age to Chris, approached Tom. Tom was wearing his U.S. Army Veteran ball cap, the one Pop had given him. Chris wore his grandfather's.

"Excuse me, sir. Were you in Vietnam?" the young boy asked, his mother a few steps behind him.

"Yes, I was."

He stepped in front of Tom, stuck out his hand, taking Tom's, and giving it a firm shake. "Thank you, sir, for your service."

Tom was surprised, yet appreciative of this young man's kind gesture. His wary eyes softened.

"My dad also fought in Vietnam. He was an Army infantryman," he stated proudly. "He died last year from what we think are the after effects of Agent Orange. No one can tell us for sure."

The boy's mother stepped up next to him. "Hi. I'm Karen Shreveport. This is my son, Ray. He's named after my husband, Raymond. We're from Kansas City, Missouri."

"Hello, Karen. I'm Tom Reilly and this is my son, Chris. We live in West Virginia. I'm terribly sorry about your husband."

"Thank you. He'd been having health issues for the past ten years. The VA couldn't figure out what was wrong. After a while, Ray decided enough was enough. He fought a good fight, but the cancer finally got him.

"I'm sorry to bother you, but he always taught my son and me to respect *all* Vietnam veterans. Ray never got the respect he and others deserved. So from me, and also my husband, thank you for your service and *Welcome Home.*"

"Thank you, Karen, Ray. Thank you for sharing your husband's story. We'll never forget what he did, along with the rest of these courageous men," Tom said while gesturing toward *The Wall*. "God be with you."

All gave some, some gave all.

As they walked away, Chris asked Tom if he had any effects from Agent Orange.

"Not yet."

But Tom had that nagging feeling that other Vietnam veterans had shared—something was not quite right. Charles had warned him that the trip to *The Wall* might produce additional anxieties. Tom would reflect on a lot of things about his own life. Today, though, he wasn't going to worry about what may be, only what is.

They passed The Three Servicemen memorial, which had been erected two years after the Vietnam War Memorial. Chris asked about the three different soldiers depicting an African American, a Hispanic, and a Caucasian.

"We were all brothers, fighting for the same cause and... we all bled red," was all Tom said.

Tom had fought with so many nationalities that at one point, it didn't matter. They were all there for the same reason. Like Tom, most fought to keep themselves and their buddies alive.

They also walked by a memorial dedicated to the women—most of whom were nurses—of the United States who served in Vietnam. Tom stopped for a moment to pay his respects. He recalled the time he'd been wounded during the same ambush that killed Sunshine.

He'd been bandaged in the field, but was dusted-off in a medivac chopper to a nearby field hospital. The nurses that took care of him not only cared for his physical wounds, but they must have known he'd lost a friend in the same firefight. Several spent time with him when everyone else was asleep, also helping to care for his emotional wounds.

They smiled with us, they laughed with us, and they cried with us. They were there for us in one of the loneliest places a soldier could find himself—alone, in a hospital bed with no close buddies nearby.

He wished he remembered their names, but they were also a forgotten part of the war.

Most nurses and doctors saw more human carnage than anyone in the war. They personally didn't know the wounded. But from his own experience, they all were aware of what happened in combat, both physically and psychologically. He hoped they came home, home to loving families *and* a loving country.

Walking toward the Smithsonian, the sun was bright and began to peer over the tops of the trees. Tom felt the warmth across his face and he closed his eyes, tilting his head toward the clear morning sky.

The sensation of sunshine was pure and sweet. He knew then and there that Sunshine would *always* be with him—no matter where his life's journey would carry him—keeping him safe.

A calm settled over him, almost like greatest burden had been lifted from his shoulders. Tom had finally been able to say goodbye to his haunted memories, his Army buddies, and the one special friend that saved his life, Sunshine.

He smiled. That thought—*that single thought*—brought him a world of peace. The guilt he had carried for over thirty years was now gone.

NEVER FORGET

ACKNOWLEDGEMENTS

While I'm a United States Navy Vietnam "Era" veteran (1973-77), the closest I ever got to Vietnamese were the refugees on Grande Island in the Philippines. Many of my friends are Vietnam War veterans. I am continuously in awe of the men and women who served in the Vietnam War.

I wanted to write a story with strong, nuanced, and authentic characters, each with a connection to war; a story that didn't focus on actual combat, but of a veteran's journey to overcome personal conflicts caused by a war.

NEVER FORGET is a work of fiction, yet many of the events and the facts are true and historically accurate, a culmination of stories from many units, both Army and Marine, both WWII and Vietnam.

My father, A.Z. Adkins, Jr., served with the 2d Battalion, 317th Infantry Regiment, 80th Division (Patton's Third Army) as a Heavy Weapons mortar platoon leader during World War II. Several of his personal experiences are reflected in this book.

My father-in-law, Dr. Rufus K. Broadaway, served with the 82d Airborne as a paratrooper section leader and landed in Normandy behind enemy lines on D-Day; he was diagnosed with dementia & Alzheimer's during his final days.

Even though they are no longer with us, these courageous men provided continuous inspiration to me as I wrote the words.

A single person doesn't create a novel like this; it is the product of research and experience, and there are many people I need to thank. I am indebted to my Vietnam War veteran friends Ernie Moyer (1/28th Marines), Stephen Dodd (Charlie Company, 1/5th(M) Infantry, 25th Division), and Fred Dunlap (Charlie Company, 2/28th Infantry, 1st Division) who not only helped me more accurately describe events and combat in-country, but also insisted that I not hold back on the after-effects of war.

I learned a long time ago to seek input early in my writing process to not only "test the waters," but also catch any glaring errors. My awesome initial readers provided insightful and personal comments, and encouraged me to continue working on this debut novel. I am appreciative of Jane McBryde, Karen Sroka, David Karns (USAF), Barbara Brockman, Petra Aldridge, MG(ret) John McLaren (USArmy), Ginny Quackenbush, Steve McGowan (USArmy), Dean Turner (USNavy), Alice Holmes, Brian Kitzman, and Cara Barfield.

I also need to thank my writing group POD: Elizabeth, Jo Ann, and Steve who, like all talented writers & critics, spent a lot of time helping me tweak the story. Thanks also to my developmental editor, Kaitlyn Johnson, who provided solid feedback before, during, and after the process, helping me to tighten the pace, highlight the characters, and to realize what a great story I have to tell.

A special thanks also to attorney Shannon Miller (USMC) who provided insights into elder legal affairs; Dr. Monika Rosier, Monica Ondrick, and John Auerback for providing practical insights into dementia, Alzheimer's disease, and PTSD; and Ernie Moyer (USMC) and MG(ret) John McLaren (USArmy) for helping fine-tune the Bronze Star Medal event.

My gracious sister, Anne Adkins Berkey, provided phenomenal support before, during, and after this challenging process. She read the initial manuscript as well as the final draft and offered critical corrections and insightful suggestions. It reminded me of the letters I wrote home during my service in the Navy. Being a middle school teacher at the time, Anne corrected my letters for grammar and punctuation, and shipped them back. It made my day.

Most of all, I thank my wife, Becky, who has stood by my side for 40+ years, listening to me "fine-tune" my Navy stories, and supporting and encouraging me to put pen to paper to create this story. For all this and her everlasting love, I will NEVER FORGET.

ABOUT THE AUTHOR

I'm actually in my fifth (or is it sixth?) career. I spent four years in the U.S. Navy during the 70s, most of which was on the flight deck aboard *USS Kitty Hawk* (CV 63) as a Crash & Salvage firefighter and a "Yellow Shirt" aircraft director. After my honorable discharge, I became a firefighter with the City of Gainesville, Florida.

By education and training, I have two degrees in electronics engineering (BSEE '82, ME '89) from the University of Florida and spent five years designing and developing microprocessor-based computer systems in the 80s.

I then turned to consulting, working with lawyers all over the country as an independent legal technology consultant. My father was an attorney, so that helped open a few initial doors. Plus, back in the late 80s and early 90s, law firms were beginning to incorporate technology into their practice. I was in the right place at the right time.

The University of Florida Levin College of Law provided an awesome opportunity and platform to establish the Legal Technology Institute (LTI), where I continued providing consulting services to the legal profession. During my tenure at UFLaw, I also served as the IT director and an adjunct professor, creating and co-teaching Law Practice Management to 2Ls and 3Ls. I left UFLaw in June 2010 with the primary goal of "slowing down." I privatized LTI and continued to consult the legal profession.

Just when I thought I was "slowing down," a previous client called, asking if I would join him as the CIO for a large West Virginia law firm. We loved our time in West Virginia; though, being a lifelong "Gator," it was a little hard to say, "Go 'Eers." After four years, we moved back to Florida intending to retire.

However, a previous employer called, asking if I would join him in a new software venture. I spent a couple of years working with a great group of folks.

Now, I'm "retired" (again)... I hope I'm slowing down.